A family historical novel by

Allen E. Goldenthal

(Book Five of the Kahana Chronicles)

What could possibly motivate a family to challenge insurmountable odds in order to pursue the fragile and fleeting illusion of freedom generation after generation? I can only respond with but a single word, ZUTRA. In this century, it bears no significance, the name being lost to the recesses of time, but once it was a rallying cry synonymous with the word freedom. In a time when people weighed the value of life against the cost of death and found that to die in the pursuit of liberty, was never to be considered a loss so great that they should be unwilling to lay down their lives. Mar Zutra loved life, he loved freedom, and he loved his wives and children above all else. I dedicate this book to my beautiful and lovely wife, Ying-Hui. Each time that I look into her dark brown eyes I experience the same exhilaration and overwhelming love that my ancestor felt when he beheld his dazzling Xanbei Princess from Northern Wei.

Author's Note

The people and places that you are about to experience all existed. The events described herein occurred to the best of anyone's knowledge as presented. The Buddhist traveler Hsuan-tsang records how a Chinese princess headed west to marry an unnamed king in Khotan (Persia/Iraq) and the cave paintings at Dan-Dan-Uiliq depict such an event happening as described around the turn of the 6th Century AD. Could these cave paintings be the visual confirmation of Princess Ti-Ping's eternal love for her Mahozan Prince? I believe it so and there is little reason to doubt it once you have read their story as it unfolds in this novel.

My own personal investigations have taken me to the city of Shenyang in China's Northeast, formerly known as Manchuria, where the tomb of an unknown general was discovered, and a replica of the findings put on display. Most noteworthy was its construction and decoration in the typical style of those used by Jews in the Middle East. Most historians have chosen to separate the people and events of distinct cultures as if they were happening without any bearing on each other, their timelines never crossing. I understand their motives for doing so. As I have often written, history is disseminated for public consumption and therefore is the prerogative of the victors. However, none of these entities or events existed in a vacuum and their impact upon each other was both monumental and undeniable. From the story I'm about to reveal, one might even deduce that our world as it exists today was entirely the result of events set into motion by a little unknown kingdom that established its independence alongside the Tigris River for a duration of no more than seven years. In the manner of a jigsaw puzzle, I have attempted to reconstruct the events and have interwoven the people accordingly, carefully recreating their history, much in the manner, as it would have actually transpired. Once completed it becomes quite apparent that these were never three separate stories of Byzantine history, Persian history, and Jewish history. Instead, they were a singular story of humanity and its perpetual pursuit of freedom. The story you are about to read, may or may not change your thinking regarding the history of our world but it should at least convince you that Love is the greatest power that binds us all, no matter which world we originate from.

Dr. Allen Goldenthal

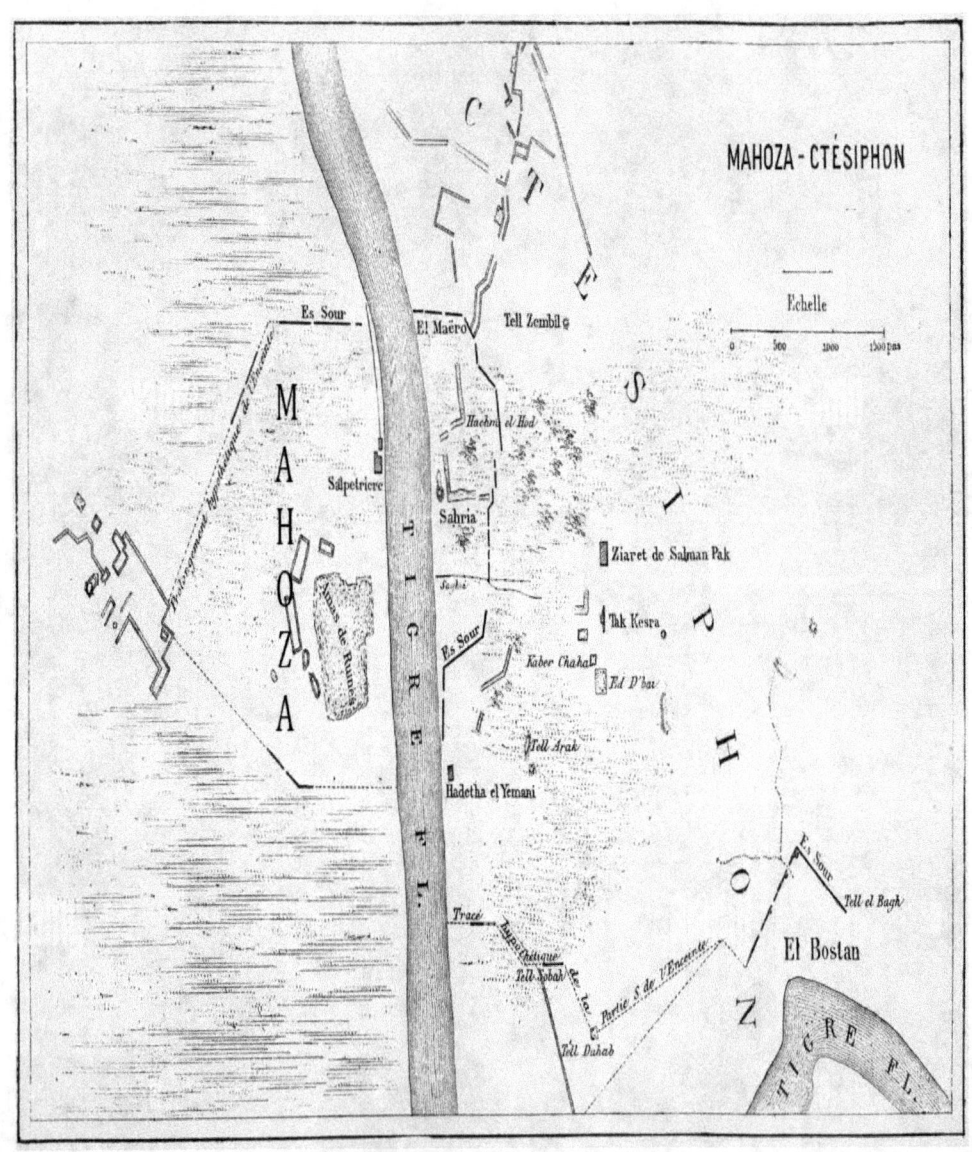

MAHOZA - CTÉSIPHON

The City Kingdom of Mahoza

PROLOGUE

"Nice digs, Doc."

My jaw dropped as I swiveled in my chair to face the man I have considered since we first met a friend and an antagonist, the one and only John Pearce. "Did I just hear you correctly, John? Nice digs? Did you actually say that? Who in this universe says something like nice digs anymore? You've been watching reruns of Happy Days or something?"

"Well, they are," John insisted, as we sat in my apartment's study. "I'm totally surprised. I didn't expect that they were like this in China," he said half apologetically.

"So, what are you suggesting? You thought I'd be living in a mud hut with a yak tied outside my doorstep. Is that it?" I inquired.

"Sort of," Pearce shrugged his shoulders.

"And here you are a media man and you actually believe some of that crap you and your cronies spew about life in China. Tell me, when do the media ever report the truth? I thought at least you would have known better."

"I'm in the print media Doc, remember? Can't help it if I watch the 6 o'clock news and they show peasants being washed away in torrential flood streaming through the middle of cities whenever they do a feature on China."

"Well, welcome to Shenzhen, John; truly an architectural marvel of the world. I think you'll find that the city outshines a lot of our western cities. In my opinion it even out Kongs, Hong Kong."

Pearce gave a little nod of his head. "Yeah, it did look pretty modern as I drove in from the airport. Still can't get over the fact that you're living in China now. Life certainly isn't boring when it comes to your travels and adventures."

I screwed my face into a perplexed mew. "My adventures? Not sure, I follow you John. I tell stories about the adventures of others. Why would you say my adventures?"

Pearce gave me that little nod and wink he did so often in the past as if to suggest that he was somehow 'in the know'. I didn't like it in the past and I certainly don't like it any better now.

"You know what I mean Doc," he smirked. "Different life, different wife," he practically tittered.

Aha, so that was it! I must be providing quite a bit of gossip around the water cooler in his office. "Shit happens," I edified him. "But regardless of what you might be thinking, all things happen for a reason. God does have a hand in this world even though you try not to believe it. And by the way, my last wife didn't like you very much." Figured I might as well get my knives stuck in while I had the opportunity.

"No kidding! Sort of figured that one out all by myself, Doc. Every time I visited you in New Zealand she either was storming up the stairs or throwing something at me. It was sort of obvious."

"You think?" I visually recalled some of their past meetings; yes, he was accurate in his recollections. "Let's face it John, you don't exactly have a winning personality," I jibed, turning the knife blade a little further.

"Well, hopefully the new missus will like me better. When do I get to meet her?"

"Of that I can assure you. Jenny is an amazing woman. From the first moment I met her I knew she was special."

"Have to be if she puts up with you Doc." Pearce's turn to do a little twisting.

"She'll be home a little later. The hours she puts in at the hospital are quite exhausting. One thing I have to admit about life here in China, the people do work extremely hard. I have to admire her for her dedication. In the meantime, you will have to tolerate my hosting capabilities or lack of them as the case may be. So drink you're instant coffee and eat your Oreo cookie because that's all you're getting from me."

"That's all I get," Pearce protested.

"If you don't shut up, you won't even get the story you flew over here

3

for," I cautioned him.

"Hey, that's not exactly fair! I just flew over twelve thousand kilometers so holding back is not going to be an option as far as my editor is concerned. Furthermore, this story better be some epic that outdoes J.K. Rowling, or else my editor will probably pull the plug on any future stories from you. He's claiming you've lost your touch and your stories aren't selling any more."

Touché! John is finally learning how to play this game. It was my turn to smirk at John's hollow threat. "How many times have I heard that one before?" I asked. "Let me see; like every time you've ever showed up on my doorstep. You know it's never going to happen. Your editor wants my story just as badly as I want my signing bonus."

"Signing bonus? What signing bonus?"

"The one you're about to call home office about John," I smiled devilishly, "if you want this story." The hook was in. Now I just had to reel in my catch.

Chapter One

Mahoza: 496 A.D.

"Their souls will talk to you, if you will only listen!"

"What nonsense are you mumbling about now, old man?"

"If you wait long enough and listen carefully, they will talk to you from the other side," the man replied sternly, cuffing the youth lightly on the ear.

"Hey, what was that for?"

"That's for not respecting your elders. Now listen to what I have to say for your own good."

"So, are they talking to you now, Mordecai?" The boy's words were laced with an insolent, mocking tone, typical of all teenagers at that rebellious age. "Anyway, I thought talking to the dead was a mortal sin."

"They are, young master," the wizened old sage responded more kindly now that he had gained the lad's attention. Though his beard was still streaked with black hairs and barely a wrinkle creased his brow it was rumored that Mordecai may well have been into his eightieth year. Perhaps even older; no one actually knew for certain. "And I'm not talking to them. I'm listening!"

"I have looked upon his face for hours and I have not heard a single word," the youth continued to dismiss the old man's banter as meaningless drivel.

"It's because you don't know how to listen. They are talking but you aren't listening!" Mordecai raised his hand as if he was about to strike again.

This time the boy thought better of challenging his elder. "So what are they saying then, if you can hear them?"

"Your father wants you to heed his advice!"

6

"Listen to him or to you, Mordecai? I know that anything you claim he is saying is merely coming from your lips. My father's days of talking are over!"

"You are still a youth, barely sixteen," the old man grappled with the teenager's refusal to accept his words, "And as such, I will forgive you your transgressions, this time, but whether your father forgives you or not, that is another question."

"Forgives me?" his voice rose an octave. "I have done nothing to him that he needed to forgive." The lad shook his head in disbelief and his pained expression made it obvious he was growing tired of the harassment he was suffering at the hands of his elderly advisor.

Equally frustrated, Mordecai scowled dismissingly at the boy. "Exactly! You have done nothing! That is what your father is saying to you right now. Heed his words!"

"You're a crazy old man," he launched into a verbal barrage, the tears beginning to well in his eyes. "In case you have forgotten, that is my father nailed up there on that cross. Not yours! Mine! A stinking, rotting corpse, being eaten by the crows and I am helpless to do anything about it! So don't try to pretend to me that he is anything more than dead!"

"He died for his beliefs. Are you willing to do the same?"

"To die?" The youth waved his arms menacingly in front of Mordecai's face. "Why don't you take a look at my father or what's left of him and tell me that his beliefs were worth the punishment he received? Why would any sane man choose such a fate over life?"

"To him they were and to you they should be as well."

"Let's not forget Avital," the boy responded indignantly. "Is she not the reason he's hanging above our heads from a wooden tree?"

"Do not be fooled, she was nothing but an excuse. Your father gave them a reason to execute him, and they seized upon it."

"It was nothing but sheer stupidity," he railed against his advisor. "And now we're all going to suffer for it. I loved my father, but let us be honest with each other, which one of us needs to forgive whom. She was intended to be my wife since I was twelve. I was the one affronted. Not him!"

Mordecai was unfazed by the accusation against the dead man. "Huna merely exercised his rights under our laws. His wife, your dear mother, God bless her soul, has been dead for close to three years and as the Exilarch, it is written that that the Resh Galuta must be married to guarantee succession in the House of David. You could die before you reach your age of majority. A ruler must have many sons to secure the succession. Even now you are still not old enough to be the Exilarch therefore, it was only right that your contract of betrothal was transferred to your father.

"Parrhi!" the boy shouted using Persian slang as it was far more expressive.

"Bullshit has nothing to do with it. It is the law. And if anyone knew the law, it was your father."

"More parrhi!" the boy exclaimed. "Why don't you tell it like it was? My father couldn't resist the opportunity to stick his withered old cock inside a beautiful young girl less than half his age and for that reason he's now dead."

The old man's hand moved so swiftly that the boy didn't have an opportunity to block the blow. The slap across his cheek stung more from the bitterness of what Mordecai didn't say than the physical pain.

The tears welled in the lad's eyes, but he refused to cry, instead letting the words flow like a burst dam. "He was like every other man that wants a woman. In two more years, he knew she would have legally become my wife and he couldn't stand the thought. Therefore, he used his guards to practically drag her from her home into his bed where he rutted her like a dog pursuing a bitch in heat. That's more than the community would tolerate, even from the Exilarch and you know it! That's why he's hanging up there!" The lad pointed up towards the dangling corpse then folded his arms in front of his chest. His chin dropped in a single nod. "And that's the truth! Don't deny it."

"I will forgive you this outburst against your father. I should not have slapped you but know well that you speak stupidly like a child!" Mordecai scolded shaking his head in admonishment.

"What else did you expect? In case you haven't noticed, I am only a boy!"

"Then it is time you grow up! Do you really believe what you have just said? Do you hate your father so much that you will pretend that the version of events they spew is the truth?" The old man frowned. "I would have thought if you had learned anything from your father it would have been to never trust anything you heard spouted by the lips of the Beth Din. Had you asked him, he would have told you the truth. Had you asked me, I would have done so as well. You should know better. The story they spread now has nothing to do with the truth."

"Well, it certainly looked that way to everyone else, didn't it? How else should I interpret it? My betrothed, taken from me by my father, and in turn he is put to death by her father. If it wasn't about her, then what was it about? You tell me!"

"It was about power and who wielded it; nothing else. The girl was just an excuse used by Reb Hanina to gain the support of the governor."

"And why should the governor care about a rabbi's daughter? That is even more absurd!" Zutra still refused to believe that any other reason existed.

"Oh, he wouldn't; not in the least," Mordecai confirmed the correctness of the boy's assertion. "But he does care about maintaining the balance and peace in his province. You know that the Sassanids have persecuted us for years now and the magus, Mazdak, has the ear of Great Shah Kavad at all times. It has been recently proposed by Mazdak that the Beth Din should be disbanded and that all matters for judgment be taken to the civic courts. The governor has no desire for such an act and so conspired with Hanina to instead elect a member to the Beth Din that was a supporter of all things Sassanid. In that way, the Beth Din would be effectively converted into nothing more than a pale reflection of the civil courts and the governor didn't have to take any further action. However, your father, he would have no part of such a miscarriage of justice. He was not willing to have Jewish law suddenly contaminated by the Gentiles after our having resisted the Persians, the Greeks and the Romans for so many centuries. He refused to recognize the nomination and in so doing earned the animosity of the Governor. Just as I suspect Reb Hanina knew he would."

"You make it sound like they had no other choice but to crucify my father?"

"The choice was your father's, not theirs. It would have been easy to acquiesce to their request for a particular judgment, but he knew that would only be the beginning of the end. He made the only decision that he could have possibly made. He had grown tired of the distortions to the Torah made by the Rabbis. He laid down his life to protect the word of God from further corruption."

"You're suggesting that he knew it would end up this way; that they would kill him?"

The old man stared vacantly up at the cross. "Did he think that Hanina had the fortitude to pass the death penalty on an Exilarch; I don't know. Reb Hanina is a coward. Cowards rarely can carry out a threat. Perhaps your father underestimated the governor's resentment for him."

"I hate them all! I will make them pay for what they have done to my father!"

"Not so fast young master. Your father would not wish to have you join him up on that cross so soon. You must use your intellect and think this thing through carefully." Mordecai tapped his temple with the tip of his index finger to emphasize his point.

"The time for thinking is over. Now is the time for action," Zutra insisted.

"Just what I would expect from a rash and impetuous teenager but certainly not what would be expected from the next Exilarch."

"What are you saying?"

"Just what I said," Mordecai's response was firm and obdurate. "Your father is dead, that makes you the next in line for Exilarch. As such, my advice to you is that you think this through more carefully. Why do you think I have hidden you away these past few days? Not because I didn't wish for you to know what happened to your father but because I knew that in all the confusion, they'd try to have you eliminated as well. No one would try to stop them until it was too late."

"Me? What did I do?"

"You live. You breathe. That is enough of a reason," the sage slapped Zutra across the back of his head. "Is none of this sinking in with you? Have you not heard any of the words your dead father is trying to whisper to you from the other side?"

"I don't understand," Zutra protested, keeping his distance not wishing to be slapped again.

"He died because of what he was, who you are going to be, now that he is gone. Both of you became unnecessary the day your half-brother was born."

"Hanai, what does he have to do with all this? I still don't understand."

"Little lord, I mean no disrespect, but as soon as Avital gave birth to a son to your father, you no longer had divine protection. That baby, Hanai, will be the entire focus of Reb Hanina. He will be determined to see that baby becomes the Exilarch and that makes you expendable, just as your father was."

Zutra turned pale as a ghost, the realization finally dawning that his advisor was right.

"Now do you believe me when I tell you the dead speak? Your father is practically shouting at you to listen!"

The youth was still speechless, suddenly aware that a dagger could be waiting for him around every corner. "But...but..." was all that he could sputter.

"Reb Hanina will raise that child as his own. He will groom him to be exactly what he wants him to be. As a result, the Exilarchate will become nothing more than an appendage on his little finger. That is what this has all been about! That is why he conspired with the Governor to change the structure of the Beth Din. That is why your father did what he had to; why he took Avital to his bed. Not to offend you, but to try and save you. He thought that by wedding Hanina's daughter, his new father-in-law wouldn't dare raise a hand against him or you. He underestimated the evil of that man. I will not."

"What can you possibly do," Zutra had finally regained his voice.

"I can give you my last bit of advice. Moreover, it is imperative that you listen to me. Heed every word knowing that they will preserve your life. Do you understand?"

The youth nodded his consent.

"Reb Hanina has petitioned the governor to take control of all your father's possessions and properties. You are underage and therefore by law, you will require a guardian. Since Hanai is a full son to your father as well, it was not difficult for Hanina to explain the appropriateness as maternal grandfather that your custody be granted to him. The governor readily consented. From now on, you will be living in your home but it will not be your home. It will be the house of Rev Hanina and he will be in charge of your life."

"But that can't happen. Not if he wants me dead. You can't let that happen."

"I can't stop it from happening. The die is cast. It is done!"

"Surely you can think of something." Zutra was mortified. "After all, you're Mordecai; Mordecai the all-wise. They say you know everything."

"Oh, so now you're willing to listen to me. If that is the case, then this is my advice to you. You will be a good grandson to your adoptive grandfather. You will heed his every word. You will be so good that he cannot find fault in you. You will be exemplary. Kindness and respect will flow from your mouth like a fountain of honey. So much so that people will praise Reb Hanina for how lucky he is to have you at his side."

"He killed my father!" Zutra cried out.

"Yes, he did," the old man attempted to console the boy, "And that will make it necessary for you to put on the greatest performance of your life. You cannot leave any doubt in any one's mind as to how much you revere and love the Judge."

"And then?"

"Ah, now you're beginning to understand. Hanina will have no choice but to name you as the new Exilarch when you come of age. The Beth Din will insist upon it and he will have to acquiesce to their wishes. One thing the Beth Din cannot change is the tradition of the firstborn. And that is when the tide will change!"

"And then…?" Zutra continued the line of questioning.

"Then you will have your life back. You can make amends for what was done to your father. But it must be done wisely and with no hint of malice. Are we agreed?"

"I will do what must be done."

"That is not what I asked of you. It is not what your father is asking of you now. Will you follow my instructions without question?"

Zutra reluctantly nodded his head in agreement. "I will do as you have instructed me. But I swear there will come a time when I will avenge my father. Those responsible will be made to pay. As God is my witness, I swear it!"

"Of that I have no doubt. Now come with me. It is time you return to your home, and we put our plan into motion. They will probably try to stop me from seeing you, but that is not a bad thing. If I am not around, it will make it easier for Reb Hanina to believe you have swung completely over to his side. In two years, when it is time for me to make my reappearance, I will seek you out."

"Until then," the boy reached out to hug his old mentor.

"Until then," Mordecai embraced in return, "May God be with you. Remember, not a moment before or everything will fail."

"You have my word."

"Swear it to God, not to me!"

"As God is my witness, I swear."

Chapter Two

Shenzhen: Present

"To be honest, I didn't think you were going to make it this time," I interrupted Pearce's train of thought as he sat mulling over the details of the story I had just recalled for him.

"How could you even think that," he scoffed. "When have I ever not kept my word?"

I took a moment to reflect on it. "There was that one time when you told me you weren't going to reveal any details regarding my whereabouts and you told your entire readership that I was living in New Zealand. I'd think that would count as at least one example."

"That doesn't count!" Pearce dismissed my complaint completely. "They just had to google you and they'd find out you were a Kiwi. By default, any information in the public domain doesn't count as me breaking my word even if I do disclose it. Anyway, you're in China now so that's all in the past now. It doesn't matter."

"So, you're a lawyer now," I ridiculed him. "Making excuses through technicalities."

"Hey, I'm here, aren't I? Let's just accept that and move on, why don't we?"

"No problem," I agreed. "So, what do you think of the story so far?"

"It's got me interested but I thought you said it was going to be a story about China when you called the office. Where's the Chinese part?"

"Oh, maybe you misunderstood. I thought I said I would give you a story 'in China'."

"Why do you always have to give me a hard time? You know that's not what you said."

"My enjoyment is proportional to just how hard a time I give you

John! That's when we do our best work together. You should know that by now."

"So there really is a Chinese story in your family then Doc?"

I nodded repetitiously. "Yes, there really is a Chinese story in my family."

"So where did this one come from."

"Same as always, buried deep inside my genetic memories and it surfaced a few weeks ago. That's when I called you; almost immediately, in fact why the details were still fresh."

"Any particular reason for this one to pop up suddenly?"

"I can't say for certain but I think living in China may have had something to do with it. Perhaps it was meeting Jenny, a remnant of a Jewish past that has been buried in China for centuries. Do you know that she still was clinging to the belief in one God and abstained from eating pork but didn't have a clue why? Try to picture someone not eating pork in China, John, and you can see how difficult that was. She had lost all connection to a Kaifeng past, yet she held on to those two beliefs."

"And then somehow you two came together," Pearce mused. "Eight hundred million Chinese women and you found the one that shares your beliefs. Amazing! But I thought you said these memories are triggered by traumatizing emotional events. How does that apply?"

"Well, Zutra was definitely a troubled personality which would mean that he'd have very intense memories but why his life surfaced over everyone else's is hard to say. But I have my suspicions."

"So did he do something special?"

"Led a rebellion; killed a lot of people; conquered an empire. Does any of that qualify?"

"Guess so."

"Well then the answer is yes. Mar Zutra was probably one of the most significant personalities of his time but history has tried to completely erase his existence."

"How can he possibly be that significant if no one's ever heard of him?" John mocked in that aggravating tone he used so often.

"They did a pretty good job in making him invisible, don't you think?" I queried Pearce. "Like you said, no one's heard of him. Imagine the effort they had to go to in order to achieve his anonymity after all that he did. Think of how hard the Church had to work to bring about the Dark Ages and make everyone forget all the scientific advances made by the Greeks and Romans until the Renaissance and then you get a picture of how it can be done."

"So, what was so special about this one that made him any different from your other ancestors?"

The answer to that question was easy. "Unlike all the others, he was motivated by a completely different set of values and emotions. I think that's why his memories were able to supersede all the others. Can't say for certain but the hypothesis fits. That's my only explanation."

"You lost me there, Doc. I'm not making heads or tails out of what you've just said."

"Remember what I told you a long time ago concerning GLEEM and that there has to be a trigger to bring the memories to the surface, just like you said."

"Not that I'd ever forget? Plus you remind me every time we sit down to have a chat."

"Well, I think I've gained a better understanding of the entire trigger concept. In many ways, it's closely related to déjà vu. If you happen to be experiencing an event or an emotional episode that is similar, or better yet, practically identical, to an experience in your ancestor's life, then it releases that stored genetically linked memory. The parallel prior existence surfaces so that it exists almost simultaneously with the occurrence of the real-time events."

"So, if that's the case," Pearce thumbed his lip as his mind processed the explanation I had just provided, "Then that would mean that you were sharing something in common with this Zutra fellow right now."

"Exactly!"

"You know it really bugs me when you say that," Pearce grumbled.

John had this long standing hang up with my use of that particular expression. Possibly one of the reasons I seem to say it more frequently whenever he's around. "Could be worse," I told him. "I could start using one that my kids use on me that sends me up the wall."

"Which one is that?" he quizzed.

"Whatever."

"No seriously, which one?"

"That's it, 'whatever'," I emphasized the word for his benefit. "They pull that word on you and how are you supposed to respond to that?"

"Yeah, I guess that could get up your nose. So you going to tell me what it was that you had in common with your ancestor that brought this story out?"

"No," I responded. "You're just going to have to listen to the entire story and solve that riddle for yourself. But I think it will be pretty obvious when I finish. Now sit back and start recording because this story is going to take quite some time to tell."

"What if I need a coffee break or something," Pearce agonized.

"I already thought of that. So that instant coffee you're drinking came out of a big box of Nescafe instant coffee packages. The 2in1 is pretty popular here in China."

"Oh, great. My favorite," he thanked me sarcastically. This is going to be a long story, isn't it?" Pearce reflected upon the size of the box.

"Yes it is, now let me get on with it."

"What about a toilet break?"

"Tie a knot in it, John."

Mahoza: 496 AD

"To the Exilarch," everyone gathered in the great hall heartily hailed the new political leader of the community. Cups were raised to the ceiling in a rousing toast to the Scion of David and Rod-bearer of Aaron, praises sung in his behalf, glorifying his name and calling down the blessing of the Lord upon the invisible throne from which he ruled.

"This is a great day," Reb Hanina, regaled in an ermine trimmed black robe addressed the crowd. "Once again, we have a descendant of David to guide us. May the Lord bless his days and number them a hundred and twenty years."

"To Mar Zutra," the assembly chanted in a single unified voice.

"While he has lived in my care, he has been like a son to me," Reb Hanina continued. "No father could have asked for greater love or devotion. This is a proud moment for me, and I feel the fruits of my labor to guide him and educate him in both the body and elements of our laws have all come to a ripe harvest. I present to you our new Exilarch, Mar Zutra bar Huna. Lord grant him wisdom and righteousness as our leader for all the days of his life."

Cups of sacramental wine were held aloft once more, a silent benediction uttered and then the toast was completed as the cups were pressed against their muttering lips.

"And furthermore…" Hanina began to speak again.

"Enough! Let Mar Zutra speak. Sit down already," the head of the Beth Din interrupted the Rabbi's monologue.

"I was only going to say," Reb Hanina continued, "That I know he will always walk in the ways of the Lord and do right by all of us."

"Fine!" the chief justice affirmed Hanina. "Then there's no reason for you to say anything further, you've said it all. Now sit down I beg you and let the boy speak for himself."

Mar Zutra fought bitterly to suppress the sneer tugging at his lips upon hearing himself described with the derogatory expression, 'the boy'. His fingers pensively stroked the short pointed brown beard that hung from his chin.

"Sit down," the other sixty-eight judges pounded the top of the tables in agreement with their chief justice.

Begrudgingly, Hanina sat back in his chair, folding his arms across his chest petulantly, trapping his wiry graying beard beneath them as he did so. It was obvious to everyone that he had not yet finished; in fact, he had hardly begun.

Mar Zutra stood up to a thunderous applause. "Esteemed members of the Beth Din," he held up his hands signaling for silence. "It is with great appreciation that I accept the title of Exilarch bestowed upon me but which was always mine by birthright. I know for certain that my ancestors up in heaven are looking down upon me at this moment with pride, both satisfied and delighted that the position has been dutifully restored to its proper place and family!" He gazed upon the solemn faces of the august assemblage, judging their befuddled expressions and knowing that he had confused them with his opening remarks. He was quietly amused; they could not tell whether he had just praised them or admonished them for either their fulfillment or dereliction of duties for the past two years. Precisely what he intended to achieve.

"I recognize that the power of the Exilarch has been curtailed over the past two decades, but I intend to restore my position to its former glory. My father had laid the groundwork for such an undertaking and now it is up to me to finish what he had started."

This time his comment certainly let the judges know exactly where they stood as several felt cold shivers dance up and down their spines upon the mention of the dead Exilarch Mar Huna. Had they looked close enough, they even would have seen the faint creases of a smile forming at the corners of Zutra's lips. He was relishing every moment.

Rumblings from amongst the judges began to surface now that some clearly appreciated that they had unwittingly unleashed a fox in their hen house.

"Seriously, Mar Zutra," the chief judge cleared his throat, "You are not suggesting that we turn back time and relinquish the powers that this court has gained legally. Justifiably I might add!"

"How can words such as legally and justifiably roll so easily off your tongues when you know that what you have achieved was gained through deceit and murder! What is the punishment for regicide according to the Law?"

The responding outburst from the assembly was deafening as they thumped their desktops and protested their innocence, demanding that the young Exilarch apologize immediately.

"You murdered my father," he pointed directly at Reb Hanina. "And the rest of you remained quiet as mice and let it happen. There is blood upon all your hands! All of you share in this sin!"

"Come, come now," the chief justice tried to calm the inflamed feelings on everyone's part. "You know there is no truth in such an accusation. This court has no authority to put a man to death. Therefore, it was impossible for this scenario you imagined to even happen as you supposed. Who has filled your head with such nonsense?"

"You need not waste your breath to explain the laws to me. I am well aware of what you can and cannot do. And because of your limitations, that man…" he continued to point at Hanina, "Went to the Governor and had him pass sentence on my father. You had the Pashah do your dirty work but even so, it was still necessary for you to provide the evidence in order to have the Pashah pass sentence."

Horrified by the remarkable change in personality that consumed Mar Zutra, Reb Hanina was too shocked to defend himself. Instead, he floundered, searching through a plethora of excuses and explanations. "I did not think that the Pashah would sentence your father to death. I had no way of knowing that he'd do so. It was not what I asked!"

"You can lie to the rest of your colleagues here, but you cannot conceal the truth from me. There was no other reason to bring the charges of kidnapping and rape to the Sassanids unless you wanted them to pass sentence through their legal system. Now I ask all of you here, what is the Sassanid punishment for kidnapping?"

The room grew frighteningly quiet. Not a single voice pronounced the sentence to which they all knew the answer. The Empire's answer for the crime was simple, death.

"Ever since the days when Khusro was the Great Shah of the Empire, the Sassanids have been our tormentors, taking from us all the rights and privileges that had been bestowed upon us by the Parthians. And Kavad who rules presently has not been any different, ruling over us with a mailed fist. Can you not see the irony?" Zutra gesticulated his expression of amusement. "These are the same people you would ask to pass judgment in a legal matter. What possible verdict could you have expected against the leader of a community that they despise? When you passed my father into the hands of the Governor, you knew exactly what sentence the Pashah would pronounce. Death was the only punishment they would administer."

"Why are you doing this to me?" Hanina pleaded, the shame of his guilt exposed for the heinous crime it truly was. He clutched his chest as if Zutra had put a dagger through his heart.

"Doing to you? To You!" Mar Zutra screamed. "You had my father killed! You gave away my betrothed! You took control of my family wealth and possessions and moved yourself and your entire family into my home.

You dare ask how can I do this to you? Did you really believe that I would just forgive and forget?"

"All I wanted was to have your father removed from his position. As you said, he was trying to restore the Exilarchate to its former position of supremacy. That would have been a transgression that the Sassanids would not have permitted and we all would have been punished."

"But knowing full well that the position is hereditary and it cannot be removed simply by having the reigning Exilarch eliminated. That would only place his closest male relation in his stead. Moreover, you knew that I wouldn't have served you any better, didn't you? What you required was a plan, premeditated long before the charges you laid against my father even existed. So you had Mar Huna marry your daughter and no sooner than when she bore him a son, you had him arrested. You now had in my half-brother a future Exilarch that you could bend to your will. Clever but flawed. As long as I'm alive it rendered your plan unachievable unless it was your intention to have me killed as well?"

"How can you even suggest a thing?" The outburst from Hanina appeared genuine. "I have loved you these past two years as if you were my own son. Reb Ezekiah," he held out his hands placatingly to the Chief magistrate of the Beth Din upon calling his name, "Obviously the new Exilarch has become ill or is bewitched; he is not in control of his mind nor responsible for what he says. Let him be removed and taken back to his house immediately. Let us seek medical attention for his affliction."

"No, what you truly mean is that I have treated you with such unwarranted respect that I made it impossible for you to raise a hand against me lest there be an outcry from the people against your perfidy!"

"Never, never," the Rabbi beseeched the assembly to believe him. "Never would I have caused him any harm. Any such claim is baseless and an insult to my reputation. I must insist that I be given an apology clearing me of any such foul accusations. But I will be considerate under the circumstances; I can wait until his mind is no longer befuddled by this sudden madness."

"You demand nothing! But I demand everything; my estates, my inheritance, my home! I want it all back. And now that I am of legal age, I shall have it restored immediately."

"Such things take time," the chief justice intervened. "Perhaps you should be taken home young prince where you can rest. Reb Hanina may be right that you are not feeling well. We will look into the matter of documentation regarding your property and then there will be a ruling by the council. It will take several weeks even if we were to begin right away. "

"In a matter of hours two years ago you stripped everything away from me and now you have the audacity to speak of weeks to restore what is rightfully mine. I will show you how the wheels of justice should be turned." Raising two fingers to his lips, Mar Zutra blew a shrill whistle that rang in everyone's ears. The response was immediate as the numerous sets of double doors that ringed the assembly hall flew open with such force that several shattered on impact. Pouring through the openings, the 'Four Hundred' made their first reappearance in the city in well over two years.

"You cannot bring armed men in here," the chief justice challenged the breech of protocol. "It is not permitted!" he shouted.

"I am resurrecting the old laws," Zutra countered. "When the governing authorities have lost their way and no longer administer on behalf of the people, then it is the responsibility of the monarch to wrest control from those that no longer govern honestly and to restore justice to his people."

"This is not possible," the rumblings and objections issued from the assembly.

"How can this be happening?" the chief justice buried his face in the palms of his hands.

"Explanations I will leave to my newly appointed advisor. You all do remember my distant cousin Mordecai bar Kahana. I believe you all saw him last time just before you took all my possessions 'legally'." Mar Zutra emphasized the last word for obvious effect. "All my possessions except for the Four Hundred, that is. I personally placed them under Mordecai's direction until such time that I could resume their command as part of my inheritance. I am actually astounded that you assumed that they had just vanished into the ether for these past two years. You never even bothered to try to locate their whereabouts; a serious miscalculation upon which Mordecai and I depended. During their absence from Mahoza we managed to keep their skills highly honed and trained on the northern frontier. You will not find them wanting in that regard. More so, they have never forgotten their primary objective; protect the Exilarch, even at the expense of their own lives. They failed to do so when you took my father, and they would prize any opportunity you afford them today to eradicate the bitter memory of their failure to keep Mar Huna safe."

"Your father ordered them to stand down at the time," the chief justice reminded him. "It had nothing to do with us."

"Only because the Governor used a threat of using his forces against our community if he didn't do so, as I recall. My father valued his people more than his own life. How much do you value your life Reb Ezekiah? Will you lay down your life for what you believe in?"

"What are you intimating?"

"You have sinned against God," Zutra clarified.

"Ridiculous! That is an absurd accusation," the chief justice refuted.

"Then tell me where I am wrong. Does the Torah not state that the scepter of David and the rod of Aaron shall not fall from between the knees of our sacred line? However, by enforcing the execution of my father, you permitted that very thing to happen. You defied God's will for your own personal ambitions. And by God's law the punishment for such a crime should be death."

"You would not dare! It was all Reb Hanina's idea. I was merely a pawn in his plan!"

"For the fact that I am merciful, you should be grateful. Cousin Mordecai on the other hand argued that by not fulfilling God's judgment, we'd be in defiance of the law ourselves, but I am a believer that God only gave us guidelines by which to establish our laws. Not necessarily dictates on how they must be enforced. For your own sake, I think you should agree. Therefore, for the time being, I will be lenient. I accept your confession of Reb Hanina's culpability."

"We are still the law," Ezekiah insisted. "The Beth Din does not recognize the charges you have leveled against your guardian Hanina or me."

"Let's see if you are still the law." Taking the sword from the guard standing closest, Zutra scored a line across the ornately woven carpet that covered the hall's floor. Those of you that had no part in my father's death, I bid you now to step to this side of the line. You will be my cornerstone upon which I will rebuild the justice system."

"Brethren, do not agree to this madness," Hanina urged but it was too late. Already many of the sages were shifting their chairs and moving towards the side of the room where Zutra was standing. "United he can do nothing to us. Do not let him divide us!" As he was finishing his words, already half the assembly had moved across the line to join Zutra. By the time they had finished shuffling across the cut in the rug almost fifty of the judges were standing behind Zutra.

"I can only presume that those of you that have not bothered to take this opportunity to express your innocence have instead declared your guilt or as Reb Ezekiah so exquisitely expressed himself, your willingness to be pawns of Reb Hanina."

"That is an absurd accusation," the chief justice protested on behalf of the twenty-three judges that remained seated. "We're not bothering to cross your line because there is nothing to support your trumped-up charges. We can't even be bothered to acknowledge such ridiculous accusations."

"Good," Zutra countered. "Then it doesn't really matter to you that I'm dismissing the lot of you from your positions."

"You cannot do that!"

"The choice is entirely yours. If you choose not to believe that I have the authority to do so, then I will have you all executed for the murder of my father. You've admitted your complicity by remaining in your chairs and not crossing over the line, so I am justified in whatever action I take. Dismissal or death? I leave the choice to you, Gentlemen."

"This is intolerable," Reb Ezekiah exclaimed, but from the look on the prince's face, it was obvious that whether it was absurd or not, he was quite convinced that the new Exilarch would carry out his threat.

"And just what do you intend to do with me?" Hanina choked on the fear and realization that he had been stripped of all his worldly power.

"You may return to wherever you came from. You will leave everything that belongs to me behind and go! Do not tread my patience or I will begin to regret my mercy."

"But I sold my home two years ago," Hanina explained.

"Then surely you have enough money left over from the sale to find yourself another place. My estate has catered for you long enough, but no more."

"You can't throw my daughter and her son onto the street. She is still your stepmother. She doesn't deserve to be treated like that," he argued.

"And I won't," Zutra informed him. "She will stay at my home. After all, she was pledged to be my wife years ago; I am demanding fulfillment of that contract."

"Impossible!" her father screamed. "She was married to another. The contract does not exist any longer."

"No, you're wrong. When you had my father killed for his crime of forcibly taking her from your house, his marriage was nullified. Not even an annulment to even suggest there was a marriage at one point but instead a crime of theft, confinement and rape. You had her declared defiled, which means the contract was never fulfilled and more importantly, never voided. And as a woman that has been violated, what other man would want her any longer? Be grateful that I am willing to give shelter to such an undesirable. I have removed the problem entirely from your hands."

"It is perverse to marry the woman that bore your brother," Reb Hanina stated abhorrently. "You cannot marry your father's wife. It is forbidden! And what about my grandchild? What will you do to him, he is an innocent?"

"Hanai, bastard that he is after you declared him so, is still the offspring of my father. I will raise him within my household. As for his being my brother, should he prove himself worthy then one day I might just grant him that legal consideration. But you will never see him again."

Mar Zutra turned to old Mordecai and instructed him of his next intentions. "I need you to find me twenty-three new judges to take the place of these disgraced men. Furthermore, find me an authority on the 'halacha'. I want to know exactly what the ruling is on marrying a stepmother whom because of the crime my father was condemned for, their marriage was never considered to have taken place. Have my guard escort these criminals home and place them under house arrest. They are not to be seen on the streets again unless I grant them permission. I want the crimes they have confessed to posted throughout the city. Every citizen is to know what has transpired this day. See to it at once!"

"What about Reb Hanina," Mordecai asked. "Where shall they escort him now?"

"I don't care. Take him to Reb Ezekiah's home. I'm certain the two of them will enjoy each other's company."

"You do not have the authority to do this," the chief justice blustered still attempting to assert some degree of power.

"What is the pronouncement on my authority?" Zutra inquired of his elder cousin and advisor.

"As Exilarch, you are the supreme authority. Your power comes from the people over whom you govern. You are only answerable to them and to God."

"But what do you say?"

"God says that these men are guilty of contributing to murder. As for the people, I would suggest we go to them directly. I will arrange for a festival and we will present their new monarch to them. Then we will let them pronounce whether you should have been as merciful as you have been."

"A fair comment," Zutra nodded. "Let the people decide whether you should all live or die."

Chapter Three

Mahoza: 496 A.D.

"What are you looking at?"

"I wanted to have a good look at my jailer before he has me imprisoned in a tower where none will be able to look upon me ever again," Avital curled her top lip into a feral snarl as she defended her bone-chilling stare.

"What nonsense are you spouting about now woman?" Zutra sighed.

"Only the truth," she shouted, "You've jailed my father and his fellow judges and now I am being punished for sins I haven't even committed, and you want me to accept the punishment without complaint!" Her hazel eyes lashed out with the fury of a thunderstorm; specks of gold flashing lightning bolts shafted in his direction.

"No! I want you to accept our betrothal without complaint and when you're prepared to do so, I will permit you to leave your chambers."

"Then I will see you into your grave because it will be a very long time before I come seeking you," she challenged him, crossing her arms so that they rested upon her ample bosom.

"Do not think my patience is without an end woman. We will be married and one way or another you will bear me a son," Zutra fired back.

"Like I did for your father?" the words cut like a hot-forged blade. "Am I some beast of burden to be ridden by all the members of your family?"

For the moment Mar Zutra failed to find an appropriate answer. His mind was reeling as he tried to repudiate her statement. Were her words crafted from pure malice, were they merely ridicule, or perhaps tinged with something even more painful such as loathing? How could such an angelic face conceal such a frigid and treacherous heart he wondered?

"You were promised to me. We had a contract! Now finally you are where you legally belong. I am only taking what is rightfully mine!"

"Take? Like as in a dog or perhaps worse, like a whore!"

"No, taking as in my wife as I was promised."

"The moment your father took me as his bride I became your stepmother. How can you even contemplate lying with me? It would be a sin!"

"There is no sin; only the lies your father told you can be deemed such. There was a ruling by the best legal minds in our city. There is no sin. You are neither blood nor legally even a widow. Your father saw to that by having your marriage rendered non-existent since you were forcibly taken from his house as he charged my father. You in turn became nothing but one of the 'unclean'; a victim of rape and the bearer of a bastard child!"

"You know that is not the truth!" she screamed.

"What does it matter about truth? Since when does your family care about the truth? Your father created this situation and now you must abide by it. All the world sees is the act of mercy I am showing to you for even having one so unclean in my home. Moreover, the fact that I am caring for little Hanai makes me appear even more magnanimous. There's your truth. Make of it what you wish."

It was the first time since Zutra had taken control of his father's estate that Avital began to reveal a few of the cracks in her tough and formidable veneer. As much as she prayed that Zutra was incorrect in how their situation would be perceived by the people, she knew he was right. Her father had destroyed any future she might have had, yet she bore him no ill-will. Instead, all her anger, all her frustration was hurled at the one man that offered her a chance to have the semblance of a normal life; even if she found it impossible to answer a simple question of why?

Whatever the look on her face may have been at that particular instant, Mar Zutra interpreted it to be a moment of indecision and chose to press his advantage. "Avital, think about your situation. The law has branded you as a violated woman. It does not matter that by definition you were the victim even if it were true. To your father you are the 'boisha,' the shame that he bears when he is among his brethren. You are the embarrassment that weighs upon his heart whenever he discusses you. In addition, you know yourself, that your father is very good at publicly winning support for his affronts. That is all that you have become for him; a tool which he can use to achieve greater support from his followers. Is that all you wish to be, a sympathetic vehicle for your father?"

Minutes passed before Reb Hanina's daughter spoke a word. During that time she took account of her life, her desires, especially her failings. In essentially a whisper she finally responded. "I objected to marrying your father. I want you to know that."

"Why should I care?" Mar Zutra said rather aloofly. "In the end, whether you objected or not, you did marry him. That is of course ignoring the fact that the law has ruled that there was no marriage at all."

"I want you to know because your father had no part in the matter. He never came to my father's house and asked for my hand. I thought you should know that too."

This time Zutra was taken completely by surprise by the revelation of this previously unknown information. He never knew for certain how the marriage contract had been altered, but he had always assumed that it had been at his father's bequest. "I'm not certain I understand," was all his faltering lips could say.

"It was my father's idea, completely his. One day he just marched up to me and said that I was going to marry the current Exilarch and that I should be overjoyed with the opportunity that he was about to engineer for me. He was on his way to see your father to discuss the arrangements."

"So, you admit your father lied to the governor! He alone was responsible for your appearance in my father's home. He neither kidnapped nor raped you as the courts were told."

"I admit nothing. Only that it was never with my consent. That is exactly what I told the Governor."

"It matters not now. What has been done, has been done. I cannot turn back the sands of time. My father is gone and your hand played a part. So let me understand correctly, your father forced you and that's when you objected?"

"Yes. I told my father that I would not do it. Your father was almost thirty years older than I was. How was I to be the wife of someone that shared nothing in common with me?"

"But your father wouldn't listen," Zutra surmised.

"He beat me," she blurted as she hid her face in her hands.

Zutra tried to search for her eyes between her splayed fingers to see whether this was nothing more than another performance designed to manipulate his own feelings and responses. After all, she was her father's daughter and over the past few days, he had grown accustomed to her attempts to ensnare him in webs of lies and deceit. However, no matter how hard he tried, he could see nothing sinister in those bewitching hazel eyes that he had tumbled so deeply and willingly into years long past.

"It was not the first time he had done so," she continued. "When my mother was alive, she was able to protect me, but then she often bore the brunt of his anger. Everyone thinks my father is such a bastion of morality, but when no one is looking he is nothing more than a tyrant."

"As are so many that veil themselves in robes of religious righteousness," Zutra added. "But why tell me all this now."

"I don't know," she shrugged her shoulders. "Perhaps because I thought of how you had become disparaging of your father for sins that he had never intended himself. In the short time I had been with your father, I knew him for a man of integrity. A day never passed when he did not comment on how much he loved and cared for you."

"Thank you. You're right. I do appreciate knowing that. But it does not erase the fact that even though the marriage to you may have been entirely manipulated by your father, it was still agreed to by my father. He had no right in doing so."

"Did you not just say that my father could be very convincing when he wished to move mountains in a certain direction? Why would Mar Huna be any less influenced than are all the others? He may have been the Exilarch, but he was still a man, susceptible to all the same flatteries and desires as any other man."

"That is where I disagree," a surge of anger flushed across Zutra's face. "As the Exilarch, we cannot be subject to all the same frailties as other men. The people must see us as much more. That is where my father failed. He let himself become consumed by the pleasures of the flesh."

"It was not that way," she turned her face away from him. "You wouldn't understand."

"Then make me understand. Give me a convincing argument of why a father that you profess told you how much he loved me every day would still lie with the promised bride of that same son. Explain it to me so that I can understand. Give me words of comfort woman, if you can!"

"He was lonely. He felt so alone. Can you condemn him for that?"

"Yes! A thousand times, yes! He had his life. It was time for mine," Zutra countered in a rage. He took that from me!" he pounded his chest. "He stole from me!"

"And now you take that from me!" she screamed back, not willing to tolerate any of his self-indulgence and childish petulance.

"You have nothing to give," he shook his head in condemnation. "Take a look around you. Everything you have is from me. Everything from the food you eat to the clothes you wear. Your father certainly took liberties to spend my inheritance freely. On the other hand, you have no dowry. Even your family name has now become disgraced and cursed. Your father's crimes have been brought before the people and although they did not demand his head, they still spit at the sounding of his name. You offer me nothing. But still there is one thing I can take from you, and I intend to do so!"

"Then you are an animal," she spat, her prior expression of pity transformed instantly back to one of intense hatred. "I will not be some beast to spread my legs so that you can force yourself inside me. Find a she-goat if that's what you want!"

Zutra emitted a hushed laugh, more so from exasperation than from ridicule. His first instincts had been correct; she had been playing him and doing so quite effectively. She had drawn him in completely, compelling him to feel sorry for her, however, it was nothing more than a performance, a charade that she so cleverly manipulated. "Then you will find it very lonely in your quarters. Here you shall stay until you recognize that I am your lover, not your jailer."

"I want to see my son," she demanded.

"You mean my father's bastard child," he sarcastically corrected her. "A child that only through accident and circumstance is my brother. As his elder sibling, I will raise him to be the man my father would have wanted him to be. You will not see him! What can you offer him to suckle upon other than milk laden with bile and hatred? I will see to it that he learns of a better world and comes to know that his father was a great man that fell prey to your father's greed and your stone-cold heart. He will know the truth of how our father died and when he is a man, perhaps he will choose to come and see you better equipped with that knowledge."

"You are a monster!" she screamed like a harpy. "I will never love you! Keep me prisoner for a lifetime and still I will not let you enter me. Never! Do you hear me? Never!"

Zutra turned to leave her chambers. "I will see to it that the servants provide you with everything to keep you comfortable. You shall not be wanting. After all, I am not one to trade in death, which surely was your matrimonial present to my father. You say your own father forced you? I can tell from the essence of your nature; no man could ever force you to do that which you do not willingly of your own choosing. Perhaps once you recognize your own guilt in my father's death, then you'll pray for forgiveness. Maybe then God will hear you and extend His mercies." Without looking back, Zutra exited from the room, slamming the door behind him with a force that reverberated around the room. Avital in her despair could hear the tripping of the locking mechanism as he turned the ornate brass key.

Chapter Four

Mahoza: 497 A.D.

"Are you ready," Mordecai inquired.

"About as ready as I'll ever be," Zutra answered nervously. "And cousin, I probably haven't told you enough, but thank you." Zutra raised the hem of his gold and green brocade tunic as he climbed into the open sedan. The floral design was woven from a luxuriant brown wool interlaced in a continuous pattern that ran the length of the robe. A bejeweled dagger with carved ivory handle hung on his right hip, while a gold scabbard encrusted with rubies dangled from the shoulder baldric on his left. The gold diadem upon his brow was of the design worn commonly by the house of Aaron as Zutra was more than just the Scion of David but descended from the High Priesthood as well. Two families that had been intermarrying for so long and so often that no one could say for certain which was the paternal line and which the maternal line any longer.

"For what?" Mordecai finally responded after considerable effort to scale the steps and settle into the sedan chair on Zutra's left. Dressed in a white silk robe sashed at the waist with a band woven from gold threads, his head coiffed with a turban comprised of the same material; there was little doubt that he held the position of second most powerful man in Mahoza.

"For everything," Zutra filled in the blanks. "This day wouldn't be possible if it wasn't for your methodical planning and hard work. You've organized every detail down to the most infinite aspect. I do not know where you found this carriage, but I must say that it's absolutely spectacular; a marvel of artisanship long forgotten. Who does it belong to?" Zutra scanned every intricate detail of the magnificent two-seater sedan, the driver elevated on a bench seat at the fore, dressed in the elaborate formal garb of one of the four hundred.

Mordecai smiled broadly. "This old thing? It's been around for several hundred years actually. It belongs to your family."

"Then it's almost as old as you are," Zutra laughed slapping his hand against the top rail of the door. "Why have I never seen it before?"

"Almost!" Mordecai smiled in agreement. "When your ancestor Mar Ukba prevented the forces of Septimus Severus from conquering all of Parthia, this carriage was presented to him by the Great Shah Valogases, in order that he could be carried throughout the Empire proclaimed as its hero and the people could shout his praises. It matched every detail of the Shah's carriage except one. Where that one was trimmed in gold, Mar Ukba's is only trimmed in silver."

"I was under the impression that the Romans actually won that war." Mar Zutra rolled his eyes upward as he gave thought to the history lessons of his youth. "Was I mistaken?"

Mordecai chuckled to himself. "That was always the way. Let the Romans think they had won and they would leave us alone. It happened over and over again throughout history."

"But they took Ctesiphon and robbed the treasury of everything it possessed."

"How is it that they could take everything and yet the city is still rich beyond measure?" The riddle was posed to Zutra, but it was rhetorical in nature. "Don't rack your brain so hard," Mordecai teased him. "Septimus Severus was paid a huge ransom to pack up his troops and leave. But to the Great Shah, it was nothing more than a business deal."

"I'm confused, cousin," Zutra confessed. "If the Romans were paid to leave, then how did Mar Ukba encounter them?"

"Severus was not honoring the agreement as promised. Rather than pack up his troops and head home, he began to think that if one city was worthy of such a hefty ransom in payment, then how much would another be worth? He set the city of Mahoza in his sights."

"I've never heard of the Romans attacking Mahoza?"

"They didn't," Mordecai confirmed. "Because Mar Ukba attacked them before they ever had the opportunity. They fled before him and never looked back until they reached safety in Armenia."

Zutra still found it difficult to accept. "How was our ancestor able to rout several Roman legions with only the Four Hundred? I can't believe that. Surely you are spinning tales again?"

"Oh, he had a lot more men back then than just the Four Hundred, but they weren't really necessary. As the story goes, the Romans were so busy celebrating and drinking, they couldn't tell if there was one man charging down the hill towards them or a hundred thousand. They never stopped to count as they turned their backs and ran for their lives."

"Unbelievable!"

"Of course when Mar Ukba described his rout to the Great Shah, he added a few details regarding the description of the battle. However, a few white lies here or there didn't matter to Valogases. He was pleased by the results and the carriage was his way of showing how pleased he truly was."

"I'm surprised Reb Hanina didn't get his hands on it and melt it down while he had the opportunity."

"It has been well hidden all these years as has much of your family fortune. I made certain that you would not be left destitute in my absence while the rabbi plundered your coffers. There are still many that are loyal to the royal family and will have no bar of these rabbis that try to usurp your power and privilege."

"I presume these bags of coins are part of that hidden treasure trove as well?"

"Consider them a gift from the Romans, my liege. Septimus Severus was a very confident general as well as Emperor," Mordecai ridiculed. "Perhaps overconfident best describes him. Having come from this part of the world, he anticipated the populace would be grateful for his attempt to liberate them from Parthian rule. He never understood that the concept of Roman rule was even more foreign to us than the dictatorships we have always lived under. He was the invader and therefore considered the true enemy. All these denarii he had minted in advance to celebrate his victory. When Mar Ukba routed his army and sent him back to Armenia with his tail between his legs, the stash of coins was left behind. We sort of kept it as part of our service fee for fighting on behalf of the Great Shah."

"Sort of kept it?" Mar Zutra questioned suspiciously.

"Okay, he never reported all the takings from the battle," Mordecai admitted. "Was that such a crime?"

"There was no battle," Zutra insisted. "You said so yourself."

"But there was a lot of the ransom left behind as they fled too drunk to transport all of it back to Rome. Don't look at me like that. He would have been granted a reward regardless whether he did or didn't mention it to the Great Shah. These are the ways of the world you will learn as king."

"Such as this carriage," Zutra patted the rail of the vehicle once again in admiration.

"He couldn't spend the carriage, now could he?"

"You have a point." Zutra took a deep breath as the carriage began to pull away from the yards, the team of two dappled grays ringing in their belled harnesses, while the coachman cooed softly to them as they pranced.

"Relax," Mordecai loosely gripped his cousin's shoulder. "Remember, these are your people. They are eager to shower you with their affections. Give them the opportunity to love you. You have nothing to worry about."

"Perhaps we waited too long. They're probably wondering why it took three months for us to announce my ascension. What if they're angry about the members of the Beth Din I placed under house arrest? Our going out with so little protection through the heart of the city could prove dangerous."

"Exactly the reason we waited three months; time for any hot heads to cool down. And do you really think that anyone is going to be angry at you as you toss these coins into the crowd. Not to mention you are spending a fortune to feed them all today at the festival. The banquet tables in the town square are bursting with more food than they've seen in a lifetime. Already my agents have reported back that the people are dancing in the streets, singing your praises. They are being fed, paid and entertained. For that they will love you!"

"And the Pashah agreed to all this?" Mar Zutra questioned.

"The Governor after all is a businessman. He's been well paid for his consent. Don't worry. Everything has been taken care of."

"What about…"

"Nothing about," Mordecai reassured him. "Smile and wave to the crowd. That is all you have to do. When we get to the square, I will do all the talking."

"Just smile and wave, that's it," Zutra's tone sounded doubtful.

"That's everything. To the townspeople, they only want to know that you looked them in the eye, smiled and waved. Then they will go merrily back to their lives, happier than they've been in years. Royalty has that effect on the common people."

"Really?"

"Especially after the speech," Mordecai winked. "The Parthians and Pontians will probably become your most loyal supporters after today. I will make a few promises in your name guaranteeing them an equal status with your own people and they will kiss your feet. In fact, every outcast of Sassanid society living in our city will become ardent supporters, just like in the olden days."

As the carriage rolled away from the estate lands, turning down the road to the town centre, Mar Zutra found his arm rising automatically into the air, waving at the crowds that had lined the gravel road in eager anticipation.

"Throw them a handful of coins. They'll love that," Mordecai urged.

Zutra did as he told, and just like children at a lolly scramble, the people raced around upon their knees, searching for the tiny silver discs amongst the stones and grass. No sooner had one been found, the would-be treasure hunter would stand up and shout with jubilation as if he had found a rare and precious gem. Watching their antics only made Zutra smile more easily and wave more enthusiastically.

All along the route Mar Zutra tossed handful after handful of the denarii, the reaction and adoration far outweighing the value of the small bits of silver.

"See. Already you have become the most popular man in the city, and you haven't done anything. It will be enough to spark the telling of legends about this day."

"Granted," Mar Zutra agreed, "It would appear that I have won them over for the moment but what about tomorrow?"

"Tomorrow will be another day," his elder cousin advised. "But they will never forget today! I know the people and I know what they want! Tomorrow will take care of itself!"

"If as you claim you know people so well then tell me what I should do about Avital?"

No sooner had Mar Zutra uttered her name, his arm fell to his side lifeless as if all strength had been drained from his body. Mordecai immediately grabbed his elbow and held the limply hanging arm up high once more, flapping it in a half-hearted wave. "Keep smiling," he instructed Zutra. "Just because you mention her name doesn't mean you have to forget everything else."

"What should I do?" he repeated.

"Will you follow my advice if I tell you," the wizened advisor questioned.

"It depends."

"On what?"

"It depends on you telling me what I wish to hear."

"Then you probably won't listen because my advice to you is rid yourself of her. She is nothing but a dark cloud that hangs over your house. She only bears you ill will. No good will ever come from her. Lance the boil before it swells and bursts into an ugly sore."

"That is your advice?"

"You asked and I have told you. Do with it as you wish."

It was easy for Zutra to tell that there was no love lost between his cousin and his betrothed. "Then give me some other advice," Zutra frowned. "I will not release her."

"Give me a good reason why not," Mordecai scowled in return, ensuring that no one in the crowd could see his face.

"Because I love her!"

"Bah!" Mordecai snorted with derision, the sound bursting through his pursed lips. "No one could love such a vile creature. She's her father's daughter, of that there is no doubt. She has no heart. Just a black hole that sucks the life from everyone and everything she touches. How could you love such a woman? My advice to you is to take a bride from the hundreds of other families of high bearing; one that can love you without conditions."

"I have loved Avital from the first day I laid eyes on her," Zutra explained in desperation. "She was twelve and I was only ten, but I knew then that there could be no other woman for me. When I was told that the marriage contract had been drawn up when I was thirteen, I was the happiest boy in the world. Now that she is a woman, she is lovelier than ever. How can I give up what I desire most in this world? Haven't you ever loved in that way cousin?"

Mordecai's eyes became downcast and distant; a cloud crossing over them like a storm swept sea. "Once," he answered. "A long time ago."

"What happened to her," Zutra pursued the issue.

"My father, Kahana, forbade the union. She was only a servant girl. It didn't matter to me. What difference should it have made? I was not in line for the Exilarchate. It shouldn't have made any difference!"

Zutra found himself consoling his elder cousin with one hand while his other swayed back and forth outside the carriage in greeting. "So where is she now?"

"When my father found out that I had been secretly meeting with her, even after he forbade me to do so, he had her sent away. He never told me where and I never forgave him."

"So, you never gave up hoping to find her," Zutra guessed at the cause of his cousin's bachelor status.

"No, I never stopped punishing my father. That was his punishment for what he did to me. I swore I would never give him grandchildren. And I kept my oath."

"So, what should I do," Zutra pleaded for an answer. "You understand what the pain of love can do."

"If this is what you truly want; if you recognize that what you have fallen in love with is nothing more than the physical and empty shell. A mirage which only remains as long as the body retains youth and vitality, and if presented with that knowledge you are still willing to accept that you may never know true love's embrace in return, then you must overwhelm her with the only force she respects; Power!"

"You're still talking in riddles," Mar Zutra shook his head. "For those of us more naïve in the ways of love, what are you saying?"

"Listen," Mordecai's expression became quite serious. "You've tried everything else. You've showered her with every kindness possible in the hope that she would turn but in fact her heart has only become more like hardened stone. She's a prisoner within your palace, yet every whim and craving is granted to her. Who then is the actual prisoner?"

Defending the extent of his actions, Mar Zutra explained, "She is, of course. She's not allowed out of her quarters. She has no one to speak to other than her maidservants. How much more could she be imprisoned? It's not necessary that I torture her further."

Mordecai brushed back the strands of silver hair that laced his scalp and remained exposed beneath his turban, all the while frowning disappointingly. "Keep waving, Zutra. There are children over there that want your attention. Throw them some coins. Win the hearts of the children and the parents follow. A simple philosophy but it has forever been true."

"Is that your advice? If I win my brother Hanai's favour, then his mother will learn to love me as a result?"

The elder statesman made a clicking sound with his tongue against the roof of his mouth, admonishing his pupil. "No, that means throw some denarii the way of the children and they will adore you, nothing more. Avital is a different matter completely, which you have obviously failed to comprehend. You keep her confined. So what? Her father did the very same thing to her. You keep her from talking to anyone else. It matters not! She had no friends of any merit that ever wanted to talk with her. She has been alone her entire life after her mother's death, surrounded only by her servants. You aren't torturing her," he imparted, "You merely carry on the lifestyle she has been accustomed to."

Zutra's mind swirled from the comments by his cousin. All these months trying to break her will but now his cousin was informing him that he had achieved nothing but reinforce her adamant nature.

"She sees you as weak; pathetic. She despises weak men. She sees you as insignificant and that demeans you even further in her eyes. You appear indecisive and that only encourages her to force her will more belligerently. If she was a camel, you would have beaten her senseless with a rod by now. You must teach her otherwise."

His jaw dropped practically to his chest once he fully grasped the meaning of Mordecai's words. "I couldn't," he stuttered. "I cannot hurt her. It is not in me."

Mordecai practically jumped on him. "And she clearly knows that. You are too predictable, cousin, another reason she despises you. Now do you want my advice, or don't you."

Not knowing how to answer without admitting to his weaknesses, Zutra remained silent for what seemed ages before nodding his head in consent.

"I know that you are incapable of beating Avital," Mordecai acknowledged. "Although she deserves it and God only knows how much I would love to do it for you, I will not suggest that you do so. I cannot make a fish fly. But there are other ways."

Listening intently, the Exilarch begged his advisor to continue.

"Your future bride respects only power, as I already mentioned to you. Power denotes strength, stability and contentment. Right now, whether you accept it or not, she has all those things within her command. Unwittingly, you have provided those to her without marriage, so why should she give you love if she already has everything she craves."

"Then I am doomed," Zutra sunk his head into his shoulders, resigned to defeat.

"Nonsense! You are more in control than you realize. The answer is simple. With the wielding of two emotions, you can wipe away all her delusions of power; fear and jealousy. Those are your weapons. They are the two emotions by which you can dominate any woman!"

"I cannot strike her," the Exilarch quickly inserted. "You already know that!"

"Who said anything of beating her," Mordecai smiled devilishly. "Others would have done so by now, but I agree, it is not in you. However, what you do possess is a quick and steely mind. That is your weapon with which to strike your blows. Make her fear that she will lose everything that she believes she already has. Make her fear that she has lost control. It is easy enough to do. As Exilarch you have the privilege of taking more than one wife."

"None has done that in centuries."

"There is no law against it," Mordecai reminded him.

"But I don't want more than one wife!"

Mordecai looked sternly into Zutra's eyes. "I said you can take more than one wife. I didn't say that you necessarily would! Make her believe that is your intention. Leave it to me and I will arrange everything. How many satraps exist in the empire? Eleven? Multiply that by the number of daughters their monarchs would give their right arm to have an alliance with you right now. We could throw a banquet every week and still there would be more princesses than we could accommodate."

"Do you think that will be enough to melt her heart?"

"No, but it will be a good start. Moreover, you will come to see that there are more beautiful women in this world than just Avital. The first thing you do before we invite a single ruler to send us his daughter is to move your harpy out of her quarters. Send her to one of the furthest chambers from where you reside. Make certain that all the servants refer to it as the concubine's quarters. Place at least four beds into the chamber so that she thinks there may be others joining her shortly. Hire a eunuch to manage the affairs and to watch her movements. His presence alone should send shivers of fear down her spine."

"You want me to set up a harem," Zutra gasped.

"Whether you fill it or not I leave that up to you," Mordecai winked. "But let her stare at those empty beds for a while and I guarantee she will start fearing for her favored position."

"This just might work," Zutra mused, twisting the spike of his pointed beard between thumb and forefinger.

"Of course, it will work. As soon as Avital realizes you are searching for a true queen, a woman of high stature and royal birth more deserving than she is, she will abandon any semblance of haughtiness. She might not love you, but she will don every pretense to make you think so in order to secure her position."

The dour look on Mar Zutra's face soured into a sorrowful pout.

"Now what's wrong," Mordecai questioned.

"I want her to truly love me. Not a pretense. Real love! Is that not achievable?"

Scornfully, the advisor directed an index finger pointing like a shaft into the Exilarch's heart. "You want real love," he fumed, "then marry one of the daughters of the foreign kings we invite to our feasts. You want Avital, then settle for what is available. Who knows, given enough time, and enough familiarity, not to mention penetrating her upon every whim that you have, you may just find that she manifests a degree of love in that block of ice sitting in her chest that she calls a heart. But I would not bet on it."

"And then I can take her into my chambers and stop the ruse of seeking other marriages?"

"Never," Mordecai bellowed loud enough that it drew the attention of some of the onlookers lining the streets. "Quick, throw some more coins. They must not think there is any discord between us."

Zutra did as he was told, intrigued by the people scrambling for the bobbles tossed their way.

"You must never let her think she has gained the upper hand. The only way she will spread her legs for you any time you wish is by making her think that if she doesn't then another will. She must always stay in the common bedchambers so that her status never rises above that of a secondary wife. Every now and then, I would suggest you have a young girl or two reside in the chambers for a couple of nights. Then remove them and say to Avital that you did not find them to your satisfaction. It will keep her constantly fearing that you are still searching for the perfect bride. But sincerely cousin, I do pray that you eventually find another though you do not wish to hear me say it."

The gloomy expression on Zutra's face transformed miraculously into a gratuitous smile. "I think you have provided me with the solution cousin. This will work!" Zutra was delighted with the plan.

"I still think she is not worthy of you."

"How does one explain why their heart quickens at the sight of another, even if no one else feels it or understands it? Were you able to explain your love you had for the servant girl to your father? It is impossible for others to see through your eyes, dear cousin. Though you may not understand my longing, all I truly seek is your blessing."

"Cousin, you will always have my blessing. And one more bit of advice if you permit me."

"Of course," Zutra assured him.

"I fear that you will be unable to maintain the charade of actively searching for a queen as long as is necessary. I warn you that the day she discovers it was a ruse will be the most miserable day of your life, only to be replaced by the next day, and the one after that, and so on, each worse than the previous. For that reason, I will give you the sword to ensure that she never reverts to her old ways. You must make her think that every day you

43

are considering sentencing her father to death. A public execution much in the manner your father suffered. She may lie and say otherwise to you, but I know her feelings of love and admiration for her father know no bounds. If she thinks her cause of displeasure to you will result in your carrying out your threat, she will remain subdued."

"That I can do easily," Zutra smiled. "There is not a day that goes by that I do not think of ordering that execution. I search for any excuse that he might provoke me to carry it out. I will see to it that a rumor of the threat is whispered constantly through the corridors of my palace."

"Look," Mordecai exclaimed. "To your right is a large number of the Parthian population. Throw them several handfuls of coins. I want them to feel special. Today will be a big day for the other citizens in your city."

Zutra gladly did as he was instructed.

Chapter Five

Shenzhen: Present

"Wife beating appears to have been an accepted practice in your family," Pearce commented.

"I thought we agreed that you'd remain quiet while I told this story?"

"C'mon Doc, you can't expect me to be silent while you're talking about this ancestor of yours abusing the only woman he supposedly loves. Can you?"

"Why so surprised? How do you think we achieved all those happily ever after stories?" I responded with a mischievous grin upon my lips. "There's one thing that has always been a constant in my family's history and that is our difficulty in dealing with our wives. Zutra's probably an exception. Most of my ancestors would have thrown in the towel by now."

"So, let me see if I've got this straight. Zutra is king of this city Mahoza. However, Mahoza is inside this Empire. So he's not really a king at all."

"But he is. That's why they were referred to as satraps; mini kingdoms within a much larger kingdom. The Great Shah was often referred to as the King of Kings. Zutra was just one of his lesser kings."

"King of a city?"

"Exactly!"

"You know that word still continues to bother me," Pearce reacted. "So, when is a city a kingdom?"

"It wasn't that uncommon. Look at Jerusalem. Five hundred years from the time of this story, it was set up as a kingdom by the Christian crusaders. If a city is big enough, it can be a kingdom. That's why we have the expression that every man is king of his castle when he's at home."

Pearce thumbed his chin. "Okay, I'll accept that. I get the point. Sort of what you explained to me in ***Blood Royale***."

"Exactly."

"There you go again with that word. Give it a break already. So where's this Mahoza?"

"Interesting you should ask. It's in Iraq. I believe they call the area now by the name Al-Mada'in. However, there were two ancient cities there, one on each side of the Tigris River about twenty miles south of Baghdad. One city was referred to as Ctesiphon, the capital city of the Sassanids. The one across the bridge from it was Mahoza, formerly known as Seleucia when it was under the control of the Greek Seleucids. Two major metropolises separated by a bridge."

"Why would they build two major cities across from one another? Seems like a waste of resources," Pearce commented astutely as if he was a civil engineer.

Simple. The Parthians wouldn't occupy it after they conquered the Seleucids. The city was considered too unclean. So they gave it to the Jewish exiles when they fled Judea after the war with Rome in the first century."

"If I recall correctly, you mentioned something about that in ***Dominance***."

"I briefly mentioned that when Joseph freed the twelve hundred prisoners, two of them were the wife and son of the High Priest, Jeshua ben Gamaliel."

"That's right, Martha and her son Joseph, your ancestors. I recall the story now."

"The name Mahoza tells the story. It's one of those words in the Hebrew language that has multiple meanings."

"Such as?"

"Such as, 'those from the outside' or 'from the pact' or 'from the prophecy' or one of my favorites, 'from those that repent and return'. As you can see, whichever translation you use for Mahoza you arrive at an apt description of how the city fell under control of my family. They had an existing pact with the Parthians for their escape should they lose the war against the Romans. The city was populated by outsiders according to the ruling class, not to mention that the location was very familiar to the Jews as they had been there six hundred years before during the Babylonian exile, so they were returning where they could repent and hopefully the ancient prophecies would carry them back to Judea in the future."

"And that's exactly what happened eighteen centuries later," Pearce calculated.

"See, there's that magic number eighteen again," I commented.

"It's a coincidence," he insisted.

"By now Pearce, you should know there's nothing coincidental when it comes to my family. Now let me get back to telling the story!"

Ctesiphon: 497 A.D.

The Sargon Bridge with its hugs stones spanning the Tigris River had been there as long as anyone could remember. The name implied that it had first been built by the ancient Babylonian King bearing that name. Stretching two hundred feet in length, it strctched over one of the narrowest crossing points, as for most of its meanderings the mighty Tigris averaged over five hundred feet in width. It was also one of the shallowest points, with some of the old-timers recalling long ago a particularly dry season when the river could be crossed by merely walking across it, the water never reaching much above the waist. Nevertheless, no matter how wide or how deep it may have been at any particular time, throughout history the river had been the lifeblood to the Empire. He who commanded the Tigris ruled Mesopotamia and it was a lesson that had not been lost on Mar Zutra.

Built from huge ashlars transported from the far-away Taurus Mountains to the head of the river, the bridge was a viable testimonial to man's engineering skills from a bygone age. Wide enough to permit sedans and carriages to pass each other, yet not so massive that the series of stone arches that spanned the river would ever collapse under the weight of the thousands that traversed its expanse daily. Rafts and small craft sailed freely up and down the river, passing beneath the interlocking stones that literally hung in the sky above their heads.

A wonder of the world, as it was labeled by the many travelers that had traversed its steps, not because it was any more magnificent or impressive than many of the other bridges that bore such an accolade across the known world, but because of the two worlds it joined. Two cities could not possibly be more different yet living harmoniously side by side. Almost as if their god, Ahura Mazda had conjoined night with day.

Ctesiphon had grown into a modern marvel, a megalopolis, on the east shore of the Tigris, where a multitude of civilizations had come together in the most cosmopolitan city of its time. Towers scraped the sky, their ornate architecture rising like needles shooting towards the heavens. Golden spires shone with the brilliance of bursting suns, casting rainbows of light though the wide tree-lined streets. Parks interlaced the city with their fountains and small man-made lakes stocked with spectacular panoramas of colorful fish imported from the orient. Synonymous with a playground for the rich and powerful, offering every earthly delight to the wealthy nobles of the Empire that tended to use it as their winter resort, choosing to stay in the northern capital city of Susa during the summer months. Though it may not have been entirely a matter of choice, since the seasonal migration was the preferred arrangement of the Emperor Kavad, and in their eagerness to gain his favor, the aristocrats of Persia tended to do whatever their Emperor decided, especially if it meant being close to his magnificent presence.

On the other bank, stood Mahoza, old and stale, like a dried piece of moldy bread. Neglected for over two hundred years, the ancient buildings were scarred by crumbling edifices and faded murals. A central sewer system similar to Ctesiphon's was noticeably absent, instead a quagmire of cesspools warrened beneath the residential districts, occasionally collapsing and swallowing an entire tenement into the yawning maw of the fetid earth below. Here lived the outcasts, the immigrants, the undesirables. Oddly, some that resided in its districts and cast as immigrants were from families that predated the Sassanids by centuries. However, their Greek or Jewish customs rendered them different and therefore unacceptable to the mainstream that could never understand why these foreigners held on so tenaciously to their ancient traditions. Yet, to Zutra it was the most wonderful place in the entire world. It was his city, his capital, though he could never publicly declare it, and to his overlord he was nothing more than a vassal mayor that ensured that Mahoza remained unobtrusive within the

Empire.

The ride to the palace in Ctesiphon was only a few miles from his own residence, yet the journey was a lesson in life, especially when Mordecai was in charge. Accompanied by a small platoon of men, lightly armed to discourage any bandits along the way, the Exilarch and his cousin rode upon the same two horses that had pulled their carriage the week before. Sitting high in the hard leather box saddles typical of the mountain tribes, Zutra constantly readjusted his position, vainly searching for a rare modicum of comfort.

"We could have walked?" Zutra protested.

· "Kings don't walk," his cousin quickly rebuked him.

"But there are other means of transportation without sitting on horseback. We could have considered a few of the alternatives."

"I am an old man and yet here am I sitting on this horse's back and do you hear me making one word of complaint?"

"Why would one old nag complain about another?"

"Hush Zutra," Mordecai was losing patience but only for the moment as he loved Zutra as the son he never had. "This is a very important summons," he continued. "It's not like the Pashah to invite us to the palace unless he wants something very badly."

"Perhaps he is upset by last week's banquet for the citizens. The people are still very excited over it. Who knows, perhaps he sees me as a possible threat to his authority."

"I don't think so," Mordecai's mind was running through an entire series of possible scenarios. "He was paid handsomely to permit the banquet. I doubt he would complain. Events in Mahoza hardly register with the Pashah unless there's trouble. The people are happy and content. That means he is happy and content. So, it has to be about something very important."

"Then perhaps he just wants to confirm my position as Exilarch. Have the final stamp of approval so he can report back to the Great Shah that it was all his doing."

Mordecai contemplated Zutra's suggestion carefully. "Possible," he drew the word out as he considered it. "But I don't think so," he blurted a second later. "He wouldn't need to see us to do so. I've known him for years. If he wanted to claim an event or achievement as his own, he'd do so without hesitation. No, there's definitely something more important taking place that we're not aware of."

The palace guards stopped the entourage at the gates, but upon recognizing the new Exilarch, waved his party on without even a search. They had already received their orders to let them pass without delay.

"Obviously, he doesn't want our presence here to be too noticeable."

"Is that good or bad," Zutra questioned.

"All depends," Mordecai replied cryptically. "If he wanted to do away with us, then the fewer people that know we were here, the easier it would be."

Zutra looked at his cousin with growing apprehension.

Mordecai shook his head, indicating that there was no need to worry. "Had that been the case we would have been dead as soon as we passed through the gates. He has something else that he wishes to keep quiet. I think the Governor is up to something far more sinister."

Zutra began to finger the hilt of his short, curved sword that hung on his left hip.

"Not against us," Mordecai quickly added cautioning Zutra to release the tightening grip on his weapon. "I believe there is a game afoot here and he wants us to play on his side."

"You've deducted all that just from the fact that the guards ushered us into the palace without any delay."

"That and from the fact that the Pashah is very anxious to greet us. Look up! He's on the balcony waving to us as if we're old friends."

Mar Zutra raised his sights towards the row of balconies that hung from each of the palace chambers. As described, there was the Governor, warmly waving and smiling, which was not his typical demeanor at all. "Most disconcerting," Zutra muttered.

"Isn't it," was Mordecai's sole reply as the horses passed beneath the architrave, where the palace grooms held out their hands requesting the reigns, while other's ran forward with small sets of steps with which the two of them would dismount.

"His Excellency, the Governor of Ctesiphon welcomes his honorable brothers most favorably," the bald chamberlain, his neck burdened by a heavy gold chain, announced.

"We are delighted to be here as guests of the most exalted Governor," Zutra saluted in return.

"Please follow me," the chamberlain instructed. "He's requested that I take you directly to his private chambers."

Ordering his guard to stay alert and watch over the horses, Zutra and Mordecai fell in step behind the portly official as he led them through the corridors of the winter palace. For Zutra, it was the first time he had seen the inside of the Great Shah's palace with its ornate furnishings and elaborate tapestries. Some of the most beautiful rugs ever commissioned, each room decorated differently from every other, covered the marble tiled floors. The display of wealth was overwhelming to those unfamiliar with the trappings of being the King of Kings. At that moment, Zutra was thinking about his ancestor Mar Ukba, squirreling away the bags of denarii he had confiscated from the fleeing Roman emperor and how he thought Mar Ukba must have agonized over that decision to steal the money as a reward for his victory. Now he recognized the truth. The Great Shah probably would not have even cared about losing such a trifling amount. What would twenty or thirty talents of silver mean to someone that had wealth beyond measure?

Beyond the two ivory inlaid doors, the Pashah stood ceremoniously attired in his crimson and purple kaftan, awaiting his invited guests. His black beard had been freshly curled and oiled in the manner of the Persians; threads of gold interwoven among the fine strands of his hair.

"Welcome, welcome," he held his arms outstretched in open greeting. "I am so glad that you could make it," his heightened level of excitement obvious to his guests. "You can leave now Mered," he instructed his chamberlain dismissing him with little concern. "And kindly shut the door behind you as you leave." As soon as the official had left and the Governor heard the click of the door latch, he invited his guests to sit down on the pillowed couches that formed a square at the centre of the room. "I've taken the liberty to have the food and libations prepared for you in advance of your arrival; all according to your dietary laws. I hope you will find them to your liking." The Governor raised a golden chalice in honor of his guests. In response, both Zutra and Mordecai raised the goblets that were arranged on the table in front of them. "A toast," the Governor exclaimed. "To the new Exilarch of Mahoza, friend and companion of the Empire. May he reign until a ripe old age."

"To the Empire," they both chirped back simultaneously before sampling the aromatic blend of wines.

"It is so good to see you once again Mordecai bar Kahana. It has been years since we last met. I must confess you don't appear to have aged a day. Ahura Mazda has blessed you with a gift."

"It has been several years Pashah Gurzam. Not since the day I requested that the Great Shah accept myself and the Four Hundred as a mercenary force in his army to fight the Ephthalites," Mordecai clarified.

"We have not done too well on that particular front," the Pashah reflected disheartened.

"The White Huns outnumbered our forces in the north.," Mordecai explained. "As long as we continue to spread the army over several fronts we can do little but try and keep them from invading. Even if we were at full force in the north, I don't honestly know if we could withstand their attack. I have never seen fighters like these before. They ride as if their horse was a part of them. Fused into a single being from which they fire their arrows in a constant stream, all the while controlling their horses with only the slightest pressure of their legs. Archers with that level of mobility are practically unstoppable."

"So, I have heard, so I have heard," the Pashah nodded his head knowingly. "And will your youthful Exilarch be thinking about taking his forces up to the Northern provinces to test his metal?"

"Not at this juncture I'm afraid," Mordecai answered on behalf of Mar Zutra.

"Is that so," the Pashah pursed his lips tightly together. "Perhaps you have another reason why you'd want to keep your cohort in Mahoza for the time being?"

Mordecai was about to answer when he felt his cousin tug at his elbow. Zutra wanted to speak for himself, and though having his reservations, the elder statesman conceded.

"My cousin fears that the rashness of youth has not given me the adequate time to speak as well as I should on the issues of state. Therefore, I hope you will have the forbearance to overlook any errors of etiquette that I perchance might make."

"Have no concerns or worries," the Pashah reassured him. "We are all friends here. Formalities aren't necessary. Speak as you wish."

"I appreciate your kindness," Zutra accepted.

Mordecai looked relieved. So far his young ward had handled himself properly with the proper deference to the Governor. Perhaps it was time for his charge to speak for himself.

"I think the Governor should be aware that my ascension to the Exilarchate has not been without some resistance from within my own community."

Feigning to gasp, the Pashah pretended to be shocked by the revelation. "I did not know. I am sorry to hear that!"

"Yes, it was most unfortunate. but I can assure you that the few dissenters to my assuming my legal and proper position have been dealt with. I have had them arrested and they are now confined to their homes under detention."

"Do you think it wise to permit them to live? I can bring your situation under our authority and use our laws to have them dealt with properly."

The Pashah's cavalier attitude in executing Jews of the aristocracy was a bitter reminder and Zutra felt a surge of bile at the back of his throat as the rage began to swell in the pit of his stomach. The Governor would have been just as callous when he passed sentence on his father. Nothing had changed. He took a deep breath and permitted a wave of calm to flush over his body. This was neither the time nor place to unleash his true feelings. His voice calm and unwavering, Zutra redirected the question back to the Governor. "Why would you think that I should fear a small group of meddling troublemakers? In death, they would probably be more of a problem to me than when they are alive. However, you can now appreciate why the Four Hundred will be staying close to me in Mahoza. Not only do they enforce the house arrest but they are a deterrent to anyone thinking of supporting the dissenters."

"Yes, yes, I can see that," the Governor agreed.

Mordecai breathed a sigh of relief. He watched intently as Zutra had recovered his calm.

"Please my friends partake of some food. I have a tale to tell. I believe you will find it to your benefit to bear with me."

"I'm afraid that tales were not what we had expected," Zutra cared little for games.

"This one will be of interest to you. I assure you. The magus Mazdak is the author of this tale."

The mention of the magi's name definitely heightened their interest. For the Pashah to share his concern over the wizard was a risk that clearly marked his desperation. For any man that ran afoul of the magus instantly declared himself an enemy to the Emperor. "Do I have your word that what I am about to tell you shall remain in confidence only between us."

"As God is my witness," Mordecai proclaimed.

"You say nothing Exilarch?" the Governor was surprised.

"My word would mean so little whereas my continued presence assures you of my confidentiality."

"Good," the Pashah relaxed. "For the moment you had me concerned."

"As we should be," Zutra confided. "If you are going to speak ill of the magus and bring us in to your confidence then it means the three of us are walking a path close to death."

"If it makes you feel any better, then let me add dozens more. All of the nobles of Ctesiphon know of what I'm about to tell you. Does that make a difference?"

"More for the Great Shah to place beneath his executioner's axe," Zutra smiled.

"Though I do not understand it, Mazdak weaves some kind of spell over the Emperor Kavad. He bends the Great Shah to his every whim. I know not how he does it but we are helpless against him."

"It is evil magics that are being used," Mordecai explained. "There have been many that have wielded them since the dawn of time and that man is no different."

"But now those magics have seized the throne and we must do something," he beseeched his guests.

"What would you want from two Jews of Mahoza?" Zutra inquired.

"I've asked you here not as Jews but as nobleman of the Empire. We share this in common, do we not? I need your support if we are to undo this evil."

"You have yet to tell us what we should be so concerned about," Mordecai suggested.

"There are new laws that are about to be announced by the Emperor; laws that Mazdak has written. All property is to become communal. There will no longer be a difference between rich and poor. The poor shall come into your house and take what they wish and the rich shall give it to them freely."

"Noble but foolish," Mordecai dismissed the unpronounced law as nothing more than an imprudent notion that would never take root.

"Don't dismiss it so easily," the Pashah warned. "The definition of wealth and property has been extended to include your women as well. All men shall be entitled to lie with any woman they wish; married or unmarried, virgin or mother. It matters not."

"And you fear that the Emperor would agree to this? Absurd!" Zutra rose to leave. "Do not fear this tale never was spoken. We will say nothing of it."

"I do not fear that he will agree to it. I know that he has agreed to it! He's even offered his queen as the first to participate in the new law. Mazdak is to bed her at his leisure."

Mordecai covered his mouth with his hands in shock.

"This has to be a mistake," Zutra fell back into the lounge. "No one in his right mind would permit such a thing."

"Now you can appreciate that this problem is not just a Sassanid one. These laws will apply to everyone living in the Empire. And your women will be considered some of the most desirable, since no one, pardon my expression, has ever had the luxury of having one unless they were part of your community."

"You have obviously caught my attention," Zutra was stunned by the revelation. "It is utter madness! But identifying the problem was not why you asked us here."

"Of course not," the Pashah admitted. "We have a plan but to make it work we need the support of all the people of our two cities."

Zutra held his hands up to pause the Governor before he spoke any further. "I can imagine what you are going to suggest. Before you say anything that will condemn us all to death, I need the time to confirm everything that you have told me. Then, if I'm convinced things are as you say, we will discuss strategies."

The Pashah Gurzam turned to Mordecai placatingly. "We do not have time to wait," his eyes were haunted with fear.

"Don't waste your time trying to convince me," the old man advised. "I'm convinced, but Mar Zutra is the Exilarch, and if he says we wait, then we wait."

"I pray you do not take too long. Time does not favour us in this matter. Within the fortnight, the law will be ready for his seal. Once affixed it may be too late."

"Two weeks at the most," Zutra offered.

"No longer, please, I beg you."

Chapter Six

Mahoza: 497 A.D.

The never-ending processions of caravans descended upon the sleepy city of Mahoza, journeying from far off lands with exotic names that few people would even attempt to pronounce. Laden with gifts, borne by chieftains, princes, kings and ambassadors, they all flooded through the Lion Gates of the city drawn to the well-circulated rumor of a Persian king looking for his first queen. The possibility of being first queen raised the values of those daughters in their father's eyes tremendously.

Mordecai made every preparation so that there would be a festival atmosphere greeting the royal guests upon their arrival, a gaiety and splendor that practically rivaled the Great Shah's court in every way. Dancing girls, jugglers, acrobats and magicians competed tirelessly for the crowd's attention and for the few dinars they would toss their way. Children sat around the grizzled old story tellers with their high peaked turbans and gnarled canes. This was the enchanted land of fantastic tales, of the jinn and demons, which would mesmerize young minds for the rest of their natural lives. The atmosphere in Mahoza felt electrified, effusing the metropolis with new life that it had not experienced in several centuries. Every citizen shared the exuberance, knowing that a royal wedding would mean a weeklong feast and entertainment, all at the expense of the young monarch. Therefore, for their own personal happiness, they prayed rigorously that Mar Zutra would select at least one wife from the many candidates being presented from across the Empire.

Out of the desert sands journeyed daughters of tribal chieftains, land barons and Arab sheiks, their fathers seeking any opportunity of getting closer to the mighty Shah, even through a marriage to the lesser prince of Mahoza. There also came the daughters of the mighty as well as the forgotten; desert princesses from the small kingdoms that dotted the landscape. The offspring of the new-men that had made their fortune, initially as desert raiders but now trading in livestock and merchandise, as their caravans transported the bounty of an Empire throughout the Far East and the lands of the Huns along the Silk Road.

From his bedroom balcony, young Zutra watched the endless parade of nobleman, accompanying the shielded sedans bearing the young woman about to be offered in the same manner that a merchant sells his wares. Speaking aloud, though no one else was present, he needed to hear the sound of his own thoughts in order to analyze the magnitude of the situation that his eyes beheld. "What have you done to me now, cousin?" he wondered. Mordecai had advised him earlier that morning that he was staging a magnificent ceremony in the evening, instructing him to wear his best suit of clothes for the occasion. "Could he actually be expecting me to choose a bride before all these guests tonight in a public display?" Zutra pondered. Though he had pledged solemnly to follow his cousin's advice faithfully, there were certain things that he considered too great an intrusion into his life; whom he married was one of them. Nevertheless, he had no other choice but to dress appropriately in his finest arraignment for the banquet. To offend all these chieftains and kings that had come to dine at his table would be a greater offense than refusing to select a bride. An eastern potentate could more easily accept the slighting of one of their daughters than an obvious discourtesy by failing to demonstrate proper decorum. Over the latter insult and incursion, they would gladly go to war.

Fortunately, as far as he was concerned, there were still several hours before he would be summoned to make his grand entrance into the great hall. Just enough time to walk the streets of his city and forget his pending predicament, at least for the moment. Few of the previous Exilarchs would ever dare to walk through Mahoza's districts without armed escorts but few of them had ever gained the love and admiration that Zutra had achieved in such a short time. Mordecai's clever use of Mar Ukba's appropriated fortune had the desired effect that they had hoped for. Every faction, all the nationalities, and each displaced culture that resided in Mahoza professed their undying loyalty to the young prince. The Parthians especially prayed that Zutra was their returning Surena, the man to lead them to victory over their oppressors so that once again they could rule in their own land. Only his own community remained divided in their loyalties, some still secretly supporting those former judges that he kept under house arrest.

Walking along the banks of the canal that channeled the life giving waters of the Tigris into the heart of the city, Zutra contemplated how the ancient tributary could be harnessed to carry the city's effluent back to the river, eliminating the ancient cesspools that riddled the ground beneath his city, just as they had done in Ctesiphon. How to create a reverse flow without contaminating the fresh water sources was the actual dilemma because part of his city sat well below the riverbed? It would take some of the best minds among the Empire's engineers but for every problem, he believed there had to be a solution. Totally preoccupied with thoughts of designing his new project, he failed to notice the rapid approach of the gilded litter with its heavily armed and sizable escort heading directly towards him.

"You there," the captain of the guards shouted in heavily accented Greek," Clear the path!"

Zutra looked left then right quickly to ensure that he was the one being spoken to; no one else was present. Having deliberately worn very ordinary attire for his stroll, his appearance was not unlike any other petty aristocrat in the city, a mistaken identity accentuated by the fact that he had ventured without any personal bodyguards onto the streets. To any foreigner he encountered, he would at best be viewed as a menial bourgeois of little consequence. "There is more than enough room to pass," Zutra responded curtly in his refined Greek a clear indication that he should not be confused with a paltry citizen, no matter what his appearance.

"Did you not hear me," the captain blustered. "Make way for the Princess Ti-Ping, favored daughter of the Emperor Hsiang Xiaowen, Sun Lord of the Sin, or bear the consequences since no man is permitted to approach her litter!"

"But I am not approaching you, good sir," Zutra continued to act the part of a mere aristocrat, "It is all of you that are approaching me," he corrected the officer.

"I will not have the princess mocked in such a manner," the soldier sounded flustered as he reached for the hilt of his sword.

Zutra refused to step aside. "And I will not permit to have a citizen of Mahoza threatened by any foreigner, no matter what their diplomatic status. Tell your princess that she is now in Mahoza and here we make no distinction between kings and nobles. They are all to be treated with respect."

"I will not permit the Princess to be insulted," the captain began to withdraw his curved scimitar from its scabbard.

Mar Zutra made no effort to clear the path even as the glint of the metal shone in his eyes. "I have an even greater weapon," he cautioned the soldier. "Would you like to see it? Here, come closer and take a good look at this ring." Zutra held out his hand encouraging the Captain to take a better look at its engraved insignia. It was then that he took note of the officer's slanted eyes and somewhat Asian features. "Do you recognize it?" Zutra was not quite certain the appearance of the ring would be familiar to someone from so far away. "It is quite famous they say, and it will blunt your sword with but a slight wave of my hand. More importantly, it will eliminate any opportunity of your Princess ever being presented to the King in Mahoza. Do you not agree?"

The captain of the guard stood in stunned silence, waving to his second in command to be quiet when he approached to investigate if there was going to be a problem.

"What do you think the Emperor Hsiang will say when you return to the Sian and tell him that his favored daughter never even had the opportunity to appear before the King because of your blind insolence?" Zutra waved the black onyx ring in front of the commander once more, making certain that he saw the intricate detailing of the carved fly insignia. "Even one as lowly and as far away as I, good sir, have heard of the tempestuous temper of your great Emperor of Sian."

"And even to someone as lowly as I from the East know this insignia," the captain's jaw dropped as he went down on one knee before Mar Zutra. "Forgive this ignorant and foolish servant, your Majesty."

While kneeling, it provided Mar Zutra the opportunity to scrutinize the soldier more closely. The Captain's uniform though peculiar and somewhat ancient in design suggested that he spent most of his time serving on the Indus. Zutra had taken a calculated risk that anyone from such distant lands would still have seen the wax seals imprinted with the fly for which his family was famous. His hunch had been correct. Had he misjudged the extent of his family's reputation then he could easily have been another notch on the Captain's well-used sword.

"Rise Commander, you need not fear me. I am not a king like your Emperor."

Rising silently, the captain slid the sword back into its scabbard.

"I am glad you did not try to remove my head, Commander," Zutra smiled.

"Captain, your Majesty. Just a humble captain."

"See to it Captain that you men do respect my laws while they are in my land. Otherwise, I will send you on your way and you can return from whence you came."

"Forgive me your Majesty, I swear I did not know."

"Of that I am certain," Zutra pardoned. "A lesson hopefully learned. Next time do not be so hasty in making a judgment solely from outward appearances. Otherwise, I would be equally entitled to make judgment based on your own tattered uniform."

"Valentius? Valentius?" the voice surfaced from the veiled litter followed by a stream of strange sounds in a language Zutra had never heard before. Even the timbre of her voice was unusual but upon his ears, it sounded like heavenly chimes. The young Exilarch tried to peer through the drawn curtains, but he could not see past the heavy linen shades.

"Please explain to my mistress?" the horrified officer beseeched, praying that Mar Zutra would forgive his offense and assist his plight. "She will not forgive me if I have offended you."

"I thought it was forbidden to approach your princess," Zutra teased the panicked Captain.

"Not for one such as you, your Majesty."

"Then simply tell your princess this, 'that I look forward to seeing the divine face that would match such an angelic voice.' She has intrigued me and I do not wish to unveil the dream by approaching her litter. Let her know that she has already made an impression upon this humble servant."

Bowing to take his leave, the captain strolled towards the litter and leaned towards the curtains, speaking in the same foreign language that sounded like raindrops to Zutra's ear. The drapes parted slightly and Zutra strained to peer through the mere slit of an opening, desperately trying to catch a glimpse of the Sian princess, though he still wished not to spoil the surprise. The conversations transpired quickly at which point the Captain backed away from the litter and ordered his men to prepare to march to the palace. He then stepped towards Mar Zutra until only inches separated the two men. "The Princess says that she like you. She begs your forgiveness for our ill manners and hopes that our poor behavior in your land has not provided you with any misgivings."

"Perhaps I was wrong and I should see your Princess?" Zutra practically pleaded.

"She agrees that she should not spoil your surprise, your Majesty. Tonight she will unveil the dream, as you suggested. Forgive my impudence once more and please do not permit it to impact on how you perceive my Princess."

"All is forgiven Captain."

"One more favour your majesty," the Captain requested in a voice desperate not to be overheard by anyone other than Zutra. "When my Commander arrives this evening, please do not say a word of this event! He is far less forgiving than even the Emperor."

"Agreed," Zutra consented to the captain's wish. "He must surely be a terror if you fear him more than your Emperor."

"But he fears me more than even my father," the sweetest sounding voice in perfectly tutored Greek emerged from behind the litter's drapes. In spite of his hushed voice, the Princess had overheard every word.

"Should I fear you too, your Highness," Zutra responded with a laugh.

"Tonight, you shall see, my Lord. All dreams are unveiled in the night," her taunting voice faded into the distance as she was borne towards his palace.

"What have you done to me?" Zutra sounded hysterical as he paced back and forth in his chambers.

"Try to relax," Mordecai advised his young cousin. "If you don't keep still, you will ruin a perfectly woven rug. I told you that I would arrange everything. All you have to remain is a very polite and gracious host and everyone will go away happy when the festivities are over."

"Everyone?"

"Well, mostly everyone. A few may remain behind with their daughters once you choose."

"They are not coming here to just go away happy," Zutra refuted. "Nor are they here to see me have a dalliance with their daughters only to dismiss them after they have been bedded. They are expecting me to pick a wife. I never anticipated you'd invite them all at the same time! What were you thinking? This has turned in to a veritable circus!"

"It wasn't how I expected it to happen either," Mordecai apologized. "When I dispatched the invitations, I didn't think they would all be sending their daughters to you immediately. But it would appear that as soon as one monarch heard that another had responded it became a race to see who would get here first. Such things happen among royalty. They cannot afford to let their rivals get the better of them."

"In your dispatch did you by chance explain that that I was not necessarily selecting a wife? That I was simply taking it under consideration."

"And how was I to explain that in my letter. That you were merely appraising their merchandise. Perhaps you wanted me to say that you only wanted to sample the produce, squeeze a few melons," Mordecai's words dripped with sarcasm. "These are the kings and chieftains of the Empire, Zutra! It is time you started acting like one yourself. They don't think in terms of taking a wife. They deal more with the question of how many wives they should take. Every marriage represents a business transaction, an alliance, even a transfer of land and expanding borders. That will be what they are contemplating at the banquet tonight. How many of their daughters will you accept will be the likely topic of discussion? See to it that you do not disappoint them!"

"You have deceived me!" Zutra shouted. "You knew this would happen all along. You have probably even negotiated on my behalf with some already."

"I am your vizier. I look towards the future well being of your kingdom," Mordecai responded harshly.

"And if I choose none?"

The old advisor looked sternly at his ward. "This is not a game, Zutra. We are dealing in politics at a level far beyond anything you have dealt with before. We need allies. We need trade routes and markets. But most of all we need protection from the Magus."

"So, what are you telling me, that I have to take all of them? Have you seen how many caravans have arrived? You said you were only inviting the daughters from the eleven satraps. At this rate I will have more wives than Solomon!" Zutra continued his pacing around the room even more frantically.

"It wouldn't be unwise to be prudent," Mordecai shook a finger knowingly.

"And exactly what does prudent mean?"

"It means take the ones that offer you the most benefits. Those kings and chieftains whose daughters you refuse would understand that completely. After all, they are businessmen too. They would do the same in your shoes and would harbor no bad feelings." The old sage held out his open hands, gesticulating in anticipation of Zutra's reply. "You're a king, why not enjoy your life and take advantage of what it affords you?"

'You're serious? You are actually suggesting that I take on a harem."

"Why are you being so obstinate? Most men dream of this opportunity, knowing it will never happen. And here you are being handed that dream and all you can do is act as if you are being tortured." Mordecai shook his head in disbelief.

Zutra became furious, his face flushed and the veins popping on his forehead. "I told you that there was only one woman that I love!"

"Ptah!" Mordecai spat at the thought of Avital. "Well, learn to love another because from what I've seen so far cousin, she certainly isn't endearing herself to you."

Zutra clenched his fists. "It is just a matter of time!"

"Time," Mordecai chuckled. "Take it from a man that has reached the end of his time; you do not have that much time to wait. Do you understand my role? Do you know what my responsibilities are?"

"You are my advisor as you were my father's advisor," Zutra snapped abruptly. "But overstepping that boundary is not advisable."

"You fail to see what lies in front of you."

"What are you talking about?" Zutra felt his temper simmering.

"The obvious! We are blood, but your line is destined to rule and my line has always been destined to serve as my father did, and his father did before him. As far back as anyone can remember; even back to the days of Solomon. Those of us destined to serve did so best by understanding the ways of the world. Moreover, when the king listened to our advice, all was well within our world. However, each time they refused to listen, we perished. So what do you intend to do, cousin?"

"This was no accident that so many have come at once, was it dear cousin?"

"Now you are beginning to understand my role," Mordecai cocked his head towards his king.

"The same way the princess from Sian did not just happen to hear about some eastern potentate searching for a wife through the talk in bazaars from caravan traders.

The Vizier continued to nod his head in appreciation of Zutra's sudden enlightenment. "It is not easy to get a message through to the Sun Emperor. Do you know how many favors I had to call upon to deliver such an invitation? Or appreciate how much of your ancestor Ukba's treasure I had to part with, in order to impress a ruler of such high standing? All this I did for you! For your city! For the continuance of your family! For the sake of your dynasty! That is what my family has done for hundreds of years, served yours even at the cost of our own happiness."

The Exilarch felt an overwhelming sense of shame flood across his thoughts. "What will you have me do?" Zutra acquiesced to his wizened advisor.

"Firstly, you will get dressed for the banquet. Then you will smile and greet everyone in the great hall as if they were your best friends from ages ago. Every monarch here is to feel special and believe his daughter will be the chosen one. We will eat, we will make merry, and when the night is over perhaps, you will tell them how difficult the selection is going to be. How beautiful and talented all their daughters are. How difficult they have all made this by having such lovely flowers in their households. And you will beg for their patience and their understanding while they indulge your slowness in making your decisions."

"For how long?"

"Weeks, if necessary. Months. It matters not."

"Why so long?"

"Because as long as they are here with their entourages, they will spend money and the markets will profit greatly from their purses. The people will love you for it. They will bless you for the good fortune you have brought them."

"But even with the seemingly vast wealth left by Ukba, how can my household afford to feed and keep all these guests for weeks or months?"

"That is why I encourage you to make your decisions a little more hastily," Mordecai snapped.

"And then?" Zutra accepting the words of advice without complaint.

"Then if you do not choose a few then at least you will choose one bride. She will be the daughter of the most powerful and important ruler; an alliance so astute and cunning that all the other kings and chieftains will acknowledge your choice without argument or resentment."

"You mean the daughter of the Emperor of Wei," Zutra understood immediately.

"There is no other that compares in rank and stature."

Donning a cynical smile, Zutra felt compelled to ask, "Is it even possible that all the other monarchs will accept such a decision? After all, she is so foreign to this land."

"If she proves to be the right one not only in standing but in intelligence, devotion and modesty, then yes!"

"And how will I know that?"

"I will let you know if she proves herself worthy," Mordecai winked.

"And if I object?"

"You will not my King. That is how our two families have worked successfully over the hundreds of intervening years. We advise and you will listen."

The wine flowed freely throughout the evening, drawn from the huge vats stored in the caverns beneath the great hall. Few of the kitchen servants could ever recall the last time the massive oak casks had been uncorked in so great a number. Truly, they thought, this must be an occasion upon which God smiled, for how else could so many rulers, many known to be hostile to one another, gather beneath a single roof in unbridled harmony.

While the guests ate their fill, dancers and musicians plied their arts while magicians performed their craft of trickery and deception to the amusement and awe of the onlookers. Throughout the early hours of the evening, the rulers presented their gifts one after the other, splaying them at the feet of the Exilarch. Chests of precious jewels or glittering gold and silver coins stacked one on top of the other as the suitors bargained on their daughters' behalves. Some gifts given freely, others to be dowries should their daughter be the lucky one. With each gift, Zutra thanked them profusely and enjoined them to share in his hospitality but never gave any indication if they had swayed his decision with their honeyed words or lavish presents.

Several hours into the festivities, the herald raised his voice and announced the late arrival of Pashah Gurzam from the neighboring city of Ctesiphon. The Exilarch rose from his high-backed chair and walked to the edge of the dais. He looked sternly into the Pashah's dark brown eyes, as a cold calm fell upon the hall sensing the unspoken tension towards the unanticipated guest. Zutra broke the heavy silence with a broad smile and a witty quip. "I did not know you had a daughter!"

"No, but I wish I did. Will his Majesty have me as a guest?"

By this time Mordecai had ambled up to Zutra's side and whispered into his ear. "I have asked the Governor to be here tonight. He has something of great importance to tell you."

"Come, Gurzam, sit with me. You are a most welcome guest." Zutra let the past be buried where it belonged. "Tonight, we drink and feast to my future."

"Thank you, Exilarch, you are most gracious."

Much to Mordecai's delight, the two men strolled together on to the platform and the Pashah took the seat of honor at Zutra's right hand to the applause of the other satraps and chieftains.

As Mordecai sat himself on the left, Zutra slapped his old advisor softly across the back and spoke quietly so not to be overheard. "Another surprise, *eh* cousin? You are a crafty one, Mordecai bar Kahana. As always my heart is won over by its kinship towards you. But such audacity as to invite the Governor without my prior agreement, that is treading a fine line."

"Whatever enmity you might bear from the past may vanish when you hear what he has to say. Trust me," he pardoned himself. "For your own sake you must listen to him."

"This better be good!" Turning to face the Governor, Zutra raised his goblet of wine in salutation. Whatever secret was being revealed this night would have to wait. There were guests more in need of his attention at that moment. The time had come for them to parade their most treasured and precious gifts before his eyes; the bridal train.

Each courtier, prince, king or chieftain, stood up at his appointed turn to sing the praises of the princess, duchess or noblewoman being offered for the matrimonial bed of Mahoza's new king. Some dark, others fair, some pleasantly plump, while others were as thin as wraiths. The many offered that one might consider attractive were only outnumbered by those that were counted amongst the plain and uninspiring. Zutra did as he had been instructed, smiling pleasantly to ensure that each one felt very special, followed by a compliment and word of praise to their fathers or escorts as the potential brides paraded their wares and then were led away to retire to their appointed chambers in the palace. He could barely remember the words that any of the girls had spoken; their little prepared speeches and performances intended to sway his heart and win him over. Some he thought would make suitable concubines, but never would he think of selecting any he had seen so far as a wife. If their fathers were agreeable to such an arrangement, then they could negotiate the terms later. More correctly, that would be a job for his vizier since Mordecai was responsible for placing him in this situation in the first place. Even those of stunning beauty and pleasant personality could not find a place in his heart from which a seed of love could grow. Perhaps he didn't have a heart he reflected, tapping his chest lightly as the most sultry and seductive failed to stir any passion in his loins as they paraded before his eyes. Was it possible in the years since his father's death that it had just shriveled and died, leaving nothing but a hollow in his chest, he wondered? Not a stir or even a flutter of excitement and anticipation surfaced, all the while Mordecai searching desperately on the young King's face for any glimmer of hope.

Lost in his own thoughts, Zutra looked down while he continued to tap the left side of his chest more resolutely to see if it sounded with an empty ring. His moment of silent contemplation was interrupted by the loud clearing of a throat calling everyone's attention. Dispersing his wandering daydreams, he gazed toward the striking commander now holding centre stage. The man was dressed in armor similar but far more recent to that of the Asian captain he had encountered earlier that day. Immediately, he focused his attention, realizing this could be what he had been waiting all evening for but didn't realize it until now.

The soldier cut a tall and distinguished figure, exuding immense power from his imposing stance. Zutra understood why the captain feared displeasing such a man.

"Noble king, grant this humble diplomat the opportunity to speak, though I fear they be the clumsy words of an old and crusty soldier rather than the prose of a dignitary. My Emperor extends his condolences that he was unable to attend himself and has given me the difficult task to effuse loquacious on behalf of his daughter." The spoken Greek that flowed from this man's lips was flawless, and certainly was not the common vernacular or pedestrian form currently used throughout the east. This man had a story to tell, of that Zutra was certain.

"Pardon any insult that the Emperor's absence may cause for it was not his intent to do so!" the commander continued.

Zutra nodded his approval. "It is well known that the Sun Emperor has much of the world beneath his gaze to look after and Mahoza would take him far away from those responsibilities. I readily accept his ambassador to speak on his behalf."

Removing his helm, the commander revealed a head full of braided silver locks. Scars of former battles crisscrossed his left cheek. In spite of the telltale wounds, they only made him appear more distinguished, looking every bit the soldier's soldier, his bearing admirable and heroic. "I have served in the courts of many rulers from Byzantium to the Sian and have gazed upon the rarest treasures coveted by men throughout the known world. I have known love and I have known loss, and I can speak truthfully when I say that no man should move through this life alone."

They were the first words spoken the entire night that actually stirred the Exilarch. It was true, no man should move alone through this life. "Philosopher-soldier, give me your name," Zutra instructed, entreated by the man's oratory skills, which belied the earlier statement of being only a simple soldier that could not wax poetic.

"I am Patricius, son of Flavius Ardabur Aspar." He stated his name with authority, knowing the effect it would have on those assembled.

No sooner had he mentioned his name than a chorus of whispers circled through the room with the force of a small tornado. "The Samatian, warlord," several murmurs echoed. Having disappeared over twenty-five years ago after the assassination of his father and brother, most had assumed that Patricius had surely been killed during the insurrection as well. At the time, Leo, Emperor of Byzantium feared that Aspar, who had risen to the position of consul, was intending to usurp his throne. Using the palace eunuchs as his assassins, he had both Aspar and his eldest son Ardabur killed. The other son Patricius, it was now apparent to all, had escaped but under orders of the Emperor, his marriage to Leo's daughter, Leontia was annulled and she was married off to his rival, Marcian. Ironic as fate often proves to be, seven years later Leontia and her new husband were arrested in a failed palace revolt against the then Emperor Zeno and both of them sent into exile. Whether they had survived their exile into the rugged interior of the Taurus Mountains, no one knew for certain though rumors abounded. However, Leontia's sister Ariadne had become Empress Consort to Zeno and after his passing was now the consort to the current Emperor Anastasius. The story of intrigue and murder within the Byzantine palace was well known to everyone. How then Patricius remained placed within this hierarchy of intrigue kept everyone in the room guessing.

"Welcome noble Patricius. As you can obviously overhear, your presence is well acknowledged." Zutra's remark was enough to stop the incessant whispering. "Most certainly you have had an adventurous life that intrigues everyone. We must sit and talk about it at some length over the next few days."

"It would be my pleasure, Excellency." The smile was genuine. Whatever the bond of mutual respect forged from first impressions between these two men, it had entrenched itself deeply. Mordecai observed the exchange with keen interest. In his eighty odd years, he had become an adept at sensing the mystic auras that weave themselves between men's souls. Moreover, he knew with certainty that a strong tie had formed between these two men for whatever reason upon first sight. He nodded silently to himself. This must be the sign he had been looking for.

"Please, carry on with your charge," Zutra requested. "I wish to hear more!"

"For the last eight years I have been in the service of the Emperor Hsiang Xiaowen of the Wei Empire. A vast land that covers most of the Eastern world; where the people number in the millions upon millions from all races between the Indus River and the Great Sea that few from your land have ever seen. The great Sun Emperor Hsiang Xiaowen sends you both his fraternal greetings in friendship and his favor. Even in his own land, he has heard of the royal line of the Exilarchs that extends back to the beginning of recorded time. The blood of the ancients he calls it, and such a heritage would do him proud if you were to mingle it with his own. The chests he has sent are a mere trifle of what he is willing to offer."

Clapping his hands, Patricius signaled for the bearers to enter the great hall carrying the train of gifts. "He offers these without precondition even should you not select his daughter as your wife. The cities he will provide to you within his own empire are mere baubles to peak your interest." On the platform before the dais the gifts began to pile in a small mountain. Woven bales of cloth made from the finest silks, chests filled with jewels and ingots, mulberry trees, each in its own little ceramic pot. Several oddly constructed wooden crates remained closed but were placed in close proximity to the mulberry bushes. "The silks he will wrap you in will be nothing but pale adornments for your own pleasure. In these boxes he has sent you the means to make yourself rich beyond compare. The very worms from which these silks were made and the threshers and spinning wheels by which to blend the threads. Here too are the looms upon which to weave your bales of cloth. No other man outside of the Sin Empire has ever been granted these special gifts and the secrets of how to do so. From the trees upon which the worms feed, to the servant girls to do the work, they are all yours without question, but they matter little to the Emperor of Emperors, for today he offers you his greatest treasure, his most prized possession; the most beautiful jewel in all of the Three Kingdoms. He presents for your heart's approval his favorite and most beauteous daughter, the Princess Ti-Ping."

Upon pronouncement of her name, the princess and her handmaidens entered on cue, pirouetting into the great hall with the grace of silver swans, while peacock feathered fans and rainbow-coloured ribbons twirled about their bodies and high above their heads with unparalleled skill and grace. Everyone felt the rustling in the air, which sparked with electricity, all present exhaling in a single combined gasp. Circling their mistress, the fans and ribbons whirled and danced mid-air, while the luxurious flowing robes worn by each performer accentuated the reflective shimmering silk robe worn by the princess. The guests were mesmerized into an entranced state by the dazzling display of spectral radiance. The chieftains inhaled the jasmine scented air and sighed with lewd desires upon viewing the princess's unrivalled features as the veils fell from her head and shoulders one by one. Every detail of her face was a veritable feast for the eyes designed to overwhelm and exhaust the senses of even the strongest willed man.

While every guest lay spellbound, unable to draw their eyes form the Princess Ti-Ping, she sang a melodious scale of notes, so high and perfect in pitch that one could only assume it was the music played upon the harps of angels. This was followed swiftly by a playful medley ranging between two octaves, played upon gourd shaped flutes until each note fell upon the ear as a cascade of incredible sound, so light and joyful that it lifted all their hearts until they were bursting with sublime happiness.

Zutra had become totally enthralled by the rare quality of her voice. The same melodic vibrancy that he had briefly encountered by the canal was now being unleashed upon his ears without constraint. Combined with the swirling colors, his senses grew unworldly, his mind spinning dizzily, and for the moment he felt as if his soul no longer was bound to its earthly existence. Others in the hall had the same reaction; a feeling not unlike the men in Homer's fabled Odyssey when Odysseus's crew succumbed to the siren's voices luring them to their deaths against the crashing rocks.

Nor could he draw his gaze from the princess's alabaster skin and sensuous red ochre lips. From her almond eyes, accented with blue shadow, to the long slender fingers, the nails of which were tipped in gold leaf, he etched every feature she displayed into his heart, which for the first time that night he could feel thumping wildly within his chest. The breath exhaled forcefully from his lungs as she twirled ever so slowly, the unknown lyrics dripping from her rubied mouth like fresh honey. Closer and closer she twirled her lithe, enticing form steadily rotating towards the platform upon which he sat. At that precise moment he knew he was prepared to promise her anything; his entire kingdom if she wished, as long as she would stay with him. His arms reached out automatically towards her floating veils, drawn uncontrollably into the invisible web she set for him. Just when he felt his fingers caress the floating edge of her gown, the trance was broken by the shrill scream of a wailing banshee.

In fact, the sound of the intruder's voice shocked all the guests from their induced delirium; their euphoric mood recklessly destroyed, leaving them now bitter and frustrated, infuriated by the sudden intrusion.

"How dare you let this…this creature lure you from the fulfillment of our contract!" she screamed at Zutra. "Is this what you're seeking? Some unnatural looking woman to dance and fondle your groin to make you feel like the man you're not!" Avital stormed towards the platform raging like a tempest that blew away anyone in her path. "Keep me locked away like some imprisoned animal while you entertain yourself with seductresses from the four corners of the Empire. Is it any wonder your father claimed me to be his own? You were not fit to have me!"

Unable to determine how he should respond to the intrusion, Zutra fumbled as he tried to rise from his chair, words escaping him the very moment he needed them most.

Standing a couple of feet away from the princess, Avital drew back her hand preparing to deliver a blow to the Princess Ti-Ping. As her clawed fist flew towards its intended target it was intercepted in full flight by Patricius's own hand shooting forward like a cobra. "Be warned, you will not touch the Princess," he growled at her as he tightened his grip. "To do so will mean instant death. Whether my host approves of it or not, I will most certainly kill you."

"How dare you talk to me that way? Do you know who I am?"

Squeezing her wrist tightly he forced her to grimace from the pain he inflicted. "You are nothing. Compared to my Princess you are less than nothing." The murderous tone in his voice forced Avital to relax her hand instantly, at which point Patricius released his vice-like grip. She turned towards Mar Zutra, her eyes looking pleadingly into his. "Are you going to let this soldier speak to me in that way? Are you?" she demanded to know.

Zutra was still unsure as to what he should say. All the rulers and aristocrats in attendance waited attentively to see how the Exilarch intended to deal with this embarrassing situation. Any decision he made now would ultimately determine how they would view this young monarch from this day forward, either with respect or with disdain. Zutra knew his measure was being taken and the future of his kingdom teetered ominously upon the words he selected. Through sheer will he found his voice.

"May I present to all of you the Lady Avital," Zutra began, forcing a smile to his face in order to ease the situation. "It is true; by contract she is my betrothed. I apologize for her outburst, but we all know what women can be like. Obviously, there is some concern on her part that she may fall from grace with my selection of a first wife. It would appear that she does not fully understand nor appreciate the term, second wife," he jested. "How would you suggest we educate her in this matter?"

"She should be worried," one of the guests shouted in condemnation. "She is nothing compared to any of our daughters! She is nothing more than a common wench! Remove her head and be done with her!"

"Now that would be entertaining," another shouted.

The others murmured in agreement with the expressed sentiments. The insult paid to the Princess Ti-Ping was equally an insult paid to all of their daughters. Others began to shout out a variety of punishments to be administered prior to her execution. Punishments that made death sound the more preferable of punishments. Their mood was growing blacker as they waited for Zutra to announce his decision. Their severe condemnation had exceeded his expectations to diffuse their anger.

Sensing his inability to deal with Avital, Mordecai stepped in quickly to handle the volatile situation. "Gentlemen, gentlemen, who here has not had to deal with the fury of a woman scorned? If there is such a man, then a most fortunate man he must be, because he never had to deal with the emasculation that any woman can do merely by keeping her legs crossed. But the presence of this harpy is a constant reminder of why we are all gathered here. So do not feel pity for my good King, but rejoice now that he has seen your beautiful and desirable daughters. From this moment he can do not more than dream of lying with them until such time that he takes one or several to wife. In the meantime, the braying of this she-wolf will make your daughters more and more desirable, especially since you see what he must currently contend with. The more she keeps her legs crossed, and I can assure you her legs will definitely be crossed tonight, the more he will long to pleasure in the gardens of your beautiful daughters. A king can rule a kingdom far easier than the mind of a woman. Are there any that would disagree? Let her live because her very presence increases the stock value of your daughters!"

It was a calculated risk to make a jest of the situation but as Mordecai had expected, there had been enough drink in the evening thus far to encourage laughter more than anger. "Guards," Mordecai shouted to the men posted to the door.

"That's it!" one guest exclaimed. "Throw her to the guards. They'll certainly pry her legs apart."

"Yes, to the guards! To the guards!" others began to shout in unison thinking it would be great fun. "Let them have their way with her."

The outburst of their laughter was a reassurance to Mordecai that the moment of danger had passed. "Better we let our guards keep their testicles from being mangled than have this lioness shred their manhood. Any of you that have angered your wives know how easily a woman can do it when they're riled. Let the guards escort the Lady Avital back to her chambers and see that she is kept locked away within them until we decide how to best punish her. If she is not willing to spread herself for the king tonight then she is of no use to him until she is willing, however long that may take. She might as well be kept where she can do no harm, as an imprisoned reminder to all your daughters that to please the king is the role and duty of his wives", he laughed, which only encouraged everyone else to laugh along with him. "As for now, we have weddings to forge and feasts to celebrate. Which one of your daughters will tantalize my King and show him what a real woman can do?"

"Zutra, how can you let him talk about me this way?" she shouted.

Mordecai interceded before the king could comment. "Send her to her chambers, my King. Lock her away for days, weeks, even months, whatever it takes. Let her know that she is not welcome here until she accepts her rightful place as a secondary and obliging wife. Perhaps the role of concubine would be more befitting of one so base born." The old advisor paused and then added, "Tell her now, my King, before she finds herself lowered to the rank of a common strumpet and I will then most assuredly hand her over to your guards! Then you will have need of not only first wife but second, third and even more!" His comments were intended solely for the distinguished guests in the room. The meaning was quite clear, convincing them that the more Avital fell from favor, the more likely that Zutra would be selecting several wives to fill his harem, rather than just the one. Avital's intrusion was turning into a most welcome opportunity for them all.

"Yes, take her away," Zutra commanded the guards. "The longer she stays here, the further she is distanced from second wife. Now be gone from my sight for your presence here is offensive."

"And he will deal with you later!" Mordecai added.

"Yes, I will deal with you later," Zutra parroted much to the delight of the assembled guests that could only imagine the punishments that would be administered.

Waiting until the guards had removed Avital a safe distance from the great hall, Mordecai clapped his hands, giving a standing ovation as if Avital's unexpected arrival had instead been cleverly orchestrated. "Well, I guess now you have no doubts as to why you have all been invited here with your daughters!" The outburst of laughter and applause indicated that they all appreciated and understood Zutra's situation, many faintly mumbling that it was all too familiar in their own households. How lucky they now all considered themselves that Zutra's father had made such a terrible choice for his son's original wife.

"Make her your concubine and then take all our daughters for you wives," one satrap ruler shouted through his intoxicated haze. "That will put her in her place. Matter of fact, I'm in need of a new wife too. Who here wants to give me their daughter to wed?"

"Shut up and sit down Lucinius. You already have too many wives," some of the guests shouted at the baron.

"Here, here," another of the local chieftains agreed. "Mordecai, use her as serving wench in the harem. It better suits her disposition. Teach her, her proper place!"

"An excellent idea," Mordecai indicated that the suggestion would be given due consideration. "The King and I will have much to discuss over the next several days, my Lords." Seeing that Patricius still stood protectively over his charge, Mordecai marched up to the princess and held out his hand so that she would place hers into his of her own volition. Bowing his head courteously to Patricius, he sought the soldier's permission to touch the Princess. Pleased with the display of proper respect, Patricius bowed his head in return, at which point the wise sage led the princess onto the platform and sat her in his own chair to the left of Mar Zutra. Stepping back down from the platform, he positioned himself beside Patricius and confided privately to the commander, "I think that is where she belongs, don't you?"

Patricius snorted his approval. The situation had been rectified to everyone's satisfaction, at which point Mordecai bowed once more to the commander signaling that everything would be taken care of and not to worry. Whatever had been written in Mordecai's original message to the Emperor had now been silently reaffirmed. The elder statesmen walked behind the long row of tables, assuming a position behind Mar Zutra.

"Thank you cousin," the Exilarch reached out and patted Mordecai's hand that rested on his shoulder. "Once again you have rescued the day."

"That woman brings you nothing but trouble," he responded in a low voice not to be overheard. "You should have let me take care of her a long time ago! I warn you cousin, one day she will be the death of you!"

"We've been through all that before," Mar Zutra groaned. "I love her. I can't help it. I know none of it makes any sense to you but it is as if she can do no wrong. I cannot even bring myself to discipline her or send her away."

"But I saw how you look at the Princess Ti-Ping," Mordecai winked. "You cannot deny what I see. Tell me there aren't feelings stirring inside you even as we speak."

"You know me too well, cousin. But Avital still occupies my heart."

"I want you to listen to me, Zutra. Listen to me well and do as I say! That man over there," he pointed inconspicuously towards Patricius, "is the key to our survival. He knows more about military matters than anyone alive today. Not only does he have the reputation as the foremost military strategist, but he also knows how to conduct a coup from his prior experiences."

"You mean failed coup, don't you cousin," Zutra corrected him as a precautionary notice.

"It matters not! What is of value is if he will lead us if we should consent to support the Pashah's plan. You need this man! I need this man! Your people need this man! Perhaps you don't realize it this very moment, but this woman and her protector have been sent to us by God. I know it! When I depart from this world, he will be the one to guide you. I am certain this is all God's handiwork. Why else would he have sent us not only one of the most beautiful and enchanting women in the entire world to of all places, Mahoza, but placed her in the charge of one of the most brilliant political and military strategists of our time? It has to be the Lord's will! Do you think you have the privilege or prerogative to disagree with the Almighty God?"

"I do not disagree with you Mordecai. I know there are forces far greater at work here than my understanding."

The King's candid response actually surprised Mordecai. "So I was right, you do desire the Princess Ti-Ping," he whispered into Zutra's ear while patting him on the shoulder.

Speaking softly so that only his Vizier could hear his reply, Zutra confessed to his desires. "Yes, Avital may occupy my heart, but this woman has somehow made my soul come alive. I look at her and it is if I am lifted towards heaven." He offered a warm smile to the Princess on his left who in turn blushed and then smiled angelically in return. "I only ask that you give me the opportunity to explain to Avital the reasons behind my taking another wife. I need her understanding."

Waving an angry finger at Zutra, Mordecai listed off his frustrations. "Firstly, you are not as yet married to the Lady Avital therefore you are not taking another wife. The Princess Ti-Ping will be your first wife that you have married. Secondly, we are politically maneuvering and that means that she will have to accept the situation whether she likes it or not."

"And thirdly," Zutra inquired, seeing that his cousin had not yet finished.

"And thirdly, you will speak with Pashah Gurzam before this night is through. He has something to tell you that I believe you will want to hear before you go visit Lady Avital in her
chambers. Promise me you will talk to the Pashah. Promise me!"

"Alright, I promise."

"Swear it to God!"

"I swear it to God. Now are you happy? What can be so important that the Governor has to speak with me? Can we at least now proceed with this banquet, this happy occasion that you arranged?"

"Of course, my king," Mordecai replied, ignoring Zutra's sarcasm.

Once again Zutra turned in the direction of Ti-Ping. "Please Princess, may I offer you some refreshments?" Zutra snapped his fingers to ensure that the Princess's cup was immediately filled. "My gratitude to your father," the king smiled broadly. In response she returned his smile and the look in her eyes said it all.

Chapter Seven

Mahoza: 497 A.D.

Ranting insanely with every determined stride taken along the marbled halls, Mar Zutra pushed his way aggressively past the two guards that stood outside the chambers belonging to the Lady Avital. The shocked sentries crept behind the fluted columns fearing that the Exilarch's fury would somehow settle upon them if they were not careful. Neither man could recall ever seeing their king in a rage anywhere close to the one they now beheld. Gazing cautiously from behind the pillars, they watched and waited for an opportunity to resume their posts unnoticed, as Zutra violently flung open the doors into the apartment. The massive oak slabs shook upon their hinges, threatening to tumble with disastrous effect after colliding explosively with the walls. The guards stood nervously by the columns, making themselves as inconspicuous as possible. Whatever was about to transpire was not intended for their eyes or ears.

Brushing aside Avital's maidservants as if they were milkweeds floating on the wind, any that dared to raise their voice in protest he merely gave an icy stare that froze them solid in their tracks. Zutra stomped towards the sleeping quarters where he found Avital stretched out on her gossamer draped and postered bed apparently asleep despite the loud commotion he had created. Seizing her by her ankle, he dragged her forcibly from her down-filled mattress, letting her body crash heavily to the floor.

Startled, she sat up immediately, now fully awake but displaying no sign of fear of the snarling assailant standing above her with clenched fists, drops of spittle drooling from the left corner of his mouth.

"What? You didn't appreciate my little disruption of your party tonight?" she taunted him. "Go away; you don't have my permission to be in here." Her voice sounded calm and commanding, totally in contrast to the obvious threat looming directly over her.

Mar Zutra did not make a reply. Only a loud hiss passed through his thinly stretched lips. He clenched his fists even tighter and his face began to glower red as the anger coursed the entire length of his body, the capillaries veining his face in a latticework of madness. Every sinew along his arms and across the back of his neck tightened synchronously until they stood out like ropes beneath his flesh. He had become a coiled spring, waiting for the moment to release the pent fury trapped within.

"What, you going to hit me now? Is that what you intend to do? You're not man enough!" she mocked him further. "Go away and pretend to be a man somewhere else little boy." She added an infuriating little laugh, accentuating her insults and taunts.

His right hand snaked out like a serpent, seizing Avital in its vice-like grip, encircling her delicate wrist. Resisting his pull, she latched one arm on to the corner post of the bed, embracing the solid mahogany spindle with all her strength but it was to no avail. Driven by the madness, he twisted her body, thereby lifting her completely off the ground, breaking her grasp and launching her halfway across the room from the sheer force of his attack.

Painfully colliding against the polished stone floor, Avital for the first time realized her own fear, her expression betraying a mask of terror. She suddenly recognized that the man standing across from her had moved beyond all reason. The Zutra that stood over her was not there to lecture or scold, as she had grown accustomed to since he seized control of his own estate. No, in this Zutra's eyes she detected an animal ferocity, a blood thirst that he had never revealed before. Neither her wiles, her glib tongue nor her normally condescending manner would deter the Zutra that now faced her. His ice-cold eyes, penetrating deep into her flesh said it plainly.

"Have you gone utterly mad!" she screamed in her vain attempt to reason with him. She rubbed her throbbing wrist with her other hand. Welts began to show not only on her arm but also along her side where she had broken her fall. "I'll summon the guards to have you thrown out of here. Who do you think you are? I'm not your wife. You have no right to be here! It is against our laws. I can have you charged for this!" Even as she listened to her own voice she knew her threats were hollow and meaningless.

"Like you laid charges against my father," he growled back in a voice that was barely human, the first words he had spoken since he barged into her room.

"What are you talking about?" she placed her arms in front of her to act as a shield as he approached.

"No more lies", he howled. "I've had enough of your lies!"

"This is madness! Who has told you such things? They're the ones lying to you. Can't you see that?"

"I can see clearly now. For the first time in my life, I see all too clearly! And I see you for what you are!"

He bore down upon her and she sensed he was well beyond any rational discussion. "This is Mordecai's doing, isn't it? He's always despised me. He wants you to marry that pale-skinned creature and this is his way of achieving that. Can't you see, it's all a trick," she pleaded, her eyes filling with genuine tears of fear as she continued to hold up her arms to avoid being struck.

"This is none of Mordecai's doing," Zutra became coherent as he struggled to reign in his seemingly uncontrollable rage. The sudden change in his demeanor was even more terrifying to Avital. Transforming from berserker madness to clarity of thought could mean only one thing, that he had crossed the point of no return. She watched as he reached into the fold of his tunic. Turning her head, expecting at any moment to feel the blade she assumed he had concealed to come slashing down across her throat. She had no desire to witness the approach of her own death.

Seconds passed without the cut of cold steel against her skin. She turned her head to see that he had only withdrawn a tightly wound scroll with brass cylinder knobs at either end. Zutra flung it directly at her, a blow that glanced off her high cheekbone before it fell ominously to the ground beside her. The impact made her wince, but the sight of the scroll made her tremble even more; she recognized it.

"Do you need to unroll it?" he bellowed, pointing towards the scroll that lay between them.

"You don't understand," she tried to explain. "You have to listen to me." The tears flowed freely but they no longer had any effect on him.

"What's not to understand," he howled once more like a wounded animal. The sound of his voice reverberating against the chamber walls with a haunting echo. "Is this or is it not the document you signed before the Pashah? Is it not the death sentence you pronounced on my father through your lying testimony?" He could restrain himself no longer; the vision of his crucified father driving him back to the edge of madness. Swinging his right leg, he caught her with a forceful blow to her hip that rolled her over twice. "I know it all now. How your father came with delegates from the Beth Din but Gurzam refused to accept their charges. It was all secondhand information; insufficient to put a man to death under Sassanid law. They require that someone that was directly involved with the alleged offense make the charge of a capital crime. It had to come from the victim. It had to be laid by you!"

"He made me do it!" she cried.

"I am tired of your lies!" The snarling rasp of his words assuming a more guttural tone as he descended once again into the depths of his bestial rage. He prepared to kick out with his leg as she curled into a ball in an effort to protect herself. He hesitated, a last self-effort to retain his humanity while he challenged her further. "I've read your words, your lying, filthy words! How my father raped you. Stole you, beat you into submission. My father! One of the gentlest men this world has ever known and you lied so that he would be put to death!"

"I'm sorry, I'm sorry!" she wailed.

"Sorry!" It was the wrong choice of word to use against the feral rage that consumed Zutra. Just the sound of the word rolling off her lips infuriated him even more than her lies. He kicked out and sent her sliding several feet across the floor. She wailed in pain. "I told the Pashah that I have my father's ketubah of your marriage, signed by all those 'great men' that were party to his execution. How could there be a signed marriage agreement and then this foul lie that you signed." Zutra bent down and picked up the scroll from the floor, holding it like a club.

"I don't know….I don't know…." the tears streamed from her eyes and rained down upon the floor. "They made me. I had no choice," she sobbed.

"You know what the Pashah said to me? Since I possess the ketubah that would make this document perjurious, he explained. Moreover, perjury involving capital punishment is murder and the penalty for murder is death. He graciously granted me permission to carry out the sentence." The scroll pendulated back and forth in his arm like an axe ready to fall, the only thing staying his hand for the moment was the indecision as to whether he should kick her again before he began clubbing her into submission.

"It wasn't my fault! Please! Please believe me!" Through her sorrow, she beseeched him to listen, but her words fell upon deaf ears.

Standing beside her, Zutra placed the knob of the scroll beneath her chin and raised her head so he could look directly into her eyes; doe-like hazel eyes that had captivated him all these years but concealed the festering pool of hate that lay behind them. In what remained of his sanity he knew that it was necessary to look into those eyes and break the spell that had immobilized him for so long. "You are dead to this world," his voice grated. "Do you understand? If I let you live for now, it is only by my graces. You have no rights, no legal status any longer. I do with you as I please and the first moment you make me regret my decision, I will carry out your sentence. As for your father, I have no such tender mercies. He will be put to death immediately. I will make him pay for what he did!"

"Please, no," she cried out. "I beg you! I will do anything. Just let him live! Please! I will give myself to you in exchange. You can have me! Look, look. Please just let him live."

"Clearly you don't understand," Mar Zutra snapped back. "You have no choice but to give yourself to me. Your life belongs to me and there are no options for you to trade. Your father dies because it is my right to avenge my father! You will service me like the whore you are because it is my right!"

"Wait," she held up a hand begging him to listen. She then began to strip her sleeping gown from her shoulders, exposing her voluptuous breasts followed closely by her curvaceous torso and hips. "You can take what you want; I can't stop you. I know that. However, only I can give it freely to you. In exchange for my father's life, I will give myself to you. I will open myself to your embraces. I will let you feel the warmth of my womb. Otherwise, I am nothing but an empty shell, a whore like you said and what good would I be to you if that is all you received in return?"

As much as he tried to resist, Zutra became transfixed by the intoxicating lure of her body. He loathed himself for his obvious weakness. He detested the power she still wielded over him. In his imagination he had pictured her naked by his side, but none of his dreams had even come close to the true magnificence of her reality. The breasts carried so proudly, upturned upon her chest, ripe and firm as if she had never suckled his half-brother; her stomach flat and hard; not a single line betraying her youthfulness. Her pelvis wide but welcoming with short tufts of hair crowning the pubis while taut tendons extended towards slender thighs that displayed each sensuous curvature of her well-developed musculature. It was as if she had been carved from marble by a great artisan striving for the perfection of womanhood. Nonetheless, what was so beautiful on the surface concealed a blackened heart that leached its ugliness, and its beating was enough to shake him from the stuporous spell her beauty had cast.

"You will give freely of yourself," Zutra negotiated but I will make no long-standing promises. Reb Hanina will live out this night because you will have purchased a single day of his life. How long I wish to continue this negotiation is at my discretion. Are we in agreement?" Even as he uttered the words, he hated himself for them. Once again, she had stripped him of his rightful privilege and once more, he had made a deal with the she-devil.

Avital rolled over onto her back, removing the remainder of her sheer gown so that her legs flexed and spread invitingly. Zutra could clearly visualize the path leading to her open labia beckoning to him. Kneeling to the floor, without expressing a single word, he raised the hem of his tunic and centered between her arced thighs. Grabbing the chiseled cheeks of her hips, he elevated them slightly above the ground and slid Avital forcefully backwards until he felt the shaft of his member disappear into the darkness behind the parted lips of her vagina. He rocked back and forth, driven by a strange combination of rage and lust that made him pound the insides of her legs and her mound until they began to swell from the bruising. All the time he roared like a lion on the hunt. A blood-curdling cry that masked the shame he felt for succumbing to her alluring beauty. She bit her lip as she stifled her groans of pain, which only made him thrust even harder and faster. He wanted her to cry out in pain. She had to be punished! For the salvation of his own sanity, she had to bear the punishment of her crime.

The sound of his hips slapping heavily against her inner thighs masked any sounds of protest she may have initially expressed as he unleashed the pent-up fury he carried for so long. However, a few more strokes and any pain she experienced was vanquished by her body's own craving for the raw excitement and exhilaration. Never before had she experienced sexual urges of this intensity and she grew ashamed of her own seemingly unquenchable sensations. She bit even harder down on her lip, drawing a drop of blood, more determined than ever to show as little emotion as possible to her assailant.

She was failing miserably in her attempt to quell any pleasure as her body began to quake and shiver under his savage onslaught. She felt her back arch involuntarily and as much as she tried to convince herself that she would not show him even a trace of orgasmic pleasure, she could not stifle her subconscious responses. She began to gasp and then forced the back of her hand inside her mouth to silence the sounds she feared she might make. Sounds that told him otherwise, but it was too late. Already she was shouting out words and squeals of delight and despising herself for it. Focusing on the series of growls and grunts emanating from Zutra, she pictured in her mind that she was being brutally mauled by a wild beast but even that could not stem the shivers of orgasm that shot through to her core each time he sank deep within her. Every muscle of her body began a rapid sequence of tensing like a drawn bowstring, only to be released, flaccid and relaxed with each unleashed arrow and then drawn again; over and over until she felt faint from the heady experience. The pleasure was insurmountable, unstoppable. She hated herself even more for it. "She would endure it for her father," she lied to herself. It was all for him. "It was not for her!" the voice screamed inside her head. "Not for her!"

Having spent himself, Zutra felt the last of his fluids ebb from his engorged penis. As he withdrew from her inner warmth, he sensed an eerie feeling of disgust flush across his soul. The anger had subsided and with it the living embodiment of rage that permitted him to finally stand up to Avital's domination. Looking down upon her beautiful body, her exquisite features, he felt the shame of betraying his father. Once again, she had overpowered him, steered him away from a proper course of action and enslaved him to her will. He had wanted her to pay for her crime, and now she would remain free of her sin; he wanted her father dead and now he would live on another day and another until he could no longer feel the need to lie with Avital any longer. Furthermore, after so many years of desiring her, craving her, the day when he would no longer desire her seemed infinitely distant. Already he felt an urge to take her again. He knew for his own sake he had to resist. He forced himself from between her legs and rose from the floor.

"Get dressed and clean up this mess," he spat as he lowered his tunic and progressed towards the door of her bedchamber.

"Yes, master," she lowered her eyes sarcastically, mocking him with her obeisance.

He chose to ignore her ridiculing deference. It only helped in rekindling the disdain he held for her and provided a brief respite from the overpowering lust that surfaced each time he looked upon her.

"And furthermore," he turned before leaving her presence, "You will prepare for a wedding. I will not have it said that I rape the servants in my house. You will be given the status of second wife!"

As he closed the door behind him, he heard the smashing of some delicate object that she had hurled in his general direction.

Chapter Eight

Ctesiphon: 497 A.D.

The Imperial chambers within the palace were even more magnificently decorated than those allotted to the Pashah. This particular section of the winter palace retained much of the original Greek architecture from the time when it was first constructed several hundred years earlier. The vaulted ceilings frescoed with elaborate paintings of the ancient gods should have been covered up long ago with layers of white paint during the ascension of Ahura Mazda as the one and only true god of the Sassanid Empire, but all the Imperial Shahs loved the artwork too much to have done so. The pictures of Zeus chasing naked nymphs through the forests still appealed to these new rulers. After three centuries, the brilliance of the Greek artists still smiled down upon them with all their glory.

"Do you like it," Pashah Gurzam inquired as soon as he noticed everyone's attention drawn to the ceiling.

"Very un-Christian," Patricius frowned, expressing a twinge of disdain.

Mar Zutra said nothing as he continued to explore the panorama spread across the vault.

"I guess for someone about to wed two women at once, it has its educational merit," the Governor made light of the commander's comment and deferred to the Exilarch. "And what would you say, good friend Mordecai?"

"This fellow is too old to even remember such things," the wizened sage jested. "Though I must admit that I wish I could remember them."

"I am so glad that you have returned to discuss the issue I raised almost two weeks ago," the Governor continued. "I thought you were no longer interested. Have you apprised the commander of the situation?"

"Without Commander Patricius, I did not believe there was even a chance of success," Mordecai explained. "Then when he showed that night with the Princess, I realized that God had certainly answered my prayers. There are no coincidences, only the Lord's quiet ministrations and manipulation of our fates."

"Praise be Ahura Mazda," the Governor added.

"Let's not move too far ahead of ourselves," Patricius counseled. "I agreed to listen; not necessarily join you in this insurrection of yours."

"You are here," Mordecai answered, "That says enough on its own."

"Only because the Princess Ti-Ping has instructed me to do so as a gesture of good faith to her newly betrothed, let us not overlook that!"

Finally concentrating on the matter at hand, Zutra lowered his gaze from the overhead depictions and spoke up. "I am in agreement with the wise counsel of Commander Patricius. Let us listen first and then we can decide."

"But ...but," the Governor sputtered, "I thought we were in agreement already," he turned to Mordecai indicating that he was somewhat confused.

The elder spread his hands to indicate that he was likewise surprised. "Gentlemen, perhaps it is best that we should discuss the matter at hand more deliberately. It is vital to all of us," he urged placatingly.

Turning to Mar Zutra, Patricius directed his question directly to the Exilarch. "If we were to do this thing, would there be any advantage to you?"

"To me," Zutra answered honestly, "Probably not. To my people, it would release them from their oppression. They have been nothing but the gravel that the Sassanids have ground into the dust. They are taxed exorbitantly, and their lives are made a constant misery."

The Commander weighed out the answer carefully, taking the measure of the man as he spoke. "A king is nothing without his people. If he does not take care of those from which he draws his power, then he is not worthy to wear a crown."

"You say that with conviction." Zutra was also engaged in evaluating the measure of the Princess's guardian.

"It is a lesson my father taught me long ago. That the only fight worth fighting is that which safeguards the people you have sworn to protect. That is what he was trying to do when the Emperor Leo had him assassinated. My father fought and died for the people he loved and served."

"As did mine," Zutra expressed his total comprehension.

"We are brothers in spirit," Patricius smiled. "If you swear to me that this battle is truly in aid of the people, then I pledge my sword to your cause."

The atmosphere in the room became quite solemn until Mordecai purposely spoke to break the mood. "Well, aren't you going to say something?" He pushed his king to respond while the opportunity existed.

"I swear to you Commander, I have no other reason to do this but for the sake of my people. I seek no further power, nor any throne that is not mine by birthright."

"And that is exactly why we are gathered here gentlemen," the Governor interceded. "I have asked you to meet in the Royal quarters because we have a very important ally. The nobles have likewise supported the cause, not for their own glorification but for the sake of their people and the Empire. May I introduce to you the brother to the Great Shah, Prince Jamasp." Upon the mention of his name, the prince entered the lounge accompanied by his bodyguard. It was a startling contrast; the thin, wisp of a man, quite effeminate in appearance, his face rouged and powdered standing beside the enormous guard, completed shrouded in a black cowl that concealed most of his features.

Those assembled in the room bowed their respects to the prince as he sat on one of the empty divans. "Prince Jamasp, we are pleased that you have come," Gurzam greeted the young royal, a man perhaps no more than thirty by Zutra's estimation.

The prince gesticulated as he spoke, his fingers constantly weaving in front of his face in order to emphasize his every word. "Governor, you understand that I'm only agreeing to this as long as my brother is not harmed." His voice was highly pitched, carrying with it an annoying nasal whistle.

"Impossible," Patricius negated the request immediately.

Rising from his seat, the prince moved quickly towards his standing bodyguard taking a protective position behind the hulking figure. "Who is this impertinent man, Governor?"

"This is Commander Patricius, Excellency. He is here as representative of the Emperor Hsiang of Northern Wei, and as an advisor to the Exilarch Mar Zutra."

"Why do I not find that terribly surprising," Jamasp said scornfully. "You rulers from Mahoza do find the most obstreperous individuals to serve your causes."

Zutra leaned over and whispered in Mordecai's ear. "I think I should be offended by that, but I can't imagine whom he's referring to."

"Shhh," Mordecai cautioned, eyeing closely the bodyguard whose hands could not be seen beneath the black cloak.

"Excellency, please," the Pashah beseeched the prince. "It is not by the Exilarch's will that we are gathered here. I am representing your own nobles. All of them have asked that I speak on their behalf."

"Then speak away Governor, but I will not be party to any attempt on my brother's life."

"I think we can accommodate your wishes, Excellency. It is only that Commander Patricius has been in this situation before and speaks from valuable experience. Perhaps you should give him the opportunity to explain himself. Then we can search for the middle ground. What we discuss today is for the good of the Empire. You know that the Magus intends to harm us all."

Placing his hands on either side of his mouth, the prince adopted an expression of alarm upon hearing the mention of the Magus. "Oh, that evil, evil man," he tutted. "I don't understand why my brother even listens to him."

"He is under a spell, my Prince and that is why we have to remove him from power," the Pashah explained. "Your brother doesn't realize what he is doing and we must save the Empire before the Magus has gained too much control."

"And that is why my brother cannot be killed," the Prince argued. "He is not in control of the decisions he is making. He cannot be held responsible for the things he does."

"Then kill this Magus," Patricius saw an easy solution to the matter.

"It is not that simple," the Governor confessed. "Mazdak has been given a cohort of men to protect his own person. The estate granted to him by the Emperor is one of the most impervious in the land. He rarely if ever comes out from behind its protection."

"Instead of telling me what we cannot do, why can't any of you tell me what it is that we are meant to do," the Commander's voice resonated with the growing frustration.

"Remove the Emperor. Eliminate the Magus. Free the people, and put the Prince, here, on the throne. That's it," Zutra said a matter-of-factly.

"Is that all," Patricius responded flippantly. "Why didn't you say so in the first place?" the Commander's ridicule was obvious to all.

"Can you do this?" The Governor overlooked the sarcasm in the Commander's response.

Patricius laughed. "With you lot? Not a chance in Hades. I mean, look at you. You're divided, uncertain of what you want. You have no army of your own except for your Four Hundred and whatever Scythians and Parthians you can scrounge up from your city," he alluded to Zutra. Then facing the governor, he continued his assessment. "And as for your nobles, whatever men they had available would probably be like the Prince here and switch sides as easily as a leaf blows in the wind. All Kavad would do is have to say 'boo' and they'd jump out of their boots. If you can't bring yourself to kill your enemy, then you certainly aren't of a mind to challenge him. I would rate your chances of surviving a coup at almost zero!"

"What about the Emperor Hsiang's forces. Can he send us several divisions?" Mordecai was already thinking on how he could rectify the downward spiraling situation.

"He's probably wondering the same thing," Patricius informed them. "How many men are you able to send him? Practically every province has some claimant to be the Emperor of China. We are constantly fighting just to keep hold of our kingdom in Northern Wei. Don't expect any aid from that venue."

"Then what should we do, Commander?" Zutra placed his entire future in the hands of the Samatian.

"Are you all willing to heed my advice? If not, then I am just wasting my time here."

Mordecai and Gurzam nodded in agreement, then they waited on the Prince to indicate his approval but it was not forthcoming.

"My Prince," the Pashah pleaded. "Some things are beyond the value of a single man. I know he is your brother, but he is permitting the ruination of this Empire and he must be stopped before it is too late!"

"If I agree to this, then will I be allowed to choose how my brother is to die?"

The Governor looked about the room and the delegate's faces for their responses. "It is agreed," he replied to the Prince.

'Then carry on and tell us of our plan," Jamasp commanded Patricius.

"Quite simple," Patricius started, "We let the Emperor of Byzantium do most of the work for us."

"And why would he do that?" Zutra inquired, his interest peaked.

"Several reasons actually. By rights I am still his brother-in-law through my marriage to Leontia.

"That was annulled," Mordecai reminded him.

"By her father, the Emperor Leo, but not by us. I signed no such document. Moreover, her sister Ariadne always had a place in her heart for me. Now that she is Anastasius's empress, she owes me several favors."

"Do you think she really cares about what she owes you twenty-five years later?" Zutra sounded skeptical about Patricius's reasoning.

The commander donned a broad smile as he reminisced. "Like I said, she always had a special place in her heart for me. I do not think she'll have forgotten me that easily. She will aid me if I ask."

"Oh," Mordecai chuckled fully appreciating the Commander's intimation. "The stories about you have not made mention of this aspect of your life."

"From what I've heard recently, something else I share in common with your liege," Patricius smiled.

The inference forced Mar Zutra to fall back into his seat. Exactly what was being gossiped within the palace about his relationships he wondered? Yes, a few of the daughters he had personally selected to remain behind in the role of concubines but those were primarily to serve as handmaids to the two future queens. What was the content of the conversations exchanged between his Vizier and the Samatian, he wondered.

"But I believe Anastasius will even be more willing to help us because now that the truth is known that it was really Marcian that was intending to seize the throne, from both Leo and Zeno, he'll think he can win me back to lead his armies."

"So much has changed in almost three decades. Without intending to be rude, why would he want an old soldier back to lead a modern army?" Mordecai analyzed the suggestion and found it wanting despite Patricius's reputation as a master strategist.

"Have you bothered to notice how successful the Byzantine army has been in the last twenty-five years? Not since my father's command have they had anything to brag about. People may forget, but soldiers don't. They remember who last led them to victory. They remember me! And I can guarantee Anastasius will not have forgotten me either."

"So, he will do all that we request because he wants you to lead his army?" Pashah Gurzam sounded doubtful.

"For that and for certain other concessions that I know you will grant him willingly."

"And do you intend to tell us what these certain concessions are, or do we have to guess?" the Pashah pressed for an answer somewhat impatiently.

"Everything will be explained in its proper time. Now is not the time to discuss these concessions, Governor. You and I can do so later in private." The Commander gave a slight tilt of his head towards Prince Jamasp.

The Governor caught the drift and nodded politely. "Later then."

"So what's your plan?" Zutra was now intrigued by the change in the meeting's atmosphere.

"We go as a delegation to see Anastasius; you, me, and the Prince over there."

Jamasp looked alarmed. "I can't go anywhere. He is our sworn enemy. What if my brother should find out? He will be very upset with me."

Exasperated, Patricius turned to Gurzam for help. "Is this the only brother we have available?"

"The only one left alive," the Pashah conceded.

"I can see why." Patricius shook his head. "Advise his Majesty that unless he goes, Anastasius will have no reason to believe that we can pull off this insurrection or deliver on the concessions. He needs to know who is going to be his ally ruling the Sassanids. I can't very well tell him it's going to someone he can trust. He needs to see for himself what he'll be dealing with."

"Do you think that's wise?" Mordecai interjected.

"Trust me. When he meets the Prince, I know he'll be delighted with our choice of ally. He'll know immediately the level of control to expect from within both your governments. This is the point that you have to trust in my knowledge of the Byzantine court."

"Excellency, it is imperative that you go." Gurzam stated firmly. "It is your duty as a sovereign. The salvation of the Empire is now your responsibility. Only you can do so. Your brother has fallen too far under the control of the Magus."

"I really don't think it's a good idea," Jamasp attempted to excuse himself. "My brother will notice my absence. He will know we're up to something."

"The Emperor Kavad is far to the north at his summer palace. He will be there for some time. And to be honest with you, Excellency, most of the time he can't be bothered to know if you're even alive."

Zutra and Patricius both fought hard to stifle a laugh. The prince seemed oblivious to the ridicule carefully expressed by his Governor. "But if we were to leave with a large contingent of men, it would be reported back to him. He'd inquire immediately as to our destination. He would find out through his spies that would follow us, even if we were to lie to him."

"And that is why, Prince Jamasp," Patricius interrupted, "We will not travel with a large contingent of men; a small group of travelers perhaps ten at most. You may bring your tall and brooding fellow with you. I'm certain he must be good with a sword."

"But what about my comforts," the Prince protested. "Surely you cannot be serious that I leave my attendants behind. Who will dress me, curl my hair, or tend to my bath?"

"While on our mission, you will be a soldier, Excellency," Gurzam drew himself back into the conversation, "just as you've always expressed your desire to be. You will take on every aspect of the soldier's life; from sleeping on straw mats to bathing in rivers just as you used to pretend in play when you were a small boy. Do you remember? It will be the fulfillment of your ambitions."

"I remember those games," Jamasp reflected on what must have been a happier childhood. "They were fun, but my father would never let me stay in the barracks with any of his soldiers. It was very disappointing."

Zutra had to turn away as he let his mind wander to think about the young prince amongst all those soldiers and the games they would have played.

"You no longer have to be disappointed, my Prince. Commander Patricius will give you the opportunity to live out your fantasy. You will become a real soldier."

"I would, wouldn't I?" the Prince grinned proudly.

Mordecai and Patricius glanced towards each other, and it was obvious they shared the same thoughts. Both had spent years in the service of administering to others with more power than the intellect to use it wisely. Such was God's peculiar sense of humor when elevating men to positions of authority.

"And when are we intending to begin this mission?" Zutra grew excited by the promised adventure as well.

"As soon as possible," Patricius informed them.

"But what about my planned weddings?" the young Exilarch suddenly felt conflicted.

"First the mission, then your weddings," Patricius laid out the schedule. There was no room for argument. "If my plan is to succeed, we need to see the Emperor immediately and the weddings will play an important part."

"Weddings?" the prince's ears pricked. "I didn't know of any weddings. Am I to be invited?"

"You are to be one of the guests of honor," Patricius let him know. "Your good ally Mar Zutra won't accept no for an answer."

"I do so love weddings," the Prince informed them.

"I don't know if the Princess Ti-Ping will happily agree to a postponement," Zutra cautioned the commander that he may be acting counter to his own mistress's wishes.

"Once I explain my intended plan to her, she will support our decision to postpone whole heartedly. After all, you will be inviting the King of Kings as an honored guest."

"I am?"

"Yes, you are, and I am certain he will make a point of attending once he hears about whose daughter your first wife is going to be."

"Ah, I think I'm beginning to see this clearly now," Zutra tapped his forefinger against his temple as the imagery became clearer. "Very clever Commander. Then let's be away before this week ends."

"Your wish is my command," Patricius consented with good humor.

Mordecai just nodded appreciatively; finally, they all understood.

Chapter Nine

The Palmyra Road: 497 A.D.

They rolled their sleeping mats, tying them securely to the back of their saddles. Regrettably, they felt a reluctance to leave the makeshift camp by the lake where they had spent their first night away from the city. An inexplicable calm pervaded every nuance and facet of the area, from the tall grass, to the insects, to the wading birds that lived by this small crystalline blue body of water.

"You feel it too, don't you," Zutra inquired of Patricius.

'It is very strange," the commander evaluated the paradisial surroundings. "I feel like the entire world has ground to a stop, and all that exists is this lake and us. Everything else has vanished. I have never felt that before. In truth it is rather unsettling."

"We call this lake Habbaniyah," Zutra informed him. "It's an old Hebrew expression."

"Then I'm surprised the Sassanids have kept it. It's not like them to let anything, even a name, survive from the old civilizations."

"They won't change it because they fear this place," Zutra smiled. "It was here that the ancestor of my people, Abraham was given the promise by God on his journey from the Chaldees. He was told to continue on towards the Middle Sea where he would be given a wondrous land and become the father of a great nation."

"So, what exactly does the name mean," Patricius inquired as he brushed the few leaves that had adhered to the quilted cotton of his brown flannel trousers.

"It has a duo meaning." the Exilarch explained. "Read one way, it signifies that 'I understand my God.' But it can also mean 'My God understands me.' It signifies that the bargain between man and God went

98

both ways. Hence, it is a very special place."

Patricius wiped the gathering sweat from his forehead. "There is definitely an odd sensation about the lake; overpowering yet oddly comforting."

"That is the nature of God. He fills us with awe, but reassures us through His love."

"So, if it's so special why have you not built a temple here?"

"That is where your beliefs and mine differ," Zutra quickly explained. "God is in our hearts. That is the only temple he seeks. The stone monuments that men build are cold and lifeless like the rock they are hewn from. They are constructed to glorify the builder and designed to fill men with awe of man's own creation; not God's. And each builder, be they priest or king, is only concerned with out-doing one another in their degree of vanity."

Patricius wanted to say something to defend his faith, but he found the words weren't easily forthcoming. All that he could think to say for the moment was, "I understand," and as soon as he said them, he fully understood the hold that the surroundings had on him.

Zutra clasped him on the shoulder. "If you find yourself at a loss for words, don't worry, it is the magic of the place. We have all experienced it."

"It is a shame that we have to leave it so quickly, but we've only been on the road a day and we have a long journey ahead of us. Mount up everybody," Patricius shouted his orders to the other riders. Everyone climbed onto their mounts, all of them dressed in the same quilted flannel pants and short jackets that suggested to any sentry or traveler they passed that they were nothing more than a band of Eastern merchants on their way to secure goods at the Western port cities.

"I don't think I can go any further," Prince Jamasp protested refusing to let his bodyguard assist him into the box saddle. Unlike everyone else, the Prince and his guard had refused to dress in similar attire. He considered it too common and chose instead to wear garments sewn from a rich brocade cloth that would at least suggest that he was a rich merchant and therefore most likely the leader of their tiny group while his bodyguard wore the familiar black robes he had always worn.

"I don't care your highness, but if you don't get your royal ass into that saddle, I will strap you into it myself." the Commander warned him. "Do I make myself clear?"

"But it hurts," the prince whined. "How can I ride if I'm going to be sore all the time? Why couldn't I have a carriage?"

Patricius moved threateningly towards the Sassanid prince at which point Jamasp's bodyguard moved quickly between them.

"Tell your man to stand down. I'm not about to lay a hand on you."

Jamasp waved his bodyguard to the side.

"We've been over this. I told you, we have to reach Antaradus in nine days if we are going to make our ship to Constantinople in time. We cannot afford to wait for another sailing vessel that may or may not be going in that direction. In order to make our deadline, it is necessary that we travel on average fifty miles a day. You can't do that with a carriage. So don't bring it up again!"

"You can't talk to me like that," Jamasp puffed up his chest defiantly.

"On this trip I am in command. You are simply one of my soldiers, remember? As one of my soldiers, I'm ordering you back into that saddle. Do we have that clear?"

"I don't think we are going to be very happy with each other on this journey," Jamasp replied bitterly as he indicated to his bodyguard to kneel down so that he could step on his back and climb into the saddle. Easing himself into the saddle, the Prince rocked his hips back and forth in an effort to find a comfortable position, all the while groaning to highlight his plight.

Muttering to himself while he readied his own horse, Patricius wondered about his decision to lead this mission. "At least you don't have any complaints, do you?" he turned to Mar Zutra, who was already mounted and prepared to move out.

"You'll be the first to know when I do," the Exilarch replied jocularly. "Mind if I ride with you?"

"Be my guest," Patricius waved him alongside.

"I'm afraid we royals from the East aren't trained for cavalry like your Romans and Byzantines. Delicate asses I'm afraid."

The commander appreciated the humor, belching out a coarse laugh. He was equally impressed by Zutra's attempt to cover for the prince, even though he knew that the young Exilarch probably held the Sassanid royal in as much disdain as he did. "You're defending him," Patricius suggested.

"Actually, I'm reminding you that this was your plan," Zutra still wore his infectious smile that contagiously spread to the commander. "At first I questioned your reasoning, but I think I understand your strategy now and the reason we three had to appear before Anastasius."

"Do you really? Why don't you tell me what you've figured out?"

"The way I see it," he continued, "You want to demonstrate to the Emperor that you'll be able to control the Sassanid Empire on his behalf, as an ally, by showing him that he has nothing to fear from the reigning kings. That is if, he helps to remove Kavad, leaving Jamasp and myself to fill the vacuum that would create."

"Continue," Patricius was intrigued by the Exilarch's train of thought.

"It would not be too hard to do, once he meets the both of us. He'll see that as King of Kings, Jamasp will be totally reliant on his nobles as advisors, and those nobles are smart enough to pursue a path of peace or why else would we be undertaking this journey."

"And what will he think when he meets you?" the commander asked slyly.

"I would hope he will see me as an ally worthy of granting me the autonomy and military support that I might preserve the independence of my kingdom within the Sassanid Empire."

"Oh, I think he might see more than that." Patricius urged his horse into a trot, which automatically signaled the other riders to pick up their pace. The road they traversed ran parallel with the Euphrates river, heading northeast across barren flat land; perfect for making good time. Zutra spurred his horse forward in order to catch up.

"What else should he see," Zutra was intrigued to know.

Surprised to see how easily he had caught up to him, Patricius looked somewhat bemused. "I thought you said that you Eastern monarchs weren't accustomed to riding horses?"

"I believe my precise comment was that we weren't trained for cavalry. I never said that I couldn't ride a horse."

"Is there anything else I should know?"

"Only that I may appear young but don't be deceived. In my short existence I think that I have already suffered enough to last a lifetime;

perhaps even as much as you have."

The comment made the commander think about his own life to that point and he realized that Mar Zutra may have been correct to a degree. The coincidences were alarmingly similar. "I doubt you will ever bear as much as I have endured but I have heard people say that there are many commonalities," Patricius admitted. "There is also one major difference. You've taken back the throne that was rightfully yours, and I will never have that chance."

"By people I presume you mean Mordecai," Zutra guessed as to Patricius's source of information. "Perhaps your return to Constantinople will set you upon that course. I know you are trying to earn back your good favor with the Emperor, and if you do that, then anything's possible."

"A remote possibility," Patricius conceded. "I think I have a better chance being imprisoned for the crimes my father never committed."

"You know that's not going to happen," Zutra read his thoughts. "Those that made those accusations are no longer alive."

The commander tired easily of the conversation. It was one he made a point to rarely converse about and he was surprised that he had opened as much as he had to the Exilarch. Remorse was a weakness and he despised it in himself. "We still have a long journey ahead of us. It will be three days until we reach the town of Husaiba. You'll have plenty of opportunity to tell me what you see in store for all of us. After all, I heard rumors that your family has inherited some unique ability to foretell the future."

"I wouldn't believe everything you hear from my Vizier. If we had that ability my father would still be alive and I wouldn't be in love with a woman that despises me." Zutra's expression was self-deprecating as he recounted his failure to avoid tragedy.

Patricius burst out laughing, catching the young Exilarch by surprise. "At least you have another woman that will love you beyond all expectation. You will learn to appreciate the Princess for the woman she is rather than the crown she bears. But take it from me; our stupidity when it comes to women has nothing to do with reading portents. Just look at me, I fell in love with a woman that was conspiring with my protégé to seize control of the throne and my family ends up on the wrong end of an axe for it. And what's worse, is that twenty-six years later, I think I still love her."

"You poor bastard," Zutra shook his head once more as he tutted.

"Almost as much of one as you are," Patricius insulted Zutra then laughed uproariously.

"We will see which one of us over time is more pathetic," Zutra howled.

Shaking Zutra by his shoulders, Patricius abruptly roused the young Exilarch from a heavy sleep.

"What is it," Zutra asked drearily, rubbing the sleep from his eyes as he looked around and saw that it was still the middle of the night, the stars forming a studded canopy over his head. The fire in the centre of their camp crackled excitedly as the flames danced upon the logs that were stacked several layers high. He had surprised himself with how much he enjoyed sleeping on his straw mat in the open, the warmth of a fire nearby and the camaraderie of the soldiers that Patricius had selected from his unit that escorted the Princess.

"One of my sentries thinks he heard footsteps in the distance," Patricius whispered. "Could be nothing but then again, this road is famous for its thieves and bandits. Better if we're prepared."

Zutra found the news strangely exciting. He reached for the curved scimitar that he kept under the wool covers. Feeling the hilt rest in the palm of his hands, he sat cross-legged, resting the blade in his lap.

"I presume you know how to use that?"

"Do I know how to ride?" Zutra retorted to the Commander's inquiry.

"Well, I hope you know better how to kill than you do how to ride," Patricius slapped him affectionately on the shoulder.

Moving towards where the Prince and his bodyguard shared a tent Patricius passed on the warning of unexpected company. Zutra heard the prince's voice raise an octave at the sounding of the alarm, but only long enough to order his man to stand ready to defend him by the flaps to the tent. Jamasp would remain concealed within his tent until the crisis had passed.

"So, what now?" Zutra asked as he saw the Commander resurface from the tent.

"I've ordered eight of my men to conceal themselves in the bushes.

At half strength, we should be a tempting target and able to draw these bastards into the open."

"What if they outnumber us?" Zutra began running through his mind everything that could possibly go wrong.

"Trust my experience," Patricius comforted him. "I have never seen bandits ride in anything greater than a dozen. More than that and they tend to slit their own throats over their booty. Every one of my men is worth at least ten of theirs. You probably won't even have to get your sword bloodied."

Pulling his mat up alongside of the young Exilarch's Patricius suggested that he lie back down and feign sleep. That way the bandits would brazenly walk into the clearing carelessly being illuminated by the brightly burning flames.

Gazing around the camp, Zutra counted that there were now only six of them, including the Prince, waiting in the open. "Shouldn't we at least move to where the light is dimmer so they can't see us as clearly?"

"Shhh…" Patricius tried to make as little noise as possible. "They are almost upon us."

Only the sound of an occasional twig snapping beneath a footfall could be heard. Mar Zutra was amazed that the Commander had even detected it over the roar of the hissing flames. He wanted to close his eyes, to complete the charade of a sleeping traveler, but he found he could not do it. The fear of one of the raiders sneaking up on him because he didn't see them was enough to keep his eyelids pasted to top of his sockets. He curled himself into a ball, the sword tucked neatly at the ready, the moment he would leap to his feet.

True to their nature, the brigands bellowed a shrill war cry as soon as they found themselves outnumbering their intended prey, a common practice intended to intimidate their victims but also designed to embolden themselves.

"Now," Patricius shouted out to his men that were concealed. A volley of arrows rained from the bushes towards the bandits the moment they were illuminated by the dancing flames. Launching himself on to his feet, Zutra stood with his scimitar balanced and ready in his hand. Standing at the ready, he had nothing to do but watch with utter amazement as arrow after arrow sunk with pinpoint accuracy into the chests of the attackers. It was even more amazing that each of the archers knew instinctively to select a target of their own without duplicating their efforts. In an instant, five of the brigands were writhing on the ground, clutching at their chests in an effort to dislodge the two and a half foot long projectiles. Those of the attackers still standing seemed fixated on the Prince's tent, more than the half-dozen defending inside the camp. It was likely they were still thinking about the objects of wealth contained within it, oblivious to their own impending deaths.

Dressed in black keffiyehs that masked their faces, the bandits had left only slits for their eyes uncovered. Zutra did a quick count. Seven pairs of eyes were now rushing towards them brandishing knives and swords, having forgotten about the booty within the tent. Patricius had been accurate in his assessment of their strength. The attackers were now too close for the archers to release any more arrows, and the eight troopers now rushed into the clearing to join the battle, swords in hand.

There was a sense of panic amongst the remaining bandits as they found themselves surrounded by the thirteen powerfully armed men. Even Jamasp's bodyguard had left his post by the tent to join the fight. The giant swung a massive blade, almost three cubits in length, that completely severed one assailant's head from his shoulders before the thief had time to blink. His companions froze as they watched for what seemed ages before the headless body of their comrade buckled at the knees and fell to the ground.

"Good man", Patricius shouted to the guard then threw himself into the forefront to engage another of the bandits that now rushed towards him. All around him, Zutra heard the reverberation of ringing steel as blades hammered one against the other, the bandits now fighting in desperation. Men facing the inevitability of their own deaths fight with an almost supernatural strength and Patricius knew the enemy would be at their most dangerous because of it. He shouted encouragement and warning to his men. "No unnecessary risks," he cautioned them. "Double up if necessary," but at no point were they to place themselves into a dangerous situation. Having said that, Patricius found himself entangled with an adversary who was clearly a master swordsman, parrying every thrust and blow directed.

The commander was equally adept, and the two men danced around each other, neither finding an opening with which to take the advantage. Patricius failed to notice that one of the bandits had taken the advice that he had offered to his own men and was approaching from his blind side so that there would be two swords against one.

It was then that Patricius saw the eyes of his opponent dart to the left, as if staring at something or someone directly behind him. He feared for the worse, unable to turn away from the man in front that lunged repeatedly with his curved blade but knowing that danger loomed to his rear. He braced himself for the fateful blow praying that his armor would blunt the stroke.

The unseen blade tapped him lightly on the shoulder from the rear, like a feather carried softly on a summer breeze. Suddenly, his assailant to the front appeared startled, expressing just enough hesitation for Patricius to press his advantage. Lunging forward he ran his sword clean through the bandit's abdomen until it protruded out his back. The man's mouth dropped open as death came quickly without a sound, as the Commander ripped his blade upward and to the left, severing the man's aorta as he did so.

Retracting his blade, Patricius leaped and twisted in the air a hundred and eighty degrees to face the threat from behind, now lying on the ground, neatly dispatched by Mar Zutra's bloodied scimitar.

"No respect for the rules of fair play I'm afraid," Zutra grinned.

The commander silently nodded his appreciation. The clearing had grown silent, no longer ringing out with clashing blades in the dark of the night. Patricius rapidly assessed the situation. Twelve men down; none being his own; the battle was over. He leaned over the attacker he had disemboweled and removed his headdress. Then he quickly looked beneath his black tunic to see if there was any identifying information. Nothing other than a couple of knives still tucked neatly in his belt.

Once the sounds of battle ceased, Prince Jamasp emerged from his tent and surveyed the scene. Walking past several of the corpses, he kicked at them repeatedly. "That will teach you," he scorned them, still retreating a safe distance after each kick just in case one still had some remaining life.

He approached the commander who was still kneeling over his victim. "So, we are clear of danger from here on," Jamasp half stated and half inquired.

"Not certain," was Patricius's only reply.

"But Commander, surely they are all that haunts this part of the province. There would be no others from their group in this vicinity."

Patricius rose to his feet to address the prince as an equal. "This is definitely all of them, but these were not bandits,"

The Prince appeared astounded by the revelation. "How can you say that? They attacked us. They would have taken everything had we let them."

Folding his arms across his chest, Patricius prepared to give everyone the benefit of his reasoning. "They aren't wearing any jewelry. They would be the first thieves that I have ever come across that didn't adorn themselves with the best they have stolen. That's their way of gaining bragging rights amongst their own kind. But more importantly, look at the way they're dressed."

"Like thieves if you ask me," Jamasp tried to make a little joke.

"Like your man there," Patricius pointed out. "I've seen this style of dress before. I recognized your man was from the assassin's guild just as were these men. Someone hired them to follow us and kill us. These men had no intention of robbing us."

"That would mean that someone knows of our mission," Zutra interjected.

"Apparently so and that someone had to pay a lot of money to hire a cadre of assassins. The question is who? Perhaps your man knows something about this?"

"I can assure you that my man had nothing whatsoever to do with these men," the Prince defended his bodyguard.

"What make you so certain?" the Commander continued to have his doubts.

"Well one reason is he's never away from me. He has no opportunity to pass information to someone without my knowing about it. And more specifically, in case you haven't noticed he doesn't talk."

"Perhaps he made an exception," Patricius was not letting go of the possibility the guard was guilty.

"No, I mean he can't talk," Jamasp explained. "He no longer has a tongue; courtesy of these men lying at our feet or their associates. Poor fellow had it torn out by the assassin's guild when they accused him of betraying them. Turned out to be another man so they let him live. Their loss, my gain. He's completely loyal to me."

"Okay, we can eliminate him as a possible suspect," Patricius conceded. "What about you?" he turned on Zutra. "Have you spoken to anyone regarding our mission?"

"Just everyone in my palace," Mar Zutra stated. "After all, I'm disappearing for a month. Don't you think I'd have to say something about my absence for that length of time? I am the king after all."

"But did you say where you were going?"

"Of course not," Zutra dismissed the question. "But how long do you think it would take for one of them to notice in which direction we were heading. It doesn't even necessarily have to be someone in the palace. Perhaps just someone that they talked to, who then kept an eye on us afterwards. It wouldn't take much to figure out our destination once they saw the three of us together."

"No, it wouldn't," Patricius agreed. "Then I'm afraid we have to expect the possibility that they will not easily give up in their attempt to have us killed. Next time we may not be so fortunate. They could hire a hundred men if their pockets are deep enough."

"So, what are we to do?"

It didn't take long for the commander to come up with a plan of action. "We have to hide the bodies. Can't leave any trace so best if we bury them. If they can't find their hirelings, then they'll presume that they're still following us. That will buy us some time."

"Will it be enough?"

"Hard to say. We still have over a week to travel by land. Would be at least a couple of days before they realize they failed in their first attempt. Add on to that the travelling time it would take to catch up with us and we just might squeeze through by a day or two at the most."

'Oh dear," Jamasp felt his heart flutter. "I don't like this. I really don't like this at all."

Chapter Ten

Husaiba: 497 A.D.

News of the small troop of merchantmen crossing the barrens from the Euphrates River buzzed through the border town of Husaiba. It was not a town per se, more of a village that stood on the crossroads of two great empires as far back as anyone could remember. At the time the Seleucid Empire started to falter, ownership of the town became contested between the Armenians and the Scythians. Soon afterwards, the claims were between the Romans and the Parthians and now finally the Byzantines and the Sassanids. Nevertheless, through it all, Husaiba stood as the one place where the scum and miscreants of all lands could sit down over a tankard of mead and let the politics take care of itself. Therefore, the arrival of fourteen men from the east should never have raised an eyebrow or be considered anything unusual for the townspeople of Husaiba.

Riding down the main street, all eyes were peeled to the weary travelers.

"You almost think they were expecting us," Mar Zutra commented to those around him.

"That can't be possible," Patricius insisted. "Even if those that hired the assassins knew that we were still alive, there is no way that they could have sent word ahead of our arrival. It has to be something else."

"Tell that to whomever has stirred up this hornet's nest," Zutra scanned the windows and doors of the surrounding buildings only to see the town's denizens watching from each portal. "They are definitely weary of our presence."

Patricius ordered his men to keep riding as if nothing unusual was taking place but those orders were quickly countered when immediately ahead of them, a group of townspeople assembled in the central square, blocking any further progression.

Just as quickly, he barked new commands. "Be prepared for the worst, gentlemen. This is beginning to look ugly." Everyone in the group reached towards the hilts of their swords. "No one makes a move until I order it," he commanded. "Just stay calm and leave your swords in their scabbards until I say it's time. Until absolutely necessary, I don't want anyone saying or doing anything without my say so."

His men listened and obeyed unconditionally. Both Mar Zutra and Jamasp's bodyguard were more reluctant to release the grips they held on their weapons. "It will be alright," the seasoned commander reassured them. "Had they wanted to kill us they would have placed archers there, there and there." Patricius pointed to three strategic locations where the higher ground would have given them full line of sight."

"So maybe they didn't have any archers," Zutra picked a hole in the reasoning. "You're a military man, they're not."

"Not if we are dealing with assassins. Killing is what they do. In that respect they are better than military men. They wouldn't have missed that opportunity. These people have a different bone to pick with us. Everyone stay here. Let me talk to them."

Separating from his wary band of travelers, Patricius kept his horse at a slow walk and strode forward to meet the assembled mob. Zutra watched from the protection of his escort that had positioned themselves into a defensive circle around both him and Jamasp. The discussion appeared highly animated, with the leaders of the people frequently pointing in their direction and shouting in voices that could only be described as extremely agitated."

"This isn't looking good," Zutra whispered to the prince, who had ducked low in the saddle trying not to be seen.

Dismounting, the people surrounded Patricius but at no time did he appear overly concerned; very little seemed to bother the general. All his life he had been groomed to deal with the careful deliberation and accommodations of state. Even at this level he considered there to be little difference. Assess, propose and finally agree. They were the three fundamental steps of any successful negotiation as he argued point after point until the leaders of the mob all seemed satisfied and then were seen shaking his hand. The crowd dispersed and everyone returned to their normal routines as if nothing had taken place. Zutra found himself simultaneously both dumbfounded and incredibly impressed by the Commander's masterful feat of diplomacy.

Lowering themselves from their saddles, they led their horses through the street, which had become deserted almost as quickly as it had filled earlier with the angry townsfolk. "Where did everyone go?" Zutra inquired as he looked about to see that even the faces had disappeared from the open windows and doors. "What did you say to them?"

"Back to doing whatever it is they do in this town."

"But what was that all about?"

Patricius pointed towards the giant bodyguard that stood beside Jamasp. "Him, or at least others dressed like him."

The prince came to the defense of his man. "He's done nothing. Whatever they claimed was a lie." His voice became even higher pitched than usual. "He's been with me all the time. Surely you all know that!"

"Relax your Highness; no one is after your bodyguard. At least not now."

"So, what's their story," Zutra inquired. "Why him?"

Patting the air with his hands, the commander urged everyone to calm down for the moment and he would explain. "The assassins that attacked us didn't come from Ctesiphon. They came from the west, passing through this town on their way. As much as this place is reportedly the domain of the worst that our civilizations have to offer, apparently the scum we faced provided them with an entirely new meaning to depravity. They did horrible things to some of the people here, women and girls in particular. Naturally when they saw your man, they assumed he was one of them and wanted to exact their revenge."

"But everything is fine now?" Jamasp was still worried.

"I have convinced them that we had nothing to do with their suffering?"

"Why should they believe you," the Prince panicked. "They could still be waiting to attack us as soon as we lower our guard."

"We are safe," Patricius insisted. "For several reasons. One, we are fortunate that your man towers well above the height of an average man. They wouldn't have forgotten someone his size so quickly. Therefore, they had to concede that he was not one of them. Secondly, I told them who I am. The name of Flavius Patricius still commands some respect in these parts even after so many years.

"You didn't," Zutra was shocked. "That means we've lost our secrecy!"

"Young King," Patricius's voice became very stentorian as he spoke, "When you have assassins on your tail, it's time you realize your cover has already been blown. Now it becomes only a matter of controlling just how much information is released. My identity is not so great an issue as long as they don't find out exactly whom I'm traveling with. But I believe that information is already widely dispersed where we're heading."

"How do you know?" Zutra questioned.

"Just think about what I said."

"How so?" Zutra turned the discussion over in his mind. "You said they came from the West. What exactly does that mean?"

Holding off on answering, the commander looked around at the shops lining the main street. "I feel like a drink," he informed his companions. "Let us find a tavern and I'll give you my thoughts on that matter." Not waiting for their consent, Patricius led his horse briskly through the street until he identified the most likely establishment to be a serving a draught of his favorite ale from times gone by. Hitching their horses, they followed their leader into the tavern. At this time of day, the tavern was essentially empty, much to the relief to both monarchs who still were not one hundred percent convinced of the townspeople's change of heart. Squeezing himself onto a bench surrounding a circular table in the corner, the commander waited until all his charges had gathered around and sat themselves down before he shouted to the tavern keeper to bring them each a drink.

"Well?" Zutra had grown impatient waiting for an answer to his question, drumming his fingers on the oak tabletop.

"What it means is that I have to apologize to both of you for thinking that either you or Jamasp had told someone about our destination. I was a fool not to have seen it earlier. The culprit was actually me!"

"How do you know?"

"When I hired our passage on the ship, I did it through my old contacts. I had to confide to them who I would be travelling with and how many. I trust them explicitly, but they had to talk with someone in Antaradus when they hired passage on the boat. It's a major port."

"And what exactly does that mean," Zutra pressed for an answer.

"A single word there becomes news in an instant. I believe that's where the loose connection exists."

"I knew it wasn't me," the Prince was pleased with the revelation.

"Though you could still be the target," Zutra suggested.

"As you could be, or even myself," Patricius postulated. "That can't be determined as yet."

"Does it matter?" Zutra questioned.

"Of course it matters," Jamasp objected. "I don't want to be killed if they're only after either of you."

"Thank you for your concern, your highness," Patricius raised his mug in a mock toast.

"Wait, wait," Zutra reviewed the details. "I think we're missing the main point. The question is not who they were trying to kill but why. There's something they fear more than anyone of us individually!"

"You're right," the commander agreed. "Either they know about our mission and then we would have to presume that we have been compromised and it's your brother, Kavad that has tried to have us killed," he intimated to Jamasp, "Or there's someone else that we haven't bargained on that doesn't want us reaching Constantinople because they fear we might succeed."

"Oh by the mercies of Ahura Mazda, let it not be my brother," Jamasp prayed. "He would have us boiled in oil and peel the skin from our bones if he catches us!"

"That's a better alternative than the other options I foresee. What if we're actually walking into danger rather than away from it? Perhaps the one trying to stop us is waiting for us in Constantinople." Zutra cocked his head waiting for the others to acknowledge his suggestion.

"It doesn't make sense," Patricius argued. "Who would want to stop a mission that could actually bolster the peace efforts of the Empire?" He racked his brains trying to decipher the enigma.

"This coming from a military man," Zutra scoffed. "Ending a war is not necessarily in everyone's best interest. Your sudden reappearance after all these years and assuming the key role in this endeavor is going to put several noses out of joint. Who's in charge of Anastasius's armies?"

"Take a pick. Information regarding the Byzantine Empire is severely scant out east. It could be his brother Paulus, whom he appointed as his Chief of Staff. Then again, his nephews, Secundinus, Hypatias and Pompeius were each made magistri militum from what I heard. Not much of a military man amongst the bunch from what's been said. Like I said, news reaching Sin was very sparse. If any of them were as bad as the stories described, then any one of them I would suspect would be very protective of their position right now. Their war efforts against Longinius's Illurrians have been a disaster from day one!"

"You've done well to dwell in the Far East for so long, and still manage to stay informed of what's occurring in the Byzantine courts, even if you call it sparse," Mar Zutra was impressed by the Commander's ability to monitor events from so far away.

"Let me extend you a little bit of advice," Patricius leaned over the table. "Knowledge is power. Without it, you won't survive very long in this world. Moreover, as a king you'll survive even less than others. Your enemies will number among them those that have no other reason to despise you other than the fact that you are a king."

"A terrible way to live fearing every shadow that looms from behind," Zutra rejected the advice.

"Better than not living at all," the Commander wagged an all-knowing finger in his direction.

The Prince straightened the skirt of his tunic, while he listened intently to the conversation. "I know that you both probably think me the fool but if you examine carefully, you will recognize the fact that of all Kavad's brothers, I am the only one still alive. Always let your enemies underestimate your true potential."

Both Zutra and Patricius were dumbfounded, jaws dropping at Jamasp's very astute suggestion. Had he been playing them for fools all this time; not just them but the entire court of his brother. There was possibly far more to the prince than the overt pomposity they had observed thus far.

114

Jamasp had nothing further to add, leaving them guessing at what was his full potential.

"Well put, your Highness," Patricius saluted Jamasp. "Know your enemies but never let them fully know you!"

Jamasp offered a wry smile in return which betrayed nothing of his inner workings.

"But then again, Ariadne's nephew Diogenes is a general, as are Justin, Johannes and Apsikal. Those four are fairly competent," Patricius continued. "And they would have an entirely different motivation for wanting me dead."

"Well, that puts a different perspective on things," Zutra calculated. "We may not be the welcomed guests in Constantinople that I had anticipated."

"Where did you ever get that foolish notion from?" Patricius questioned over the rim of his tankard as he swallowed deeply. "Let me forewarn you. No foreigner is ever welcome in Constantinople."

By noon the next day, Husaiba was far behind them in the East. They had slept the night without incident and there was no further discussion of how and where the threat may have originated. Each had their own illusions in that regard, the myriad of possibilities practically driving them mad. However, they had agreed to free their minds of such speculation, waiting instead until they confronted the true source enmity, which still lay far ahead. It would be another one and a half days until they reached Palmyra and Patricius was convinced that the answers would be awaiting him there.

Palmyra was considered an ancient marvel of the Syrian province, known simply to the rest of the world as the City of Palms. It was rumored to have been built by King Solomon as a gift to one of his many wives, but whatever its origins, it was a city with fifteen hundred years of inglorious history. As a prize, it had been fought over since the day it had been built, much of it now laying in ruins since the conquest over Queen Zenobia by the Emperor Aurelian. The rebellion had greatly disturbed the myth of Roman invincibility and a decision was made to turn Palmyra into little more than a Roman base for military operations so that it would never serve as an outpost to challenge the Empire again. With the rise of Sassanid power, the Emperor Diocletian reinforced the city with additional troops and even built a wall around its perimeter to protect it from the barbarian world. As the last bastion of the Roman Empire before entering hostile territory it stood as a reminder of Rome's constant and repeated failures to extend further east. As a once great merchant centre it acted as the marketing hub for the legendary Silk Road, but those days were long gone, and use of the famous route had declined dramatically of late with the rise of the Sassanids. Now under the control of the Byzantines, other than a few new churches scattered here and there, no evidence of any such revival in Palmyra was evident.

Patricius led his party to a familiar inn that still stood in the old Armenian Quarter. The structure was at least two hundred years old but well maintained for its age, a fresh coat of whitewash recently applied to its plastered walls. "Still here after all these years," he sighed as he stared up at the ornately carved sign, swinging in the slight breeze. "Inn of the Oasis Palms, I can't tell you how many times I've spent a night in here."

Precisely at that moment, several ladies of the evening exited through the swinging doors to the inn.

"I bet you did," Zutra commented much to the amusement of the other traveling companions.

"Believe it or not, I was as young as you, once." Patricius appeared to get misty eyed as he recalled some of his past conquests.

"Yes, it is hard to believe."

That comment earned a playful shove to the shoulder. "What would you know about love? You're about to marry two women at once. That's not love, that's madness! Where's the common sense in doing that at your age? You should be ploughing fields, not planting seeds!"

Zutra thought about a suitable reply. "Should I let the Princess know that you said that?"

"Why, do you want to see me dead as well," the Commander retorted.

"That's the second time someone has warned me about how dangerous she can be. Is there something you haven't told me about the Princess Ti-Ping?"

"Only that she is very talented in what the Orientals refer to as the Shaolin Kung Fu. Whatever you do, do not make her angry. You might not live to regret it."

Zutra laughed at the mere suggestion that someone so petite and slender could even knock over a stalk of wheat. He was still laughing when he realized that Patricius was not participating with the jest. The Exilarch's expression dropped immediately into a frown. "Really? You're actually serious?"

"I would not even wager that Jamasp's man could withstand her full onslaught longer than a few minutes."

"What kind of woman could do that?" Zutra was flabbergasted.

"One that you don't want to make angry," Patricius pointed out as he watched several other young ladies stroll through the central foyer of the inn. "As for me, I don't have those worries. A true shame that you do!" he ridiculed his young companion.

"Patricius?" the shout rang through the halls. "Is that really you? No, it can't be! My God, it is you!"

"Belarius," the Commander shouted as he ran to embrace the stout, bald headed man waddling towards him. "I can't believe you're still alive," he hugged the innkeeper. "You must be ancient by now?"

"Me?" the man hugged back, "How could someone like you that has offended so many in so short a time still be breathing, you old war dog?"

"Too tough and miserable to let anyone get that close," he laughed as he patted his old acquaintance on the back.

"It is so good to see you again," Belarius smiled. "You know they say you're dead!"

"I've heard the rumors too. Good to see you, old friend."

"Come, you must tell me all about your adventures. I believed them. I really did think you were dead when you disappeared so long ago."

"That was the idea my friend. No one comes looking for a dead man?"

"Come, come!"

"First you must find lodging for my companions. A few rooms should do it. That one over there is getting married, so make certain that your girls leave him alone."

"All the more reason I should send a few to his room so he can find out what he should do in order to please his new wife."

"No, no don't do that. He's Jewish. They're somewhat prudish about those things!" Patricius quipped as his voice dropped to a hushed whisper. "Has several beautiful concubines in his harem and from what I've heard still hasn't laid a hand on even one of them."

"Hey, I can still hear you, you know," Zutra protested.

"And that one, I don't think will be interested at all," Patricius said quietly on the side in reference to Jamasp.

"Is he Bithynian? Perhaps then a boy or two?"

"Don't encourage him," Patricius shuddered at the thought. "Let him have a room to himself with his bodyguard."

"And what about for your soldiers," Belarius inquired, running through the charges in his mind.

"Of course, they'll want some entertainment. They've been on the road quite a long time; all the way from the Sin Empire. That's a very long time to be celibate."

"Sin? Is that where you've been all this time? You've been to the ends of the earth, my friend. You must tell me all about it. I'm insisting!"

"We'll have plenty of time to talk tonight but first I have to make a few visits. I'll be back later. See to my companions in the meantime."

"Are you certain that who you're looking for will still be here? After two decades, things change. People move away and some of our old friends have even died."

"Oh, this one's around," Patricius was purposely vague. "He's expecting me."

Chapter Eleven

Palmyra: 497 A.D.

Moving swiftly through the streets of the city, Patricius relied on his old memories to point him in the right direction as he negotiated his way through the crowds. Anyone seeing the cowled figure knew instinctively from his gait that the hood concealed a seasoned warrior and steered well clear of his path. Having lived beneath the shadow of the Roman infantry for so long, the citizens of Palmyra knew what a trained sword arm could do in a confrontation. Not even the thieves were that bold that they'd take the chance of an encounter. Cutting a wide swath, it wasn't long until the Commander found exactly what he was looking for; a very unremarkable building that served as a warehouse for goods moving back and forth along the fabled caravan routes.

The old limestone building sat on the corner of two merchant lanes, which ran only a short distance in each direction before ending abruptly against the stonewall that now encircled the city. Once upon a time, before the wall had been built the two roads would have led into the suburbs, which were now converted into nothing more than the slums where the majority of the new immigrants resided. This particular merchant house served as agents for the Emperor Hsiang Xiaowen, handling the goods that flowed down the meager remnants of the Silk Road then onwards to Europe. Patricius never had a reason to doubt their loyalty before, but he was positive that any leak of information regarding his current mission had to originate from this building.

Pushing his way past the staff that ineffectually tried to bar his progression, Patricius burst through the doors into the offices located to the rear of the first floor. Several men, all in their fifties and sixties were thrown into a state of shock as the burly soldier stormed towards them.

119

"We have only a little money here, but take it all," one of them shouted. "Please, don't hurt us, take whatever we have," another cried out in fear.

"Which one of you is Masserio?"

The men looked one to the other then quickly pointed in the direction of their associate with the oversized girth and balding head. "He is!" After making the identification, the others drifted towards the edges of the room and out of harm's way.

"I am Flavius Patricius son of Aspar, and you and I have a lot to discuss."

Masserio's expression relaxed upon hearing the stranger announce his name. "Master Patricius. It is so good to see you. You had us worried that you were some kind of ruffian."

"Do not underestimate me," Patricius warned. "If I don't get the answers I want, I could very well seal your doom."

"Master Patricius, what could possibly be the problem. Your patron has always been one of our best clients. For the past twenty years, we have dedicated ourselves to meeting all your needs. What disagreement could you possibly have with us?"

The Commander stood over the frightened merchant and hammered a gloved fist hard against the table. "I entrusted you to prepare my passage to Constantinople, but you have betrayed me to my enemies."

"No, no," Masserio shook his head, denying the accusation. "I betrayed you to no one. In all the time we have served your Emperor, we have never even disclosed your whereabouts or even that you were still alive. Why should we suddenly talk to enemies of yours that we don't even know? Moreover, for what possible gain imagined? There'd certainly be no advantage to this firm. I must disagree; I don't understand your accusation at all!"

"You don't understand?" Patricius mocked Masserio's driveling tone. "What's so difficult to understand? The only one that knew of my travel arrangements was you. Then coincidentally a band of hired assassins happens upon our location a couple of days out of Ctesiphon; that's not a coincidence. That had to be planned at least a week in advance of our starting out since the assassins came from this region. That means they had to know both when and where we were going to be on any particular day. Only you knew when we were beginning our mission because I sent you that information as well as the route I'd be taking. So once again, if you're desirous of living, who did you speak to about my voyage?"

The other managers of the business slowly crept towards the door in an effort to escape but they did not go unnoticed. "Nobody moves!" Patricius shouted. "After I'm finished with Masserio here, I'll be starting to ask the rest of you the same questions." Like obedient dogs they stopped in their tracks, remaining motionless.

Cowering beneath the threatening shadow cast by the Commander, Masserio had no idea what he was to say or do. "I swear to you Master Patricius, I only spoke to three captains before I found a ship sailing to the port you required. "

"And you told them all who was to be their passengers, didn't you? Didn't you!" he shook the merchant violently.

"No," Masserio pleaded. "I only told the one captain that said he had passage for you. There was no need to tell the others. I swear, I'm telling you the truth."

Tossing the merchant backwards into his seat, the Commander was still not satisfied with his replies. "You swear you've said nothing to anyone else!"

"I swear," the tears welled in Masserio's eyes, as he feared and prepared for the worst.

"Any reason that this captain we've hired would be bearing a grudge against me? What can you tell me about him?"

"We've used him for years," the merchant exclaimed. "The owners of the boat are based in Joppa. Antaradus is their last port of call along the coast before they sail west. They have always been very reliable. Never a problem for as long as we've hired them."

"And you told them about the passages I was booking."

"I had to," Masserio admitted, "But only what you told me, fourteen men, including yourself, an aristocrat from the Sassanid royal family and a member of the Exilarch's family. Nothing else but that!"

"And just how did they react to the mentioning of any of this information?"

Masserio thought about it for the moment. Patricius thought he spotted a change in his demeanor as the merchant's eyes lit up with recognition.

"It was odd," he recounted. "When I mentioned the Exilarch's relative they became very excited. I thought it was only because being from Judea, the Captain was ecstatic to be of service to his own royal family. These Jews tend to be very protective of their own kind."

"Excited in what way?" Patricius pushed harder for answers.

"He began jabbering to his first mate in that language of theirs. I don't think he realized I understood a few words. You pick languages up in our line of business."

"And... what did you hear man? Get on with it!" Patricius grew impatient.

"Only that he said they have to tell their owner immediately/"

"And you didn't think that was significant?"

"Well," Masserio explained, "It is a little unusual to feel you have to inform the owner of the shipping line about a passenger. Normally captains don't even talk to anyone except the company officers. I only figured they got excited about it being someone from the Exilarch's family. Perhaps they had to find out if they needed to arrange something special. How do I know? I'm not a Jew. Maybe they need a special blessing or something. Am I supposed to know the proper etiquette they must provide to their royals?"

"And then what?"

"Just that!"

Patricius moved in closer like a lion to the kill. "Think harder. I need to know exactly what they did after you spoke to them."

"Nothing. Wait! I did get a message several days later, but it was more of a confirmation letter that the passages had been approved and they asked if I had made any other arrangements for your travels between Ctesiphon and Antaradus."

"And you didn't think that was perhaps a little strange?" Patricius was furious with the merchant's failure to read between the lines.

"Not really," Masserio's bottom lip quivered as he sunk down in his chair. "They were giving passage to three very highly placed people as representatives of three different Empires. I thought they were wishing to extend themselves and offer their services to make your journey as pleasant as possible from the time you began your travels."

"But instead, you told them that we had not made any arrangements, which would have immediately informed them that we'd be camping in the wilderness."

"It didn't seem to matter at the time."

"Of course not," Patricius raised his voice in a howl of derision. "You know our standing instructions. If there were any inquiries into Emperor Hsiang's business or mine, you were to report to me immediately. You failed miserably in carrying out that responsibility."

"But...but...it wasn't our fault. It was entirely innocent," Masserio tried to defend his company.

"Let me see that letter. I want to see who is behind this!"

Without hesitation, the merchant rifled through his files desperately searching for the letter while Patricius stood over him with arms crossed.

"Here it is," Masserio practically shoved it into the Commander's hands, relieved that he was able to find it so quickly.

Patricius stood silently as he read each paragraph and then deciphered the signatures at the bottom. "Do you know these people that signed this letter?"

"Of course I do," the merchant stated positively as if to say he could vouch safe for every one of them.

"Tell me about this one," Patricius demanded, pushing the letter in front of the merchant's face and pointing at one name in particular.

"That is the major owner of the fleet of vessels. Why would you have picked him out from the rest?"

"Because of the title and monograph he placed after his name. It's a little unusual, don't you think?"

"Oh that, Masserio chuckled, "his family has been using that thing for over three centuries now. It's completely harmless. No one really gives it any serious attention."

"No one but his followers I would guess. But that would probably be most of the Jewish community still residing in Judea."

"It's a very small community," the merchant was quick to explain. "If they wish to view this man's family as some royal bloodline by default what harm could that possibly do?"

"Combine the delusion with immeasurable wealth and you have a very dangerous mixture."

"Do you wish for me to cancel your passage and seek another ship?"

"No, don't do anything," Patricius advised all the men in the office. "Not a word of this is to escape from this room. If I should hear that any of you had even the remotest communication with this individual or anyone else, I will personally see to it that they are the last words you ever spread. And gentlemen don't ever think that I'm not capable of seeing through on my threats." Turning, Patricius stormed from the office with the same pounding military gait with which he had entered, slamming what was left of the door behind him.

Riding alongside each other along the road to Antaradus, barely a word passed between them for the best part of two miles.

"Is there something I have done that warrants this wall of silence," Zutra could not tolerate being ignored any longer.

"Yes and no," Patricius was enigmatic with his reply still buried deep in thought and reflection.

"That is not an answer."

"I'm afraid it is the only one I have to offer right now. As Jesus is my witness, I do not have all the details, but I will soon."

"Not wishing to be offensive but rather than wait for Jesus to give you an answer, why not see if we can work this out together?"

"That could be taken as offensive," Patricius responded gruffly.

Zutra shrugged his shoulders. "You've been waiting almost five centuries for his return. I don't think you want to wait another five hundred years for an answer to your question. Perhaps that special quality regarding my family that you heard about can be of assistance?"

"I have a possible lead regarding who sent the assassins," Patricius acquiesced and revealed his secret.

"And why would that cause you to brood in this agonizing silence that you've displayed all morning?"

Patricius grew reticent once again, not wishing to divulge any further information.

"If you're trying to spare me the concern that their target was actually me, then spare yourself the guilt. I already know."

"You couldn't know. I only found out yesterday,"

"Actually, I didn't know positively until just now," Zutra admitted his ruse. "I played a hunch and you confirmed it."

"You tricked me!" Patricius didn't appreciate being toyed with.

"And you were concealing the truth from me," Zutra countered. "That makes us even."

Tossing his head from side to side, Patricius thought about it for the moment and then roared with laughter. "You're right. But I only did so for your own good."

"You've been avoiding talking to me for my own good? I can definitely see how that would work," Zutra's sarcasm was equally evident. "So, what's this big secret you found out?"

"It's flimsy at best," Patricius pulled the letter from beneath his waistcoat. "I believe the assassins were hired by the people we've booked passage with. I believe that you may be familiar with the owners of this particular fleet of ships." Passing the letter over to Mar Zutra, he didn't have to wait long for a response.

Passing the letter back, Zutra looked disheartened. "It wouldn't surprise me. Gamaliel ben Judah has inherited the hatred for my family over more generations than I can count now."

"Explain to me the use of that monogram. That's what clued me in the first place."

"They are a family that has absolutely no right to claim anything above their station as rabbis but that has not stopped them for the last three hundred years."

"They're claiming to be your family from what I can interpret," Patricius deciphered that much from the insignia.

Zutra shrugged his shoulders as his horse kept to its steady pace. "Few would take it seriously."

"I've been told that already except that this family uses in their company motto 'In Services to the Emperor of Byzantium'. Only companies that are officially recognized by the Empire can make such a statement, which in turn means that the legislators have officially recognized this Gamaliel's claim to be 'Prince of Israel'. A country can't have two masters sitting on the same throne. Therein lies the problem that I have to work out before we meet with Anastasius. That's why I haven't mentioned anything to you yet."

"It's not as serious an issue as you think. They have not a drop of royal blood amongst the lot of them. The only time they could even say they were related was when one of my ancestors would marry one of their daughters."

Pointing his finger in Zutra's direction, he waved it menacingly. "You're not appreciating the seriousness of this situation. This Gamaliel is recognized by all the legal systems that exist in Byzantium as whom he claims to be. You are the complete unknown in this situation. Therefore, you will be seen as the claimant, not him. And do you know what happens to claimants?" It was a rhetorical question that Patricius didn't wait for his companion to answer. "They disappear, so that no one has to bother with the legal paperwork if there actually should be a legal claim. That's how they clean up the mess. Do you understand now?"

"That's absurd," Zutra protested. "I am the Exilarch. Everyone knows that."

"Apparently this pretender in Judea doesn't and he's willing to have the problem eliminated before it becomes a sore spot for the Emperor to decide upon. I need you to tell me everything there is about this pretender. Right from the beginning when it all began."

"It goes back quite a way," Zutra sighed.

"Everything about you Jews goes back quite a way," Patricius scoffed. "About time you all start living in the present!"

"It started a few hundred years ago."

"Even more of a problem for us. Time has a way of giving a claimant legitimacy. If he can show that his family held the title for generations then he can make a pretty good case in the courts that he's whom he claims to be."

"But everyone in the Jewish community knows that he's nothing more than a descendant of the sage, Hillel; a rabbi; nothing more than that. Just because he calls himself Gamaliel VII doesn't make him anything more." Zutra attempted to defend his position.

Patricius shook his head in disbelief. "So, he's the seventh one in the lineage to bear that name. And I'm assuming that there are others in the line that would have a similar number after their name. Right?"

"Judah the fourth, Hillel the second, Simon the third, but they're just names. Meaningless names within a family that became self-aggrandized."

"And while this family was busy calling themselves Princes of Israel, what was your family doing? Nothing! You allowed it all to take place right under your noses."

Zutra begged to differ, "It wasn't like that. After the Bar Kochba revolt, there were no traces of my family left behind in Judea. We had all relocated to Parthia. That left behind a lacuna that the first Judah in that family stepped in to fill. He was the first to call himself 'the Prince.'"

"So why didn't you stop him? Does your family have absolutely no understanding of the workings of affairs of state?" Patricius still couldn't understand how the Exilarchate allowed it to happen.

"We bore title of Exilarch in Persia. Why would we worry about Judea?"

"I don't know," Patricius continued to shake his head in disbelief, "Maybe because your family was in Persia and their family was established within the Roman Empire and both those Empires happened to be at a perpetual state of war. Perhaps that would be reason enough?"

Guilt was probably the main reason we did nothing," Zutra explained. "My family didn't support the revolt. The last of us fled across the border before the Romans put down the insurrection. We felt guilty about leaving behind the remnant and therefore never asserted ourselves over their lives again."

"And you failed to support it because…"

"It was suicide. Anyone with any intelligence could have seen it."

"Obviously there were those that didn't perceive it that way."

"You're a military man. Tell me how you would view it. Hadrian was Emperor of Rome at the time. He had already pacified the rest of the Empire. He had brought prosperity to all the countries that he ruled over. However, he refused to let the Jews rebuild the Temple in Jerusalem. To the rabbis this was their sign that their world was at the end time, so they anointed themselves a messiah to be their savior and started a war that lasted three and a half years. By the end of it, the Romans had slaughtered us in the hundreds of thousands, burnt our towns to the ground and turned the Temple Mount into a refuse dump. We were practically wiped from existence within our own homeland. We gained nothing. We lost everything."

"What does this have to do with the rivalry between your family and this other?"

"We left Judea to these rabbis and their war mongering messiah. We wanted no part of him or them. They in turn blamed us for their destruction because the descendants of David had abandoned the country. They say we caused God to doom their revolt because we turned our backs on them. They then declared we no longer had any role in the future of Israel and proceeded to nominate a family from amongst themselves to be their spiritual leaders. That was the House of Hillel. And that is how this all began."

"Your right," Patricius agreed, "It was insane. Everything about you Jews is insane. It wasn't bad enough that Vespasian slaughtered you and enslaved your people, you still had to believe you could take on Rome a second time. Even the Gauls had enough sense of when to lay low and abide their time and we all know they're not exactly the brightest thinkers when it comes to strategy."

"Except we have God on our side," Zutra interceded.

"Do you now," the Commander gave Zutra a quizzical glance. "From what I've seen, you've been subjugated by the Babylonians, oppressed by the Seleukids, enslaved by the Romans, and now you're getting it up the ass once again from the Sassanids. Explain to me where you believe God is actually fighting your battles, because if He is, then He's not doing a very good job of it!"

"We survive!" Zutra fired his response. "How many other civilizations or people do you know of that can make that claim? Long after everyone else is gone, we will still be here. That is how you know God is on our side."

"For how much longer? Even if you had defeated the legions, they only would have sent more legions. Perhaps a year, maybe even five, but they would have come, and any freedom would have been short lived. In the end, these battles you wage will seal your destruction. But back to the point, it was also foolish for your family to have permitted what followed because of some misplaced guilt for not wishing to die with the others."

"Let's not elevate the situation beyond its true merit. This latest Gamaliel isn't even recognized by his own community in Tiberias as their spiritual leader. It all ended with his grandfather, the sixth Gamaliel."

"If it ended than why is he an issue today!" Patricius demanded to know. "And believe me, anyone that tries to have us assassinated is an issue."

"Any real authority was stripped away from them by Theodosius seventy years ago. He executed the sixth Gamaliel and made it illegal for any further claimants to the patriarchy. This last patriarch's grandson has no legitimate claim to any hereditary position."

"Theodosius is dead," Patricius reminded him. "He died a long time ago and the things he said and did, died a long time ago with him. Strangely enough, I do recall something of this execution of that particular Jewish leader but otherwise any people that may have remembered the Emperor stripping the power from this family are probably also dead. And if this current Gamaliel wants to call himself Prince of the Jews, no one is going to remember why he can't!"

"I know this is all sounding very foolish to you but that's the way it was."

"Foolish isn't the word I would use; more like dangerous!"

"What can I do about it," Zutra shrugged.

"It has to end."

"And just how is that going to happen?" Zutra inquired, failing to appreciate the nuance in the Commander's voice.

"I intend to end it!"

"Do I even want to know how you plan on doing this?"

Spurring on his horse, Patricius raced forward to join his troops, ignoring Mar Zutra's question.

Chapter Twelve

Shenzhen: Present

"Alright, that's it, time for a break," Pearce yelled as he dragged himself out of his chair.

I was actually beginning to wonder when Pearce was going to interrupt my story. The fact that he sat as long as he had without calling a time out was a world record for him.

Moving towards the kettle, he poured himself another cup of hot water and added the packet of Nescafe. "Let me digest this latest tidbit. There's another family that laid claim to the Kahana heritage, eh? You never told me anything about that."

"Actually, I have. You know I've always mentioned that there was this rivalry between the Kahanate and the rabbis. It was the premise behind *Shadows of Trinity* if you recall."

"But you never exactly said why. I just presumed it was a jealousy thing. It's taken on a whole different complexion now."

"Envy was still a primary motivator. Don't discount it John. But I will admit that there was this something else you're alluding to."

"And was this something else significant enough that they had a justifiable claim? Perhaps your family isn't as unique as you've been telling me all these years."

"Not at all!" I insisted. "The family of Hillel was most likely as they claimed from the tribe of Judah. But so what? So were most families that lived in Judea. Even if they had a distant tie in to the Davidic monarchy, what they didn't have was the bloodline like that of the Kahana constantly mixed into their milieu. That was and is the major separation point."

"Touchy, aren't we?" Pearce knew he was pressing all the wrong buttons with me.

"They didn't have anything close to the same bloodlines. End of story!"

"But they ruled in Judea for a few hundred years nonetheless." Pearce always had to be the spoilsport.

"Not until approximately 200 A.D. That's when the first one took the title of Prince Judah ha Nasi. But he was no prince, and he was never officially recognized as one. Subsequently, his descendants all took on the title of 'the Prince'. By the time of Gamaliel VI, it got out of hand. That Gamaliel started building synagogues and mansions believing he really was some Eastern potentate and that's when Theodosius pulled the plug on him. In 415 A.D. the Emperor stripped him of all his authority, but when that didn't stop Gamaliel, Theodosius had him executed in 425 A.D."

"Meanwhile your family had moved themselves to the outskirts of Baghdad and completely ignored events as they were transpiring back in Israel."

"That's a little harsh," I confronted him. "It wasn't as if you could move freely back and forth between the two empires. Even if we wanted to intercede in Judea, we weren't permitted to. You have to keep in mind there were political circumstances that kept us at bay."

"But in essence, this family of Hillel was the only leadership the people had."

"You're beginning to piss me off John," I threatened though truthfully I was only minorly irritated.

"Whatever Doc, they still were the rulers of the community."

"Yes, but that doesn't mean they had the right to claim the title."

"If you say so," Pearce cooed satisfied that he got in the last word.

Tiberias: 497 A.D.

A pale gray mist swirled above the gently rolling hills that surrounded the rippling waters of a shimmering lake. Summer was coming to an early close in this northern province of Palestine and already the tendrils of silvery frost could be seen quickly vanishing as the sun rose over the ranges that divided it from the Syrian province. Patricius pulled the collar of his mantle as high as it would go to stave off the morning chill.

He traveled with only two men, the most trusted of his soldiers, having left the balance of his squad to safeguard the two monarchs back at Antaradus. By riding through the night, he calculated it would only be two days at the most before he was back at the Syrian port city. Patricius never even bothered to consult with his companions regarding his little diversion, only saying that he had personal business to take care of and that he would be back in time for their ship's sailing. Mar Zutra had his suspicions, but he knew better than to try and make the Commander accountable to him. Worrying was something he would leave to Jamasp, who he knew fretted over every detail and little change in plan. Sometimes it was best not to know, Zutra concluded. Successful and powerful men left the hard decisions to those best qualified to make them he continually reminded himself. It also allowed them to distance themselves from the consequences.

As the three riders approached the city, they scrupulously surveyed the surrounding countryside. There was little to remind a visitor to Tiberias of its ancient stature as one of the most beautiful cities of the world. Sadly, it had never recovered from the destruction visited upon it when it was burnt to the ground during the first revolt against Rome. What little rebuilding took place since then was a frail shadow of its glorious past. Over the centuries, it had remodeled itself into an educational centre where the remaining Jews, the last of fifteen hundred years of continuous existence in the land, relocated their centre of government. Several synagogues had been built as well as the yeshiva where new rabbis would be trained and then dispatched to the Jewish communities around the world. However, the radiant magnificence that had once crowned the jeweled city on the Sea of Galilee had faded forever.

In the hills above the city, Patricius found a little grotto, where a trickling brook passed between etched crevices in the rocks, as it made its way to the blue waters of the lake below. Surrounded by lush ferns and shady palms, his presence was concealed from the road as he tied the reins of his horse to the stump of a fallen tree and then stretched himself out on a bed of basalt, basking in the early rays of the rising sun. He turned to his two men and instructed them to carry on with their task; he would wait for them there. Without a moment's hesitation the soldiers saluted and then carefully picked their way down the hills towards the town that stretched out on the horizon at the end of the roadway.

The respite gave Patricius time to reflect on the quarter of a century he had been away from this part of the world. He dreamt of Leontia; his beautiful, seductive Leontia. An offering made to him by the Emperor Leo only after he had snatched away his true love. His forced marriage to Leontia was a clear signal that all was not well concerning his father, Aspar, whom was designated to be the next emperor of Byzantium. Nevertheless, though she had been foisted upon him as a bride, there was no doubt in Patricius's heart that he had grown to love her. Alas, when his world crumbled all around him, she was the first to abandon him, not willing to sacrifice her prestigious place in Constantinople society by being married to an alleged traitor. Love, what a strange and wretched emotion he mused. More than even the death of his father or the murder of his brother, it was betrayal by those he loved that proved to be the final straw, making him flee to the farthest corner of the world. The pain and anguish that pierced his heart from those that turned their back on him drove him to the brink of madness and despair. It wasn't until he reached the ocean at the far side of the world that he finally stopped running.

Searching for a release from his misery, Patricius succumbed to the somnolence offered by the humble poppy; his days passing seamlessly within an opiate haze that he wished would last forever. Lying in a soiled cot, numbed to his surroundings was exactly how Valentius had found him. Recognizing what remained of Patricius's Byzantine armor, he felt compelled to give assistance since Valentius considered himself to still be a Roman captain, though by outward appearance he was most certainly Asian. A Roman that had never seen Rome, born within the colony of exiles that had escaped from the clutches of Shapur's Persian army when they had taken the Emperor Valerian prisoner, over two hundred years prior. Though the product of well over two centuries of intermarriages with the Chinese population Valentius still considered himself Latin by birth, thus suffering from all the delusions of Roman heroics and chivalry. His chance encounter with Patricius when he went in search of one of his own man that had strayed days before into the opium dens was in his own words 'divine providence.'

An opportunity for penance was more like it. Whereas his ancestor had abandoned Valerian, leaving the Emperor behind to be cruelly slain by the Persian monarch, skinned and preserved as a trophy on display, he was now provided a chance for redemption; an opportunity to regain his family's reputation and honor. How else could it be explained that a commander serving the throne of Byzantium would be found in the heart of Sin, desperately in need of his help. Forgetting about his missing trooper, Valentius had his men drag Patricius from the opium parlor and carried back to their camp where they eventually nursed him back to health over several weeks.

The withdrawal period was most excruciating, persisting for seven days of writhing and screaming torment. At times Patricius had to be staked to the ground, completely immobilized, in order to prevent him from harming himself or anyone else as he recovered. The attending soldiers mopped the sweat from every inch of his body, keeping him under a constant vigil while Valentius brewed a mixture of phu and sow thistle, an ancient Chinese remedy. The therapy was reputed to relieve the pain and nausea that addicts endured as they were weaned from their narcotic cravings. They repeated the process endlessly until one day when Patricius stared Valentius directly in the eyes and spoke in his deep stentorian voice, "I believe you have a lot of explaining to do soldier!"

The cheer that rose from those in attendance when they heard Patricius' first words was deafening Untying his wrists, Valentius aided Patricius into a sitting position, holding a cup of the herbal remedy to his parched lips.

"This stuff is absolutely vile," Patricius protested. "What do you call this swill?"

"This time it is a tea only brewed from phu," Valentius responded, as he poured it slowly past Patricius's lips. "But it has no name."

"How is it you speak Latin?" Patricius was intrigued by this man of mixed race speaking the ancient language.

"I am Roman," Valentius stated proudly. "See; look at some of the segmentata plates in my armor. They were taken from my great great grandfather's armor. He served Valerian."

"Valerian died with all his men," Patricius sneered in disbelief. "They never came back!"

"That's true that they never came back but all did not die. They headed further east. Just like you," Valentius informed him.

"His was a name and cause forgotten to the past and disgraced. So, you're continuing to preserve the memory of someone we'd sooner forget. You talk Latin; you try to dress in bits of old armor and even think like a Roman. Why bother?

"Since our presence here is entirely the result of our failure to save the Emperor Valerian, we must strive for forgiveness and restore our honor. A family's name and honor is everything."

"Roman honor. Of course. How noble of you." The sarcasm dripping from Patricius was lost on Valentius and his men. To them the old Rome still existed, and they knew little of how decrepit and decayed the Empire had become.

"Your salvation by our hands must be directed by the gods. We could not save Valerian, but we were given the chance to save you. You want a name for the concoction that returned you to us…we will call this tea 'valerian' in honor of this moment. May your coming to us be a sign that we have redeemed our honor?"

The explanation of how and why they existed didn't fully register with Patricius who was still slightly dazed from the rehabilitation process. Over time, he became entirely familiar with the history behind this colony of Romans in the middle of the Chinese province of Han. In addition, over the next few months he even became grateful for finding a small sliver of the life he had left behind in this strange and foreign dominion.

After several years, Patricius accomplished what he had always done best; he forged the men of this small Roman outpost into an elite military machine, which soon brought it to the attention of one of the many contenders for the Emperor of China's throne. In a period of civil strife and constant fratricide between the imperial claimants, the hiring of a mercenary unit with skills that exceeded those of the local militias was a valuable asset. The Emperor Hsiang Xiaowen was able to establish himself as the chief candidate soon after he and Patricius had arrived at a mutually beneficial arrangement.

Now, thirteen years after joining Hsiang's army, he was, back in the world in which he was born, but as an official ambassador of the Chinese Emperor and guardian of both Sassanid and Jewish monarchs. Furthermore, he was on his way to visit the reigning ruler of an empire that he was forced to flee twenty-five years ago. Whatever else the fates had in store for him, he seriously doubted whether they could ever surpass the present irony. With a smile of contentment stretched across his lips, he closed his eyes and slept peacefully.

It was several hours before he was awoken by the sound of hoof beats heralding the return of his two men. Crouching down amongst the palm leaves, Patricius waited until he could clearly discern the feathered helm belonging to Valentius. As soon as he recognized it, he emerged into the open grotto and greeted his most trusted companion.

"Did you find what I sent you for?"

The second solder untied the sac strapped across the flanks of his mount and let it full heavily to the ground. The sac wriggled and turned wildly. Whatever it contained within was desperate to break free.

"There he is," Valentius responded affirmatively as he gave the sac a quick kick as both a warning to the occupant and a confirmation to his Commander.

"Did you have much trouble?" Patricius inquired.

"If you mean did anyone see us," the captain smiled, "the answer is no. Apparently, he's quite well known to everyone in town. Even to the derelict scum that reside by the town's trash heap. A couple of coins and one of them practically drew a map to the man's house. All we had to do was sit and wait for him to leave his house unescorted."

"And you're certain it is him?"

"Don't take us for fools," Valentius protested. "Calithenes here asked him in perfect Greek if he was the famous Gamaliel, Prince of Israel, before he bashed him over the head once he replied that he was."

"See Calithenes," Patricius praised, "All those years of studying Greek and it finally paid off. I told you it wasn't a waste of time."

The soldier made a few mirthful grunts to show that he appreciated the compliment.

"I guess he's regretting being so famous now," Valentius surmised.

"Well, let's see what we have. Untie the bag," Patricius commanded.

Calithenes undid the big knot in the rope that held the sac closed. As the rope fell away, a short but stout figure of a man was revealed. His clothes were a dingy grey and he wore a low cap upon his head, which concealed his balding features. His hands and feet were tied and a gag had been placed across his mouth.

"Undo everything," Patricius rotated his index finger in the direction of all the remaining ropes.

As soon as the gag was removed then the man started raving and ranting at his unknown assailants. Taking a moment to calm down, Gamaliel glared towards Patricius and spoke threateningly. "Do you know who I am?"

There was no evidence of any alarm in Patricius's voice. "The real question is do you know who I am?"

"I couldn't give a damn, who you might think you are," the Jewish patriarch replied disdainfully. "I am the leading man in this province and I am under the protection of the Emperor Anastasius. Anything you might do to me will be considered as a direct threat to the Emperor. So my advice to you is to set me free and there's a chance you won't be executed for this effrontery!"

"Blah, blah, blah. My father was the Consul Aspar," Patricius smiled in response to the threat.

Upon hearing that name, Gamaliel turned as white as a ghost, his hands noticeably beginning to tremble.

"I see you remember the name," Patricius continued. "As you should."

His knees began to buckle as the Jewish patriarch felt himself becoming faint. "You can't be," he muttered. "You're all dead. You can't be," he repeated again.

"One should never make assumptions," the Commander

advised. "The same way your grandfather never should have assumed my father would tolerate his attempt to seize power in this country without his consent. My father was a reasonable man, yet your family chose to slap him in the face by ignoring his edicts. Your grandfather thought himself beneath detection of the Emperor Theodosius. However, as both consul and protector of the state, he forgot it was actually Aspar that preserved the needs of the Empire in this region. My father was not about to let some upstart peacock strut his feathers in his face and in so doing embarrass the Emperor. And you know what he did, don't you?"

The frightened Gamaliel nodded his head in acknowledgement.

"And here we are, once again. You are doing exactly as your grandfather did, and have forced me to respond exactly as my father had to. What a shame that the lessons have not been learnt."

Tears welled up in the Jewish leader's eyes as he understood fully the meaning of Patricius' implied threat. "But I have the blessing of the Emperor Anastasius. He has granted me the rights and privileges I use."

Patricius paced back and forth in a leisurely stroll, his hands clasped behind his back as he did so, like a teacher schooling his pupils. "But that's because the Emperor Anastasius doesn't truly appreciate the severity of the threat you represent."

"I threaten no one," the rabbi's voice cracked as he pleaded with his captors. "I only serve my community. I don't make any pretense to doing anything else."

The commander shook his head in disagreement. "That's where you are very wrong. You're very existence is a pretense to claiming far more than you're entitled to."

"What have I done to you?" Gamaliel cried.

"You honestly don't know," Patricius continued to shake his head in disapproval. "How can you have made an attempt on the Exilarch's life and not known whom he was traveling with?"

Gamaliel's face contorted into a combined mask of both guilt and alarm. He knew that his planned assassination had been exposed, a fact that he obviously could not deny. "It was not my idea," Gamaliel explained in a last-ditch attempt to save his own life. There were others involved. All the way up to the Emperor's secretary. They all approved and urged me to carry it out."

"And how do you think that makes you any less guilty of the crime?" Patricius felt compelled to ask.

"Because I was only carrying out their wishes."

"Wishes that would ultimately benefit you more than most," the Commander challenged.

"Not true, not true," the captive patriarch wailed. "It was all planned by the deposed council members in Mahoza. They were the ones that first sent word to both me and to Anastasius's secretary that the Exilarch was on route to Constantinople. Then I received notice of exactly when later on from one of my captains. Those in Mahoza said that if he was eliminated on route, then they would be returned to power and would throw their allegiance towards me. And since I serve the Emperor, the Exilarch's death would give Anastasius control over a large segment of the population within the enemy's empire."

"I can see the merit in such a plan," Patricius agreed. "But there is a weakness in the strategy. As Anastasius will shortly learn, I can deliver him the entire Sassanid Empire, not just a portion of its subjugated population. It was never a matter of you being the sole leader of the Jews. It could be anyone. The key though is that there must only be one. You understand the arithmetic?"

The question was rhetorical, and Gamaliel lowered his head, knowing that the solution to the mathematical equation meant that he would not be able to convince the Commander to spare his life. The two soldiers grabbed one arm each of the kneeling patriarch, steadying him for the final blow as Patricius withdrew his sword from its scabbard.

"It ends here," he emphasized the obvious. "Are there any prayers you need to recite before I finish this?"

"A curse upon Mar Zutra's house and yours, Son of Aspar," Gamaliel spat. I pray that Almighty Go…"

"That is not what I meant," Patricius scolded as his blade sliced down upon the exposed neck with a bone breaking thwack. Tossed into the thick growth of the grotto, it would be days before any of the townspeople would find their illustrious leader and Patricius and his contingent would be well on their way to the Byzantine capital.

Chapter Thirteen

Antaradus: 497 A.D.

"This is insane!" Jamasp screamed. "I cannot let you do this. I will not let you do this!" The Prince defiantly stomped his booted feet against the stone slabs of the tiled floor performing a childlike tantrum.

Mar Zutra seized both of Jamasp's wrists in his strong grip. "I don't think either of us is in a position to tell Patricius what he can and cannot do?

"We owe no debt to this man, Zutra! He has already placed us in a compromised position. How do we know we will not become prisoners of Anastasius to be ransomed back to my brother?"

"This is an issue of trust. If we don't do this, your brother will permit the Magus to destroy our world. And should we resist, hundreds of thousands will die as a result of the civil war that will ensue. We have the power to stop that. Not Patricius! Only you and I can do this by appealing to the Byzantines and convincing them that a world of peace would be mutually beneficial to everyone. As the rulers of two great and noble people do we have the right to place our own lives above that of the people we rule over?"

Jamasp pleaded with Zutra to reevaluate the circumstances. "He has killed an agent of Anastasius! He has freely admitted that to us. Why would the Emperor forgive us for such an act?"

Zutra's eyes pierced deeply into the Prince's heart. "Because we can offer him something far more valuable than some petty and insignificant magistrate from the far corner of his Empire was worth. Can you not understand this?"

"We do not even know if Anastasius will be pleased to see Patricius. For all we know he may want to stick his severed head on the end of a pike. Perhaps we should ask for a reassurance before we sail onwards?"

"And shall they say that both Jamasp and Zutra were not men of their word. Shall they spit on both our family names because we have no honor? Without honor, we are as good as dead. I will not have them brand us as cowards! We shall stand in front of the throne of Anastasius, not as subordinates but as equals. And no man will dare to think otherwise!"

"And I fear our deaths are imminent. Nevertheless, I will stand by you, brother. Not because I consider Patricius as our protector but because I believe in you."

"Do not fear brother, we will live! Just as both our families have survived since the dawn of time. Do as I say! Let Patricius do as he sees fit without objection. No matter what you might think, he is wise in these ways of the world beyond our reasoning and measure. Do not falter in that belief!"

"I trust you, brother. I will do as you wish."

"Good, then have your man prepare your belongings and let's board the ship."

Having successfully convinced the Sassanid Prince that the journey should continue, Zutra left him with his bodyguard to pack his few remaining personal items.

Outside the inn, Patricius had been waiting impatiently, arms folded across his broad chest, while he leaned up against one of the support poles that craned the overhanging roof above the entrance. "Well, what did he have to say?"

"He's coming," Zutra stated succinctly.

"Did he give you much trouble?"

"Not really. I just had to convince him that you're not as big an asshole as he might think."

A devilish smile crept across the Commander's face. "Are you so sure of that?"

"No, but I have to put my faith in someone, so it might as well be you," the words dripped with a mixture of cynicism and fatalism.

"I don't think I've ever been so underwhelmed by someone's faith in me," Patricius laughed. "So do you also disagree with my handling of the situation?"

"No."

"Just no? Nothing else to say?"

141

"Just no," Zutra showed no interest in elaborating further.

The Commander was not prepared to let it drop that easily. "You know that it was the only solution possible. You cannot have two people claiming to hold the same title. It would only complicate the situation."

"I know."

"But you don't approve."

"I didn't say that."

"So, you do approve?"

"I didn't say that either."

"There's a new captain on board as well," Patricius informed the young monarch.

"Do I want to know what happened to the old one?" he questioned gingerly.

"He took ill," Patricius replied quickly to dispel any thoughts that Zutra might have been harboring in regard to another murder.

"That was convenient," the Exilarch commented.

"It was," Patricius agreed. "It came on suddenly last night. Fortunately, there was another captain available for hire. In fact, I hired him personally."

"And the merchant owners were in agreement with your selection?"

"They were more than happy to agree to my choice," he confirmed. "There should be smooth sailing all the way to Constantinople."

"I appreciate that," Zutra finally cracked a smile, flashing his white teeth at the Commander. "I really do."

"I wish that the Prince saw it that way as well."

"I'm certain he already does,"

"I do what has to be done," Patricius felt compelled to explain himself.

"Of that, neither of us had any doubt," Zutra nodded.

The merchant vessel sailed under the trade name of 'Heart of Zion', which Mar Zutra took as a sign of providence as soon as he saw it written at the top of the manifest. He immediately turned to Jamasp, whom he discovered had never been on anything larger than a river barge his entire life. Exclaiming that it was a prophetic message from God that everything would be all right, Jamasp tried to appreciate the divine significance in Zutra's insight but just watching the ship rise and fall at its mooring was enough to make him queasy.

Once on board, Zutra was not surprised to discover that the new captain was an old acquaintance of Patricius. He could only imagine what powers of persuasion had been used to convince the remaining owners of the merchant fleet that they should hire Captain Diocletian. His thoughts began to wander, and he shuddered to think how much more blood would stain his hands through his association with Patricius.

Carrying their baggage below deck, Patricius divided their group into three units, assigning each party one of the three rooms that had been allotted to their contingent. He would berth with Mar Zutra, Jamasp and the Prince's bodyguard, while Valentius and the other soldiers would divide themselves between the two remaining rooms. Being a merchant vessel, the cabins were far from luxurious, but at the last moment, every attempt had been made by the owners to make them as comfortable as possible.

"Well, gentlemen, I would suggest you try your best to squeeze in because this scow is going to be your home for the next ten days. Pray to whatever gods you wish that she stays afloat for that long a voyage," Patricius laughed thinking his jest amusing, especially to those that had never sailed on the seas before.

Jamasp was not amused. "Is that supposed to be funny, Lord Patricius?"

"It was an innocent musing, your majesty. There is nothing to worry about, I can assure you. She's a fine vessel and I know my ships. Everything will be fine." Over the years, Patricius had become accustomed to all manner of sailing vessels, having held the command of the navies for two different empires.

"I will hold you personally responsible," Jamasp waved his hands frantically, "If we should drown at sea?"

Upon hearing his comment, his companions burst into fits of laughter.

"What's so funny? I insist on knowing what you all find so funny", the Prince swung around to face down each man.

"If we should drown then I shall tell you about it," Zutra could barely get the words out between laughs.

The Prince thought about it for the moment and then broke into a broad smile. "I made a good joke," he covered his embarrassment, nudging his massive bodyguard in the ribs as if to suggest you better start laughing too.

"Yes, your highness," Patricius deferred to the Prince, "You did make a good joke. Well done."

"But I am still not happy about sailing. I would have much preferred we travelled over land." Jamasp was not willing to confess that the thought of sailing on the sea terrified him.

"Unfortunately, the Taurus mountains make that means of travel too difficult this time of year," Patricius explained. "I'm certain once you've stretched your legs on deck you have a different opinion."

"Oh no," the Prince was quick to correct him. "I have no intention of going on deck. I will remain in our cabin until we reach our destination, thank you."

"We're looking at ten days at sea, your highness."

"Then ten days it will be," Jamasp accepted the period of confinement nonchalantly.

"I intend to be topside," the Commander informed them all. "I'll have the stewards bring down towels and a several wash bowls. It sounds like you might have need of them."

The Prince nodded his head in an expression of gratitude for his consideration.

"I think I'll go topside as well," Zutra quickly added as soon as he pictured in his mind the prince stretched over the bowls retching until his stomach had run dry and his lips parched until they blistered and cracked. Not a sight he wished to observe too closely in their shared accommodation. The two men moved towards the open door of the cabin and then closed it swiftly behind them as they ran towards the stairs.

"When do you think we'll be able to sleep in that cabin?" Zutra asked his Commander.

"I think we might be spending most of our nights on deck," Patricius informed him. "He was beginning to already look green and we haven't even weighed anchor. I can't even imagine what he'll be like once we set sail."

"I never like confined spaces anyway," the young Exilarch exhaled in relief to be away from the stuffiness of the cabin.

Patricius watched with interest as Mar Zutra steadied himself on deck, his legs shifting their weight with the rolling of the ship. "So where did you get your sea-legs from," he inquired.

"I don't' really know," Zutra replied. "I also have never been on a ship before, yet I feel like I've done this all before."

"That is a bit strange," the Commander stated quite intrigued by the Exilarch's inherent talent to keep himself balanced.

"Not in my family, it isn't," Zutra explained. "We all seem to have that ability to do things that we've never done before in a manner as if we had done them all our lives. My father used to call it the gift of the Kahana. He used to say that his father would sometimes start speaking in a language that he never learned, only to be surprised himself once he uttered the strange words."

"And what do you think it is?" Patricius was curious.

"A gift from God, I suppose."

The commander seemed satisfied with the answer. He equated it to the speaking in tongues of his own faith; also considered a gift to those that experienced it.

"You're expecting problems once we reach Constantinople, aren't you?" Zutra stated it more as a fact than a question.

"I've been away a long time," Patricius sighed as he leaned over the rail. "I'm not certain what to expect any more."

Mar Zutra watched the variety of expressions as they flushed over the Commander's face briefly. For most others, the changes would have not even been noticed, but to the insights of the Exilarch, they were like a well-crafted book telling an endless story. "Who was she?"

"What are you talking about?"

"The woman you were thinking about."

"What? Are you a mind reader now too?" Patricius grew annoyed by the invasion of his thoughts.

"It is what you were thinking," Zutra defended himself.

"That doesn't mean you have the right to peer into my head! Some things are meant to remain private!"

"If that's the case, then don't think so loud!"

"You can be frustrating. You're a lad with too much power!"

"Perception; too much perception," Zutra corrected him.

"Alright, too much perception if that's what you want to call it!"

"Blame my ancestors," Zutra weathered the comment. "But that still doesn't answer my question. We are on a quest to achieve one goal but sometimes your mind is preoccupied with this other matter. Should I be worried that the two shall be in conflict?"

Patricius suppressed a desire to strike the young pup but consciously he conceded that Zutra was correct in his assessment. "It won't be a problem."

"It's always a problem," the Exilarch advised with wisdom garnered from far more than his years. "The more they hurt us, the more we want them. Look at me with Avital. My own Vizier tells me that I'm being a fool but do I listen to him? No! She is a poisoned arrow directly pointed at my heart, yet I yearn for her fatal touch. Now I am even forcing her into a marriage which I know I'm going to regret immediately afterwards. So be aware, I understand your feelings for this woman far more than you may wish to give me credence."

"Then you know why I wish to keep my thoughts to myself!" Patricius fumed.

"I thought that way once," Zutra continued to ramble. "The more Mordecai told me I was a fool and a madman, the angrier I became. It took me a while to figure out that I wasn't mad at him but at myself. I recognized that everyone I knew was mocking me, considering me the fool. They were right and I loathed myself even more while at the same time desiring Avital beyond reason. There was no breaking the cycle and no point in even trying."

"Perhaps you are smarter than you look." Patricius relaxed to the point that he actually found some solace in what Zutra was saying. "So how do you deal with it? I can't believe I'm asking a mere boy this! I must be going mad."

"That's how I deal with it," Zutra responded. "I freely admit that I am not in control of my faculties. That I am insane and everyone else is correct in his or her condemnation. And as I'm doing now, I freely admit to my lack of sanity, my irrational behavior, but let everyone know there's absolutely nothing I can do about it, so they need not waste their time in giving me their advice. Confessing to my insanity is liberating!"

"That sounds crazy too," the commander laughed.

"Try it!"

"You are crazy."

"No, try it. Admit it to me and you'll see for yourself what I'm talking about."

Patricius shook his head indicating that he thought the notion ridiculous. "Okay, just to get you off my back. I'm in love with a woman that broke her promises to me three decades ago. A woman that no sooner did she hear that my family was being stripped of its power and charged with treason made confessions to the council that she was aware of my plotting to kill her father and seize his throne. The same woman that provided the tribunal with enough lies that it forced me into exile for twenty-five years, destroyed my life, killed my family, stole my possessions and even after all that I can't banish her face from my dreams, and I still wonder if she's in love with me. Does that make me crazy too or just a sick, sorry son of a bitch like you?"

"Not even close," Zutra argued. "If she had married your father, then had him killed, while stealing your possessions and trying to rob you of your hereditary power before charging you with assorted criminal behaviors and doing that all within a few years instead of decades, then you'd have a case to challenge me. But as it stands, I have you beat hands down!"

The stern face of the commander shattered into a huge grin, and he slapped his companion across the back with his broad hand. "By Jesus, you are right. I feel better already," Patricius felt a heavy burden lift from his heart. "I've been feeling sorry for myself for over twenty-five years and I should have realized I was crazy and there was nothing I could do about it. Not to mention that you're an even sicker pup than I am! So, what's the point of fighting with myself any longer?"

"Exactly!" Zutra shouted.

"You can't fight it, change it, correct it or do without it. So, you might as well just accept it. Women are the bane of our existence and that's all there is to it!"

"Now you understand," the young man instructed his much older student.

"I think I can do that! I believe I can look her in the eye and confess that I still love her, no matter what she has done to me in the past. If that's a crime, so be it but similarly, if she claims I'm a fool, then so be it too!"

"But she's in exile now, I think you said and unreachable."

Patricius never responded to Zutra's comment.

Zutra looked deep into the Commander's eyes. "You're talking about someone else, aren't you? Aha! This is not your former wife you're talking about!" Zutra's eyes widened in the revelation as he pointed an accusatory finger at the commander.

"Don't push this!"

"Two women! You're right! You are almost as messed up as me!"

"Not another word!"

Smiling impishly, Mar Zutra didn't have to say another word to make his point, while he stared blankly over the rail, a huge grin painted upon his lips.

"Crazy sons of bitches, that's what we are," Patricius muttered to himself, shaking his head in disbelief.

Chapter Fourteen

Constantinople: 497 A.D.

The beautiful summer day unfolded its tendrils of Eden-like splendor across the vapor shrouded docks; the air fragrant with scents of jasmine and citrus trees that lined the canals. It was the perfect day to bring a ship into harbor, the water calm as a pane of glass. Both Mar Zutra and Patricius leaned over the rail as they watched the city slowly come into view as the morning mist lifted.

"Too bad the Prince is missing this," Patricius reflected. "The city is even more beautiful than I remembered it."

"It's still going to be some time before he'll be able to free himself of hugging chamber pots," Zutra laughed. "Let him stay where he is for now."

No sooner had the Exilarch completed his comment when a trembling Prince Jamasp, with the aid of his ever-present bodyguard came on deck, his legs wobbling excessively with every step he took. His complexion still as ruddy green as the first day he climbed on board but now his eyes were sunken behind prominent cheek bones that stood out more than ever. Having only managed to keep a minuscule amount of food down the entire voyage, the prince was now wraith-like in appearance, looking far older than his natural years.

"You've managed to find your way out of your cabin, Prince Jamasp," Patricius said jovially. "Just in time to see the splendor of Constantinople. Isn't she beautiful," the Commander spread his arms to encompass the panorama of the shoreline.

"Yes, yes," Jamasp agreed without even looking up at the city view. "A sight to behold."

"Nothing compares to it anywhere else in the world. And I should know, because I've seen most of this world."

"Yes Commander," Jamasp's voice croaked. "But more importantly, how long until we're freed from this accursed ship?"

"We'll be in port soon, your Majesty. Just a little more patience." Patricius found himself almost pitying the ailing prince.

"Oh god, I have nothing left to spew over the side," Jamasp dug his nails into the railing as he body arched. He gagged on the dryness at the back of his throat, wiping away the bit of spittle that clung to his lips with the back of his cloak. "Promise me we can return by land when this is all over."

"I'm sorry," Patricius apologized. "We have to go back by sea. You certainly wouldn't want to encounter your brother on our return. "

"At this moment, Commander, death is a far better alternative than the way I feel."

"Unless we can convince Anastasius of our worthiness as allies, death may still very well be in the cards for all of us!"

No sooner had their vessel had docked, Patricius's small entourage was met by a waiting contingent of armed men assembled upon the wharf. Their black leather cuirasses and plumed helmets clearly identified them as Alanine soldiers. They were fierce looking fighters, barbarians by local standards, and renowned for being the Emperor's shock troops in battle.

Having no concern for his own safety, Patricius strolled briskly down the pier to face down the captain of the hundred-man cohort. The officer in turn matched Patricius stride for stride as he charged towards him.

"Oh god, they are going to fight," the Prince's voice rose in alarm. "We are all going to die!"

"Prepare to be attacked," Zutra shouted to Valentius adding his concern to that of Jamasp's. As soon as the two commanders were a couple of yards apart they ran unrestrained at each other, lowering their shoulders as they both prepared for the resultant collision. From the distance, both Zutra and Jamasp watched horrified as the two men grappled, each struggling to better the other as they wrestled to their knees.

"Quick, we have to do something," Zutra's voice was alarmed as he watched. "You have to do something," he reaffirmed his previous instruction to Valentius.

"Our orders are to wait here," Valentius refused to budge. "The commander will signal us if he needs help."

"There are a hundred men over there," Zutra pointed out. "At what point do you think he will be disadvantaged and need to be rescued."

"Just wait," Valentius cautioned. "There are only a dozen of us. We'd be of little help against those odds. I am certain the Commander knows what he is doing."

"Right!" Zutra disagreed only to agree. Valentius was correct though. There was little more he could do but watch the two burly combatants entangle horns like rutting water buffalo, seeing that their own squadron was so vastly outnumbered.

The captain of the Alanines reached around Patricius, seizing him in a bear hug that lifted him off the ground. Patricius squirmed and managed to break free, then scrambled to wrap his arms around the challenger but no matter how hard he tried he could not find the leverage to take the larger man off his feet. Finally, exhausted by their efforts, the two combatants smacked each other about the shoulders with the flat of their hands.

"Wait a second," Zutra squinted his eyes as he scrutinized the changing situation. "They're not fighting! This is a ruse!"

"No, this is a greeting," Valentius informed him, "A Samatian greeting," he laughed.

"You knew all the time!" Zutra accused the Captain.

"Of course," Valentius assured him. "Do you think we'd let our Commander just charge off the ship alone? We're sworn to protect him; wouldn't exactly be doing our job if we let that happen."

Patricius waved his group of travelers to come forward and join him. Once they had disembarked, he pointed towards the hulking Captain of the Alanine guard. "Allow me to introduce to you my cousin Hermantius," the Commander shouted joyfully. "Best damn fighter in my entire legion."

Despite his wide girth, the captain was still able to bow gracefully following his introduction. "Caesar, my men are yours to command."

"Shut up, you old fool," Patricius shouted angrily. "Don't call me that! You want to get us all killed?"

The smile on Hermantius' lips was beguiling. "You will always be our Caesar. That will never change! Not until the day you die!"

"You keep calling me that and that day will likely be today," the Commander was furious.

"Can you believe this," the Alanine captain turned to his men. "For twenty-five years we have not seen each other and already he wants to scold me for the things I do. Nothing has changed! He's our Caesar," Hermantius announced. "He's still the same man that he's always been! Caesar then and Caesar now."

"Caesar?" Zutra questioned intrigued by the reference.

"Not you too?" Patricius bemoaned the continued use of the reference. "Alright, if it must be known, the Emperor Leo named me as Caesar after I married his daughter."

"But that would mean that you were the legitimate heir to inherit the empire."

"And that's why if you all don't stop mentioning it, Anastasius will have our heads sitting on top of poles before dusk. Do you really think he wants a rival to his authority? So let's this be the last we talk of this! Agreed?"

"Yes, Caesar," Zutra saluted playfully. A salute quickly followed by all the others with a mix of admiration and adoration.

"I pray we live out to see tomorrow," Patricius shook his head.

Taking the opportunity to introduce everyone in his party to his cousin, Patricius then outlined his planned itinerary. Having received no formal invitation from the Emperor, his appearance at the court was going to be as an uninvited guest and he was still not quite certain as to how he would be received considering what Gamaliel had told him just prior to his death. Knowing that blood among Samatians meant everything, he was secure in the knowledge that he had the loyalty of the Alanine legion, which would be more than enough to guarantee his security within the palace. Brotherhood amongst the Alans superseded even a sworn oath to the Emperor. He hoped knowledge of how deep those roots went amongst his people would have a leveling effect once they arrived at the palace and Anastasius would recognize that Patricius was asking for an audience with a good deal of leverage to actually insist upon being granted one.

As the squadron of soldiers moved through the corda of the city, the general populace cleared a broad path for them, awed by the spectacle of the cohesive formation that moved with fluid precision; a trademark of the Alan fighting men. Meanwhile the city was buzzing in anticipation of what this unannounced appearance of the foreign princes from the East might actually mean. Most times it meant there was a war raging somewhere on the other side of the world and these dignitaries had escaped in order to beg the Emperor for his protection. However, the talk in the streets was more curious regarding the escorting small platoon of what appeared to be soldiers of Asian stock wearing uniforms made from obsolete Roman armor from the old Western Empire. What any of this could possibly mean had everyone guessing. 'Bizarre' was the word that sailed throughout the city heralding their arrival and spurring on the wave of curiosity that surged ahead towards the palace.

Mounting the palace steps, the procession flowed gracefully towards the yawning portico thirty feet above ground level. The Emperor's palace guard hastily assembled to serve as a barrier to their entering into the columned archway.

Patricius and his cousin ordered their men to halt and the two of them stepped forward to address the sergeant at arms.

"Let the chamberlain know that Julius Flavius Patricius, son of Aspar has come to seek an audience with the Emperor, if he is so willing. I will wait here until he replies to my request and proceed no further." The message was clearly designed to express that he represented no threat.

Stepping from behind the several rows of palace guards, the chamberlain had already arrived and positioned himself at the forefront. He was a lean man with a sallow face that maintained an air of dignity but also suggested he was not one to be trifled with. "Patricius, son of Aspar? I am not familiar with that name."

"That is most likely because it has not been bandied about for at least two decades," Patricius informed him. "You were probably not more than a mere child when I was last in Constantinople. However, I promise you that the Emperor Anastasius will know it quite well. I have it on good notice that the name has come up recently here at your court. Mention it to him and you will see."

"How do I know that you do not wish the harm the Emperor?" the chamberlain eyed the oddly dressed Roman force suspiciously.

"You have my word that is not our intent. Not to mentioned I am surrounded by the Emperor's own Alanine guard."

"You mean your Alanine guard, don't you," the chamberlain corrected him.

"Oh, so you have heard of my reputation after all. As you know me, Anastasius will also know my word is my bond. You need not fear that we bear any ill will in our hearts. The Emperor's army is loyal to the Emperor. Now go tell him!"

"I will see if the Emperor Anastasius is not indisposed," he replied haughtily, then turned and disappeared once again behind the rank and file of palace guards.

"I will see if the Emperor is not indisposed," Hermantius mimicked the chamberlain in the same arrogant tone. "Where in hell else is he going to be? What kind of bullshit is this?"

"The kind of bullshit that has permitted you to rise no higher than a tribune of your own forces all these years, cousin. That happens to be the same commissioned rank I left you with over two decades ago! When are you ever going to start appreciating that you have to play the game if you want to get ahead?"

"Cousin, the day I start kissing their boney asses around here will be the day I surrender my sword," Hermantius proclaimed proudly, to the chagrin of Patricius but the acclaim of his own men.

"All these years and nothing changes," the Commander sighed. "But I still love you cousin."

"Of course you love me," Hermantius grinned, "Because you know and appreciate that I will always be the man I wish to be. I am at least true to myself!"

"I know what you're inferring but I told you on the day I left; the survival of the Empire was more important than the ambitions of any man," Patricius's voice concealed a cautionary tone purposely meant for Hermantius.

"So instead, you sent yourself into exile. Your men would have stood beside you to the very last one! You know we would have done so! All you had to do was give us the word!"

"I knew so and I feared that fact alone could have destroyed the foundations of everything I had sworn to preserve and protect. Those days are gone, Hermantius. Let them be. The world has unfolded as it was meant to unfold."

"Bah! I still say there is one good fight left in this old body of mine."

"And so there might be. Why not wait until you hear what I have to say to Anastasius and perhaps that fight will be sooner than you think."

That comment intrigued Hermantius. He had no idea what his cousin might be planning.

Still standing at the portico entrance almost an hour after their arrival on the palace steps, Patricius and the men under his command stood at attention without complaint whereas the two Eastern princes were becoming obviously disgruntled as they shifted from one leg to the other.

"Care to explain what is happening," Zutra inquired.

"Yes, what's happening?" Jamasp parroted the question.

"We are being taught a lesson," Patricius advised his companions. "Protocol says that we arrived without appointment, therefore we must wait until summoned. More importantly, the Emperor is testing our true intent. If we had intended to assassinate him, we would have broken through his guard by now, rushed the throne room, and slain him. "

"Unless we wanted him to think we meant no harm, luring him into a false sense of security by standing here all this time, only to march into his throne room where he'd have absolutely no protection to speak of."

"Are all your people so devious of mind," Patricius asked. "There is an issue of honor. What you suggested has no honor."

"There is honor and then there is reality," Zutra annotated. "Personally, I am glad that you Byzantines still believe there is a code of honour. It is more than we've experienced under the Sassanids." Zutra turned quickly to apologize to Jamasp, "No offense intended dear prince."

"None taken," Jamasp gracefully dismissed the disparaging comment.

More time passed and still no sign of the chamberlain. Not until another hour had come and gone did the wisp of a man return with the Emperor's response. "The Emperor bids you welcome, Patricius, who claims to be the son of Aspar. If you are who you claim to be, then it has been quite some time since you departed Constantinople. He will need to be convinced first that you are whom you say. Follow me!"

Walking along side of the commander, Zutra remained to his right and Jamasp on his left. To Zutra's right marched Valentius while Hermantius was on the Prince's left. Jamasp's bodyguard had been relegated to a row behind where the rest of their force had assembled into a block of close-knit bodies. The high vaulted ceilings of the palace echoed their footsteps as they proceeded through the maze of corridors towards the throne room. Its marbled walls and fluted columns were a pristine white with silver veins, unmarked through time, exactly as Patricius had remembered them, while overhead, the frescoed ceilings and plaster cornices were breathtaking in appearance.

The throne room sentries pulled back the heavy doors, allowing the delegation to pass through into the inner hall. At the far end of the room sat Anastasius and his consort, Ariadne, adorned in their matching heavy brocade gowns and gold trimmed robes, the ornate crowns of eastern monarchs resting high upon their heads. Around them shuffled an army of scribes and petty officials, happily busying themselves with the affairs of state so that there was a constant ripple of movement throughout the room.

"Step forward and let me see you," Anastasius commanded in a voice crusty with age.

The five of them stepped forward, separating themselves from the main body of their men that remained a safe distance behind.

"Which one of you lays claim to being Patricius, son of Aspar?"

"I am he," the Commander voiced proudly. "I do not claim to be him Excellency, because I am him."

"Patricius is dead. He died in the revolt of the palace eunuchs along with his father and brother," the Emperor insisted.

"Only because Leo said that I had died. No one would have ever seen the body and I am no ghost!"

"You wish for me to believe this fantastic tale that you survived." Anastasius refused to accept his existence without proof.

"The proof was the fact that Leo had my marriage to his daughter annulled. If I had been killed, then she would have been a widow and an annulment would have been unnecessary."

"That only proves that they could not find the body. To ensure no sin was committed, he had the marriage annulled so that Leontia could remarry without committing adultery."

"How can I make you believe what your eyes refuse to accept?" The tone in Patricius voice indicated that he was becoming frustrated by the Emperor's intransigence. "My own cousin recognizes me after these many years. Would not his word be sufficient?"

"Harrumph," Anastasius exhaled loudly. "The tribune is not known for his dazzling intellect. He could be easily duped. I cannot accept his word."

"I bear the ring of my family, the seal awarded to us by Emperor Leo."

"How do I know it is not a forgery," Anastasius dismissed the evidence. "Provide me with some proof that cannot be fabricated."

Patricius was at a loss. He could not think of any way that he could persuade Anastasius of his true identity. When he was last in Constantinople, Anastasius was nothing more than a petty state official and their paths never crossed. There was no common knowledge that he could relate that would convince the Emperor of his identity. Disheartened, he turned to the Empress, who remained silent all this time, but carefully monitoring the exchange.

"Dinah what should I do to convince the Emperor of my identity?"

Her hand immediately cupped her mouth as she stared at him in a moment of stunned silence. "Oh my God," she finally blurted, her face suddenly flushed with excitement. "It is you, Paddy! No one has called me that in almost thirty years. Oh my God, you have returned to us! I will vouch for him. This man is Julius Flavius Patricius."

The Emperor turned to face his consort with a look of consternation. "Ariadne, my dear, how can you be certain. The man could be a charlatan. A few choice words have drawn you in to his deception."

"Silence, you old fool," she turned on him with a fury that made him draw back meekly. It was suddenly obvious to Patricius and his companions who was the real power in Byzantium. "Only one man ever called me by that name, and it was his alone to do so. There are some things a woman never forgets. Time has altered his appearance but not the man. This is

Patricius and you will treat him as such!"

"Yes dear," the Emperor practically cringed as he turned to face his uninvited guests once more.

"I bid you welcome, Julius Flavius Patricius. But why have you returned to Constantinople after so many years and sought this audience?"

Kneeling on one knee, Patricius motioned for the other four to do likewise and then bowed his head. "Excellency, we seek your blessing for an endeavor we wish to undertake on your behalf. We request your generosity and your support in our mission. Only you have the power to aid our cause and guarantee us success."

"Let me hear your petition while the day is still young," Anastasius urged him to get to the point.

"I bring before you two great princes of the East that are willing to extend their hands in brotherhood to you in alliance that will extend from the great sea in the west to the one in the east. Before you on my left is Prince Jamasp, brother to Kavad, Great Shah of the Sassanid Empire, and to my right is Prince Zutra, royal monarch of the House of Israel, future son-in-law of the Emperor Hsiang Xiaowen of the Sin Empire."

A gasp of astonishment ricocheted throughout the hall as the retinue of aristocrats and administrators blanched from the shock of the commander's announcement.

Anastasius turned to face his wife, but the stern expression on her face advised him not to cast doubt upon Patricius' statements.

"Granted that if these gentlemen are whom you say they are, I must admit it is unusual that two such rulers of such great and grave import would be appearing before me with no retinue whatsoever to speak of. This has me confused and I can only ask what great travesty has occurred that they have lost all of their men that accompanied them on their journey?"

"A valid point, Excellency, but neither of them has come with the blessing of the Great Shah Kavad. He has no knowledge that his brother is here."

There was another disturbance throughout the room as a rumble of whispers circulated wildly.

"Silence!" Anastasius shouted to his advisors. "I need you to explain this enigma to me, Patricius. Are you saying that you have come on a clandestine mission?"

"That is exactly what I am stating, Excellency. This mission is with the approval and knowledge of Kavad's inner circle of nobles but as yet the Great Shah is unaware that we have come to you to seek an alliance on behalf of the people."

"On behalf of the people? What a quaint turn of a phrase," Anastasius chortled. "In other words, you seek to overthrow the Emperor! Is that not so?"

"The Prince Jamasp is equally entitled to rule and the nobles have approved of his ascension."

Looking the Sassanid Prince up and down, Anastasius made a quick assessment as to Jamasp's ability to rule. "You think he is a match for his brother, do you? How long do you anticipate he will hold on to the throne?"

"Once again, a valid and wise question, Excellency" Patricius affirmed the Emperor's initial assessment of the Prince. "That is why we are here for your blessing, Excellency. The nobles can deliver most of the people under their rule. And Prince Zutra can provide the support and recognition of the people that he rules over which number in the hundreds of thousands. That support alone would most likely win over most of the satrap principalities within the Empire to our cause but as long as the existing Emperor is free to attempt to wrestle the power back then we will never be able to live in peace and harmony with Byzantium as it should be."

"So you're proposing a peace pact between our two kingdoms should your Prince here become Emperor."

"An eternal peace that will bring great reward to Byzantium and to all her people."

"Tell me more of this reward!" Everyone's attention within the hall had been captured by Patricius' latest offering.

Patricius waved Mar Zutra to step forward so that Anastasius would focus his attention on the youthful monarch. "The Scion of David has much to offer in exchange for the recognition of his hereditary right to rule over his people as a distinct and separate Kingdom. In gratitude for his being granted this privilege, he will direct one half of the Temple Tax, also known as the Jew Tax to be deposited in the treasuries of Constantinople rather than all of it in Ctesiphon. Each year this amounts to several hundred talents of silver. A sizable income to the state coffers here."

"That was already in the process of being arranged," Anastasius interrupted, "Before there was a tragic accident with our Jewish dynastic representative in Tiberias."

"How unfortunate," Patricius quickly commented, "But how fortunate that the true representative of the Jewish monarchy and the only descendant that can legally make that claim is willing to see that such a wealthy tribute still becomes part of Byzantium's legacy."

"A strange coincidence," Anastasius intimated awaiting some sign of the Commander's prior knowledge of the event.

"Silence! Be grateful that your blundering in the east can be restituted through this opportunity," the Empress berated her consort, taking him totally off guard by the ferocity of her sudden attack.

"I was only trying to point out…"

"Enough of what you think or don't think," Ariadne fumed. "You have emissaries entreating you for an alliance, offering you tribute and gifts and you want to carry on about some nonsense regarding some worthless Jew that you held in your employ that got himself killed. Do not embarrass us any further with such drivel in front of these distinguished guests!" Her tongue cut deeply and the Emperor hunched his already curved shoulders so that he slunk even lower in his throne. "Now without trying to be rude," Ariadne continued, "ask our guests what they require in exchange for their fealty to your authority and recognition."

"Yes dear," the Emperor whimpered as he turned back to Patricius. "The Empire of Byzantium would be greatly appreciative of your offer of peace and the sizable tribute you will make available. Do you have anything else you would like to contribute to this Pax Monda?"

"Rather than let me bargain on behalf of two great Empires, why not let those that have the authority to actually commit, do so? Excellency, if you don't mind, may I present Prince Jamasp to speak on behalf of the Sassanids and Prince Zutra on behalf of his Kingdom of Mahoza."

Stepping forward Prince Jamasp donned an air of regal authority that quickly masked the queasiness that rumbled throughout his intestines as if he was still sailing on the seas. "It does me great honor to greet my regal brother, the Emperor of Byzantium. Your reputation for fairness and integrity is well known even within the borders of my land." Jamasp provided a polite bowing of his head signifying reverence for the Byzantine ruler. "Too long we have struggled over the lands that separate our two kingdoms. Too many of our soldiers have died for no other purpose than to shift a boundary line only a few feet to the west, only to shift it back a few feet to the east in a subsequent skirmish. Nothing has been gained; nothing has been proven other than both of our domains can squander lives and money foolishly without any benefits."

There were sounds of approval and agreement to what Jamasp had to say rising from the Emperor's council and entourage. Scribes hurriedly recorded every word the Sassanid Prince eschewed expecting this to be a most monumental occasion worthy of recording for posterity.

"I say that the time for such foolish squandering has come to an end. My brother has fallen victim to an evil Magus that has distorted his thoughts and compromised his ability to rule. All of us within the government have seen the change that has overtaken him. He is presently drafting laws that will make all wealth communal and all possessions communal so that all men will be the equal of the other."

"What matter of nonsense is this?" Anastasius roared. "Kavad has obviously gone mad!"

"We truly believe so," Prince Jamasp replied. "So much so that he has even offered his queen to lie with the Magus so that he can show to the people how committed he is to these new laws."

"Such behavior is a sin; an affront to God, Almighty. Your brother intends to bring Sodom and Gomorrah back on earth. Such evil cannot be permitted to return to our world. The Lord will not permit such a thing to happen. We will not permit such a thing!"

"And so, we also believe that our God, Ahura Mazda will not permit such a thing. Since he is one and the same with the Father of your Holy Trinity, he has advised us to seek out his other holy champion to ensure that justice prevails. He has sent us to you, my royal brother, to aid in our battle to keep evil from ruling this world we share."

"And the Lord was right in asking you to seek our aid in your time of need, my brother. What will He have you ask of me?"

"Nothing without compensation," Jamasp was quick to offer. "In

161

exchange for your support we agree to cede those lands over which we have fought for ages to your rule. Your eastern border will be expanded to safeguard your cities and the line of demarcation will run through the eastern borders of the Syrian province much as it did in the past."

An ovation of applause and joyous exclamation ricocheted amongst the royal attendants."

"A most generous offering, my brother but still you have not stated what you wish for me to do in return for such generosity."

"All we ask is that you have your forces already amassed on your eastern borders throughout Anatolia march into the no-man's land in preparation for an invasion. This will draw my brother's forces to counter attack and the rest we will take care of within the Empire."

"A simple enough request, but how will you stop this from escalating into a full-scale war?"

"My brother will be removed from his throne shortly after your invasion. Without his presence and will to commandeer the forces, they will soon withdraw from battle at which time we will institute the truce."

"Commendable," Anastasius nodded in agreement. "I think this can be arranged. You have my pledge. I will have my scribes and officials write up the necessary paperwork."

Jamasp bowed in gratitude and acknowledgement of their agreement. Both Zutra and Patricius were in admiration of how well the Prince had handled his part of the negotiation. He had actually sounded like a credible ruler, speaking with both authority and dignity. There was obviously more substance to the Prince beneath the mask that he presented to the world at large.

"Excellency, if I may take the opportunity to add to the agreement so that Byzantium may be rewarded for any losses of its valiant soldiers as they carry out this plan," Zutra stepped forward to take his place in front of the dais.

"You have already offered me your financial contributions to which I am greatly pleased. What other offerings are you considering?"

"As Lord Patricius has mentioned, my father-in-law to be is the Great Emperor Hsiang. My marriage will ensure that the trade routes to Sin are open to the west. With the ensuing peace of our two empires, access to these trade routes will be extended to Byzantium as well. There will be no restriction of trade between the three Empires that will come together along this east-west trade route. The Silk Road will flow once more like it did long ago. We will all share in this unified commercial agreement."

Anastasius clapped his hands with delight while the rest of the royal entourage applauded lavishly. The negotiations, though superficially made to appear mutually beneficial, could not conceal the fact that Byzantium was clearly the winner. The Emperor could hardly refuse.

"Your proposals have been most generous," Ariadne rose from her throne, standing at the edge of the dais. "Now I would suggest that these agreements all be notarized and the actual details of what monies and support to be exchanged and at which times be recorded to everyone's acceptance. There is a tremendous number of fine details that have to be discussed in private and for that, I don't think you require my presence. Perhaps it's best that those with the authority to speak for their governments and their people be the ones to do so. I will leave you to your matters of state. May I request Lord Patricius that you join me in my gardens at this time. There is much we need to discuss concerning your lost twenty-five years. I see no further need for your presence as they write up these arrangements. Would you not agree?"

Ariadne didn't even wait for her husband's approval as she descended the stairs to stand in front of the Commander. She extended her left hand, which he kissed lightly then held gingerly as she led him out of the great hall towards the interior of the palace. Anastasius's face contorted into a reticent pout but there was little he could say that would stop his consort from doing as she pleased.

Chapter Fifteen

Constantinople: 497 A.D.

Moving through the palace corridors, Ariadne escorted by her guards, strolled towards the centre of the palace where the scent of the jasmine blossoms grew progressively stronger, never taking her eyes off her long-lost commander as if she would lose him again if she did so.

"Just like old times," Patricius reminisced as he inhaled the perfumed aroma. "All this time and I can still remember it."

"As can I," the Empress inhaled, as she signaled to the guards to remain at the entrance to the gardens and not accompany any further. Holding Patricius's hand tightly in her own, she led him through the maze of shrubbery that enveloped the gardens. The Commander followed, a most willing captive.

Ariadne took a quick glance over her shoulder to make certain that her guards were well out of sight and hearing and then with a wicked smile upon her lips her right hand snaked out and slapped Patricius sharply across his left cheek.

"What was that for?" his voice rose an octave as he rubbed at the ensuing welt clearly outlining where her four fingers had struck.

"That's for never even attempting to contact me all the years you've been away!"

"Excuse me if I didn't think it was in my best interest. After all, you were responsible for having my family murdered."

"And who's fault was that?" she challenged. "It never would have happened if you had acted like a man and stood up to my father!"

"It didn't mean my father and brothers had to die just because you married someone else."

"Of course it did," she reached out and caressed his reddened cheek. "You know it as well as I do. The day you let me marry Zeno was the day you signed their death certificates."

"How are you able to twist their deaths into being my fault?" he protested.

"You knew Zeno as well as anyone. After becoming his wife do you think he left me with any options?"

"I never should have let you marry him," Patricius shook his head remorsefully.

"No, you shouldn't have. You could have appealed to my father."

"It wouldn't have been enough!"

"But you would have had the support of the Empress Verina. My mother despised Zeno."

"Perhaps your memory is failing you, but Verina never had the control over your father that you seem to exert over this current Emperor. What was that puppet show I just witnessed all about?"

Ariadne ignored his comment, instead focusing on his past sins. "And then later you went and married my sister. What were you trying to prove? Were you trying to hurt me?"

"You were already married to Zeno! Your father arranged that marriage; just as he arranged everything else in our lives. It was his way of playing with us as if we were chess pieces on a board. He played Zeno against my family and us against him; keeping us constantly at the other's throat."

"Only because you both let it happen," she fumed. "He knew that Isaurians and Alans both hated each other and used that hate as a means of controlling everything else you did. You all foolishly played into his hands. My father was notorious for his little games, but you allowed him to play with our lives!"

"An Isaurian never should have been permitted to sit on the throne!"

"Listen to you! Even now, you can't let go of your ridiculous ancient tribal hatreds. Haven't you learned anything? You let your foolish hatreds destroy our future!"

"I don't recall you trying to persuade your husband to abandon his squabble with my family. In fact, I recall you assisting him."

"I despised him; his touch, his scent, it all made me sick. Even thinking of it now makes my skin crawl. But you left me with no other choice. When you married Leontia and my father declared you as Caesar, how long do you think as Zeno's wife I would have survived once you took the throne?"

"I would never have hurt you," Patricius insisted.

"Do you really think my sister would have let me survive? Do you believe she would have forgiven me for possessing your heart? You still know nothing about women Paddy after all these years. How could she have ever been secure in her position as Caesar's wife as long as I lived? She would have killed me..."

"As certainly as you killed her," Patricius completed the sentence.

"She was sent into exile with her husband. No one knows what happened to them," Ariadne defended herself.

"Dinah, everyone knows what disappeared in exile means. You don't have to lie to me. I know it to be true. You know it to be true."

"And you miss her?" the Empress questioned.

"If you mean did I love her, yes, but not in the same way I felt for you. Never could I feel about anyone the way I cared for you. But in case you've forgotten, I grew up with both of you. We were all friends since childhood. How could I not love her?"

"Easy," the Empress answered, "She was never in love with you. She cared for you but that was all. So, do you miss her? I have to know."

Patricius took a moment to look down at his feet as he searched for an answer. "I don't know. I don't really think about it."

Ariadne looked relieved. "How can't you know if you miss your wife, especially if she may be dead?"

"I already told you. I was always fond of Nita. You always knew that. She reminded me of you and if I couldn't have you, then I took pleasure in your sister."

"But you didn't answer my question," she insisted. "Do you miss her? Do you still love her?"

"I loved you. I always loved you. I know now that Nita was just a means by which I could have some of that love fulfilled. In some ways she provided me with a little bit of you!"

Ariadne looked skyward as if seeking relief from a higher power. "Why not be honest with yourself?" she erupted angrily. "You married my sister because you felt in doing so you could hurt me! That's the real reason. You wanted to punish me for leaving you!"

"You didn't leave, you got married," Patricius argued. "And you already had a child with Zeno."

At the mention of her son, the Empress burst into tears. Breaking with any protocols of State, the Commander wrapped his arms around her as she nestled into his shoulder. It would have been a crime warranting execution, but the guards were far away and there was no one else in sight.

"He was so young," Ariadne cried. "My poor boy. He was so beautiful. My beautiful, darling boy. Why did he have to die?"

Patricius knew the question was rhetorical but he felt compelled to answer. "He never should have been made Emperor. Making a seven-year-old boy Emperor was just inviting trouble."

"Ten months! Ten months he sat on the throne before he was killed. And all along I knew that his father was plotting against him. And I did nothing, my poor little baby, my little Leo," the tears splashed across her lips.

"What could you do?" Patricius attempted to console her. "Zeno and your father were cut from the same cloth. If they wanted something to happen, I guarantee they would make it occur and nothing or no one could stop them. What did it matter that it meant killing his own flesh and blood as long as he could seize the throne."

"I was his mother!" she wailed. "I was supposed to protect him! He was my responsibility!"

"He knew that," Patricius reassured her. "Your son would have known that you were fighting for him. The same way that I know he knew that the fight continued well after his death as he watched from heaven."

The tears subsided as she looked up into his grey eyes. "You know about that?"

"How could I not? The stories of what occurs in the Byzantine court are some of the favorite stories recited amongst the Sin nobility. They even use them as bedtime stories to get their children to behave. I especially love the tale of how you and your mother finally got your revenge. Though I know the tale is too absurd and ridiculous to believe but nonetheless, it still made for great dinner conversation. They say that you finally found a way to drug Zeno despite his having his food tasted and everyone searched before they entered his chambers. According to the rumors you spiked his perfume with venom from the black desert snake. Went right through his skin and he fell into a coma. Everyone one thought he was dead, so you had him buried only to have him wake up in his tomb days later. And I love this best from the stories; they say that every passerby could hear his screams but everyone hated him so much that no one would answer his cries for help." He looked upon her face for a hint of a smile at hearing his retelling of the story, but her visage remained expressionless. At that moment Patricius shuddered, realizing that it may have been far more than an exaggerated tale.

"Why are you staring at me like that?"

"Like what?" Patricius attempted to avoid the question.

"You know, like you've seen a monster!"

"I see a woman that loved her son very much and was never going to let his killer go unpunished. That's all I see."

"He was my son, Paddy. My only child."

"I know," he patted her back softly. "But I'm here now and that can all be put behind us."

Her reaction to those words was unexpected, as she pushed away from his embrace and looked at him startled. "Paddy, I'm forty-eight years old!"

"So, I'm in my fifties. What does it matter?"

She reached out and stroked his bruised cheek once more. "It is sweet of you Paddy, but I'm not a young girl any longer. I don't need the things that young women crave. Those days are gone."

"Those days are never gone," he rebuked her comments. "I love you, Dinah. For twenty-five years that love has burned continuously within my heart. What does it matter if we are older? You can't tell me that bag of bones sitting on the throne can fulfill your needs."

"Dear, dear Paddy," she caressed his face tenderly. "That bag of bones as you have so kindly described my husband doesn't have to fulfill my needs. Those are long gone. They died early into my marriage with Zeno. Yes, I let Zeno make love to me, so that I could feel the life within my womb but once my little Leo was given life that was the last time I let his father

168

touch me. So, why would I need Anastasius for physical comfort if I had abandoned any such desires long ago?"

"Because we all need it, whether we deny it or not and he's certainly not going to give it to you. What is he, eighty, perhaps ninety?"

"Don't be so harsh," she reprimanded him, he's only sixty-six. Furthermore, he's very good at organizing matters. That's why I selected him to become Emperor and my consort."

"Well, he could have fooled me. His brains obviously have addled since you selected him, the way you have to tell him everything," Patricius grinned conspicuously knowing the Empress well enough that she would appreciate his intimation.

"Now you are being cruel," she attempted to sound insulted but the smile on her lips betrayed her. Folding her arms beneath her bosom, she adopted the lecturing posture that Patricius had remembered from long ago. "You know full well that I control the affairs of state, so don't pretend that you don't. If you've heard stories about my marriages, then you certainly have heard other stories regarding the political arrangements in the Empire."

"Dinah," the commander explained. "When I was a young man in my twenties, I already knew then how head strong you could be. I wanted to fight battles, explore the world, live the adventure, but that was never going to happen if you and I were to become engaged. Your sole focus even back then was affairs of State. God, I loved you, but you could be so pig-headed some times."

"Well at least I wasn't so dense, all the time," she countered. "I practically had to leave a trail of breadcrumbs for you to follow to find your way to my chambers and even then you failed to show up most nights."

"Ah, but when I did find it then you certainly knew what the pleasures between a man and woman were. As I recall, you had specific cravings back then," he reminisced with a sigh.

"So, what happened to us Paddy," she returned his sigh in unison.

"Like I told you, Dinah, you scared me. You're a powerful woman now; you were one back then too. I didn't want to give up my freedom, at least not so young. However, it never meant that I didn't love you. Not even for a second."

"You are such a fool Paddy! I was yours for the taking and because you wanted to play soldier you let another man have me. I hated you so much at the time for allowing it to happen."

"Is that why you let me live, Dinah. So that I would know how much I hurt you by taking away everyone else that I loved?"

"Don't be a fool," she scolded. "I already told you that it was the hatred between you Alans and the Isaurians that caused the death of your family. I did everything in my power to protect you."

"Love, hate, they're both the same thing. One is always in balance with the other. Call it love but seeing that I remained alive could equally be the result of how much pain I had caused you."

"What are you talking about? Have you become a philosopher now? A couple of decades in the orient and you think you can fathom the depths of a woman's mind? That will never happen. It is beyond any man's capacity. I loved you Paddy, that was all there was to it! So, what are you really trying to say?"

Patricius struggled to find the words, practically stuttering as he mulled over each one as he grasped them from the recesses of his memory. "I think what I'm trying to say is that I'm sorry. I'm sorry for being blind to the life we would have shared had my father approached yours first to make the marriage arrangements. I'm sorry for the coldness that filled your heart when I left. I'm sorry for the loss of your son, who could have been ours. Who should have been ours! I'm sorry that at forty-eight years of age you have never had the pleasure and fulfillment of being with someone you loved. And whatever you may have done or not done to assuage that pain that I have caused you, I only pray that one day you can forgive me."

"Oh Paddy, you can still be such a fool." She leaned forward to embrace him, kissing him softly as she nestled into his body. "There is nothing to forgive," she whispered. "Don't you see this is the life I have chosen for myself? There are no regrets. Who I am and what I am has been of my own choosing."

Wrapping his arms about her, he embraced Ariadne lovingly.

"Don't get any ideas," she warned him. "We are only two old friends sharing a moment together. Nothing is going to happen!"

"That's where you're wrong Dinah. Already so much has happened. I've dreamt about this day for so long that it's like an answer to a prayer.

Even if all it means is that I hold you just this once in my arms, a great weight has been lifted from my soul. My heart feels lighter than air."

"This only serves to make things so much more difficult," she confessed. "I had wished that you would come back to me and now that you have, it will only make things extremely complicated."

"Only if you chose to make them that way."

"There are no other ways, Paddy. Old man or not, Anastasius is my husband and the Emperor of Byzantium. He's not about to let you strut into his world, bed his wife and usurp his throne. Don't underestimate him."

"I never wanted the throne," Patricius made it perfectly clear. "That life would have been too confining for an old adventurer like me. I prefer to work behind the scenes."

"Like I said," she reiterated, "This is the life I chose for myself and I'm not about to give it up. Everything says we just weren't meant to be yet my heart keeps insisting that we are."

"Listen to your heart," he strongly advised.

"Then I would certainly be responsible for your death. Even if you weren't a threat to the throne, any relationship with me would be perceived as being one and the same."

"Your mother managed," Patricius reminded her.

"Verina managed a lot of things behind my father's back," Ariadne admitted. "But don't take my father for a cuckold. He was probably more aware of the situation than we thought. My father would have found a way to turn it to his advantage."

"I don't want to lose you again," Patricius held her close against his chest refusing to let her go.

"We are too old and too tired to think like young lovers anymore," she laughed. "And we both have far more to do before we depart this world, so let's not speak of our eventual parting but instead of the world that we can shape together."

"Still the same Dinah after all these years," Patricius mused. "Will you ever stop trying to rule the world?"

"Why should I?" she snapped back, "It is my destiny. I accepted it long ago unlike someone else."

"But I do accept it now," he confirmed her accusation.

"And it's about time. You sit on the apex of three worlds that have come together. You have three rulers practically eating out of your hands. They all listen to you, which in turn makes you more powerful than each of them by themselves," she speculated.

"Not four?" he asked somewhat brazenly.

"Don't be greedy," she wagged her finger in front of his face. "I will acknowledge you as my equal but never as my master. Do what you must to unite your authority over the Sassanids, the Jews and the Sin. Once you have done so you may take your place as Byzantium's friend and chief ally but never as its superior."

"Wouldn't you fear that my successfully uniting of the three kingdoms would mean that the Byzantines must beg to be part of the coalition?"

"Does the bird fear the sky, or the fish fear the water," she riddled. "I know you too well, Paddy. For you to take on this role, it will force you to be a fish out of water. Yet I will always be at home in whatever domain I choose. That is not arrogance but fact!"

"God, you make it hard to love you," he laughed.

"But you do," she insisted, "And you always will."

"I'm afraid that is my failing and my downfall. You have always known me too well, Dinah."

"Alas my love, I never got the opportunity to know you as well as I should and the paths we have set upon will see to it that I never will. That is one achievement I will always resent and despise my sister for throughout eternity. She has had what I never could."

"You asked me if I still love her, Dinah. The reason she despised and turned on me was because she knew you always had my heart."

"Then perhaps my sister and I were even in our retributions against one another. As for the present, the most I can grant you is the occasional embrace in our lives of solitude." The corners of her mouth turned down in an expression of sadness and anger. "Enough of that, now tell me about these men you have come with. I have so many questions. And where did some of your soldiers get that wonderful armor from. I don't think anyone has seen the likes of it in centuries…"

Chapter Sixteen

Constantinople: 497 A.D.

For days, they hammered away the hours, formulating the strategy necessary to set their plan in motion. The majority of the meetings were between Anastasius's military advisors and Patricius, but occasionally both Zutra and Jamasp would offer some important tidbit of information overlooked during the conversations concerning the terrain or placements of the Sassanid outposts. The plan was simple; draw Kavad's forces to the northwest and engage them in battle far from any major population centers. At the same time, the nobles in Ctesiphon would swear allegiance to Jamasp and begin an insurrection that would cut off the supply lies to the distant Sassanid forces. In a matter of months a surrender would be effected by Jamasp as supreme commander of the forces and with notable generosity, Anastasius would force a peace treaty on the Persian Empire that demanded nothing more than an armistice and guaranteed trade relations. There would be no demands for tribute, taxes or slaves; only peace.

The Byzantines would launch a two-pronged attack. From Amida in Mesopotamia, three standard legions would march across the border into Assyria and strike at the city of Nisibis. As soon as it had fallen, they were to march on to Hatra where they would join with ten thousand heavy cataphracts that rode out from Armenia Major eliminating any resistance at Nineui and Arbela. With the ranges to their backs, there was only one direction that the Great Shah's forces could use to counter attack, but in the wide open plains very little would stop the Byzantine mounted cataphracts with their heavy armor and skilled archery. In total, thirty thousand Byzantine men were to be placed in the field, a sizable army but still small compared to the forces that were at Kavad's command.

"Now tell me again, why you think this is going to work," Justin, the

Emperor's most decorated general demanded to know. Patricius drew his attention from the map spread out on the table to stare directly into Justin's cold, calculating green eyes. He knew this was the one he must convince in order to win over the others; young, ambitious, driven by a desire to replace the glories of any of his predecessors, Justin was the key to acceptance of the plan. Furthermore, Patricius knew that he definitely fulfilled the criteria in the category of predecessor now that he had returned, and stories had begun to circulate amongst the armies of his great battles fought in securing the throne for Emperor Hsiang. The war stories were unavoidable as any unit of Romans, dressed in ancient armor circulating through the city was going to be pressed to tell a tale or two of their adventures, especially over a tankard of ale. By the fifth or sixth tankard, the legend had grown in magnitude to the point where there was no greater military leader in the entire world than Julius Flavius Patricius.

"It's simple," Patricius began. "You won't require more than thirty thousand men because you're never going to truly engage in a full campaign. By the time your two armies conjoin, Kavad will already be removed from the throne and Prince Jamasp will be declared as the new Emperor and he will entreat for peace immediately."

"But if we've already crossed the border into Persia, your majesty, why don't we just claim the land at that point and shift the border. It seems reasonable to me," Diogenes appealed to the Emperor as he sat in the chair pulled close at the end of the table.

Anastasius directed the question back to Patricius who had grown weary with this repeated line of questioning.

"None of you seem to fully comprehend the true purpose of this battle. It's a sham, a ruse, nothing more! You're only purpose is to draw the Sassanid army to the northwest away from Ctesiphon. We in turn will draw Kavad and his personal guard to the south where we will subdue him. It's very simple. Let's not complicate this more than it need be."

"Simple for you Alan," Apsikal growled, "But I'm not prepared to let my cataphracts get slaughtered on the expectations that an Alan will keep his promise."

"I would think after four years of fighting the Isaurians side by side, you wouldn't have a problem with us Alans any longer. Especially since from the look of you, I'd say you're a Goth and that would mean that a promise wasn't of any importance to you since you never keep them!"

Apsikal's sword arm quickly reached to his side, grasping the pommel as he spat and cursed. "You insolent dog, I will carve your tongue out!"

Before he could even finish the last word, the point of Patricius' sword was pressed against the fleshy part of his throat. No one had even seen the Commander's arm swing through the motion, it had occurred so swiftly. "Excellency," he referred to Anastasius, "Can you please remind your general that we are all working towards the same goal here. It would be a shame that your reputation as an honorable and judicious man be spoilt by the intolerable actions of a barbarian that I was forced to slay within your palace."

This second insult was more than Apsikal could bear, and his sword slid from the scabbard only to have his motion halted by the point of Patricius' sword pressed even more sharply against his skin so that the first trickle of blood was drawn. "I will do it sir if you force me!" Patricius warned.

"Apsikal!" Anastasius screamed, "If you wish to make a fool of yourself and mess the floors of my palace with your blood, then be prepared to clean it up as well." The little jest drew a laugh from the other generals. More importantly, all were aware that the Emperor had just given Patricius permission to end this matter should Apsikal fail to withdraw his hand. The Goth's sword slid back begrudgingly into the scabbard as his shoulders hunched in resignation.

"Now, if I may have the opportunity to explain," the Commander requested their attention. "Without Kavad, the will of the army to fight will be gone. They will dig in to their fortifications awaiting orders from the capital. We will make certain that the orders are some time in coming. Nothing saps the will of an army more than having to stand at the ready for prolonged periods of time without any engagement ever occurring."

"But the same will happen to our men," Diogenes protested. "We'll have disgruntled soldiers prepared to mutiny on our side as well."

"True," Patricius agreed, "But you will also have men eager to return home, especially if they are rewarded for their endurance. There will be a payment. A onetime payment, so don't get any ideas that if you remain on

Persian soil you'll get paid even more. Your men will be told that it is a ransom, paid by the new Emperor Jamasp to free his people of Nisibis, Nineui and Arabala and the surrounding country."

"It will have to be a hefty ransom to pay thirty thousand men," Diogenes suggested.

"It will be," Jamasp piped in, "But that is a matter to be haggled between emperors. Would you not agree?"

"Most certainly," Anastasius nodded to his Eastern counterpart. "I will ensure that the men are satisfactorily rewarded Diogenes. You need not worry."

"Most gracious of you Excellencies," the general bowed his head in gratitude.

"Not to be disrespectful, but I have a legitimate concern," Justin expressed his skepticism. "This entire plan hinges on separating the Emperor Kavad from his forces, subduing him, and replacing him with his brother. I understand all that. What I don't understand is why you think it will be such a simple matter to capture Kavad in the first place. If he doesn't fall into this trap of yours, he will descend upon our forces with the full strength of his army and with our smaller force on the field, he will annihilate us!"

"A worthy question that deserves an appropriate answer," Patricius acknowledged. "And one which you will find hard to believe at first but which I assure you is beyond dispute. He will come to Ctesiphon to stop a marriage from taking place."

"A marriage?" all the generals repeated incredulously. Some began to guffaw, finding the Commander's response too unbelievable for words.

"Yes! He will try to stop a very important and strategic wedding. And that's when and where we will capture him."

"I don't believe this!" Apsikal growled furiously. "We're to put our men at risk on the presumption that Emperor Kavad will place a greater importance on interrupting a marriage ceremony than the defense of his Empire."

"To him they will be one and the same!" Patricius shouted the Goth down. "If you don't believe me, then let his brother explain it to you. No one knows the mind of Kavad better than Prince Jamasp. He will tell you that it's so."

"Is this true, brother?" Anastasius questioned his fellow monarch.

"Without a doubt, brother," Jamasp answered. "In our kingdom, the marriage between a man and woman of royalty is a political statement above all else. Whom we marry determines both fame and fortune."

"As it is here," Anastasius agreed.

"It can be both a blessing and a curse depending on what can possibly arise from the union. If the bride is from a wealthy enough family and a prestigious lineage, it can sway the balance of power over night."

"That is the true nature of acquired power," The Emperor conceded from his own experience.

Jamasp circled his index finger in the air as he prepared to make a point. "Being ruler in Persia is all about having the right connections more than inheritance. Like a game of draughts, even the lowest can be raised most high. My brother is well aware of how kings are ordained. Therein lies the definite difference between our two kingdoms. Whereas you can only make this choice once and pray that it is the right decision, we have the opportunity to do it repeatedly until we get it right. That is why Kavad's harem is filled with the wives of my dead brothers, uncles and cousins. As soon as any of them were married, if the chosen wife was seen as being a kingmaker, then he made certain that he possessed them."

"But you are alive, brother," Anastasius pointed out.

Smiling effeminately Jamasp provided the reason. "I was not considered a threat."

"Yet you threaten him now."

"But he is not aware of it," the prince made it clear that they still held the element of surprise. "When he hears that Prince Zutra is about to marry the daughter of the Sin Emperor, he will be furious. Such a marriage would claim precedence over all the wives in his harem. He would never allow that to happen. He can't allow it to take place. Do you understand? The potential change to the balance of power in such a marriage gives him no other choice. He will be there."

"Of this you are certain," Anastasius sought one hundred percent confirmation.

"I will personally send him the letter alerting him to the impending marriage. I will even tell him that Prince Zutra is considering a revolt shortly after this intended union. He will be absolutely furious! I know my brother."

"It has its merits," the Emperor informed his generals. "I can see that if carried out correctly it can be a very shrewd tactic. "This plan has my blessing. You are not all that you appear brother."

"So much the better to stay alive, brother."

Having the Emperor's blessing meant that there would be no further discussion. The matter was settled. In fact, it had been settled long before this meeting when Ariadne had ordered her husband to follow Patricius' instructions explicitly, but Anastasius could never permit that to be known by his men.

"But Excellency…" Johannes who had remained silent all this time protested, goaded by a slight tap as Apsikal nudged him in the side to prompt him to say something.

"But Excellency nothing," the Emperor shut down any further discussion of the matter. "I have spoken and so it shall be done."

'Good on you', the Commander thought silently to himself. Dinah has her lap dog well trained. His mind wandered for the moment to contemplate if he too would have been her marionette swinging from the strings attached to her fingertips had the two of them ever managed to come together. Perhaps subconsciously, his fleeing to the Far East was motivated by far more than just the fear for his life.

"Is there anything else, Lord Patricius?" the Emperor inquired shattering Patricius's moment of self-reflection.

"Yes, your Excellency. There's the matter of my legion," he responded.

Drawing his frail frame into his chair, Anastasius squared himself against the backrest, his stature growing proportionately as he did so. He let the matter hang thick in the air as he gave it his contemplation. "It is an unusual request!"

"It is an unusual situation," Patricius remarked.

"And if I don't offer you these men, what is your present situation?"

"The nobles can mount no more than a few thousand men from the city. Prince Zutra commands a contingent of four hundred superb fighters.

And I have no more than what you've seen with Captain Valentius and a small remnant that guards the princess at Mahoza."

"Harrumph!" Apsikal snorted through his nose.

"You wish to make comment General Apsikal," the Emperor took him to task.

"Excellency, there is no way that such a paltry force is going to take on the Emperor's personal escort. Kavad surrounds himself with close to five thousand of his best fighting men. The Prince's men will be slaughtered and we in turn will have to retreat as soon as Kavad turns his attention upon us."

"Consider the legion yours then, Lord Patricius. In General Apsikal's wisdom and foresight he has settled the issue."

"I said no such thing, Excellency," Apsikal protested. "I don't even know which legion we're speaking of."

"The Alanine forces under Hermantius of course," Anastasius enlightened them.

"But that's under my command!" Justin exclaimed.

"Not any longer," the Emperor appeared to be enjoying the consternation he had caused among his officers.

"Good riddance," Apsikal muttered in a growl that was clearly audible.

"What was that?" Justin questioned.

"I was only saying that they will serve Patricius far better than they ever served us. After all, they're the same blood."

"What are you talking about?" Justin raved. "If it wasn't for the Alanine soldiers, we never would have been able to defeat the Isaurians under Longinus. Or have you so quickly forgotten how close we all came to having our heads set up on pikes outside the city walls?"

"Had the Alans done their job properly in the first place, we never would have had the Isaurians to contend with at all,' the Goth glared disdainfully at Patricius for past failures.

"But your majesty, I can't afford to lose one of my legions," Justin continued his protest.

"That's not what you told me last week," the Emperor reminded him. "Last week you said you could only hope that Hermantius and his men would get lost up in the mountains and never return. Or some wording to that effect."

"Only because I was tired of bickering with Hermantius that day; he would rather argue about the most insignificant detail than listen to common sense."

Patricius suppressed the smile that tried to force its way onto his lips; all these years and his cousin had not changed one iota.

"It wasn't the first time you expressed that wish," Anastasius pointed out.

"Yes, but it doesn't mean I don't respect the fighting prowess of that particular legion," Justin attempted to explain. "The Alanine legion is well known for their ferocity. The Empire cannot afford to lose men of that caliber. I cannot agree with this decision!"

"Let them go," Apsikal interrupted his comrade's argument. "They are troublemakers. Their constant bickering only upsets all the other units. You will be better off without them," he insisted.

"Let them come with me," Patricius advised. "Now that I have returned and they know that I am still alive, they will be even more difficult than ever to keep in line. We Alans are tied by far more than blood. Between us there is a bond that we could never explain to those that aren't one of us. General Apsikal will know of what I speak because it exists among the Goths as well."

"He is right, Justin," Apsikal confirmed. "You will never have their full loyalty as long as Patricius is alive." His tone was menacing as the General stated what was evidently a well-established fact. "Their hearts will force them to find some why of joining with him, even if it meant deserting their posts. It is too great a risk to try and keep them here any longer."

"Excellency," Justin pleaded with the Emperor once more. "It's not right to just hand over four thousand men to a man that only days ago was a perfect stranger to all of us. Not only that, they will be fighting on behalf of our enemies. Who's to say we will not face them in battle sometime in the future."

"I am to say so," Patricius' voice boomed across the room. "And let no man dare doubt my word. Whether you acknowledge it or not, the title of pro-Consul awarded to me by Leo has never been rescinded. Therefore, by our own laws, I could order you to agree, but I will not do so and I will not offend your Emperor by doing so since he was not the one that invested me with my title. Thus, I ask you as a commanding officer, will you stand with me against a common enemy? Will you fight for the greater glory of Byzantium and in so doing achieve a new dawn, heralding peace between two great nations? Are you ready to etch your name into history as one of Lord Jesus' soldiers bringing the age of peace to this world? May God bear witness to what we can achieve this very moment, within this hall and in His name!"

"Well, Justin," Anastasius questioned rather smugly. "Are you prepared to do God's work?"

There was no other way to answer the question except in the affirmative. To argue any further would have taken the matter out of the military arena and into one decided upon by the religious courts. Outmaneuvered and feeling isolated, the general lowered his eyes to the floor and consented to the transfer of his troops.

"Good! Now let us talk of the timetable for this venture of ours," the Emperor moved on to the next matter.

"Spring will provide the best opportunity," Zutra finally entered into the conversation. "I say so for several reasons. First being the timing of the weddings. It will fall close to one of my people's fast days dedicated to a victory long ago of my people against a corrupt Persian magistrate. It will also remind everyone in the cities of Ctesiphon and Mahoza of that last time we had one of our own queens sitting on the throne of the Persian Empire. This will create an overwhelming sense of euphoria within the people. There will be few supporters for Kavad that would dare make their presence known on the streets."

"Go on brother," Anastasius encouraged the young prince.

"There is also the strategic advantage of the spring runoff from the rivers. They will be swollen from the melting of the snow upon the mountains. To reach your troops situated in the northwest, Kavad's forces will have to cross these rivers several times. They are treacherous even at the best of times. Should it happen that word does not reach the front in time to let the Sassanid generals know that Kavad has been deposed, you will at least be facing an army that is already exhausted from fighting the elements."

"A realist at last," Apsikal shouted. "This young Prince is at least aware that all things may not go as planned."

"General, all my life I have recognized that whatever you think will happen will likely not happen. Only a fool would leave himself open to the whims of fate. Moreover, as long as I'm aware of what could go wrong and have made allowances to counteract, then at least there is a chance of controlling the outcome to a level of certainty. If you call me a realist, then so be it. I'd like to consider myself practical."

"Anything else you wish to elaborate upon concerning the Spring," the Emperor requested further details.

"Yes, there is one more thing. Kavad will be in transition at the time moving from the winter palace in Ctesiphon to his summer palace in the north. It is a time generally of great commotion when his nobles are also moving back and forth across the countryside in order to be at the side of the Great Shah. Therefore, there will be no suspicion if he sees them moving about the countryside escorted by their armies. Nor will he be surprised by either the sudden presence or absence during that time period."

"Then it is settled. We do this in the spring!" Anastasius proclaimed.

Chapter Seventeen

Mahoza: March 498 A.D.

Seated within the conclave, the members of the Beth Din huddled nervously, awaiting his presence. Few of them had any idea of the extent of events to unfold that particular day, but word had already reached them that the King of Kings was descending upon their city with a substantial number of armed men.

"I am an old man," Mordecai began as he addressed the forum, "And I have seen much with these tired eyes but never have I seen as much cowardice as I've witnessed this day." He rotated his withered frame slowly so that his dark, penetrating stare would borrow deep into each of their pitiful souls. "Why is it that the common folk of this town have no such trepidation as you harbor? Could it be that they are already aware of our impending success that they have no need of fear? I will not permit any of you to ruin this day! You may join the festivities once they are underway. For now, you will remain here until I say otherwise!"

"You can't hold us prisoner against our will," one of the judges declared with false bravado.

"You are right," Mordecai agreed. "I can't, I'm an old man. But they can," he pointed to the dozen armed guards outside the hall. "They will see to it that none of you leave here until I say so." Against their protestations, Mordecai wheeled about and exited the chamber as the doors were shut behind and those trapped within could hear the sound of a bar being slid across to ensure they could not be opened from the inside.

"Is it done?" Patricius asked as soon as Zutra's wily old advisor had returned to the central square of the city where the wedding was soon to take place.

Flashing a fine set of pearly teeth, even at his age, Mordecai laughed merrily, "They will not present a problem."

"They will always present a problem," the Commander was quick to correct him. "It is part of their nature to whine and complain like old women. That much I have come to appreciate about your legislators. On a beautiful day they will say that there must be a rain cloud somewhere in the heavens."

"Be grateful you have not had to deal with them all your life," Mordecai enlightened him.

"Had that been the case, there would have been seventy less judges walking the streets of this city," Patricius assured the Vizier.

"And where would we be then?" the old sage quizzed him. "The only law in the city would be the sword and no one would dare raise their hand to serve on the council. However, you must always remember that these are not bad people; they are merely men that are afraid. Fear has a way of making imbeciles of even the most intelligent of us."

"You are lecturing me, aren't you?" The realization dawned on Patricius that Mordecai was purposely engaging in far more than casual conversation.

Still flashing his disarming smile, Mordecai stepped closer to the Commander as they walked the corridor. "And you are learning," he instructed. "I am not long for this world my dear Patricius. My whole purpose in life was to see our kingdom restored under Mar Zutra and now I'm afraid I will not live long enough to see that day. You must rise to the occasion. You must be the voice of reason and caution for our impetuous king. He is still a youth, and has much to learn. You who were a Caesar will understand!"

"So, you've heard."

"The lad could not stop talking about it as soon as you returned. To stand in the presence of Caesar meant more to him I believe than any power the King of Kings might have. To be Caesar is to measure your worth against all of the great men that bore that title preceding you."

"It is only a title," Patricius downplayed the honor.

"Maybe so," Mordecai agreed, "But to an impressionable young king it is everything. So guide him wisely."

"You are asking much of me. I have not even considered staying on after we place Jamasp on his brother's throne."

Wagging a gnarled finger in the Commander's face, Mordecai corrected him, "Do not try to lie to a man that has observed the mechanizations of men for all his long life. You have always seen yourself as the power behind two thrones since you've come to this land bearing the princess. You're an opportunist and to be a good vizier one must be so. You must have the vision and scope to move the Empire in the proper direction. Kings will never have the ability to see beyond their borders. That is why I have selected you."

Patricius was astounded by Mordecai's frankness. "Selected me?"

"From the day you entered the Great Hall to herald the Princess Ti-Ping. I knew at that moment that you were the one to carry on in my absence."

"And what made you so certain that I would even consider undertaking the role?"

"Honor," the old man simply replied. "You are bound by honor. Duty and honor are the principles you live by. They consume your every fiber. Your commitment to the Princess and her father was always evident. The way that you and my charge have gravitated towards each was more than I could have even hoped for. Even Prince Jamasp admires you, which is enlightening since he has lived in the shadow of his brother for so long. I had prayed for one to come in my stead and my prayers have been answered."

"Why would your God send one such as me? I don't even pray to your God."

"But you do," Mordecai explained. "There is one supreme God in the entire universe. Whether you call him 'The Father', or 'Ahura Mazda', he is one and the same and to us he is simply God. Remember that and all the mysteries of the universe will be explained to you. Only when men start making division and refusing to accept the obvious do they become blind to the reality."

Bowing graciously, Patricius felt effused with a sudden sense of purpose. "I am glad that you have chosen me," he said in gratitude. "But you must not leave this mortal world soon, as there is still so much that I must learn."

"I will not leave until my duties are done," Mordecai grinned. "And someone has to remind you to let the judges out of their sealed chambers as you may have a tendency to forget," the Vizier laughed.

"As much as I may be tempted not to, they will be released."

"And all is in readiness?"

"Hermantius is prepared. Not a single guest will know of what has transpired until it is all over."

"See, already you have the makings of a worthy vizier," Mordecai complimented him, "We work behind the scenes and no one ever knows."

It was the fourteenth day of the month of Adar and the populace of Mahoza and practically all of the aristocracy of Ctesiphon began to gather in the city's forum with the break of dawn. By the time the cock crowed, already several thousand were waiting excitedly as they shivered in the cool spring breeze. Everyone residing in the city was exhilarated with the news of the impending wedding. Announcements were nailed on every signpost within the two cities and messengers had delivered the good news far beyond the borders.

'His Eminence, the Pashah Gurzam hereby invites all
citizens of the Empire to attend the wedding of Prince
Mar Zutra, scion of the House of David, Keeper of the faith,
Monarch of the Jews, to her most Magnificent and royal
majesty, Princess Ti-Ping, daughter to the Emperor
Hsiang Xiaowen of the Sin Empire.
Let all men of good conscience and warm heart take
part in this most joyous of occasions.
In addition, it is the pleasure of the Vizier to the Exilarch
of Mahoza, to invite all men and woman of the
community of Jews to attend the traditional joining
of the houses of David and Aaron, when his
Excellency, Mar Zutra, Prince of Israel, takes as

*his second wife, the Lady Avital bat Hanina according to
the laws and customs as laid down by Moses the law-
giver.
This day shall be declared a holiday of the realm and
every person shall be granted one modius of grain and
one sac of salt from the royal warehouses in celebration.
All praise the all merciful Ahura Mazda and call down
His blessing upon these two couplings. So Mote it Be!'*

It was not by accident but cleverly intended that the public invitation was written in such a way to allude to the newfound power acquired by the Exilarch through the union of these marriages. By having the Pashah release the announcement, credence was provided to the fact that these unions constituted a state event far beyond the typical marriage of any other satrap. Ensuring that the Great Shah Kavad received news of the wedding was left to Jamasp, to do his part. More importantly, Patricius wanted the people talking about the proposed marriages as a normal daily discourse and hence the addition of the grain and salt ration. Where the invitation was purposely designed to anger the King of Kings, the gossip among the citizenry of Zutra's generosity was designed to enrage him beyond the point of rational thinking.

As noon approached, there was barely enough room in the city square for anyone to move about freely. The air had become languid, so humid that it was palpable. As the sun rose towards its zenith, the trumpets blared, heralding the commencement of the ceremony. The crowd roared their approval as the wedding procession wound its way through the one path that had been cleared by the honor guard, leading from Mar Zutra's estate to the town centre. With nervous enthusiasm the invited guests and townspeople anxiously awaited in order to catch a glimpse of the mysterious and beauteous Asian princess that they had heard so much about but few had seen. For most of the common citizenry, they had never seen anyone from the Far East and the rumor of her porcelain like skin and almond eyes was enough to draw them to the event. In the pettiness of their everyday lives, there would be a telling of this historic and monumental event to their grandchildren and to their grandchildren's grandchildren.

Summoning forth the Pashah and his elite guard, the magister called for silence from the spectators. Miraculously, though thousands had assembled in the civic square, barely a sound escaped from the crowd as the Magister spoke his first words.

"In the name of the Great Shah of the Sassanids, King of Persia, Royal Highness of the Tartarus and Armenian Kingdoms and ruler of the Mesopotamian Empire, I bid all those gathered here, peace and good will."

A great roar went up from the throng upon hearing the obligatory royal blessing for any occasion. No one within the crowd didn't catch the auspicious absence of the Great Shah's personal name, which had been purposely obliterated from the speech.

"May the All-Knowing Lord, Ahura Mazda extend His graciousness to all his children and may you find peace, prosperity and happiness beneath his gaze."

Once more, the people cheered enthusiastically. A chorus of hallelujahs and God is great rang out towards the heavens, as the Magister whipped the people into a frenzy of anticipation.

"Let the wedding begin!" the Pashah shouted his single line at which point the musicians lining the streets began their well-orchestrated performances, strumming their lyres and blowing on their flutes. Cymbals and tambourines reverberated with metallic clangs while drummers beat to the dancers spreading their petals along the path towards the central platform.

From the periphery of the square, the chiffon and taffeta veiled litter moved steadily along the road, carried proudly upon the shoulders of ten massive servants provided personally by the Pashah, each one bare-chested and wearing billowing striped pants belted with big golden sashes. As it made its way steadily to the front of the platform, as if by magic, the groom and his attendants appeared to rise from beneath the stage, seemingly materializing from the ether. Those in attendance clapped and cheered in utter astonishment, marveling at the trickery designed to amaze, entertain and confound the senses. Then, as the sun arced to its highest point in the sky, its rays caught the gold and silver threads woven around the myriad of precious jewels sewn into the groom's robes, rendering Mar Zutra into a blazing star. A star that burned so bright that those close to the platform had to momentarily shield their eyes until the sun had traversed away from its zenith. Those in the square that could still recall the ancient legends realized that the king was wearing the fabled suit of lights that had been handed down through the family of the Kahana as long as history had been recorded. One tale claimed that it was carried by Zutra's ancestor, Josef ha Cayef, from Jerusalem at the time the city fell to the Titus. Another legend told how it was designed and worn by Solomon when he was visited by the Queen of Sheba. Whatever its true origins, no man had ever seen its like before and probably never would again in their lifetime.

The honor guard outfitted in matching blue and silver turbans, their arms crossed with broad scimitars, lined the steps from the ground to the top level of the platform. Meanwhile the dancers and musicians moved through the crowds of people, encouraging them to join in the frivolity. It did not take long until the thousands in attendance were laughing and skipping to the beat of the music. This was a wedding for the people, by the people, with the people, unlike any other they had attended and surely one that they would be remembering long after.

Halting at the base of the steps, the bearers lowered the litter onto its four protruding legs carved in the shape of massive lion paws. Commander Patricius descended to the base of the platform, reaching the litter and drawing back the veils as he extended his hand to the bride waiting nervously within. A delicate, gold-painted hand reached out to grab his fingertips lightly, and as if in slow motion, the Princess Ti-Ping stepped from her carriage.

At that precise moment the world stopped. The music ceased, the dancers froze, and a collective gasp of enchantment exhaled from the lips of all who viewed the indescribable beauty of the royal bride. The interwoven fabric of white silk and thin silver threads flowed and shimmered like living water when she moved. Every step painted a picture of exquisite grace. Slowly, the Commander, adorned in his full-dress regalia, led the princess up the polished steps until she stood alongside her betrothed. Every eye in the crowd transfixed on the comely beauty of her eastern exoticness. Zutra could barely sustain the beating of his heart as he watched her float upwards to his side like an apparition from heaven.

The King's eyes were alit with excitement as soon as soon as her veil lifted and he gazed upon her incomparable features. Her skin was radiant with a brilliant glow, overpowering his senses with a vision of paradise. If ever there was a more beautiful woman in the world, no one in the square could ever recall seeing one. In but a single moment she had captured their hearts with every breath she took, their lives hers to command. Equally mesmerizing was Mar Zutra in his suit of lights, blazing like the desert sun matched only in brilliance by the Princess Ti-Ping, shimmering like the ever-flowing Tigris River. Together they united the universal elements of fire and water, binding them to a singular place on earth; Mahoza.

The entire ceremony became a blur to anyone's recollection, a dream barely bound to reality. The words of the Magister followed by the exchange of vows and the symbolic binding of their wrists flowed seamlessly into a fairy-tale of enchantment. One event melded into the next, so much so that none could exactly recall when the chief rabbi of the community had replaced the Magister and the second wedding to the Lady Avital began. Though beauteous by anyone's standards, no one was given the opportunity to draw any comparisons between the two brides, as Avital's face remained veiled throughout the ceremony, as she stood dressed in the traditional wedding gown of her ancestors. Her hands and feet hennaed as was custom, but this Princess of the Jews had been reduced to an afterthought; an aperitif to the main meal as some were overheard to comment.

To the sheer delight and fascination of the citizenry, Emperor Hsiang had sent some of his most skilled pyro-technicians to Mahoza, the very best at creating a spectacular array of scintillating fireworks. The bursts of coloured lights, with their thunderous volleys carried on well into the night. The people drank, they sang, but most of all they adored and admired the royal couple that graced their city. The twin cities of Mahoza and Ctesiphon would surely be the most eminent of cities in the world they all foreswore with each passing mug of ale. Oblivious to the outside world, the citizenry of both cities went to bed that night without a care in the world, totally unaware of the danger that had narrowly passed them by while they celebrated.

The heavily armed infantry appeared bewildered and confused by the distant sounds of drums and horns playing. Having marched several hundred miles, they were now advancing upon the outskirts of the capital city and it was beyond their comprehension that they would be making their final approach totally ignored by the t populace under threat. Not a single member of the cities' leadership bothered to emerge from the gates to greet them as was both obligatory and customary for the returning King of Kings. Notwithstanding, none of his officers or advisors dared to mention a word to the Great Shah regarding this obvious affront, fearing for their own lives should he vented his anger. One look at the foul mood clearly imprinted upon his stony features said it all. The unmistakable sneer beneath his beetling brow, the spittle gathering at the corners of his mouth, and they all knew that their king needed no reminder of his humiliation.

"It appears that we shall take them completely by surprise, my Great King," the ever cautious general attempted to break his master's gloomy silence by highlighting the situation's advantage.

"I want them all dead, Ibrahim. Burn Mahoza with its populace to the ground and teach them what it means to affront and insult their King. Stake the citizens of Ctesiphon on crosses from the bridge all the way along the Euphrates until you reach the gulf. Too many times they have ignored me and now they shall all pay once and for all for their folly."

"Is that wise, Majesty? Your brother did write that it was only the nobles along with Pashah Gurzam and the Jews that were involved. Why punish everyone else?"

Twisting in his saddle, twin fangs protruded as he curled his lips back into a feral sneer, "Are you challenging my word, Ibrahim?"

"No, no. Never, Great King!" the general sniveled.

"Then do as I have commanded." No further discussion would be brooked.

"As you wish, my King."

"But this bridegroom," Kavad quickly added. "I want him taken alive. I want him tortured as he watches me make love to his intended new bride. Only when he can't bear it any longer, I want him hung from a pole exactly like we did to his father."

"It will be so," Ibrahim confirmed his master's wishes. "What shall be done with the princess afterwards, Great King?"

The wicked grin on the King's face said it all. "If she pleases me, then I will most likely let her live but not until I've taught her father a lesson in proper conduct. He will have to pay me a handsome ransom to ensure that his precious daughter isn't sent back to him in a box, cut into tiny little pieces. Once that is completed, then I will insist he name me as favored son-in-law and heir," the growl in his voice was enough to convince the general that there was still a good chance that the princess would not survive the week. Stroking his beard Kavad contemplated how he could make them suffer further. "They will all pay for this slight they have offered me. No one makes a fool of me! Make certain your men understand my orders Ibrahim. There are to be no survivors! Rape the women, torture the children, it matters not as long as none survive!"

"As you have commanded, oh Great King," the general bowed at the waist only to have his parting platitudes interrupted by the shouts from his officers that they sighted men stationed on the road between their legion and the city.

"Who are they and how many," the general shouted to his officers.

"We think they are the Exilarch's Four Hundred," returned the reply.

"What are they doing?" he asked his lieutenant.

"That is the strange part, general; they are doing absolutely nothing. They are just standing there."

'Just standing there and nothing else?" he responded in disbelief.

Trembling, the junior officer didn't know what else to say in the presence of his commanding officer and the penetrating stare of the Great Shah. "Yes...that's all sir."

"And you're certain of this," General Ibrahim questioned further.

"There is no doubt sir, they are just standing there."

Perplexed, Ibrahim grew silent as he tried to fathom the significance of his enemy's tactics.

"General!" the Great Shah shattered his deliberations, "Is it that difficult for you to give the order to attack? Have you all become dumb as well as blind? You outnumber them twelve to one, they're standing in the open, and you are far more heavily armed. Which part of this equation don't you understand?"

"Excellency, I just need to wait on our reconnaissance of the surrounding area. My scouts should be back within the hour. If the Exilarch's men are just standing there, then there is no harm in waiting a little longer before making our move."

Kavad's eyes grew terrifyingly wild as his brow knitted into an angry furrow. The spittle flew from his mouth as he began shouting at his general. "Are you now deaf as well?" he screamed. "Do you not hear the music that is coming from the city? That is the sound of my Princess marrying an underling against my wishes. We must stop it before they exchange any vows; otherwise, my leverage over Emperor Hsiang is negated if he views me as the murderer of his son-in-law. I can only force him into accepting me as his daughter's husband if she is not already married. Are you too stupid to understand any of this?"

"No, Majesty?"

"No what, you sorry excuse for a camel's ass. No, you're not too stupid, or no, you don't understand any of this?"

"I understand the situation, Great King. But in my duty as your commanding officer, by our own rules of martial conduct, it is imperative that I ensure that before engaging the enemy, we are not entering into a trap."

"Fool! This is not an engagement of war! He only has four hundred men standing guard. Already they tremble with fear and are afraid to even move a muscle. Do you really think any of the nobles would be foolish enough to send any of their paltry forces to aid them once they've heard that I am here with a legion of hardened fighters? Use your senses General and do what I pay you for! Battles are won by instinct, not by costly delays!"

"Lieutenant," General Ibrahim shouted out to his officer, "Sound the attack. Quick march, weapons drawn at two hundred paces."

"As you command, sir," the officer saluted and relayed the orders to the non-commissioned officers.

The quick march became more of a jog, as they hung the small round shields on their sides running in tight formation directly at Zutra's guard who never flinched as they stared at the cloud of dust kicked up by the Sassanids.

Once Ibrahim's men drew their weapons, the Sassanids began to charge at full trot towards the enemy that still remained frozen like marble statues.

As soon as the distance between the two opposing forces was halved to just one hundred paces, the rain came. Not as droplets of water, but a black, deadly cloud of missiles that pelted down upon the Great Shah's legion creating a formidable barrier preventing them from reaching the Four Hundred. At first, the legion was too stunned to comprehend the devastating impact the arrows were having. Only when those still left standing looked right and then left to see their comrades who moments before were running with them shoulder to shoulder now writhing in agony, did they grasp the deadly seriousness of their situation.

"Cataphracts!" Ibrahim's men shouted in a panic as they desperately tried to dodge the continuous hail of missiles. The most feared word in modern warfare. Man and horse fused into a single entity, with the freedom to shoot an endless volley of arrows without ever breaking stride. The combined speed of animal and drawn bow meant that the range was almost doubled, enabling an attack on the enemy from a distance where the cataphract soldier wasn't even in full view by his intended victims. The heavy armor on both horse and rider was virtually impenetrable, yet articulated so skillfully, that the archer managed a two-hundred-and-seventy-degree arc in which to make his shot.

Within seconds, the cataphract unit was visible on the crest of the hills to both the right and left of Zutra's men and riding at full gallop towards the remaining Sassanid force. A thousand men, singing out with their bows so rapidly that each man had released a half dozen arrows with infallible accuracy before reaching the front lines of the enemy.

"Regroup, regroup," Ibrahim relayed the orders through his officers, trying to stem the panic that rolled like a tidal wave through the remnant of his legion. It was too late, as the horses poured through the scattering force, dispersing them without any opportunity to restore themselves into a cohesive unit.

"What is going on?" Kavad seized the collar of Ibrahim's quilted vest. "Where did these soldiers come from?"

"They're Byzantine," the General recognized the cut of their armor and style of combat.

"How can there be Byzantines here?" Kavad was practically

hysterical.

"Your Majesty, we must get you away from here before they discover your position," the general's primary concern was still the protection of his king.

"You want us to flee?"

"Great King, we have no choice. All is lost here!"

"'It can't be!" Kavad protested. "Do something! Turn the battle. Up close they're archers can't be effective."

"It's not the cataphracts I'm concerned about." the general's words were prophetic as Hermantius unleashed the next wave of his attack. As the riders waded through the Sassanid legion from every direction the remaining three thousand heavily armed Alanine units of infantry moved in for the final kill. The same command that ordered the Alanine soldiers to rush into battle was also the long-awaited signal for the Four Hundred. As if awakening from a l trance, the personal guard of Mar Zutra flung themselves upon the enemy with unbridled ferocity. Like tigers, they pounced upon the Sassanids, their bodies as much a weapon as the long, curved swords they carried. Even the Alans had to take a moment to stand back and admire the fighting tactics of the Four Hundred as they danced through the enemy lines, constantly in motion as they dodged and ducked the swing of a sword or arc of a shield with feline-like prowess. Many a story had been told of the whirling dervishes, but none would ever come close to describing the fighting style when witnessed up close.

To Ibrahim it was all too familiar. He had seen the Four Hundred when they were mercenaries under his command on the northern border against the White Huns. They were the only soldiers on the front that the Huns admittedly feared. Had he had a full legion of them under his command, he knew the war against the Huns would have been over ages ago. This time they were not shouting their usual war cry of Elohim! The word they shouted repeatedly was 'Zutra' and the louder their cry the greater it empowered them. Over and over, they repeated that single name, rolling it off their tongues until is spread fear through the hearts of their remaining enemies. Ibrahim felt his resolve melting rapidly as he observed the soldiers of the Four Hundred reenact their dance of death against his men. As an experienced commander he knew that retreat was his only option but to give the order contrary to his King would certainly bring about his own sentencing to death even if they should survive. His prayers to Ahura Mazda went unheeded as his men fell like trees logged in a forest, tumbling down one after the other. Surely, the fates had been cruel this day leaving him no other choice but to place the welfare of his men over that of his own life. Turning his back on the Great Shah, he raced towards his remaining units sounding the retreat.

Chapter Eighteen

Ctesiphon: Spring 498 A.D.

Patricius roared hilariously at the wild imagery that played within his mind as Hermantius recounted the final events of the battle. Proof that his cousin was not exaggerating was laying there before him. Bound and humbled, kneeling on the grey tiled floor of the council hall was the once great and mighty King of Kings.

"Tell me again Hermantius the part where you practically ran him down with your horse as he tried to flee on foot."

"You should have seen him, cousin. We cut off his route and realizing that the only means of escape was to race into the hills, he takes off like a scared rabbit. Only, I don't think he's ever had to run before in his life because my little sister could have walked faster. It was like watching a fish flopping about on land."

"But the stick, tell me about the stick again," Patricius could hardly hold back the tears of laughter.

"I'm getting too old to go chasing up hills after rabbits," Hermantius retold the story for the third or fourth time. "So, I see this stick lying on the ground and I picked it up. I was trying to hit him in the back of the head with it but I guess my arm isn't what it used to be. Instead, it strikes Kavad in the back of the knees and next thing I know he's rolling down the hill until he stops right at my feet. You had to see it. End over end he's tumbling and then there he is, right beside me. I didn't have to move an inch to subdue him."

"Clearly a sign that we had God's blessing this day," the Commander sounded pontifical in his assessment.

"Either that or an extremely lucky toss on my part," Hermantius downplayed any religious hand in what had transpired wanting full credit for himself.

"Luck only takes you so far, cousin," Patricius philosophized as his attention was drawn towards the Pashah taking centre stage and placing a foot across the back of the Great Shah's neck as he invoked the attention of the assembly of noblemen.

"Men of Ctesiphon," Gurzam's voice rolled across the council hall strongly and with a stentorian pitch. "What say you now about your once great and glorious leader? The godling that would have you sacrifice your wealth and possessions so that he could distribute them among the citizenry who would glorify his name at your expense. This monster that would snatch your wives and daughters from your homes so that he could feed his evil passions by tossing them to the masses to feast upon their succulent flesh and indulge in all manners of depravity. Look now! This is no godling! This is no king! This is a cringing coward that came here to slaughter us all and now begs us for mercy. What clemency would befit such a man? I say we show him none!"

The council of nobles was evenly split down the centre. For every man in agreement with the Pashah, at least one other feared taking the life of the Great Shah and the repercussions that might unleash. No matter how hard the Pashah tried to persuade them that they had no fear of reprisal, the killing of a Great Shah in the past had been associated with so many terrifying curses, that over the centuries, irrational fears of the evil jinn superseded intelligent thought. The governor's battle against their superstitious beliefs became further complicated when the newly acclaimed Emperor Jamasp requested that he take the centre floor and address the nobles.

Dressed in the resplendent embroidered floral robes of the King of Kings, Jamasp wore the high domed crown with its layered filigree tiara and cascade of little golden bells that wound their way down from the crest to the lattice inlaid brim. From the precise moment he donned the apparel of the mightiest man in the Eastern Empire Jamasp had grown proportionately in stature. Once he had been no one of consequence, either ignored or merely tolerated, but now the most prominent of dignitaries from across the empire bowed, their foreheads touching the ground as he walked by. Even

Patricius recognized that it was necessary to embrace an entirely different attitude around Jamasp, for he was no longer the awkward prince reliant on the paltry few nobles that would befriend him. Absolute power was the only intimacy he required as it could render even the feeble, dangerous. When he spoke, everyone listened.

As he moved before his audience, the little golden bells on his crown chimed sweetly, playing a melodious tune designed to silence any other voices. "In the name of the almighty Ahura Mazda, who's wisdom is that of the universe, who's majesty rises above all of creation, and who's mercy is limitless, I ask how you can violate His will by extending none of that mercy to one of His chosen?"

"I sense this is not going to go well," Patricius whispered to his cousin in the mezzanine of the great hall where they sat privately, watching the proceedings.

"Then he is truly a coward," Hermantius criticized the newly crowned Great Shah safely from any prying ears.

"I will not let you shed the blood of my brother!" Jamasp railed against the assembly. "No man, whether a lowborn or even a nobleman is fit to do so. Only by the hands of another Emperor could such a dishonorable deed be performed, and I refuse to do so! My brother shall not be harmed. Instead, he will be imprisoned at the Castle of Oblivion in the east, where he will be kept under constant guard to live out the days of his remaining life in peace. Such is the mercy of Ahura Mazda; such is the will of your Great Shah!"

"Not good, not good at all," Patricius shook his head knowing that Jamasp was making a terrible mistake.

"There is nothing you can do about it cousin. After all, he is the new monarch, but I wager it won't be for long with his brother kept alive. Why would the fool do such a thing?"

"It's a relatively safe decision on his part," Patricius analyzed the situation. "If his brother stays in prison, he wins and should their roles reverse, his brother can show him no less mercy than was extended to him."

"I say kill him and be done with him, that would have been in the little bird's best interest."

"Perhaps ours, but not in this bird's situation, I think. Establish the precedent of doing away with Emperors at the behest of the nobles and you might find yourself next on their list. Jamasp would only have been kept around as long as he remained useful. He just might be far more clever than I gave him credit for."

"I still think he's stupid."

"You would. Not all diplomacy ends with a dead body at the point of your sword."

"It does with me!"

"I know. Have you ever wondered why Anastasius was more than pleased to send you on this mission? It managed to get you and the rest of your men out of his hair because of how much he regarded your diplomatic abilities."

"I was diplomatic," Hermantius defended his past record. "Once you returned, the rightful Caesar belonged on the throne! But did you see me try to make that happen? I thought I was being very diplomatic."

"And he knew exactly what you were thinking; so now you're here, with me, and we're both getting a lesson on how to survive from this fledgling Emperor. There is an irony there."

"I don't get it," Hermantius shook his head apologetically.

"Don't worry about it. With any luck we'll not have to rely on the lesson."

"Just on our sword arms," the Alanine captain responded.

"As always cousin. Just like old times."

At his villa in Mahoza, Mordecai leaned back on the sedan chair, shifting the weight from his legs to his lower back trying to relieve the pain in his joints. "Never get old," he advised, "That is my lesson to you today." He had set aside the day in order to convey his teachings to his protégé.

"What are you going on about," Patricius murmured. "You're not old."

"Do not try to fool an old fool," the vizier waved a crooked finger in front of his face. "This body is telling me that it is old and that its time has come. I am not left long for this world. Days, perhaps even weeks, but no longer. But I have one last task to complete before I go. I must ensure that a king is not without his advisor."

"Look to your own people. I have given it a lot of consideration and decided that I have no intention to live my remaining days here. I am an outsider. I will always be an outsider. I don't even understand your ways."

"You say one thing but I read otherwise in your eyes. You will stay."

"Even if I did, I have no means to establish my authority here," Patricius protested.

"Ah, but you do," Mordecai corrected him. "If I'm not mistaken, you see yourself as the actual power in this region of the world bending the will of kings to your particular views."

Patricius belched out a hearty laugh. "I can see there's no deceiving you. You read minds like your cousin. It is true. I've had such thoughts but under present circumstances, I cannot see how it would be possible. I do see that it would be in everyone's best interest if I could bend them to my will, but how to do so may beyond my grasp, especially if Kavad remains alive."

"No. I just sense there's very little difference between the two of us. That I have always known from the first moment I laid eyes upon you. What you wish to do is what I have always done; advise kings so that they make decisions which are really mine but nonetheless which they are more than happy to take the credit for. That is what a viceroy does. That is what you do. That is what we do."

"And let's pretend that you are correct in your assumption; why would I choose to stay here in a civilization that is so foreign to me that I could never belong?"

Narrowing his lids so that his eyes danced mischievously behind dark lashes, Mordecai flashed an all-knowing smile to his counterpart. "I had wondered that too and then it came to me. You can't go back to your world. Not because of laws or enemies, no, those have all faded into the past. In fact, anyone that could even remember what charges had been laid against you is likely deceased by now. You can't go back because you won't let yourself do so. There is someone there that you torture yourself about and by not returning, you feel that you can numb the pain. Am I right so far?"

"You seem to be the one with all the answers, so why don't you tell me."

"Of course I am right. Your reputation as a great general would have made it difficult for the Emperor Hsiang to let you go, even if it was to escort his favorite daughter. Your value to him on the battlefield right now far outweighs your need as a chaperone. Therefore, I have to guess that you insisted on taking this mission and the Emperor acquiesced. You needed to get back to this part of the world with the hope of at least attempting to restore some part of your past that haunts you."

Reading the lines on Patricius's face, he could tell that the Commander was not refuting his intuition. "Ah, once again I see that I am correct," Mordecai winked. "That which keeps you away from Byzantium also draws you near like a moth to the flame. However, you know that if you get too close to the flame you will be burnt to a cinder. So, Ctesiphon allows you to be close enough and that is how I know you will stay. Here you will make your seat of power and I can see in your eyes you feel there may still be a slim chance to reclaim that, which prevents you from going home. But to do so you must make a name for yourself here!"

Rocking back and forth in his seat, Patricius nodded courteously but would not agree nor disagree with Mordecai's statements. "They say that curiosity killed the cat," he warned.

"I am already dying. So let me be curious. It can't make it any worse."

"Even if you were right, what you're describing will not be as easy as you make it sound. Jamasp is not following according to the plan. In his attempt to ensure his own welfare, he has locked the Empire into stagnation. If he tries to change the governance of the land too much, someone will get it into their mind to release Kavad and I will find myself without any power at all. Moreover, if Jamasp doesn't do enough to appease the nobles, they will begin threatening his rule and again we might find the country in turmoil. Either way I become expendable."

"I would think that you would have already found a solution to your problem."

"What are you implying?"

"If one has an itch, then they scratch it," Mordecai suggested slyly.

"I have given it some thought," Patricius admitted knowing perfectly well, what the vizier was implying.

"And?"

"And Susiana is not an easy place to reach."

"Bah," the old sage easily dismissed his concerns. "Five hundred miles to the southeast and you're there. My ancestors walked for forty years in the desert. Surely a month wouldn't prove too difficult."

"No, but a heavily armed guard would, and you know just as well as I, that if I was to send my men to carry out the deed it would turn into a full-scale battle. It wouldn't work."

Releasing a heavy sigh, Mordecai resigned himself to the argument. "I understand," he agreed with Patricius' assessment. "But it doesn't mean it shouldn't be tried by some other means. That is the purpose for men such as you and I. To find ways where other men would fail."

"The order has to come from Jamasp. It's the only way I can see it being possible. If any other soldiers other than Jamasp's men were to arrive in Susiana, they would be considered a common enemy of the Persians. It would unite them in Kavad's defense and that you can understand would have a disastrous outcome."

"So, are you saying it's hopeless?" Mordecai challenged in a tone that made the Commander feel uneasy.

"Not hopeless," Patricius was already formulating the germ of an idea, "But it will take some time to arrange, and it will have to be done by Persians or at least appear to be done by them if it is to succeed." The Commander poured two cups of water from the large, handled jug on the table in front of him. He passed one of the cups to Mordecai, who had stretched out his hand to receive it.

"Thank you," he said, his voice wavering slightly as he assessed the impact of the Commander's words. "And you can't believe that they will l ever do it, do you?"

"They elevate their kings to the status of a god in this land. At least as Christians we learned long ago that a man, even if a king, is nothing more than a man. They can be killed just as easily as anyone else."

"Which would explain why your world has left a legacy of five hundred years of regicide," Mordecai was quick to remind him.

Patricius ignored the criticism, continuing to explain why he considered Kavad possibly beyond his reach. "You can kill a man, but you can't kill an idea. Superstitions will survive long after our bones turn to dust."

"So, what you need is for one superstition to destroy the other," Mordecai transformed the solution into a riddle.

Cocking his head inquisitively, Patricius's waited for a further response. "I suppose you're not going to explain that remark?"

"It's obvious, isn't it? You have the tools at your disposal if you use them correctly," the old vizier commented but still refused to provide a straightforward answer.

"Enough riddles, explain it to me," an undertone of impatience surfaced in the Commander's voice.

"Have you never questioned what is it that binds the hearts of men to your young charge? Why would the Sin Emperor send his most favored daughter to nothing more than a vassal prince? Why a city exists in the heart of an Empire, where Jews and Scythians pay homage to a liege that is not even the Great King of Kings? Surely you must have contemplated all this and more during the time you have been here?"

The Commander gave pause to the series of questions that spun off the sage's lips. "You're referring to Mar Zutra, aren't you?"

"Good," the vizier congratulated him. "At least you acknowledge that there is something unique about the king."

"Well, it is because he claims to be descended from King David," Patricius added. "Is that not so?".

"Claims?"

"Alright, is," Patricius admitted upon being pressed further.

"So?" Mordecai drew out the word as if it was answer enough.

"So what?"

"Do you really think that these non-believers in our religion, which live side by side with us truly care a rat's ass about some ancient king that they never heard of?"

"The knowledge of the Davidic kings is universal."

"Only if you are a Jew or a Christian," Mordecai corrected him. "There obviously is far more to his inheritance for him to command such respect. So, your thinking thus far has been wrong," he scolded.

"And what thinking is that?" Patricius inquired.

"You speak of magical powers, mind reading acts, other-worldly forces beyond your comprehension. It is none of those things. It never was about any of those things!"

"Then tell me!"

"It is Shekinah; that which binds all men, regardless of their lineage. All things come from the Shekinah and all things return to the Shekinah. That is the fundamental rule of life."

"I am not an alchemist," the Commander's impatience flared again. "I know nothing of the transmutation of matter. And even if I did, I don't see the importance!"

"See, that is the undoing of you Christians. You accept all that you've been told without questioning, without investigating. If you were to do so, it wouldn't weaken your beliefs but instead strengthen them."

"That's all fine but what has any of this to do with Mar Zutra?"

"He draws his power from the urim and thummim. He is both king and priest. Does that not make it any clearer for you?"

"You're saying he's like Jesus then," Patricius sounded doubtful.

"Not like; the same! The same heritage, same family to be exact. They are both descended from Alcimus. You refer to him as Eliakim in one of your Gospels."

"You are not making any sense Mordecai. Jesus was the son of God! He was not a mortal man! Mar Zutra could never be the same."

"Are you sure? That is not what is being said behind the back of Anastasius. The Nestorians say differently about Jesus; not a God but merely a gifted man. Even here in Mahoza, an old Jew like me can know what goes on in the court of the Byzantine Emperor!"

"And they are mistaken!"

"Are they? What if it was the power of the Shekinah that gifted Jesus with his abilities that you all presumed were so miraculous? That he was nothing more than a man graced by God; the same heritage and gifts that are bestowed upon young Mar Zutra. Then you can appreciate why the people are attracted to him and why he is raised above others. It goes beyond being a Jew or a descendant of David! People sense the divine inspiration within him, caring little for what label of religion others apply."

"That all ended with Jesus. He was the last of the Davidic Kings,"

Patricius insisted.

"Does your brain deny what your eyes can see? That is not what you read in the bible. The rod and the scepter shall never fall from between the legs of Israel's two families."

"That all changed with Jesus."

"That is what you have been told but that is not what Jesus said," Mordecai reminded the Commander. "In fact he said that he had not come to change the laws of Moses but to confirm them. Therefore, he confirmed all that was in the bible in so doing."

"You are trying to trick me with your Jewish banalities."

"I am trying to make you see truth. Perhaps it is time for you to ask questions rather than close your mind to all the answers."

"See, that is exactly what we have been warned against. Such arguments only breed confusion!"

"I am not confused. Why should you be? Mar Zutra is not confused. He knows exactly who he is. He knows his lineage for the past eighteen hundred years. He is the son of priests and kings that have intermarried since the dawn of time. He is whom the oracles spoke of, the same as they spoke of Jesus and why the people were drawn to him."

"But not you Jews," Patricius corrected him.

"Oh, some were. He did not get to where he did without a following of thousands. After all, there were only the Jews in Israel to follow him. Whom did you think were present when he was feeding the masses?"

"But then you rejected him," the Commander still vigilantly defended his position.

"Only because the oracles never said that they would rest with only one man. It was a destiny, always to be fulfilled by a family, never an individual. Not just once but many times through the course of history. Had Jesus' followers not tried to make him the sole inheritor of the prophecies, in all likelihood you would be a Jew today, not a Christian!"

"It that was true, then you're his relative, so that makes you one of these supposed king-priests," Patricius challenged. "But you have none of this so-called divine gifts. You have not drawn people to you in the thousands. What you say is not correct!"

"The answer is simple; I was not meant to rule. The lines have always been clearly demarcated within the family; those to rule and those to serve. Jesus in his time was well aware of it too. Some say it was his brother Jacob that was meant to fulfill the destiny and bear the gift, but that Jesus took that away from him, just like the original Jacob took Esau's inheritance. Try to understand now why his followers drifted away when he tried to assert his ownership over the prophecies. He tried to take that which could not belong to one man."

"What has any of this to do with the problem we have with Kavad remaining alive."

"There is no more to say," Mordecai smiled. "The seeds of knowledge have been planted. The rest will grow in your mind steadily until you can see answer to that question on your own."

"You said nothing!"

"I have said it all! You need not focus on it any longer. Any power you attain will grow from your allegiance to Mar Zutra. Through him, you will achieve what you seek. The throne of the Persians is not the power that will make you the Vizier over an Empire. It is the throne in Mahoza that will do so, whether you believe it now or not. Look for your answers there!"

Chapter Nineteen

The Mahoza Palace; 498 A.D.

Princess Ti-Ping sat alone in her chambers, having dismissed her servants earlier needing the time to be alone. Loneliness had become a melancholy harvested painfully within her heart as she struggled to adjust to the world of her newlywed husband. Though married for several weeks by this time, he had only visited her matrimonial bed just once, that being the night of their wedding, performing the perfunctory duty of ending her virginity but his actions had proven mechanical, passionless and he withdrew before the seeds could be planted. Their marriage was hardly consummated, and now Zutra was barely doing more than fondling her from time to time when they were together. His heart and soul were distant and no matter how often she tried to convince him to come to their bed, they remained far beyond her reach. That one night they had been together was becoming nothing more than a bitter memory and she could not fathom the reason. All her senses told her that he desired her but his actions spoke differently.

This was not as she had been led to expect. At first, she thought perhaps it was her fault; that she had done something wrong despite following the instructions of the ancient ways. She had been tutored very well in the art of conjugal love making by her nurses. Tui-na was a mastered art that she considered herself quite adept at, yet when she performed the tantric massage on Zutra it appeared to have little impression upon him. Her expectations that she would feel the life force of his ching swell within her never materialized and it filled her instead with trepidation that she had been sentenced to an empty existence with a man incapable of making love.

Her insecurities overwhelmed the better of her and she committed the cardinal sin for any Chinese bride; on this night, she decided she would confront her husband with her fears, leaving her bedchamber and crossing the short distance to where she knew he would be resting. Such an effrontery in her homeland warranted a severe scourging as a woman was never to question her mate's manhood, but she believed Zutra would feel neither insulted nor belittled. Her intuition was correct as he welcomed her cordially, even inviting her to sit beside him on his divan, while he reviewed documents and letters from the day's judgments. Immediately, she sensed the all-consuming sadness that was devouring him from within, leaving him quiet, remote and sullen. It gave her the courage to ask the question of whether or not she had displeased him.

Leaning back on the divan, Zutra let his hand fall to her shoulder and then he softly brushed her silken black hair from her face. His lips parted into a faint smile as he studied her exquisite features. The almond-colored skin, the natural pout of her lips, the delicate nose that sloped gently between crystalline eyes that sparkled even when she was sad. Oh, how he wanted to make love to her like a raging bull, a tempest unleashed against the baleful earth that screeched and trembled as it flooded through the forests and gullies washing aside all that existed before it. His mind and body ached as he imagined surrendering to her completely, falling between her finely toned thighs and forgetting all about custom and laws, and the lines of succession that were arresting his manhood.

The faintest brushing of his fingertips across her pale skin communicated a lifetime of conflicting demons that he battled constantly. She empathized with his internal struggle, sensing that his heart was heavily burdened; nevertheless, there was little she could do to ease his personal torment. She raised her hand to his cheek, stroking it tenderly with the tips of her fingers. Responding to her touch, he emptied his inner most secret to her, exposing the fear that resided within his mind, as he had done to no other person, not even Mordecai. He talked of other lives, of past existences, interwoven into his own fiber, his body nothing more than a vessel for everyone that had come before. He then waited for her response, expecting, fear or ridicule, but much to his astonishment, she barely batted an eyelash, nodding as if she had heard it all before. In truth she had, his revelations not any different from the beliefs in her own land of the Yinjian. Her lips let the word drop from them in a hushed whisper, fearing to wake any of the ancestral spirits as she did so.

"You understand?" Zutra was both shocked and surprised. No one had ever understood the curse of the Kahana. One could only speak of it to another family member if seeking any hope of compassion.

"It is the Yinjian," she repeated, still careful not to say the word too loudly. "The spirits of the dead, they reside in a parallel world to ours. Theirs is a world not dissimilar from ours but only with the help of the living can they survive. We must interact with them constantly for their sake as well as our own. They communicate to us through our thoughts and our dreams, and if we are not careful, we fall prey to the samsara, living their existence as if it was our own, and this can happen generation after generation until all the lives become blurred without distinction."

Placing her delicate little hand within his own, Zutra turned them over and then back, admiring their lovely, refined quality. "Then you understand why I have not come to your bed chambers?"

"No!" she responded firmly. "I only know that you somehow feel bound to your ancestors, but this is your life, not theirs," she reminded him, her mouth drawn into a pout.

"Do not doubt that I love you. I loved you from the moment I laid eyes upon you in the great hall. I have never beheld such beauty in my life and I am bound to you forever." His eyes roved up and down the length of her torso. "You fill me with desire, but they will not let me have you until I fulfill my duty to them."

"Only because you imagine that they possess your soul. That is what they do. They trick you into doing their bidding."

"My love, this is no trick of specters from the past. I am the past. I am the present. Just as much as I will also be the future to my descendants. That is what being the Kahana is. Not what will be but what was. I am bound to do their bidding so that my people can survive."

"You have confused me, my husband."

"In order for my people to exist there must always be a Kahana. It is part of the natural order of the universe, a continual flow through the streams of time. It was promised a long time ago by God that there would be a son to each generation and in return we would pledge that child to serving the Lord."

"So lay with me my husband and let me bear you a son to pledge to your God. See how I open my womb to your seed." Ti-Ping spread her legs so that he could clearly visualize her welcoming embrace. "Let me bring you the pleasures you seek."

Zutra turned his head away, avoiding the enticing web of enchantment she spun throughout his senses. "You cannot be the one to bear me that son," a single tear streamed from his eyes. "I know that this must hurt you but you cannot be the one to bear my firstborn son!"

"Why?" was all she could manage to say, her own voice choking as she reeled from his rejection.

"It is written as such. Damn the fates that have cursed me so," Zutra struck the frame of the bed with a clenched fist so hard that it shook in spite of its massive weight. "Damn the rabbis that have made me the most pitiful of all men."

"Please, please, tell me what is happening," the princess pleaded, totally confused by her husband's consternation. "Written? I don't understand! How can our night together already be written down?"

"Once the Kahana were powerful and a law unto ourselves like every other monarch in this world. We would have many wives to fill our harems. Daughters of kings came from all the realms, and we made love to them freely, and they bore us children that grew to be kings, sitting on many thrones in many far off lands. However, these wives came with their own beliefs and their own gods and soon there were kings that sat on the throne of my own people that did not know our God and did not know our ways. The rabbis say that is the reason my people have suffered so much throughout history. In order to protect the people from errant rulers, the rabbis passed laws making it impossible for a King over Israel to be anything but Jewish. All throughout our history succession has been from father to son, but then they changed the law. Only from a Jewish mother can a Jewish child be born they decreed and only a Jewish child of the Exilarch can be King of the Jews. A child from any other relationship they have deemed to be a mumzur amongst my own people."

"Mumzur?" she repeated.

"A bastard!" he explained, ashamed to even say the word to her.

Affronted, Ti-Ping cupped her hand over her mouth. "Our child will be the product of two great nations. How can that child be considered a bastard?" Horrified by the situation, she found herself trapped and the princess wept openly. "Who would dare call our child a bastard?"

Zutra reached out to comfort her, but she brushed his advances away.

"Our child will be a great king but just not here," he said tearfully.

"You are saying that your second wife must bear your firstborn son. Then go! Go to her and let her fulfill your needs!" she screamed in anger. "Is your religion so blind that I am not even considered a woman by your laws? Do you also see me as some creature less than human as your rabbis have claimed?" She ranted.

"Never! Never would I believe such a thing," Zutra pleaded with her. "To me you are the light of my life; my most beautiful and loving wife. The rabbis are fools and consumed by their own prejudices. But these laws now exist and they are what binds my hands and keeps me from demonstrating how much I truly love you."

"Then change the laws!" she insisted. "You are the king. You are the maker of laws."

"I wish and pray that it was that easy, but I cannot change what has been transcribed into the religious beliefs of my people. If you were to bear me my firstborn son he would be rejected by the people, and any son born second, even to a Jewish wife would be considered unacceptable. Therefore, Avital must provide that son. Afterwards, all the children you bear to me will not threaten the throne in Mahoza." His last words a weak attempt to appease her frustration and mounting anger.

"Then go and do what you must!" she plunged her face into the pillow and cried.

"She does not want me, and right now all I want is you."

Rolling onto her back Ti-Ping's anger flashed from her dark eyes. "Here I am!" she yelled as she slapped the inside of her thighs, parting the lips of her labia as she did so. "If you truly want me then enter me now! Be a king and not some puppet of these foolish rabbis!"

"I cannot!" he cried despondently. "I must have a son to sit on my throne and I would not bear to hurt you by having any son you bore me rejected. You must understand! It is my destiny. To not do so would be the end of my existence; then end of my line. Try to understand."

Calming the fury that had been aroused within her, Ti-Ping took a deep breath and then exhaled slowly. Descended from a long line of kings, she also understood the obligations and incomprehensible facets of royalty. "Do you love her, your second wife?"

"Do I love her? I love her, I hate her, I need her, and I despise her. Take your pick, because on any day it can be any one of those emotions. On most days, it is all of those emotions. And then there are some days I'd like to kill her."

"Does she love you?"

Zutra had to think long and hard before answering. "I think not."

"Then why did you choose her as second wife?"

"The choice of wife has always been very limited to the Kahana. We are both priest and king. We can only marry someone that is of those two families if the child they bear is to be Exilarch. Avital is descended from those families."

"Surely there would be others?"

"Perhaps, but none that I had grown up with and thought for years would be my wife."

"If you had told me that it was just an alliance of state, then perhaps I would understand better because such things are common in my father's palace. But to say you wanted her only because you were denied her for so long does not speak of matters of state nor of love. It only speaks of madness."

"Exactly what Mordecai has repeated endlessly to me. It is madness and I suffer from it knowingly."

"Then you have my pity, my husband. Go to her and plant your seed inside her if you must. Then come back to my bed for I do love you husband. Unlike her, I do want to make love to you. Between these legs, you will always have a home filled with love. Know and understand that. There is duty and there is love. I will always offer you both, but it is the latter that we will cherish together."

"I have tried. I have forced myself upon her but God must not deem it a favorable union as no child grows inside her belly. It is as if her womb rejects my seed. What if it should never happen? How could I return to your bed not knowing that it would be a safe time to do so?"

"It must happen. It will happen," the Princess tried to summon encouragement for her disheartened Prince. "We are meant to be together. You know this in your heart. If it takes a fortnight of prodding her with your member, as many times in the day as you can muster, then let it be so. Ultimately, her womb will receive your child. A woman cannot help but abide by the laws of nature and she is already proven not to be barren...." She stopped mid-sentence, lost in a train of thoughts.

"What is it my love?"

"Nothing my husband, a recollection of something I once heard.

"I will lie with you as soon as the physicians tell me that she has missed her monthly flow."

"Then go," Ti-Ping dismissed him. "And do not return until I can wrap my legs around you and hold you inside me while you spill your seed without fear that you must leave again." The princess watched as her husband took one more backward glance and then crept sheepishly from his own chambers.

Ti-Ping reflected upon the conversation she held with her husband three nights past, the last time that she had seen Zutra, and her eyes began to mist over. Her own servants reported the palace gossip to her and the word amongst the palace servants was that Zutra had entered Avital's quarters on several occasions and each time the physical and verbal abuse she hurled against him was heard resonating throughout the corridors. If Zutra had forced himself into her inner sanctum, then it was not without overcoming severe resistance. Under such circumstances she knew a man would barely be able to sustain his ching and as she had been taught without the release of his ching, the seeds of his discharge would not have the strength to fertilize the egg. If such was the case then the days until she would finally see her husband again in her bed chamber would be very long indeed; too long for her to sit idly by waiting. Ti-Ping reminded herself that she was a modern woman unlike her ancestors; they were impotent and vulnerable. If something needed to be done, then it was best that she did it herself. That was the way of a modern woman!

With a sense of determination, she coiled her night robe around her body, placed a pair of gold fabric slippers over her tiny feet and crept silently from her chambers and down the hall leading towards Avital's quarters. The guards barring the doors to the harem quarters never batted an eye as she approached, especially when she slipped through the portal into the concealed chambers beyond. Passage for the females of the household were unlimited, the guard's primary instruction from their king only that the Lady Avital was not permitted to leave without an escort and certainly not without Zutra's prior knowledge and approval. No such restrictions existed for the king's first wife.

From the sounds of the water pouring from the caldarium pots it was obvious to Ti-Ping that Avital was presently in her bath, a most fortuitous opportunity since she would not be able to readily flee from her uninvited visitor. Peering through the veils that surrounded the perimeter of the marbled caldarium she saw that the Lady Avital had her eyes shut, head resting on a pillow while her handmaidens sponged the water tenderly over her body. Stepping through the curtains, she motioned with a finger across her lips that none of them were to make a sound. Being first wife, she knew that her authority far exceeded all others, even if two of the handmaidens happened to be lesser concubines from local chieftains that Zutra had selected to join his household. Even should they fear reprisal from Avital, they still respected Ti-Ping's superior position.

The souls of her feet never made a sound as she moved through the room and knelt between two of the girls, taking a position just behind Avital's head. The Lady Avital reposed peacefully; her eyes closed as she enjoyed the pleasures of the warm water lapping over her body. Placing her hands at the base of Avital's neck, Ti-Ping pressed deliberately yet delicately on certain nodes that she palpated on either side of the vertebrae. With each manipulation, Avital released a sigh of immeasurable pleasure.

"When did you learn to do this, Seritah?" Avital questioned, her eyes remaining closed as she exhaled deeply.

A titter of laughter escaped from the handmaidens' lips but still none dared to say a word. Upon hearing the laughter, Avital opened her eyes immediately, staring directly into Ti-Ping's smiling face that hovered mere inches above hers.

"Hello Sister," Ti-ping cooed in her heavily accented Greek.

Avital tried to pull herself out of the bath by grasping the stone edging, but discovered her arms were suddenly too weak and barely responsive. Beginning to panic, her eyes flitted to the faces of all the girls watching her predicament, but none dared to defy the Princess and come to her assistance.

"All of you leave now," Princess Ti-Ping commanded. They obeyed immediately without hesitation.

"What have you done to me?" Avital's voice trembled in fear.

"Do not be afraid," Ti-Ping's own voice was calm and soothing. "I am only releasing your chi. This is the art of Tui-na. I have taken you to a place between great pain and great pleasure. At first it will feel as if you are numb but soon the chi will flow, and you will float upon silk wings while your body and soul heal."

"I want to come out now!" Her voice was distressed but she was powerless to make her body respond to any mental command.

"Do not fight me upon this, my sister. Remember that you hover close to the centers of great pain as well. It would be possible if I should make an error that your chi stops completely, and you will die."

"Then if you wish to kill me, do so while you have the opportunity," Avital challenged. "If you don't, I will not waste my opportunity when it arises."

"I do not fear you," Ti-Ping laughed, "Unlike all the men of this land have all come to do. There is nothing you can do that will ever make me fear you. Remember, with a mere touch I can remove your threat at any time of my choosing."

The princess applied pressure to a specific spot at the base of the skull and Avital found herself losing consciousness. Then just as suddenly, the sensation stopped and was replaced by a warm sensation growing outward from the center of her belly.

"But I would prefer to give you much pleasure instead," Ti-Ping explained as her finger rotated gingerly upon the crest of a vertebrae at the centre of the neck. "You see, it feels so much better. And there is so much that I can offer you."

"If I refuse, then you will kill me. Is that not correct? Is this not your game?"

"Why would I wish to do that when we can be so much more than wives to the same man?" Placing her thumbs just at the roots of the clavicles, she released a ripple of immense relaxation across the expanse of Avital's shoulder muscles.

The sensation brought a smile to her face and Avital purred uncontrollably. "How did you do that?"

"There is so much more that I can do. Infinitely more," she boasted. "This is only the Tui-na. If you wished, I could show you the Tei-ta which will take you to the gates of the seven heavens."

Skeptical, Avital was not prepared to trust her oriental rival to let her do any more. "And what is it you want from me in return? You would only do this if there was a price to pay!"

"There is always a price," Ti-Ping admitted freely. "That is the natural way of things. Let me show you what is being offered and then if you like it, I will tell you my price." The Princess stood up and untied the sash around her waist. Opening her robe, she let if fall from her shoulders and drop to the tiled floor. She then slid herself into the water alongside Avital, their bodies caressing each other as she moved into position.

"What do you think you are doing?" Avital questioned foolishly, knowing full well that it was the Princess's intention to climb into the bath but not knowing what she intended to do next.

"To show you the Tei-ta, I must prepare you from within," the princess explained serenely as she lay in the warm water alongside Avital, who began to shiver involuntarily each time Ti-Ping's body brushed up against hers. Without seeking permission, the Princess left hand searched out the hollow between Avital's thighs.

Avital began to protest the assault on her senses but with each insertion of Ti-Ping's probing fingers, she found her protests drifting off into silence.

"Do not be afraid," Ti-Ping spoke softly. "There is no shame in the art of Tei-ta. The women of my father's palace practice it constantly. He has over a hundred wives. If they were to wait for him, each would have gone mad from their loneliness. This is how they ensure that it does not happen." Isolating a spot tucked inconspicuously beneath the fleshy folds of the labia, the princess revolved her fingertip around the circumference of the node.

Every muscle in Avital's body tensed with the sensation of a hundred bowstrings pulled taut simultaneously, only to release their arrows in a hail of fury. Then no sooner had they found their mark, the bows were nocked and bent even further than the previous launching. "Stop, you are killing me," she voiced in a halting speech riddled by spontaneous gasps and moans.

"No, I am releasing you," Ti-Ping refused to relinquish her control. "Feel the chi moving through your body. Let your ching flow from your womb. All this you have denied yourself and if you do not have it released it would eventually consume you from within."

Avital found herself in no condition to argue as wave after wave of indescribable euphoria rolled the length of her body from the top of her head to the tips of her toes. Never had she experienced anything of its like before and the more it overwhelmed her, it tormented her, and the more she craved it to continue, praying that the sensations would never stop.

"Do not be afraid," the Princess said soothingly in a voice as sweet as a summer breeze. "What I am going to do now is known as Ta-gong." Another finger uncoiled and slipped itself gently backwards, penetrating the sphincter like a snake burrowing its way into its nest. "Every muscle within your pelvis is about to clench. You will feel your legs as if they are chained together, shutting out any ray of light from the exterior world, yet they will not have moved at all. It is all within your mind. Then you will feel as if a dam has burst, and all the cares of this world will be flushed from you. It will strike with an intensity so great that you may pass out. But have no fear I will not let you drown in your bath," she winked and smiled with that remark.

Exactly as described, Avital could feel the compaction of every vital organ within her hips clench as if held within the grip of a gigantic vice. The tension exerted increased exponentially until it felt as if her entire being was slowly drawn through the eye of a needle. It was excruciating, it was exhilarating; it was birth, death and rebirth all at the same time. Her mind filled with images of bursting light, so intense that she was blinded by their sheer whiteness.

She had no idea how long she had been insensate. When she awoke, her head was cradled tenderly against Ti-Ping's bosom. "I thought I had died," she whispered, staring gratefully into the Princess's face.

"Some say it is so," Ti-Ping smiled warmly. "They say we go to a place that hovers between life and death and that is why we can feel sensations that do not exist in this world. Sensations for which we do not even have names."

"How did you know I would let you enter me?"

"A woman knows about other women. Men are blind to such things, but a woman can tell. They think of you as cold and heartless but fail to see that you were not a woman for men. This society of yours cannot comprehend such things and punishes harshly those that are discovered but in my world we understand completely. There is no shame that you find no excitement in a man's touch."

"Then are you also not a woman for men," Avital questioned innocently.

"As I told you, I have grown up in the wives' quarters of my father. I am a woman who seeks and gives pleasure. Undeniably my greatest pleasure is to be with the man I love." She tenderly brushed Avital's hair from her face, letting it fall slowly from her fingertips.

"How can you even say that when you have not even had the opportunity to know him."

"I know him well enough. From the time we first met on the causeway I knew that my destiny was fulfilled. What I saw and heard that day told me what kind of man he was. You have closed your heart to him, so your eyes no longer see and your ears no longer hear. To you he is just a man and you have grown to resent all men and the game they play. That only serves to breed more loneliness, more resentment in your heart but I am here now to take all that away."

"I would like you to come to my quarters again," Avital stated quite matter-of-factly.

"There is a price to do so," Ti-Ping reminded her.

"Any price! I will give you anything."

"You must lay with our husband and bear him a son. That is my price."

"You don't know what you're asking from me," Avital protested. "Any way, he has taken me by force many times and his seed is impotent. It is impossible! He is barely a man," she sneered condescendingly.

Smiling impishly, Ti-ping let her finger slide across Avital's shoulder to the cleft along the joint which sent a shiver of delight along the length of the arm. 'It is not that he is impotent, it is only that the black blades of the rye are far more potent."

"What are you saying?"

"More to the point it was something our husband said to me several nights ago. That it was if your womb rejected his seed. Such a thing is possible with a little help. There is the faintest odor upon your skin. You have used the fungus to flush any eggs from your womb. The use of these plants is documented for thousands of years by the Sian. Such a thing is easy to detect if one is familiar with its use."

Feeling like a mouse caught in a trap, Avital could not deny her complicity.

"You will lie with your husband, and you will bear his child. In exchange I will come to you once every fortnight. That is my bargain," Ti-Ping stood firm on her price. "Do you agree?"

"Only if you stay with me until morning each night that you come to me."

"We have agreement then."

"Yes!"

"Then we are truly bonded sisters," Ti-Ping laughed.

Chapter Twenty

Mahoza: Summer 498 A.D.

Word of his arrival swiftly passed throughout the precincts along the southern road. "Patricius was coming. Patricius was coming," the children screamed with delight and the young maidens swooned openly, hoping that just this one time he would let his eyes fall on them a little longer and perhaps they would attract his attention a little better than they did the last time he passed their way. Hundreds of townspeople gathered along the streets in anticipation of catching a glimpse of their hero; a living legend in their midst, who returned to them their freedom and reestablished the Kingdom of David after so many centuries.

As the subject of their adulation approached, sporting his gilded armor and escorted by his legendary Roman guard, he waved to all assembled, acknowledging their presence. His enormous strides took him closer and closer to the city's palace in answer to Zutra's summons. He basked in their admiration as they chanted his name repeatedly.

As he marched through the palace portico, a hail of salvos greeted him. Patricius was led directly to the judgment hall, from where Zutra dispensed justice over the community. Familiar faces lined the passages, all smiling, all nodding with their approval. Even his cousin along with some of his chief officers could be seen among the assembled crowd, waving their acknowledgement as he passed by. Not since the year of the Lord, four hundred and seventy, had he felt this same sensation of overwhelming adulation when the Emperor Leo had placed the laurel leaves upon his head and pronounced him Caesar. Here he was, almost a lifetime later reliving that experience.

At the far end of the procession, Mar Zutra sat upon the ornately carved throne of his ancestors, with its lion paw feet and bejeweled flowers that swirled across the fanned scallop back.

"Step forward Lord Julius Flavius Patricius son of Aspar," he commanded in a very imperial sounding tone.

The Commander did as he was instructed, standing alone in front of the young monarch while hundreds of eyes gazed admiringly upon the great general. Though the interlude was probably only a matter of seconds, it seemed to last forever as Patricius waited anxiously for Zutra to continue the prepared speech. During the pause, Patricius scanned the faces of those surrounding the dais. It was a valuable lesson in political survival that he learned a long time ago. See who was smiling, who was not. Not everyone would be pleased with the outcome of the ceremony. Those that weren't, were the ones to watch out for in the future. It made him reflect back to the time of the assassination of his father and brother. It was this particular lesson that may have saved his own life at the time. A request for an audience had come just prior to the attacks; a request from Zeno who was definitely not smiling at the ceremony of his coronation as Caesar. He knew immediately that a plot was brewing, but at the time he only thought of his own safety, not realizing that the plot was against his entire family. Now was the time to see who amongst Zutra's advisors would not be displaying a congratulatory countenance.

Behind Zutra, seated on a lower level to either side sat both of the royal wives. The Princess Ti-Ping sat in the throne to the right and slightly higher than the Lady Avital's seat on the left, acknowledging her position as royal consort and first wife. Both of them were beginning to show a little belly beneath their shimmering robes; the Lady Avital perhaps a month or so further along. "The Emperor Hsiang would be pleased," he thought to himself. He had fulfilled his obligation to ensure that there would be an imperial heir able to stride the boundary between their two worlds. Having fulfilled that duty, he felt free to move on with this next challenge in his life. The Princess beamed her innocent affections towards him. It was obvious she was content and happy with the life he had brought her to. There would be no dissatisfaction prejudiced towards him from that direction. Whatever magic she had woven over her husband, he no longer felt the need to withhold his affections from her any longer and it was obvious that they both shared in that love effortlessly from the tender way in which he now cradled her hand.

Though she also bore a smile, the turn of Lady Avital's lips confounded him. It was obvious the smile was nothing more than an elaborate mask. "What dark secret was she hiding?" he wondered. "More to the point, what was she plotting?" He had seen that look before, in the eyes of his wife Leontia, and it told him that her mind was busy fathoming the depths of some depraved scheme. Every now and then, he would see her take a sideways glance toward the Princess, and the forced pleasantry would immediately turn to a genuine smile, which confounded him, even further. Before he had an opportunity to continue evaluating the other guests present at the ceremony, Zutra interrupted with his speech.

"We have all passed through a week of great mourning, but no longer must we fill our hearts with sadness. My cousin Mordecai would not want it so. He was a great man, of that there can be no doubt, but even great men must pass on into the world beyond. Let us remember his name with admiration but know that with each sunset there comes a new dawn! Before he passed away, he asked if I would permit him to pick his own successor. An unusual request, to say the least, but then Mordecai bar Kahana was not your typical man. I never had any reason to doubt his wisdom, nor question his advice to me, so I had no reason to refuse his final request. Today I name his successor that he chose. The new vizier of Mahoza is Julius Flavius Patricius. Kneel Vizier Patricius and receive your gold chains of office."

Mounting the second step of the dais, Patricius knelt so that his right knee rested on the top of the platform. He bowed his head and waited for Mar Zutra to perform the time-honored presentation. As soon as the gold necklace was placed over his head the assembly burst into thunderous applause, signifying their approval. The Commander tilted his head, first to the right, then to the left to reconnoiter the faces of the nobleman in attendance. They would be standing closest to the platform and represent the civil servants he would have to deal with on a daily basis. Just as he suspected, not everyone was happy with his attaining the vizier's position. Several members of the Beth Din were not applauding, and they certainly weren't smiling either. He memorized their faces. He would have Valentius look into their affairs once he became firmly established in the affairs of state.

"Repeat after me," Mar Zutra instructed. "I, Patricius son of Aspar, give oath to my liege, Mar Zutra ben Huna, of the House of David, family of the Kahana, in this the year four thousand two hundred and fifty-eight from the creation…"

Patricius meticulously repeated the words without a single error.

"To do honor to my liege, to serve him and protect him, and in so doing guard and preserve the people of our kingdom…"

Once more the Commander repeated the words effortlessly.

"To give to the king my loyalty and service, as Vizier of his Kingdom of Mahoza until such time that I depart this world. This I pledge in sight of the people and in sight of Almighty God…"

Patricius' voice crescendoed as he mentioned the supreme being.

"And as the Lord is my witness, should I fail in these duties and act in such a way that I betray my liege, then I beg no mercy from the Lord, may he see that I am punished for my sins with death!"

Once again, there was no hesitation as Patricius completed his oath of allegiance.

Stretching out his hand, Zutra grasped the new Vizier's shoulder and helped raise him to his feet.

"May the Lord bless you and keep you, all he days of your life. May He watch over you and guide you, grant you wisdom and knowledge. Rise, Vizier Patricius, let all those present salute you."

Taking Patricius by the hand, Zutra paraded him from the throne room towards the banquet hall where all the guests would celebrate their good fortune of having a Vizier so courageous and gifted. As they waded through the crowd, the subjects roared their approval, singing and clapping to the music, which birthed spontaneously from the hidden cloisters built into the walls of the room.

Speaking softly, Mar Zutra spoke in confidence to his new second in command. "I know it is not the same as being anointed as Caesar, dear friend, but I will see to it that you have enough responsibility that you will not be disappointed."

"Zutra, you presume that I wanted to be Caesar. I fled from that position as you might recall."

"I pray that I do not give you cause to flee from this position too!"

"I do not think you need to worry in that regard. I am still honour bound to fulfill my duties to the Emperor Hsiang to safeguard his daughter. As long as she is here, I am here. And from what I see, she appears to be quite content to remain here." The Commander patted his belly and winked to indicate that he noticed the princess was now visible with child.

Zutra smiled with pride upon seeing the gesture. "Yes, I believe she has reason to stay for quite some time," he gloated. "If I keep her belly full you will never have the opportunity to leave us!"

"But considering the Lady Avital also bears good tidings, we both may find that leaving will be the only way either of us can find any peace in your household."

"I will keep that in mind. Perhaps there should be a limit to the size of my household. I will accept this as your first example of sagely advice, Vizier."

For days, the celebrations continued without an end in sight. When they were no longer celebrating at the palace, Patricius had relocated his personal guests to his new residence, the former manse of Mordecai ben Kahana, which had been gifted to him through the old Vizier's last will and testament on the condition that he accepted the position upon his death. Though smaller than Mar Zutra's palace villa, Mordecai's estate still consisted of a main house with sixteen rooms and fabulous gardens situated on a ten-acre parcel of land. A suitable enticement if all else failed to convince the commander to want the position. Patricius quickly discovered his new residence was well suited to the guests that formed a continuous train coming and going for many weeks afterwards, many of them staying much longer than desired.

Valentius and his troupe were reassigned as Patricius' personal guard, permanently installed at his villa, whereas Hermantius and his men were assigned the duties of safeguarding the city of Mahoza, relieving Mar Zutra's Four Hundred from that role. As for the Four Hundred, they were reinstated as the Exilarch's personal security force and honor guard, watching over the now expanding royal family. With such large numbers of military personnel in the city, it would be necessary to begin construction of suitable barracks to house them all; the first major construction project within the city of Mahoza as long as most could remember. A new age of prosperity was being heralded and Mar Zutra was its champion. Almost in anticipation of the city's newfound wealth, merchant enterprises and businesses literally sprung up over night to take advantage of the burgeoning affluence.

The same could not be claimed for Ctesiphon, which in contrast appeared to stagnate under Jamasp's reign. Fearful of making any decisions that could impact negatively on his popularity, which was never that high to begin with once he assumed the throne, he tended to leave the decision-making process to his Vizier and the nobles. Unfortunately for the Emperor, Gurzam fared no better in achieving unanimity among the nobility, who seemed more than ever intent on squabbling and trading insults between themselves than in actually instituting policies of good governance. Gurzam needed to move quickly if he was to secure both his and Jamasp's positions and he knew of only one man he could turn to.

"This is most unexpected," Patricius commented as he reclined on the couch opposite his surprise visitor.

"Is it?" Gurzam appeared surprised. "Is it really? I didn't think it would be. After all, it is not as if everything is fine within the Empire."

"I have no idea what you are referring to," Patricius sat upright in response to Gurzam's high level of agitation.

"We are going backwards, Patricius!" he exclaimed. "Backwards I tell you! The removal of Kavad from power was supposed to stabilize this government but instead it has created even more chaos. The fact that Kavad is still alive has only made the situation more tenuous. It should not have been permitted."

"Why are you looking at me," Patricius challenged Gurzam's penetrating stare. "It was not within my authority to have your Shah executed."

"Had your men done as they were instructed when they first captured him, it wouldn't have been any of our responsibility. It would have been merely an accident of warfare."

"I don't recall any instruction by yourself that he wasn't to be taken alive."

"That is because you still don't understand our ways. In the East some things don't need to be said. They're merely taken for granted. Kavad's death was one of those implied events!"

"Well, if you knew my men weren't familiar with the way men think in this part of the world then you should have just come out and said it," Patricius parried the barb.

Gurzam shook his head. "You don't understand. You foreigners will never understand. We cannot say such a thing about our King. It is not permitted to even make idle talk about killing the King of Kings. The prohibition is too ingrained into our consciences for us to disobey such an edict."

Now it was Patricius' turn to shake his head in disbelief. "Well, if you couldn't say it then you can hardly expect my men to know what you wanted. This argument is getting us nowhere! So, what is your point?"

"Agreed," Gurzam nodded. "Let us be progressive and talk about what must be done."

"So, are you going to tell me that you want him eliminated now?"

"I can't. I told you it is forbidden by Ahura Mazda to discuss such a thing."

"But if I was to arrange an accident, you wouldn't attempt to stop me, would you?" Patricius attempted to draw out the answers a different way.

"I would not know of what accident you were speaking of. Things happen all the time by accident. I am unable to prevent them all."

"I will take that as a yes," Patricius grimaced in response to this foolish game of words.

"There is far more that ails this country, but you and your king have been so busy celebrating your good fortune you have paid little attention to the events that surround you."

"If there were matters of urgency, I'm certain there was some way in which you could have brought them to our attention," Patricius refused to accept the accusation.

"Your Byzantine friends have not left our territory as was part of the original arrangement. They continue to occupy towns and land on our side of the border, which is making the people turn angry. They are beginning to blame us for their presence."

"Of course, they blame us. We brought them here."

"But we did not expect them to stay!"

"Did you give them what we promised?" Patricius questioned knowing in advance the answer to his question.

"I could not. The barons will not let me. You promised the Byzantines too much."

"I promised them what we had agreed prior to giving them," the Commander's voice grumbled impatiently. "A single payment of tribute and open trade routes; it was quite clearly expressed. It wasn't that difficult a bargaining."

"Perhaps not at that the time, but the barons squabbled bitterly when it came time to part with their gold and jewels for the tribute."

"Then take it out of the treasury," Patricius dismissed Gurzam's flimsy excuse.

"That is the problem," Gurzam was now practically pleading. "The barons haven't paid their tribute into the treasury either. Without the threat of Kavad upon their necks, they saw no need to make their regular payments. They collect the taxes from their people and then keep it for themselves. They know that Jamasp is powerless to stop them."

"I don't understand," Patricius shook his head. "You want the Byzantines off your land, but you won't pay them the price agreed upon. And you won't pay them because the barons refuse to provide the monies that were promised. But the barons won't pay because you can't force them too since they control the army which is busy preventing the Byzantines from encroaching any further on the land that the barons don't want them on in the first place."

"Yes, you understand perfectly," Gurzam shouted.

"So what is it you think I can do?"

"You have the only army within the region. "I need you to get the money from the barons," Gurzam smiled wryly.

"I suppose it can be done," Patricius contemplated the basic logistics of the situation. But naturally I have to ask what the benefit to my liege would be or to me."

He watched as Gurzam clenched his fists, a silent rage flushing across his face yet Jamasp's vizier managed to hold his temper.

"What's in it for you is a peaceful co-existence," the Sassanid Vizier replied contemptuously. "That is by far the most significant benefit. Secondly, you won't have your Byzantine brethren breathing down your back and safely behind their own borders."

"And thirdly…?"

"Do you need more?"

"You're asking me to make an example of some of your leading citizens. That will not be an easy thing to do without creating new problems and animosities amongst our two populations. We'd be putting out one fire only to light several new ones." Patricius remained calm and confident as he explained his reasoning to Gurzam, reposed on his sedan, barely flinching a muscle. "Your problem is not insurmountable. Anastasius will be content once he receives his tribute and his trade concessions. He will withdraw his armies as soon as he has his assurances."

"How can you be so certain?"

"I'm a military man. It costs a fortune to maintain forces across enemy lines. The supply trains alone would be a king's ransom to maintain. He'd be relieved the moment he hears that the men can be withdrawn."

"And what of the taxes? How can you guarantee that the nobles will pay what is owed and will continue to do so?"

"You see my friend that is your problem. Whereas Kavad inspired fear in their hearts, and they would not dream of betraying him, Jamasp is held up to ridicule. It will be necessary to make them fear him more than they ever feared his brother. That is why mine and King Zutra's assistance is going to cost you."

Gurzam unclenched his fingers and resigned himself to the fact that there would be a third price to pay. "So, tell me what you have in mind."

"In order to do this properly I will need authority for my Alanine legion to operate within your city. That places my men in confrontation with your own patrols. Any forces you have in Ctesiphon must be placed directly under my command to avoid any conflict."

"They will not like that," Gurzam was quick to interrupt.

"Call it a co-command, whatever it takes to get their agreement. But ultimately the final orders must come from me if we are to succeed."

"So how much is it that you'll want to be paid for this service you're extending into my city?"

"As I mentioned, maintaining a standing army is a costly business. I don't ask much. Those districts that are filled with foreigners, they will pay their business taxes to Mahoza's coffers."

"That is absurd!"

"No, it's reasonable and logical. As foreigners, they won't care to whom they pay their taxes, and as foreigners, the rest of your citizenry will be glad to be rid of their responsibility to them."

"His royal highness will not like giving up any of his loyal subjects, even if they are just foreigners as you suggest."

"Tell his royal highness that he won't be the King of Kings for long if he doesn't have his treasury filled quickly. There are no poor kings in this world. At least not any that last very long on a throne!"

"And the other matter?"

"I had already promised Mordecai before his death I would look into it. The Castle of Oblivion is a long way away. I need to know everything there is that you know about Susiana; streets, alleys, and possible allies. You get me that information and then we can talk."

Chapter Twenty-one

Mahoza Palace: Autumn 498 A.D.

"I don't understand," Zutra sounded worried.

Patricius paraded back and forth in front of his king, his arms held behind his back as he went over the strategy for a second time. "We have no choice; it has to be done."

"Wasn't it enough you filled their treasury. Why is it necessary that we do all their dirty work for them?"

"It would appear that they are incapable of doing it themselves," Patricius answered dryly.

"Oh, yes, their supposed fear of royal curses as I recall. It's all fabricated, you know. Has been from the time of their very first ruler. They've always been so intent on raiding the tombs of their dead kings that they started placing curses over each internment. Superstitious lot! They've actually come to believe in the curses that they had made up themselves. And now they're even willing to believe that such a curse extends to their living monarchs as well."

"Then you understand why it has fallen upon us to do this."

"No," Zutra stated flatly, "I said they are a superstitious lot but I never said I agreed with all their legends and nonsense of demons and evil jinn."

"But you agree that it has to be done."

"Of course it has to be done. Jamasp's government is powerless as long as there are factions that believe Kavad is still the rightful ruler. Not even all of Gurzam's oratory skills and machinations are going to keep them in line for long. But to do their dirty work for them, we should have been handsomely paid for that!"

"I would have thought possession of the foreigner districts in Ctesiphon would be ample pay," Patricius reminded him.

"Perhaps," Zutra sighed. "Perhaps. We will see. I still think they got away cheaply."

"We will see what, now?" their brief interlude alone interrupted suddenly by feminine curiosity.

"Matters of state, Avital," Zutra dismissed her inquiry. "Nothing to concern yourself with."

"Oh, I didn't mean to intrude on such serious matters," she apologized.

Patricius studied her carefully, considering himself quite adept at reading people's innermost thoughts. It came naturally when you had to be concerned that anyone close was a potential assassin. 'Shrewd. Very shrewd, you little vixen,' he thought to himself. 'You must have been hiding in the portico and overheard every word. Now you are pretending that you heard nothing. How are you intending to use this information?' he wondered.

Avital half-curtsied politely and smiled at the vizier. Her barely perceptible nod was an acknowledgement that she knew he was reading her mind, but she had no fear of the man. She was pitching her wits against his and as far as he could discern from her pleasant expression, she never even bothered to consider himself to be a worthy opponent. 'This one is definitely up to no good,' he recognized. He would have to make certain that he was careful in protecting Mar Zutra and the Princess from her clutches.

"What is it my dear that has brought you here?" Zutra drew everyone back from his or her thoughts.

"I ask a favor your majesty. A simple one but still one for which I still need your permission."

"Ask," he commanded, "and let me be the judge of whether it is simple or not."

"I would like your permission to leave the palace and visit my father. A simple request I think you would agree."

Not so simple, both Zutra and Patricius were well aware of the implications. Even under house arrest, Reb Hanina was still a very dangerous opponent and thus far, his daughter was his only conduit to the outside world. Mar Zutra had to evaluate carefully where he thought her true loyalties lay. Reluctantly, he consented to her request and she left immediately.

Patricius waited until her heard her footsteps disappear in the distance. "Do you think that was wise?"

"Wise? No. Prudent? Yes. She has been far more amenable of late and I think that has earned her some trust on my part."

"With all due respect, Zutra, and I do not wish to be insulting, but by amenable do you not mean she has provided you with your conjugal rights? That is hardly a reason to trust her implicitly."

"Had anyone else said that to me I'd have them lashed severely," he warned.

"No one else would have the courage to tell you the truth to your face," Patricius advised. "But that is what you expect from me."

"Just like Mordecai," Zutra stated reminiscently. "He could never understand why I never beat Avital into submission."

"I have to admit I have thought the same thing. I don't trust her. Now I fear she overheard us talking."

"Even if she did," Zutra shrugged his shoulders, "What could she do with the information?"

"Again, I think your cousin Mordecai and I would have been in agreement. It is what we don't know which makes her so dangerous."

"But don't you see? I didn't beat her and she came to me on her own terms. And now she carries my child."

"Haven't you wondered why she suddenly had a change of heart? Strange, wouldn't you think? Remember, the fox will do anything to find its way into the hen house."

"Be careful, Patricius. I love you like a brother but that does not give free reign to your tongue. She is still my wife."

"Forgive me again Majesty, I meant no disrespect, only that we must remain cautious."

"Who can really understand the ways of women? I prayed to God that He would turn her heart from stone back to flesh and He did so. That is all I know. That is all I care about. Through her womb, my lineage in Mahoza will continue. If letting her see her father is the price I must pay in homage to my ancestors, then so be it."

"And what of your lineage through the Princess Ti-Ping?" Patricius questioned. "Is that not of value to you?"

"You don't understand yet the ways of my people," Zutra attempted to explain. "To sit on the throne of David and carry the rod of Aaron, it can only be through the union of my family with Avital's. As for my union with the Ti-Ping, I believe that child will be far more. He will conquer the world."

"I only pray that you have not sewn the invitation to disaster I fear it might be. I doubt very much that the Lady Avital would permit any other child but hers to rise to such heights."

"No more than I hope," Zutra confessed after musing over Patricius's words in his mind. "Perhaps your are right and we should see where the fox is heading."

"There is someone I would like you to meet. Allow me to introduce my beautiful niece, Roxanne; she has spoken only of you since she laid eyes upon you in the procession. I think she has become one of your greatest admirers." Waving his hand, the city magistrate summoned the young woman from the shadows where she sat in conversation with two other veiled women, extending his right hand as she approached. Taking his hand at its tip between her own thumb and fingers, she floated to the side of the table where Patricius had sat most of the night drinking heavily with his two companions.

Hermantius peered past the loosely tatted lace and looked directly into the dark eyes of the breathtaking beauty wishing that it was him and not his cousin that she longed for. Beneath her cowl, raven locks fell loosely across her shoulders enticingly. "I must have died and gone to heaven," Hermantius proclaimed to his cousin, "Because I have beheld an angel."

"They say you are a great warrior, my Lord." Her voice was soft and melodic exactly as they had anticipated it would be.

Severely inebriated, Patricius parroted what his cousin had just said. "So is it true?" he added, "You are an angel on earth."

Her laugh was a girlish giggle. "Oh, my Lord, if you think I am beautiful, wait until you see my two sisters."

"I've yet to see your face fully, my lovely," his words were slurred.

"That is easily remedied my Lord." She leaned over the table and pulled the veil to one side, but partially concealed so that only Patricius could view her face fully.

"What did you see, cousin?" Hermantius demanded to know.

"Yes, yes, tell us," Valentius added.

"Indescribable," Patricius blurted.

"Let me see, let me see," Hermantius whined.

"You wouldn't be able to handle it," his cousin warned. "Helen of Troy reborn! It would be like staring into the sun. I must protect you from doing something so foolish!"

Hermantius reached out to grab the girl so as to turn her face towards him but Patricius seized his arm before he did so. "Some things are not meant for mere mortals, cousin!"

"I understand," Hermantius laughed. "Come Valentius, we are needed elsewhere."

"Go on without me and I'll join up with you tomorrow," Patricius suggested and ordered simultaneously.

"Sure you will Patricius. Until tomorrow then." Bowing clumsily both Hermantius and the captain withdrew from the Vizier's presence and exited the tavern on wobbly legs.

"And now, my little one, what would you recommend this old general who is suddenly feeling very young, do for the rest of the evening?"

"Allow me to make a suggestion," the magistrate pushed himself between Patricius and his niece. "It does not appear that you have eaten much while you were enjoying your ale. My home is but a short distance from this tavern. It is time that I brought Roxanne and her two sisters home as the hour grows late and we would be honored to have your company. I am certain that all my nieces would love to hear of your heroic exploits while I have some of my kitchen staff prepare a sumptuous meal."

"Lead on good sir," Patricius struggled to his feet only to stumble forward, his right hand slamming against the tabletop. "It would appear that I may need a little help," he snorted, only to be supported immediately by the Magistrate who placed a steadying hand beneath his arm.

Waving to the two women in the shadows, they followed discretely behind as Roxanne and her uncle shouldered Patricius along the street towards the small cottage several blocks away. His senses considerably dulled by the copious volume of ale he had been consuming all night, the Vizier failed to notice that for all intent and purpose, the house appeared abandoned, save for a few tables and chairs and several straw mattresses upon the floor in the back room where they led him. In his intoxicated condition, he wasn't even concerned. The mattresses in fact were a welcome sight.

"Some more beer, Lord?" the magistrate inquired as he and his niece helped lower Patricius to the ground atop one of the woven mats.

"Yes, flagons of it," he roared as he felt Roxanne's slender fingers work their way through the myriad straps and buttons that held his cuirass and tunic in place. "My, you are a feisty one," he laughed. "No time wasted to eat with you around!"

"Plenty of time to eat later, my Lord. Consider me the appetizer," she snickered.

"I will go and instruct the staff to prepare some food," the magistrate said as he returned with a mug of strong drink that he placed into Patricius' outstretched hand. In one swift motion, the cup was against his lips and downed in a single swallow.

"And some more ale while you're at it," Patricius burped loudly wiping his mouth with the back of his hand.

"Of course, my Lord," the man bowed and shuffled quickly from the room.

Roxanne's two sisters sat themselves ever so quietly in a dark corner of the room where they watched intently with piercing eyes shielded behind the slits in their veils. They followed closely every movement their sister made as she prepared the Vizier for their union.

Patricius groaned softly as he felt her nimble hand slide beneath the skirt of his tunic and between his legs. It was only then, when his head rocked to the side that he saw the other two women in the corner, their arms tidily wrapped about their knees, watching in silence. "Are they going to be there all the time," he sounded vaguely nervous regarding their silent observation.

"We're sisters Lord. We share everything."

"Everything?"

"Yes, everything," she purred.

"Oh, my," he grinned. "This is definitely going to be a night to remember!"

Roxanne's hand was now squeezing his member methodically, drawing the blood into his engorged penis until it stood proudly at full erection, waving like a flagpole caught in the wind. "A mighty weapon Sire," she fawned over his sturdy appendage. Between the ale and the skilled hands of the girl, Patricius could barely keep his upper body balanced on his elbows as he attempted to watch her pursed lips moving towards his unmasked manhood.

Up and down her tongue slid along the veined surface sending surge after surge of rapturous delight the length of his shaft until he groaned and shouted boisterously, unable to accommodate her attentions any longer.

"Shall I stop my Lord?" she taunted him, knowing well that his outburst was nothing more than uncontrollable urges that cried out for more.

"No, no, go on," he protested just as loudly.

Precisely the moment where he thought the shaft could extend no further without bursting at the seams; Roxanne slid a copper ring over the appendage and wedged it firmly at the base of his groin where it held snugly once she sealed the clasp. Now with each throbbing pulsation, the flesh of the penis spilt over the sides of the ring until it felt as if the metal would bury itself deeply into the muscle of his swollen phallus.

"It hurts," he winced in a childlike voice, having never experienced this particular sensation from a device before.

"Only for the moment," Roxanne reassured him. "Then it will numb the sensation and preserve the erection. The cock rings have been used for as long as anyone can remember in our country." Her voice no longer sounded like the sweet, innocent child he first heard in the tavern. Its intonation sounded more methodical, mechanical, and sterile in its pronunciation of the words. "How else do you expect to service the three of us my Lord? The ring will ensure your tool remains erect for a considerable length of time," she teased. "At least long enough for the three of us to have the pleasure of your company. Moreover, the numbing will see that you don't spend yourself too early so that the only pleasure is your own. That would be very naughty and greedy of you!" Her laugh was wicked as she took control of his body.

Patricius nodded his head in consent. He wanted to prolong the pleasure as long as possible. Through the alcoholic haze, what did it matter if his reputation as a great lover required the assistance of a mechanical device? He would prove himself more than qualified for the challenge.

With his penis buried deep within her mouth, Patricius felt every concealed movement of her tongue as she drew more and more of his own energies into his throbbing appendage but the accursed ring prevented him from crossing beyond the threshold in order to release the wave of explosive energy that his mind yearned for. He could no longer hold himself on his elbows, falling back onto the mattress so that he lay stretched out at the complete mercies of his feminine assailant praying that she would let the dam break and release the tidal wave.

Though his eyes remained closed, he sensed Roxanne changing her position. Suddenly he felt his penis slide between the moist, tight lips of her vulva. 'Virgin' he thought at first, but no that couldn't be true, too experienced and knowledgeable to be likely. He laughed with sheer delight at the thought that just perhaps he might be the first to enter this forbidden sanctuary. She sat upright, riding him like a horse, thrusting her hips back and forth until he had slid the full distance of her canal, banging at her innermost doors until he thought he was once again about to explode only to have that damn ring prevented him from doing so. His mind swirled in a cloud. How much time had passed, seconds, minutes, hours, he could not tell. It mattered little as she dug her heels into his thighs, riding high in the saddle to the beat of one continuous never-ending crescendo.

Silently he muttered, praying for a moment of relief; any chance to end the intense throbbing of his phallus and the limbo of unachievable bliss. As if in answer to his prayers Roxanne lost her balance, collapsing upon his chest, flailing like a fish out of water as she shouted her own unintelligible curses until she lay motionless on his outstretched body, panting with exhaustion. The last of her own moments of pleasure waned as she extracted herself from his swollen member and rolled over on to her side. 'Relief, glorious relief' was all that he could think of until the nightmare manifested itself once more.

The sensations along the shaft were barely palpable due to the numbing of the ring but there was no mistaking the unique sensation of a tongue lapping the secretions from around its base. He creased the lids of his eyes so he peered through the merest of slits, recognizing that the second sister was now preparing him for her own lust-filled satisfaction. Shedding her veil he could see that Roxanne had definitely not lied. If the first had been an angel then this second sister was surely a goddess. Her skin was lustrous, even in the dim candlelight that pervaded the room. Like polished bronze, it glowed with an indescribable radiance that only made the carving of her features more statuesque and surreal. "Damn,' he cursed as her unfathomable beauty rekindled a surge of lust in his mind that was now overpowering the weariness and discomfort of his groin. Rather than achieving release of the interred engorgement through sheer exhaustion, he felt himself forcing his penis to even greater lengths with each beating of his heart.

"Yes, my Lord," her eyes lit up as she watched his penis rise in stature. "Give Seritah the full fury of your desires," she cooed. Her voice tempered by a sensuous laugh that made him groan for mercy. Whereas Roxanne had been slow, rhythmic and in hindsight even tender, Seritah was a complete animal, voracious, cunning and exceedingly demanding. She cared little for her partner's satisfaction or pleasure, pushing his reddened raw flesh to its limits as she satisfied her own insatiable desires.

"Careful, Seritah," Roxanne cautioned her. "You cannot have him all for yourself. Do not be so greedy."

"Let me have him," Seritah moaned, her spirit taken over by the coupling that held her glued upon her victim as she pushed him further and deeper inside herself. "Please, please," she groaned as the orgasm ripped through her tensing muscles, refusing to release him until she had drained every last moment of pleasure from his exhausted body.

"Enough," the voice of the third sister commanded with an unexpected authority.

Forced to obey, Seritah reluctantly slid off of Patricius's still erect phallus, fingering herself as she obeyed in order to attain one last thrill before she resumed her position in the corner of the room.

"Oh God, oh God," Patricius moaned as he felt the third sister climb across his weakened, crippled frame. He wanted to throw her off, buck like a bronco, until she could stay on no longer but his spirit was too weak and there was not a single ounce of strength residing within his limbs. Entirely flaccid except for the shaft between his legs, it now contained his entire essence and he in turn had become a prisoner within his own body. Whatever state of exhaustion prevented him from fleeing, the near paralysis from copious amounts of ale ensured he could not rise from the mattress.

Something about this third sister he sensed was different. As she mounted his erection, he recognized that she was being extremely cautious as she found a position that rolled the weight off his hips while she sat practically upright upon her knees. She refused to slide down the entire length of his penis, instead carefully limiting her movements to only the upper third. He opened his eyelids further to see that she still wore her veil, concealing all but her eyes; dazzling, beguiling, entrancing hazel eyes that stared down at him menacingly. Eyes that excited him in different ways from her sisters, once again filling him with desire and providing new invigoration to his love making though his tired flesh screamed 'no more.'

Her breasts were firm and upturned; the areolas darkened suggesting that this one had possibly known motherhood. He looked again and saw that several blue veins surrounded the turgid nipples possibly suggesting that she had recently suckled a child. His gaze lowered to her abdomen, and he was spellbound by the prominent navel that was protruding well beyond the flattened stomach. Not flattened he corrected himself, but rotund. 'Pregnant' it suddenly dawned on him. It now all made sense. Her cautious movements, the restriction of his penetration, the bluing of the veins in her breasts; this third sister had to be pregnant.

Her hands reached down, and she began methodically to knead and press certain locations on his pelvis as if she was unlocking a secret code. Entirely new and different sensations coursed the length of his body. Confusing feelings surrounded by brightly colored flashes of light and unearthly sounds. His legs no longer responded to any of his mental commands. He began to panic with the thought that he had truly become fully paralyzed.

His lips struggled to move, the words slurred and barely audible as the last mug of ale finally took effect, "What have you done to me?"

"I am moving your chi." she answered. "And then I will take your ching and you will belong to me," she growled maliciously. "You should understand. After all, you spent twenty-five years in Asia."

"That voice..." his words trailed off into nothingness. Those hazel eyes, now he remembered where he had seen them before!

"Do not fret," she soothed the anxious look upon his face. "As your chi moves towards your centre, you will temporarily lose control of all the other parts of your body. You may even think you are having a stroke, but I can assure you that you are not. Within a few hours, you will have regained full control of your body once again. We will be long gone by then." She reached to the clasp on her veil, releasing it and letting it fall to one side.

Patricius stared blankly into the alluring face of the Lady Avital, beaming in her glory of tasting victory.

"Just as your Princess made me her possession, toying with me like a cat plays with a mouse, now I am doing the same to you. I have been a good student and she is a better teacher than she may realize. More to the point, you are mine now and will do as I command. That is all you should be concerned about from now on."

Sensing the time had arrived, her hands reached between her legs and she undid the clasp from the metal ring around the base of his shaft. In response, he exploded inside her, filling her with the massive ching that had been welling within. His entire essence flowed into her like a tsunami of emotion. She sat on her haunches, milking the length of his penis through tightly contracting cervical muscles until she was rocked backwards by the sheer force of his outpouring.

She regained her composure, clambering forward along his paralyzed frame until she sat upon his chest peering down directly into his eyes. "You are a powerful man, Lord Patricius. Nevertheless, I have always been a more powerful woman. I want you to listen to me well. What you have done this night cannot be undone. Nor if it was to be found out could it ever be forgiven. The magistrate truly is my maternal uncle. His name is Abraham. When I venture into the city, he is my appointed guardian. Had you paid more attention to civil matters you would have known this. You should have recognized him as my loyal and obedient custodian, but you cannot bother with such trivial details and now he will testify that you were drunk. That you became enamored with one of my maidservants and seeing an opportunity to abuse your power and privilege, you sent away your men so that you could force yourself upon her without restraint. She refused and we all fled to the safety of one of my uncle's properties nearby. You followed and forced your way in, knocking my uncle unconscious in the process. He has no memory of what happened afterwards. We tried to conceal ourselves from you but one by one you raped us, taking my two servants first and then still not satiated, you forced yourself upon me though I protested and fought back."

At the precise moment she mentioned her resistance, she raked her nails across his chest drawing blood as she did so. "See, I resisted. You thought you recognized my voice, so you ripped my veil discovering that I was the pregnant wife of your king that you had pinned to the floor. This inflamed your passions even further, releasing a torrent of your seed in an attempt to flush Zutra's child from my womb; the child that means everything to your king; the very child that he has prayed for in order to fulfill his destiny. The unborn child of the man only weeks ago you swore allegiance to and said that you would lay down your life should you ever betray him. In your drunken, lust filled daze you copulated with his wife! What kind of monster would do such a thing? What you have done should constitute a betrayal of the vilest nature. Who could possibly disagree? Who would ever question my version of the events! No one and you know it for a fact!"

Patricius absorbed every word she had spoken. He knew she was right. There'd be at least twenty witnesses from the tavern that would attest that he was drunk this night. More that would say he appeared enchanted by a woman that came to his table. More importantly, none of his captains could make a statement in his defense as to what happened next since he had dismissed them. What Vizier would be foolish enough to dismiss his own escort unless he intended to do something he did not wish for them to see? She was right; he was completely at her mercy.

"But it would be a shame to see a man of your stature lose his life for a moment of misguided lust," she reasoned. "Perhaps we can strike a bargain, you and I. In return for my remaining quiet about your indiscretion, all I ask is that you remove the guards from my father's house and those of his associates. Not for very long, just long enough so they can pack a few possessions and leave their imprisonment. Such a simple and minor request is surely worth the silence on my part. Call a meeting of your security forces, or perhaps hold a parade to create a diversion. Whatever the excuse, it doesn't matter just as long as there is enough time that they can leave the city unchallenged. It can be a blessing for you in disguise. You'd actually be ridding the city of troublemakers that have been a burden to you for months."

It was difficult but Patricius was able to force the words past his lips, "Beware of what you wish for."

"Is that a threat, my good Vizier," she laughed. Looking over the length of his body, stretched out and immovable as it were, she could not help but ridicule, "I barely think you are in a position to threaten me."

"Get off me," he winced.

"I know that you will make the right choice." She leaned forward and kissed him gracefully upon his cheek. "You're a smart man Patricius," she reminded him as she forced herself slowly to her feet, rubbing between her thighs gently to sooth the discomfort of his penetration. "My, my girls, he certainly was a big one, wasn't he," she remarked happily as she ushered her girls from the edge of the room.

"I wouldn't mind having him again," Seritah licked her lips as she took one last trailing look behind to see Patricius still lying like a corpse on the straw mattress.

"Now don't be greedy girls," Avital scolded. "We've done what was necessary. Let's leave him alone with his thoughts. After all, he has a lot to think about," she laughed, amused by the extent of her own cleverness and cunning.

"It's not fair," Seritah huffed petulantly. "Roxanne got to enjoy herself much more than I did. I wasn't finished."

Avital smiled devilishly, patting her stomach gently. "Oh, we are definitely finished here, my dear. We got exactly what we wanted! Now, not another word of this, do you understand? Not to anyone, otherwise I will have to punish you. Is that clear?"

"Yes, my Lady," they responded sheepishly, bowing their heads and following their mistress out from the cottage.

Chapter Twenty-two

Susiana: Autumn 498 A.D.

Concealed within the cavernous shadows of a long-abandoned sewage conduit, overwhelmed by the scent of moldy excrement and the odiferous remains of desiccated rats, they met, exchanging adversarial glances harnessed by forced smiles. Their own elite force surrounded each man, carefully searching for the hidden weaknesses and gauging warily the other party. Summoned together as allies on this mission, it was evident neither even remotely trusted the other. Theirs was an alliance out of necessity, nothing more and nothing less. Each leader stood motionless, fingering the handles of the knives tucked beneath their belts, waiting for the other to break the awkward silence. Finally, the assassin covered from head to heel in the black robes of his guild spoke. "You must be Captain Valentius?"

"Considering that we are both wandering through a sewer in the middle of the night, I doubt you were expecting me to be anyone else," Valentius replied sarcastically.

Ignoring his impudence, the assassin waved for the Romans to follow. "I am Rashid. These are my men. More than that you need not know."

"But you know your way through these pipes?" Valentius wanted confirmation before he followed any further.

"Does a camel know how to shit?"

"I'll take that as a yes," Valentius shrugged his shoulders in front of his men indicating he had no knowledge of camels.

"Of course, it is a yes. Gurzam is not a fool to waste his money. He hired us because he was familiar with our work."

"Then why did he insist that we be here?" the Roman captain was curious.

"We will lead you through the sewers into the castle, but as for what you do there, that is without our assistance."

"I thought being assassins, that is what you do."

"Sometimes there are assignments that are beyond any amount of money."

"And this would be one of them?"

"Correct! This is one of them."

"Then lead on and let's get this done with," Valentius insisted.

Eerie was the only description the Romans could think of as they followed in the light of the flickering torches through the warren of tunnels and catacombs that interlaced the sewage system.

Rashid raised his hand and brought everyone to a halt. He motioned for silence, placing a finger to his lips. The sign was universal, the message was clear. The guardhouse was directly above them, and any talking could have disastrous effects. Until such time as he signaled again, they were to be as quiet as rats in a sewer. They began trudging through the tunnels once more.

Slogging through waste a further hundred yards, Rashid pointed to the far wall, identifying the foot and handholds that had been carved into the smooth slime covered brick. He broke the silence but briefly to pass on his departing message. "If you climb this wall it is a waste chute built into the castle directly from the kitchens. There should be no one in the kitchens at this hour. As you exit from the kitchen there is a stairway to the right. It leads directly to the rooms where Kavad is being kept as a prisoner. Be prepared to face the guards when you reach the second doorway. Most likely, only two, but I have no way of confirming if there will be any more on duty tonight. I will remain here with my men to lead you back out of the city if your mission should prove successful. However, if you are not back within two hours, we will be gone. If it should be longer than that then you are obviously dead."

"We will be back," Valentius assured him. "Do not leave before the time is up!"

"We are not thieves," Rashid was indignant. "Gurzam has paid for the two hours and that is what you will receive."

Pulling themselves up slowly, the years of grease and slime that had accumulated on the stones made the ascent precarious. Weighed down by their armor, the squad found the climb laborious, necessitating several respites to catch their breath as they clutched and pulled themselves up the thirty feet of masonry to the kitchen portal. With only enough room to ascend one at a time through the narrow column, a half hour was lost before the last of the Romans passed through the portal and landed with a thud on the galley floor.

Valentius motioned for two of his men to secure either side of the door leading from the kitchen as he prepared to open it. Looking though a hairline crack as he swung the door outwards, the captain saw little to cause alarm. The hallway was empty as far as he could discern. He waved for the others to follow as he opened the door completely and stepped towards the stairway. Pointing up the stairs, he sent the same two advance men forward to ensure the way was clear.

Creeping slowly, one stair at a time, they made it to the top landing without incident and then motioned for the rest to follow. Reassembled on the second level of the castle, Valentius was wary of a possible trap. The living quarters were far too quiet and thus far, they had not even encountered a single guard. He signed his men to spread out and search the quarters. With their short swords drawn, each moved in a different direction, covering the entire multiplex of rooms in a matter of minutes.

"There's no one here," one of the returning soldiers whispered to his captain. The same response followed from each of the other men as they returned to their assembly point. "What do we do now?" his second in command questioned.

Valentius stroked his chin, weighing out his next orders. Already they had wasted the first hour that Rashid had allotted them, and they had achieved nothing in that time. They could easily spend another hour searching through the rest of the Castle of Oblivion and still not find their quarry. He decided on the direct approach if he was going to salvage their mission at all. "Since we're going to need answers then we better take our queries to the people in charge," he instructed. "Constantius, do you think you can find a path through the halls that would lead us to the guardroom that we passed underneath? At least we know that they have men in there. I doubt it will be more than a handful. We need to go in quick and dispatch them before they can send out an alarm. Do it now!"

"Yes sir," he responded while snapping his forearm against his leather breastplate.

"Good. I want everyone prepared for a brief skirmish. We're the enemy here so they will have the advantage of knowing this building. The only way we can take them down is if we can take them by stealth."

"What if they should have sentries posted outside their barracks?" one of the soldiers inquired.

"We won't waste our time with them. No prisoners; dispatch them immediately. If we want answers, then we'll get it from whoever is left inside their room. Let's move it people!"

Descending the staircase, the elite squad of troopers wound their way behind Constantius who took the lead. Using his acute senses of hearing and smell, the core traits of an invaluable tracker, he led them directly to the section of the castle where the guards had established their quarters. Remaining hidden in the alcove, Valentius removed a small, polished brass mirror from his sack and held it with his arm extended so that he could see around the corner into the next room. He withdrew the mirror and silently held up two fingers to his men, then indicated that they were in luck as both sentries were fast asleep at their posts.

Using knives only, two of Valentius's men moved in silently for the kill. Before the guards were even able to assess what was taking place, they had one hand firmly sealed across their mouths while the other one brought a blade swiftly slashing across their exposed throats. Squatting outside the door into their barracks, Valentius listened intently to the voices from the other side, trying to determine the number of adversaries they were about to face. The effort proved futile. Though he only heard a couple of men talking, he knew there would be far more waiting inside. Most were probably asleep but that would only be until such time that the door was kicked inwards. Looking around the outer room he spotted the set of shelves with the two tiers of spindles: eleven spindles for the corresponding eleven helmets in total. Excluding the two sentries that were now dead, Valentius determined that there had to be at least nine men on the other side of the door. Their numbers were equally matched; however the Romans held the element of surprise.

A heavy boot broke the door off its hinges as the elite Roman squadron burst through the opening, forcing those inside to automatically retreat to the far corner of the room. One of the guards had been asleep under blankets near the doorway, remaining undetected as they rushed past him. With their backs turned, he drew his sword from under the covers and prepared to charge the Romans from the blindside before they could defend themselves.

The heavily mailed fist appeared from the blackness of the corridor landing squarely on the overconfident guard's left temple. Falling to his knees, the guard momentarily lost consciousness until he was forcibly dragged back onto his feet by Captain Valentius. Always the cautious one, it was not Valentius's custom to charge blindly into the action with his men, preferring instead to mop up the rear for this very reason. In his experience, there was always at least one enemy that managed to avoid the initial charge. Susiana he figured would be no different from any other situation back in the Sian.

Regaining their composure, the Castle of Oblivion guards slowly began to push back their invaders, having calmed their initial panic. But, when the first two of their comrades fell with barely a fight to the superior swordsmanship of the Romans any bravado and momentum that they may have mustered was quickly lost.

"Unh-unh-ah," Valentius waved a cautioning finger towards the remaining guards. "Not a good idea. You may think you match us in numbers, but I can assure you this is far from being an even battle. Trust me; you don't want to lose your lives in this manner. Lower your weapons now!" he shouted at them. "There will be no more killing today unless you force our hands. You understand me, don't you?"

Though his Persian was less than fluent, the guards nodded their heads in affirmation.

Still holding the one guard by the scruff of his tunic, Valentius spoke directly to him. "You my friend and your mates here are in a lot of trouble in case you haven't realized it yet. You were assigned a very simple task of guarding one prisoner and he doesn't seem to be here any longer. Now I would suggest you start explaining very quickly what has happened to him!"

"He has left," the guard replied contemptuously.

"I am very aware that he has left. I want to know how he was able to do so and don't forget to mention where he's gone."

"His freedom was paid for and we released him," the guard sneered in response.

"Under whose authority?" Valentius demanded to know, his patience wearing thin with the belligerent attitude of his adversary.

"His own, of course. He is our Great Shah, and we are his trusted servants."

"A few weeks ago, he wasn't anything to you," Valentius reminded him. "Just another prisoner. Jamasp is the Great Shah and you serve him now!"

"Then you are as big a fool as the rest, foreigner! You are nothing. You are the dirt beneath our feet. You don't even belong in this part of the world. We will sweep you away and you will be gone forever. We will wipe you and your kind from the earth. Do you truly think you are strong enough to fight against our rightful King when he returns to us? No one is that strong! Not you, not the Byzantines, no one!"

Valentius plunged his short sword through the guard's chest until it emerged from his back. Placing the sole of his hobnail boot against the man's torso, Valentius used the leverage to pull the weapon free, the blade dripping with blood. "Okay, you forced my hand. I warned you not to. Now are there any among the rest of you that would like to tell me how we are going to be crushed by your superior forces?" he turned on the remaining castle guards, "Or would at least one of you like to live and tell me how Kavad managed to escape from here!"

"What is this?" Patricius asked as Valentius lay the chest in front of him.

Flipping back the lid, the captain exposed the contents of gold and silver coins as well as a sprinkling of jewels. "This is the price that was paid for Kavad's freedom!"

The Commander flew into a rage, kicking the chest over and scattering the treasure across the tiled floor. "Now I am fully aware of the price for stupidity!" he ranted but the meaning of his statement was lost on Valentius. "I want Zutra here when you explain all this to me. I don't think

I could stomach hearing it twice!"

Not long afterwards, Zutra stepped into the room, tip-toeing gingerly though the strewn coins so as not to trip. "Is this some new custom of yours?" he joked seeing the coins strewn across the room. .

"No," Patricius practically bit his head off. "This is the price for my error in judgment. Had I understood your father-in-law better, I would never have relaxed the rules of his house arrest."

"Don't be too hard on yourself," Zutra comforted him. "He deceived my father, whom most considered a very shrewd judge of character and he in turn lost his life over it. You still have yours. But what is this all about?"

"Valentius, you tell our King. I cannot!"

Bowing, Valentius began his retelling of events in Susiana. He brought the story forward to when his men had confronted the castle guards in their barracks. "And then one finally started to sing like a bird," he described.

"I would guess so," Zutra commented. "After seeing five of his colleagues gutted for not cooperating, I would think he would have become very compliant."

"I was only surprised that after he told us everything that they had not fled the city with their ill gotten gains. It was a week already since the visit from Reb Hanina and his associates and the guards were still lodged at the castle."

"Not too surprising," Zutra analyzed the situation. "They never dreamed that anyone else would be coming to the castle to check on their prisoner, at least not for the foreseeable future. They would have kept up their charade of guarding Kavad until such time that they weren't able to hide it any longer, drawing on their wages for the duration. Greed rules men, not logic!"

"Apparently when they saw the gold and jewels that Reb Hanina had brought with him," Valentius continued his story, "they still went to Kavad and asked what they should do?"

"In other words," Patricius interjected, 'They wanted to be reassured that he wouldn't kill them as soon as he returned with an army! Even greedy men want to stay alive long enough to enjoy their ill-gotten rewards. Had they been smart, they should have killed Hanina and his allies, taken the money, and kept Kavad imprisoned. No one would have been the wiser."

"None of these guards were what I would describe as intelligent. They were barely capable of putting up any resistance," Valentius added.

"I hope you taught them what we do to traitors?" Patricius checked to see that his captain had left no loose ends.

"After we learned what we needed, they were of no use to us," he confirmed. "I only promised they'd live if they fully cooperated. That was not forthcoming, so they all paid the price. At least we have their fee as consolation."

"Take some of it and distribute it to your men," Patricius advised. "Let them know that they did a good job!"

"And where are the traitors from my community?" Zutra inquired, still calm despite the obvious concern showing on the face of his Vizier.

"From what I understand, the Jewish leaders went with Kavad to seek out the White Huns."

"At least they were smart enough not to return here. I should have had Hanina executed for the murder of my father a long time ago! So you see, this is entirely my fault."

"It wouldn't have been necessary had I not been negligent in my tasks and reduced the guards posted to watch him," the Vizier apologized, searching for Zutra's forgiveness.

"You are not at fault here," Zutra reemphasized. "I've already told you that. I have been the foolhardy one, allowing my wife to exploit my benevolence for the sake of her father. Had I not been weak of mind, she never would have had that power over me."

"I just wonder where Reb Hanina managed to get all the money and jewels?" the vizier speculated.

"Another unfortunate display of my foolhardiness; the treasure was mine or I should at least say from my family's estate. Reb Hanina and his cronies were not the only things that went missing at the time. I should have mentioned it to you. Together we may have figured out what they were up to." Zutra shook his head in regret.

Patricius quickly changed the topic, not wishing to discuss the Lady Avital and her deceptions any further. "An interesting alliance, don't you think?" he proffered the question to the young king. "I am stunned by the possibilities. To seek aid from your sworn enemy is the sign of a desperate man."

"Certainly not an alliance made in heaven. Kavad has been fighting the Ephthalites for years but he would not have gone unless he thought he had something to offer. He will have to crawl on all fours if he is to gain their favor and obviously offer them more than they could have ever gained through continued war. "

"To get back his kingdom, he'll drink their piss if he has to," the Vizier stated sarcastically. "We must not take the threat lightly. We have not heard the last of Kavad!"

"We have time," Zutra sounded encouraged. "It is not as if we are without allies either. I think we must start with a war council in Ctesiphon. It is imperative that Jamasp take control of the situation before it can no longer be contained."

"My sentiments exactly," Patricius agreed. "Our best defense is to go on the attack. Now we just have to convince our own King of Kings of it. I fear he is not up to the task."

"It may prove even harder than you think," Zutra's lips smacked with disgust.

Chapter Twenty-Three

Hastings: Present

Pearce was busy mixing himself another cup of coffee and forgetting as usual to offer me one. With the cup precariously balanced in one hand, he waltzed about the room, searching for his next question. He spun on his heels to face me.

"Are you suggesting that Avital knew all along what her father's intentions were?"

"Why presume that they were her father's intentions?"

"You think she masterminded the whole thing?" Pearce asked finding it hard to believe that she was capable of doing so on her own.

"Women have been some of the most dangerous political manipulators throughout history. Remember Cleopatra, Lecretia Borgia, Mata Hari? So don't discount her."

"What could she possibly gain?"

"Think about it. Revenge could be a starting point. She's the second wife of a satrap prince ruling a city kingdom. A life that's practically non-existent for a woman that wants to be a major entity and player. The odds were pretty good that her father would weasel himself into Kavad's favor and at least become an advisor if the Shah should be restored to power. She'd obviously be a widow if that came to pass and that would make her a very eligible woman in the eyes of the Empire. Daughter of a confidant to the King of Kings, family sitting on a fortune as a result of Kavad's generosity for their liberating him, not to mention what they would confiscate from Zutra's estate, and she wasn't a bad looker either. There'd be a lineup of kings within the Empire wanting her hand in marriage."

"But she was Jewish? Would her father even permit it?"

"Remember Esther?"

"Oh, yeah. Well, heaven help any of them that married her."

"We may never know who the mastermind behind Kavad's release was but my money is on Avital. She was far more nefarious than we could even imagine."

"You sound pretty sure of that!"

"Let's just say there's a lot in common that I share with Mar Zutra and leave it at that."

Ctesiphon: Winter 498 A.D.

Gathered around the conference table, the arguments and insults seesawed back and forth without any progression on the matter raised by Mar Zutra. The division among the Sassanid noblemen was evident. Even Pashah Gurzam appeared to be questioning his initial commitment to the revolt, disgusted by the lack of support from those that had gained most from the overthrow. With hindsight, many were claiming that they had backed the wrong candidate for the throne. Jamasp was of little value in his own defense, choosing instead to moan over and over again, 'Ahura Mazda help me!' unable to raise his head from the cradle of his palms. Clearly a sign that he was willing to leave his fate to a finicky god whose moods changed as much as the wind he was credited with creating.

Gurzam banged his staff against the flagstone floor repeatedly in order to restore a semblance of order. "Gentlemen, if you please!" he shouted several times until the din faded and he was permitted to speak further. "Clearly these are troubled times, but it does not matter what we did or did not do. Yes, we let Kavad live, but who amongst you was prepared to take his life at the time? As I recall, no one! We must endure the consequence of our failure to act at the time. However, we do have the opportunity to act now! There is no need to wait and see what happens in the future. Our destiny is within our own hands! We are the lords and masters of this Empire and until that authority is wrested from us, we can prepare to safeguard that authority by setting in motion the necessary defenses to do so.

Now more than ever we must stand unified!"

"A brave speech Gurzam," one of the barons challenged but take a good look at our valiant King of Kings. How can we prepare any military stratagem, when our ruler can't even take charge of this meeting?"

All eyes immediately turned to Jamasp who sat curled in his chair unable to focus on anything other than the visions playing within his mind of the eventual return of his brother.

"We all knew when we elevated Prince Jamasp to the position of King of Kings that it was in name only," Gurzam refuted the comment. "Who amongst you truly believed that he would rule with an iron fist? Was there any man that saw a vision of his Highness riding at the forefront of an army, waving a scimitar above his head as he engaged the enemy? We elected him king based on the knowledge that he would never behave like Kavad and mistreat his people. We knew he would leave the administration of his government to us. So why demand he act like a King now?"

There was an outburst of jeering from some of those assembled as they tried to visualize Jamasp at the head of an army. The thought was incomprehensible.

"As I thought," Gurzam acknowledged their amusement. "It was not even considered a factor at the time. Nor should it be considered one now! We have generals to lead our forces. We have strategists to design our plans. And we have people willing to fight to ensure that we do not return to corruption and oppression that an entire nation felt under Shah Kavad."

"Maybe he's learned his lesson?" another of the barons bleated.

"And maybe the leopard has changed its spots," Gurzam ridiculed the inane comment. "When you find your severed head sitting atop a pike, then you will be able to say that Kavad is Kavad and that is the way he will always be. Only a fool would believe otherwise!"

"You have no proof of that!" the same baron began to argue, angered at being called a fool, only to be subsequently enjoined by several others that shared the same opinion.

"Don't I?" Gurzam's face glowered brilliant red as he fended off their accusation. "What do you think he's saying to the Chieftain of the Ephthalites right now? Do you think he's asking for a little cottage by the sea so that he can live out the rest of his days in peace and quiet? Or do you think perhaps the only reason he would even parlay with our fiercest enemy is that he has guaranteed to help them crush us underneath their heels?"

A small skirmish broke out between those noblemen that knew that the picture Gurzam had painted was accurate and those that had thrown their lot in with the dissenting baron.

"This is going nowhere," Patricius leaned over Mar Zutra and whispered into his ear. "The situation is hopeless!"

"Perhaps we should tell them of our plans," Zutra suggested to his vizier. Lord Patricius thought about it momentarily and then shook his head in disagreement. "Until we know where every man's loyalties lie, I think it best we keep that quiet. We will lose any advantage if our plans should fall into Kavad's hands because someone in this room double crosses us."

As Zutra witnessed more and more of the august assembly of nobles join in the scuffle, he appreciated his Vizier's cautious advice. "We'll wait then. I can see you have a valid point."

Banging his staff, Gurzam tried repeatedly to restore order but there was no one willing to deal with the issues through words any longer. Chaos had taken control of the august assembly.

Seeing a large terracotta urn in one corner of the room, Zutra quietly left his seat and walked over to it. Raising it high above his head, he carried it back to where he sat then hurled the massive pot into the centre of the room. It hit the ground with a resounding crack, spraying shards of glazed clay in every direction. The sharp projectiles hit some of the barons as they scattered, causing them momentarily forget their little skirmish and turn to see what had taken place. Most returned to their senses, permitting the mighty crash to overturn their arguments.

"Look at your Empire!" Zutra scolded them. "See it in pieces. Recognize it as the ruination of everything you have dreamed of. Together each piece formed a beautiful urn. Separated they are nothing but useless debris. Who amongst you thinks they will be anything more than broken pieces of pottery should Kavad be restored to power? If you do, then you're a bigger fool than any of us that choose to fight and defend what we have already won! Your lands and your women will be handed over to his new allies. Their nobles will settle in your homes and father children on your wives while you serve as footstools at their table should they decide in their mercy to let you live. Look at the urn and see your future should you decide to bicker and feud amongst yourselves rather than unite. I have no illusions of how I will be received by my enemies should they win. Here I will make my stand and here I will die before I let my people fall under the hand of oppression! If any of you think otherwise, then now is the time for you to flee to the northern lands and beg for forgiveness. Stretch your necks before Kavad and pray he does not loose his sword upon them. If that is how you are so inclined, then leave now and do not waste our precious time any longer!"

Several of the land barons made their way to the exit. No more than a half dozen but they were the most vitriolic of the dissenters in the assembly. "We will not have some lesser king of an empty throne tell us what we can and cannot do," one baron shouted in disgust as he exited.

Patricius rose from his seat and walked over to his cousin who had remained inconspicuous at the room's perimeter since the onset of the meeting. "Hermantius, you know what to do. See to it that none of them returns to their villas," he snarled in a hushed voice.

"Consider it done cousin," Hermantius saluted and wheeled about on his heels, leaving the hall immediately to carry out his pre-assigned task.

Returning to his position beside Zutra, the Commander's face failed to betray any trace of malicious undertakings.

"Is the gardener doing what's necessary?" Zutra asked very casually, unconcerned if any others happened to overhear.

"Yes, I believe the gardens will be free of weeds by the end of the day," Patricius answered in their mutual code.

"Good!" Zutra nodded in satisfaction. "Then now would be a good time to tell everyone that remained of our plans." Rising to his feet, Zutra clapped his hands to draw their attention. "Pashah Gurzam, if I may have the floor once again," he requested.

The Pashah was more than happy to divert the speaker's role to anyone else.

"Of lesser kings, I agree, I cannot claim to be any more than the ruler of Mahoza. Nevertheless, even a lesser king should not be underestimated. For how many lesser kings can claim that they are the son-in-law of the Sin Emperor and therefore able to call on his assistance in time of need? In addition, how many lesser kings can claim that their vizier is also a former Caesar of the Byzantine Empire and therefore capable of summoning their aid in time to do battle with our enemies? Yes, I am a lesser king but what of it? Measure my kingdom not by the size of my throne but by the size of my allies. Then you will have a better understanding of what I can achieve. Plans are already underway to send ambassadors to both empires in pursuit of forces to fight alongside us against the White Huns. Be not mistaken, it will not be your own brethren that you must take arms against should Kavad return but our most hated enemies from the steppes. Furthermore, both Kingdoms to the east and west of us understand that if we should fall then one of them will be next. It will be only a matter of time. The war to come will be a long and bloody one but if we are to survive then it cannot be without the help of such allies. Pray that my men are successful in their missions for they leave on the new moon. Bless them in the name of the Almighty God. Our future is in His hands."

Zutra's closing remarks were met by loud cheers and a round of applause. He had given them the breath of hope that they wished to hear when they first entered the assembly hall. Even Jamasp was revived from his state of lethargy and applauded enthusiastically.

"Well put, my Lord," Gurzam congratulated him. "You have inspired all of us! How soon until your ambassadors to both courts are selected?"

"I would think that both entourages can be assembled and organized within the week. By the start of spring we should have our answers."

"Perhaps I might suggest that we send some of the leading men of our communities along with your envoys, bringing gifts of friendship to both Emperors," Gurzam indicated the need for a contingent of Sassanids to be present and heard.

"I had no intention of excluding your emissaries Pashah," Zutra reassured him. "As long as you can have your men picked and ready at the same time, I see no issues that prevent us from making these official state visits to both capitals."

"I will have everything in order in a matter of days," Gurzam promised. "Better yet, I will provide you with two flagships from the royal navy. They will sail from Meseoe into the Persian Gulf and then around the Indus and Jin mainland. Your envoys will be In Northern Wei within a month and not face any of the dangers of taking the overland routes"

"Most generous of you, Pashah," Zutra thanked him. "If we can expedite their journeys then so much the better."

"You must already know who will lead your missions?"

"As I said, the plan has already been in the working. Patricius will head the entourage to Constantinople, and I will place Valentius in charge of the one to my father-in-law. Both men are familiar with the courts they've being assigned to which will hopefully work in our favor." Valentius with his ability to speak the language and his more polished mannerisms was the better selection over Hermantius though the latter outranked the other and had expressed a desire to see the East. Zutra did not bother to mention that to Gurzam.

"Excellent choices," Gurzam agreed. "I will send Baron Attard with Patricius and I have several in mind for the mission to the Sian but prefer to see which of them agree before I name names."

"Very good," Zutra commented. "By the new moon they will be off then."

"It is agreed," Gurzam confirmed.

Chapter Twenty-Four

Mahoza: Winter 499 A.D.

"What's wrong?" Zutra affectionately patted his wife's protruding belly, which had grown considerably over the last trimester of her pregnancy.

"I'm worried," Princess Ti-Ping bit her bottom lip.

"The baby is fine," he reassured her. "The doctors have said so. You're as healthy as a horse!"

"And eating like one too, is that what you're trying to say?" she pouted, poking him in the side until he had to grab hold of her wrist as his muscles were beginning to hurt.

"No matter how much you eat it never shows. It is all going straight to the baby. If anything, he will be the one built like a horse. You still remain beautiful without even trying." He caressed her face with his free hand, looking deeply into her dark brown eyes as his head lay on the down-filled pillow beside hers. "So tell me what worries you."

"I thought we'd have heard from my father by now."

"It's a long journey. Even by sea we knew it would be months before Valentius would return."

"And not even a word from Patricius either," she moaned.

"Alliances take time," he reassured her.

"Like marriages," she quickly inserted the comment.

"There is nothing wrong with our marriage," his voice became raised and tinged with concern. "I fell in love with you the moment I laid eyes on you and my love has continued to grow stronger with each passing day."

"I know that," she interlocked her fingers with his.

"Then why worry about our marriage?"

"I was not referring to us," she brushed his face softly. "You have two wives, but you don't seem to remember that. You have only lain with me since Avital conceived."

"I am where I want to be," he sounded wounded. "Since when does one woman actually wish for their man to lie with another woman? I'm confused."

"A woman abandoned can be a very dangerous person. You should reconsider. I can accept you in her bed if I know it is to our benefit!"

"Is there something you are aware of that I'm not? She has already proven to be a very dangerous adversary."

"No, it is nothing new that I know of," the princess shook her head.

"Then what? Has she expressed her displeasure to you," Zutra demanded to know. 'Has she threatened you? I will make her pay dearly if she has!"

"Quite the opposite," Ti-Ping continued to stroke his face. "She has said nothing and has done nothing to offend me. That is not a good sign. Silence only confirms a woman is having malevolent thoughts. Trust me. A woman knows this about another woman."

Wrapping his arms around his beautiful wife, he pulled her close to his body, or as close as her swollen abdomen would permit him. "It really doesn't matter. She has already done her damage. What more can she possibly do?"

"Again, you underestimate the power of a woman, my love."

"She thinks herself too clever to be caught. No one has come out and said it but I've known Avital for too long and too well not to see her hand behind the escape of the Shah and departure of her father."

"I cannot understand why she would do such a thing?" Ti-Ping questioned his instincts, not seeing any advantage to her companion wife should Kavad be successful in regaining power.

"That is because you are too logical in your thinking. You look for purpose and advantage behind every act. Why does Avital do anything?" Zutra riddled back. "Because she can! She is a primal force of nature. Is that not what you have taught me about the Yin and the Yang from your world? That for everything that is positive there must be a negative. It is the balance of life you said. One cannot exist without the other."

"You consider her the balance of your existence?" the princess questioned trying to make sense of Zutra's explanation.

"No. I believe she may be the balance to your existence," he laughed loudly. "But more like the bane of my existence. Maybe that's why I desired her all those years, because I saw her as a force of nature that needed to be tamed."

"And can you tame the wind?" his wife drew the comparison of futility.

Moved by her compassionate expression, Zutra kissed her tenderly on her full red lips "Only God can control the forces of nature, but I think even He would have difficulty controlling this one! She would even drive God to His wit's end."

"What will you do with her?"

"Do? Nothing of course. One cannot break Avital like a horse. The more you pull in one direction, the harder she will pull in the other. I will not break her but instead show her what her true position is in life."

"And what do you have in mind husband?" Ti-Ping was not willing to let him retain any secrets when it came to matters of his marriages. She had learned too well in her father's household that the tumult of one relationship always impacted negatively on the others.

"When she gives birth to the child, he will be removed from her and raised by the same wet nurses that will raise our son. She will not be allowed to influence this child any more than she did my father's."

"Are you making all the decisions now, even the ones for me?" She gave Zutra a short jab to his side once more to emphasize her displeasure.

"What? What did I say now?"

"Of course you wouldn't understand you're a king. You're a man. What would you understand of a woman's desire to suckle her own child?"

Zutra was at a loss for words. The use of wet nurses by his family went as far back as anyone could recall. It was more a tradition than a practicality, permitting the wife of the Exilarch to move back into the social arena as soon as possible following birth. "I am certain that will be fine."

"Of course it will be fine," Ti-Ping pushed her turgid nipples hard into his chest as if they were two knives digging into his flesh. "Do you think that these are only for your own pleasure?"

Gazing down upon the darkened and enlarged areolas, Zutra found them erotically attractive, smacking his lips to emphasize his arousal.

"Behave yourself, husband," she pushed him away in mock anger. "There will be none for you with two tiny mouths to feed!"

"What? Are you suggesting you'd take Avital's child as your own?" Zutra sounded surprised.

"No. I am willing to accept a baby of yours as my own. Your child is my child. Any child royal by birth should not be abandoned to be raised by servants. Nor should they obtain their nourishment from the milk of strangers. They need to learn how to behave from the first moment of life, not when they are at age that suits your convenience. And the nourishment offered by a princess is far more blessed than one living from the scraps of your kitchen."

Mar Zutra picked up immediately on his wife's reference to how he had cared for his half-brother Hanai thus far. At five years of age, Hanai had been raised in virtual isolation, away from his mother and barely a visit from his much older brother. There were no other children in the palace his own age to play with, so although Zutra provided him with the finest tutors and caregivers whose entire purpose was to play and amuse, for all intents and purpose, Hanai was nothing more than a prisoner in his brother's home.

"What would you have me do," Zutra petitioned her.

"Do you want me to tell you in order to do what is right or are you merely wishing for me to say what it is on my mind so that you can then forget it and everything moves on as if it was never mentioned?"

Rolling his fingers across her pale shoulder, she reveled in the sensation that his fingertips produced as they stimulated the bundles of nerve endings under the skin. "You have been paying attention to my techniques," she praised him.

"I only assumed that if they worked on me, they must also work for you."

"It is very pleasant, but you cannot avoid the question this way. You have not answered me. I am not to be so easily dismissed," she purred coyly.

Zutra smiled in response to her clever perception. "I was not avoiding you in the least. In fact, I was giving you my answer. You are too beautiful for me to ever dismiss your advice so casually. Every word from your lips drips like honey. I savor it."

"My husband has become a poet," she tittered. "A sly and clever poet."

"And my wife has become a sage," he responded in kind. "I will see to it that I spend more time with Hanai. I will try to be the older and wiser brother that he needs so badly."

"Do it for both of you," she counseled. "You need him almost as much as he needs you."

"How did one so beautiful become so wise?" he sighed.

Gazing downwards towards his hips she laughed delightfully. "Put that away husband, there is nothing you can do with it for now!"

"I have a few mystical techniques of my own," he growled and winked slyly.

"You are insatiable," she blushed.

"Only because you are too beautiful for words. It's entirely your fault!" He placed his hand behind her hips and let their bodies softly collide.

Disembarking, Valentius inhaled the heady land-based breeze laden with the heavy scent of lotus blossoms. It had been so long since he had enjoyed that simple springtime pleasure of his youth. After so many years, he had almost forgotten the unequivocal beauty of his homeland. He had been following the Commander on one expedition after another, with little attention to his own wants and desires. This diplomatic mission provided him with a rare opportunity to recall what had been sacrificed for so many years.

The two Persian galleys found themselves escorted by a convoy of the Emperor's flotilla the moment they rounded the coast off the Southern Chi but their deep hulls prevented them from sailing up river unlike the more shallow keeled junks. The Han admiral offered to take them up river on his boats but Valentius declined, choosing instead to make the long march so as to engage the people en route. From the port city to the new capital at Luoyang would take several hours but Valentius and his men didn't mind. It felt good to have solid ground beneath their feet. As anticipated, throngs of people gathered by the roadside, lining it several rows deep in order to greet the strangers as they traversed the main highway. Some of them even remembered Valentius and his men from years long ago when they lived amongst them, but the members of the envoy sent by Gurzam piqued their curiosity the most. With their tightly curled beards and long hair braided in ringlets and intertwined with colored beads and painted tubules, the people couldn't help but stare and point at the fascinating men with their intriguing adornments.

As soon as his men passed through the perimeter gates of the palace, Valentius felt the uneasiness that hung heavily over the complex of ceramic bamboo peaked green and red tiled buildings. From the time they began the march, not a single word had been exchanged with the Chinese escort during the sojourn to the city. The captain had been trained too well by Patricius not to rely on his instincts over substance. This particular silence was enough to suggest that all was not right within the kingdom. Raised in the ways of the court he knew that questioning any of his escort would be pointless. The Han had a code of silence when it came to strangers, and he had determined from their attitude that officially he was no longer considered to be one of them.

The entourage was herded directly to the Hall of Justice, the customary room in which one would seek an audience with the Emperor. Like most eastern palaces, the Emperor's residence in Luoyang was no different in its construction. A series of buildings, each with a distinct purpose laid in a spoked pattern radiating from the central hub where the Emperor's residence was located. The residence was often the simplest of structures, consisting of separate sleeping chambers for both the Emperor and the Empress. The lesser wives would reside in a communal harem that was located on the farthest side of the building from the Emperor's bedroom. The other buildings, numbering around thirty, were far more elaborate and represented a variety of architectural styles from around the orient. Each building had a specific governmental or religious purpose so that at no time could matters pertaining to one temple's function be dealt with in another. To the western mind the process of rotating from building to building in order to deal with matters of state often seemed incredulous, but to the Sin, it hard a far greater significance. It was a representation of the universal order, everything in its time and everything in its proper place. To do otherwise would upset the structure of the universe.

Valentius ordered the men in his company to kneel before the empty throne on both knees and keep their heads bowed with their foreheads touching the tiled floor until such time that they were instructed to rise. At all times they were to remain motionless and silent unless spoken to. To do otherwise would be considered an insult to the Emperor. The Sassanids at first objected to the humbling position, which they associated with the posture of slaves but quickly agreed once Valentius made them aware that the punishment for an insult to the Emperor was death. Following that comment, they quickly assumed the position.

With foreheads to the ground, they could not see but only hear the ringing of tiny bells approaching from the hallway as the Emperor entered the room accompanied by his entourage of advisors. He sat himself confidently upon his jade encrusted throne. Valentius kept his head down waiting patiently until the chief minister instructed them to rise in the Han tongue, saying, "To our respected guests from Persia and the welcome return of our Roman son and his men, in the name of the Emperor Hsuan Wu Ti, we welcome you."

Valentius almost lost his balance as he tried to stand, the shock of the announcement catching him totally unawares. He needed a moment to catch his breath and then relayed the instruction to the Sassanid ambassadors to stand up but to remain silent. The party rose to their feet and stood motionless while Valentius returned the salutation in the High Chinese language. "I, Valentius son of Valens pay homage to the new Emperor. On behalf of my men, I swear allegiance to Hsuan Wu Ti, son of Hsiang Wen Ti. As we have served his father so shall we serve our new liege. May his ancestors smile warmly upon him."

"Your warm wishes are greatly appreciated, Valentius," the Emperor spoke directly to the Captain, a privilege that few men were afforded. "I guess it must be somewhat of a surprise old friend to see me sitting here." The expression of familiarity brought about a scornful look from the chief minister, which did not go unnoticed by the Emperor. "Pay him no attention, Valentius; he is cemented to the old ways. We are living in troubled times when an old and friendly face is a joy to behold. If my familiarity is to be considered contemptible, then so be it. I cannot afford to lose any friends at this critical time." The Emperor made a wry face at his minister that did not go unnoticed.

"What has happened here, your highness?" Valentius was still confused by the ascension of his boyhood companion to the throne.

"My father was unwell, which only made his lesser wives more eager to see him pass on into the realm of my ancestors so that their sons could vie for the jade throne. His illness was probably not fatal but when he saw his sons dividing the Empire into slices and warring against each other, destroying everything he had spent his life building I believe his heart just gave out. He lost the will to live."

"Why didn't he just put an end to their bickering? He could have done it with a single command. They would have been routed in a matter of days."

"And then what, my friend? Was he to watch his sons be slain for their treason? You knew my father better than that! He chose to die rather than witness the failure of his children. He considered their fracturing to be his own failure. He dreamt of creating a dynasty and instead it became his nightmare."

"And so it fell to you to end the fighting," Valentius surmised.

"If only it was that easy," the Emperor sighed.

At the sound of Hsuan's exasperation, his chief minister cleared his throat in admonition.

"What old man? Should I hide the truth from my oldest friend who has returned in my time of need? There are powers at work here that you are not appreciating! For Valentius to return at this precise moment is the will of fate and fortune."

The minister turned his head away indignantly without uttering a word. Unlike his father, the son did not adhere as stringently to the old ways. Valentius easily discerned from the minister's look of disdain that the old man was not pleased that he had returned, probably blaming the presence of foreigners within the Sin Empire for causing their problems in the first place. The old ways still feared the outside world.

"Perhaps we should speak in Xianbei," Valentius suggested knowing that the minister was not one of the tribe, and therefore unlikely to speak their boyhood language.

"No," the young Emperor was emphatic. "The Xianbei are history! My father insisted that if we were to unite all the Sian people then we are to speak one language and that is Han. The only reason we have a rebellion now is that there are those that still insist that we are Tuoba and not true Chinese. To speak our old language would only confirm their misguided beliefs that we are separate peoples."

"Apologies, my Emperor. I have been shown to be in error, your Highness," Valentius deferred as he lowered his head and bowed apologetically.

"The only reason my half-brothers have been successful in their insurrections is because they have played upon the prejudices of the people, insisting that I am still more Xianbei than Chinese. Furthermore, they insist that the religion of Buddha that we have instituted within the empire is evil and designed to steal the free will of the people. How can the teachings of Buddha ever be considered evil? Yet they spread these lies and they gain adherents."

"The people are gullible, Your Highness. That is the way it has always been. The bigger the lie, the more believable it becomes!"

"My ministers say the same thing," the Emperor laughed.

"How bad is it your Highness?"

"It's bad old friend. Where once there was only Northern Wei, now I must contend with an Eastern and Western Wei as well. Another one of my brothers attempts to unite the tribes in Southern Chi in a revolt and make that province a kingdom of its own. Everywhere I look I have a half-brother proclaiming himself as Emperor of the Sian."

"And obviously there is some bone of contention here regarding myself, if I read your minister correctly."

"Don't mind him," Emperor Hsuan dismissed Valentius concern as if his minister didn't even exist. "Your return had been foretold to me in a prophecy. Many of my ministers are still Confucian though they outwardly pretend to be Buddhist when they are around me. Such are the lies of politics," the young Emperor flashed a look of derision specifically at those ministers that he knew only maintained a pretense of being Buddhist. "They refuse to believe in such things as prophecies since they consider them to be illogical. It was said that my throne would only be preserved when the eagle came and devoured the lesser dragons. I never doubted the truth of the soothsayer. As soon as I had word that your ship had rounded the peninsula, I knew that the prophecy is now being fulfilled. One of my scouting boats returned to say that they saw your eagle insignia standing proudly at the bow. Jian-jou here still refuses to believe it though it is as plain as the nose on his face."

"Your Highness, I did not come here to fight in your wars. Your sister's husband has sent me and these other men here to seek your aid in a battle of their own."

Folding his hands together, the Emperor Hsuan digested what Valentius had to say, the look on his face betraying little emotion. "How fares my sister?"

"She is well, your Highness. In fact, she is with child."

"How wonderful! Is she happy?"

"Yes, I believe she is."

"Then she is not desperate, whereas I am. You are still a citizen of this land, old friend. Must I remind you that you have just sworn your allegiance to my throne and therefore I am your Emperor, to command you as I see fit. I have no men that I can spare at this time to send to the aid of my brother-in-law. Suppress these revolts for me quickly and then the availability of my men is without question."

"But your Highness, we could be talking years."

"I would suggest you start immediately then. You and your Commander were victorious time and time again for my father because your ways of warfare are different from ours. Command the men as you did before, and we should be talking months instead of years. Then I will give you an army to take west with you but not before then."

All of Valentius's men that were overhearing the conversation understood that they would not be returning to Ctesiphon any time shortly. None were actually too upset by the news. After all, this was their home, the land where they had fathered children by their wives and girlfriends, and they had been away far too long. They followed Patricius out of loyalty, but Northern Wei was where their hearts resided. As yet, the Sassanid ambassadors were not aware of their mission's failure. Within a few days, it became quite evident to them, as they were loaded back on to their vessels, returning without the hoped for legions of soldiers, provided with several chests of gifts to be presented to the Emperor's sister and her husband upon their safe return. Along with the gifts, they also carried an official letter from the Emperor explaining why Valentius and his men had not made the return voyage with them. The new Emperor's decision had been final.

Propped on her elbows, Ariadne made certain that their points were pressing forcibly against Patricius's chiseled abdominal muscles.

"That hurts," the Commander protested.

"As well it should," she scolded. "How could you have been so foolish to have allowed your cock to do all your thinking? I had always considered you to be a little smarter than other men," she continued to berate him.

"It wasn't like that at all Dinah," he defended himself against her diatribe.

"Tell me how it is different then," she challenged. "You stuck your little member where it didn't belong and because of that, your most lethal enemy is on the loose and preparing to take back his throne. Tell me where I'm mistaken!"

Patricius found that not only his argument had lost any support but also his manhood had gone completely flaccid as it fell limply from between Ariadne's hips.

"Should I remind you that the only reason you are even in my chambers is that I said if you return to me as the most powerful man in your world then there would be a place for you within mine if only for a fleeting moment."

"There was no way that I could have known that the trap she had set for me was in any way linked to freeing Kavad from his prison!" he still protested his innocence.

"And that is why you're in the predicament you find yourself because you should have known!" Rolling herself off his chest, on to the bed and then over the side and on to the floor, she felt around on the ground until she located her discarded robes which she then immediately slid over her head, tying the belt snugly around her waist. She took a long look at the naked body of her lover and admired how even three decades later it was still firm and well-muscled, despite the lines of scars crisscrossing in every direction, just as she had remembered it. She shook her head and sighed, "I had been looking forward to the moment that we'd lay together and now all I have is a bitter aftertaste. The dream has soured for me, Paddy."

"Don't say that Dinah. Come back into the bed and lie with me." He patted the mattress hoping to entice her back into his arms.

"Paddy what have you done," her voice was heavy with tears that she refused to shed. "You've committed adultery with your King's wife, you've released a nightmare of warfare upon yourself and your allies, and now you've come to me hoping that I can resolve it all for you with but a magic wave of my hand. There is no simple spell in my arsenal to achieve what you wish for!"

"You have already granted me one wish by being here with me," he quipped trying to lighten the heavy atmosphere. "You cannot deny that there is still magic there."

"Do not flatter yourself," she pricked his confidence. "I never claimed to be a nun and Anastasius does not insist that I behave like one either. However, he will not tolerate my being involved with anyone. You are nothing more than a recaptured memory. Cherish our coupling for what it was but do not try to make anything more of it, or as I warned you upon your last visit, not even I would have the power to save you."

"You say that but when your chest was up against mine, I felt the trembling of your heart, and I know it is not true. You desired our union as much as I did!"

"Have you not done enough damage fornicating with one King's wife to last you a lifetime? Don't make your situation worse than it already is!" she chastised him, absolutely furious that he had apparently learned nothing from his previous experience.

"This is different," he argued. "We are different!"

"Paddy, Paddy," she sounded frustrated. "Impetuous as always. How is it you can be such a brilliant tactician yet lack the common sense that is necessary to lead a people in peace time? If I didn't know better, I'd swear you wanted to let Kavad escape just so that you'd have another war to fight. The calm only makes you restless; it causes the flame within you to flicker and die out."

"And that is my point," he reaffirmed his position. "With your aid we can destroy our enemies; both Kavad and the White Huns that are his allies. At some point, in the near future both you and I know the Huns will launch an attack into the heart of Byzantium. Now is our opportunity to force them into combat before they're ready. The advantage will be ours."

"Only if I can persuade the Emperor," she reminded him. "But you're lucky in that regard. I'm still willing to lie on your behalf."

"See, you still love me," he grinned openly.

"Only because you're such a damn fool," she reiterated. "And don't you forget that. I've backed you since you first returned to this court and I'm not about to make myself look foolish for having done so! Nevertheless, fortune still smiles upon you. Our spies have informed us that Kavad has become married to a niece of the Hun chieftain. It makes it more likely that his release was all part of an Ephthalite strategy to prepare for war. This way we can claim your only incompetence besides letting Kavad live, was letting Hun spies deep within your lands so they were able to conduct their espionage and liberate him. Anastasius may forgive you for that. He's experienced the same within our own borders, so he knows keeping the Huns out is not an easy task. If you're lucky, he won't condemn you for it."

"But still, you'd be able to influence him," Patricius suggested.

"My empowerment over the Emperor only goes so far. We are now talking military matters and the generals do not appreciate my interference in an arena they consider their domain. So for me to even suggest that we should preempt an attack by the Huns by invading them first, will require your providing me with sufficient reasons to do so."

"That will not be difficult to do," he reassured her. "I know their initial movements will be against the Sassanid territories in the north, so that means Armenia will provide them with the first impasse along the invasion route. As I recall, Armenia is already a bone of contention between your empire and that of Jamasp so I don't believe your generals would be pleased to see a third kingdom laying claim to it."

"You have to do better than that." Ariadne instructed. "Armenia has always been a bone of contention. Losing it does not immediately threaten

Byzantium."

"Then let them chew on this for a while. Originally, it had been our intention to sail across to Constantinople through the Black Sea. We would have left from the Port of Batumi. We had to change our plans when we heard that it had fallen to loyal followers of Kavad and is now occupied by a cohort of Huns. Now why would you think the Huns would want a port town?"

The revelation was quite obvious and equally distressing to the Empress. She fingered her lower lip nervously. "Certainly not to attack Ctesiphon," she analyzed. "They're thinking of launching an attack by sea on Constantinople."

"That's what I would surmise," Patricius agreed completely with her assessment. "My lands are all landlocked. Unless they find a way to sail ships across the sand, they'll be useless in a battle against us. So do you think Anastasius will be concerned now?"

"How long do you think it would take the Huns to master the skills of sailing?"

"They're quite a resourceful people," the Commander complimented them. "After all, who ever thought a horde of nomads would be able to challenge our civilizations for mastery of the world. I'd say about a year until they have their own flotilla on the sea."

"Then we must be ready to attack them within months," she calculated. "You wouldn't have already formulated the plans to do so?"

Patricius brayed, "You know me too well Dinah. I have it all worked out. We can trap them between the Black and the Caspian Seas with a three-prong attack. We will cut off all routes of escape. In less than a year we can wipe them out completely."

"Give me all the details," she instructed.

"If I was in command of your troops, I would transport at least thirty thousand men across the Black Sea; one half to Odessa, the other half to Anapa. In the meantime, I'll advance from the south and seize Major and Lesser Armenia. Just in case we run into difficulty, you'll send another thirty thousand Byzantines across the Tarsus ranges and back us up by providing a secondary line in the south."

"But all they'll do is withdraw to the north," Ariadne picked at the plan.

"That's where we have the real surprise waiting for them. We've also sent emissaries to the Princess Ti-Ping's father. He'll be just as eager to rid himself of the Huns. Valentius will be in command. His instructions are to bring them across the steppes and attack from the north. Meanwhile your troops stationed at Anapa will start sweeping east taking out any resistance they encounter. Marching at double time, the forces from Odessa should be able to unite with the Anapa forces at about the same time Valentius comes sweeping down from the north shore through the Caspian depression. We won't let a single enemy unit escape intact."

"It sounds like an excellent strategy. I can't wait to see the war council's faces when I tell them."

"I thought you said the generals won't listen to you."

"They will when they realize I'm the only one with all the information and a suitable plan to counteract the enemy. They'll claim it as their own of course but I will never let them forget who gave it to them."

"An enviable position," Patricius congratulated her political astuteness.

"Hopefully there's a lesson here for you in the future. Always be on top, not on the bottom."

Patricius picked up immediately on her sexual nuance.

"Now get dressed before someone sees you lying there like that and links my presence in your chamber and your being naked with something a little more than a strategy session."

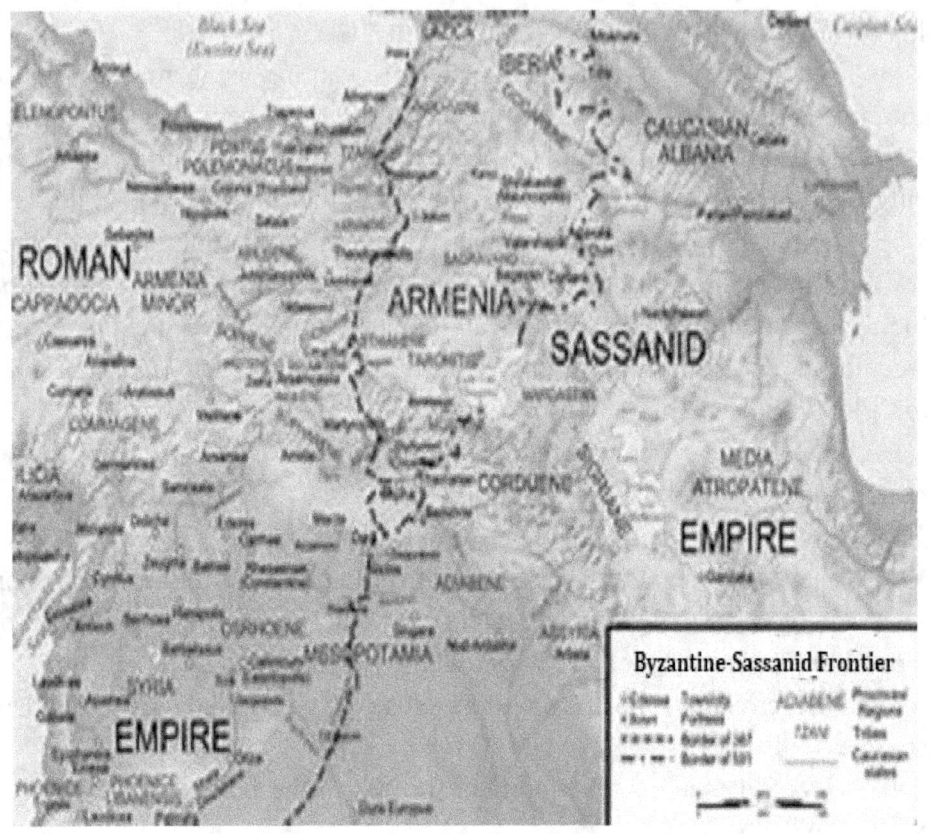

Division of the Empires

Chapter Twenty-Five

Mahoza: Spring 500 A.D.

The mop-haired, bright-eyed boy sat nervously on his half-brother's lap, fidgeting restlessly under the scrutiny of the mysterious stranger, who paced back and forth across the room. This time, it was not a joyous occasion, which brought Gurzam to the palace but quite the contrary. Events of the past week had proven a traumatic experience for all, but for none more so, than the Pashah who found himself besieged by angry nobles that were convinced the return of their colleagues from the Sin Empire, without Valentius and his men was another ill omen. Some already spoke openly of throwing themselves at the mercy of Kavad and his Ephthalite allies. At the moment it was only hollow and empty talk, all of them knowing that to do so would only be met by the cutting edge of a sword as Kavad was not one to forgive, nor were his new wife's relatives interested in preserving the old order of barons. Kavad had made it crystal clear that he promised his new masters that he would replace all of his former barons, seizing their possessions and awarding them to Hun replacements. As long as the nobles were fully aware of that fact, they still remained firm adherents to Gurzam's strategy but they were not pleased with the current situation.

"And why is this boy here," Gurzam grumbled.

"It is time that young Mar Hanai starts taking an interest in the affairs of state."

"Since when have you had an interest in your father's son?"

Zutra ignored the disdain that emanated from the Pashah. "Since my wife pointed out to me that I have been neglectful in my duties. As you said, he is my father's son and that makes him next in line to my throne."

"Not any longer," Gurzam was quick to correct him. "You now have two newborn sons. They will inherit your kingdom."

"My sons are less than two months old. With war looming, I'm preparing for the short term in case there is need for an heir to take my position before my own son's are old enough to inherit."

"What are you indicating?" Gurzam became infuriated by the intimation. "If you begin thinking that way, then you're as bad as those weak-kneed barons I have to deal with daily. It means you have already accepted defeat!"

"I am only being practical," Zutra assured him. "I am thinking only of who should rule in my stead should I fall in battle. Not the end of my kingdom but instead it's insurance for the future."

"Battle? What battle are you talking about?" Gurzam sounded petrified by Mar Zutra's latest comments.

"The coming battle," the Exilarch reconfirmed. "I intend to be at the forefront of my men."

"Are you mad? What do you know of warfare?" the Pashah questioned in a semi-mocking tone. "Your place is on your throne and safe in your city!"

"I know this much; if you want men to fight for you then you better be willing to fight for them as well. And what I don't know about combat, I'm certain that Patricius can teach me."

"Still, what is the boy, four years?"

"Five," Hanai snapped back immediately.

"Five then," Gurzam conceded. "Still too young to rule."

"Let's not place me in the grave so quickly," Zutra jested. "From what I understand, it will be several months before we march north, and even then, it will be many more months before we enjoin the enemy in any battles of significance. I would think that I'll be around for quite a while longer."

The Pashah nodded his head agreeing in part to the speculation. "It definitely won't be a quick war. Without the advantage of the Sin forces, I suspect we'll be engaged in a stalemate for quite some time. Our forces will be too evenly matched and stretched over too many front lines. You should think about returning as soon as the attrition starts."

"Any delay will give us more time until the new Emperor Hsuan, will be able to send us reinforcements."

"I am not one to think in definite terms. Your brother-in-law is an unknown entity to me. It appears he has far more concerns than our welfare."

"Which is why you worry too much," Zutra advised. "If you doubt from the onset, then you will fail."

"I had no doubts when we had Kavad as our prisoner. I would have had even less doubts if we had killed him when we had the opportunity."

"It did not happen that way. We have to live with the consequences."

"Consequences brought about by his grandfather!" Gurzam pointed an accusatory finger at the boy.

"An error in judgment, nothing more." Zutra was not willing to discuss the matter further.

"No, actually at least two errors in judgment; yours for not dealing with the murderer of your father when you had the opportunity and your vizier's for deliberately providing the same murderer with the opportunity to escape."

"There was a lapse in the guard. The numbers had been reduced and assigned elsewhere."

"Believe what you wish, but I have my own reports," the Pashah challenged. "If by reduced you mean that the entire contingent of guards was pulled from that sector of your city for over an hour, then you'd be right. Why would you suspect such a thing should happen?"

Zutra's body stiffened upon hearing Gurzam's words. He silently lowered the boy from his lap and walked over to one of the windows in the room, staring blankly towards the horizon.

"You heard me?" Gurzam questioned awaiting a response.

Wheeling about on his heels the expression in his dark eyes was ferocious as they bore down upon the governor. "Yes, I heard you!" he snarled angrily. "There is no disloyalty in my house if that is what you are inferring. If the guards were pulled on purpose, then it was not done with the knowledge that Kavad would be freed, that I can assure you. There was no betrayal by my men!"

"Suit yourself," Gurzam interlocked his fingers then bowed slightly. "I can only inform you of what my own spies relay to me. This was no accident."

"Go Gurzam! I will speak to you later when I have discovered the truth!" he dismissed the Pashah unceremoniously.

Bowing at the waist, the governor shuffled two strides backward, then turned and left the room.

"Run along to your quarters, Hanai. There is someone I have to see." The boy hurriedly did as he was told.

Racing through the palace corridors, the Exilarch flew toward the women's quarters where his second wife resided. Passing through the double doors, he screamed out her name. "Avital! Avital come to me immediately!"

Her voice sailed back from one of the many rooms that broke off from the central chamber. "Am I a dog that I am to come running when my master calls?"

"You are less than a dog," he bellowed in rage. "Not even a dog would betray its master no matter how cruel he believed his master to be."

Without a trace of fear, the Lady Avital emerged from the room where she had been resting, ordering her attendants to remain behind the locked door. "Betrayal! Who speaks of betrayal? Oh, the man that has taken my second child from me," she ridiculed him with her accusation.

"I will leave you with nothing! Nothing, do you understand me?"

"You have given me nothing," she screamed back. "There is nothing left for you to take from me." She weaved in and out, circling him continuously in a challenging dance that infuriated him further.

"Even nothing is too much for someone like you! You are only an empty vessel to carry my seed. A stew pot for the flesh! An animal to be bred no different than a prize cow." The words spat from his lips with venomous fury as he gesticulated angrily with his hands.

"If you were a real man you wouldn't need to fill the pot so many times before it takes," she ridiculed him further. "I've had much better fill my womb."

"Of that I have no doubts," he snarled in derision. "I know you were behind the release of Kavad. How did you get Patricius to agree to your scheming! What did you do to him?"

"He betrayed you!" she screeched like a banshee. "He raped me and then he helped let my father escape." Her laugh bordered on insanity.

"After he spread me like a common tavern wench, he was compelled to do anything I asked of him. He betrayed you, cuckolded you, and now I'll see that the whole world knows it! But best of all he was more man than you could ever be. I loved riding his cock! Do you hear me? His big, throbbing, Scythian cock!"

"Whore!" Zutra ranted. "I will have you put to death for adultery. I will see you dead before you sully the name of such a man who is your better in every way. You will ride the end of a sword! Make love to that!"

It was not the response she had anticipated, this sudden twist in her own fate, as a result of her revelation caused a momentary setback. She had not even considered that her husband would actually accuse her of adultery and side with his vizier. So certain was she that he would be enraged by the accusation of rape and would immediately execute Patricius, she had not thought of any other possible course of action nor contingency should the tables turn against her. From the wild look in his eyes, she knew he meant every word he spat at her. She had to think quickly before it was too late. "My uncle was there too," she tried a reasoning tactic. "He will confirm that I was raped."

"Then I'll have him executed as well for being a willing participant. I will wipe your entire family from existence. They will all die for your sins."

"You're an animal," she screamed, realizing that there'd be no persuading him otherwise. "No wonder the only thing that could love you is some pale skinned half-human creature."

Of all the insults, none of them stung as deeply as her insult of Ti-Ping. Losing any reservation, he may still have held, his right arm swung in a full arc but catching her with only a glancing blow as she moved inward that very instant in her encircling dance. It had not connected solidly but it was enough to knock her backward several steps until she collapsed back onto her haunches.

Launching herself like a panther, she practically leapt the length of the room her nails extruded like eagle's talons ready to rake across the face of her prey. Thrashing like a wild beast, her arms flailed in front of his face as Avital clawed against the flesh of his arms, ferociously trying to break through his defenses. Instinctively, Zutra seized her by the wrists and then turning in a full arc flung her hard against the wall. Once again, as if a cat, she twisted in mid air, her feet delicately touching the stone walls before she sprung at him again. This time she had moved so quickly that he couldn't block the savage attack and her nails struck home. He felt the blood ooze down the side of his cheek from four tiny rivulets that spurted. Standing back, she licked the blood from her fingernails, laughing as she did so.

"Hardly a man and your blood tastes weak as well," she mocked, preparing to strike again.

"Lying bitch," he roared, rushing to the attack rather than waiting to defend. He lunged in an attempt to grab her by the neck but moving faster than he thought her able, she bent under his grasping hand so that he caught the collar of her robe instead. The momentum of his attack carried him over her back so that he somersaulted in the air landing hard against the floor. Still holding on to the collar of her dress, it tore down the seams so that it hung limply from her waist, exposing the upper half of her torso. She kicked repeatedly at his arm while he lay on the ground, trying to free the piece of the robe he still clutched so that she could break free. Though his arm took the brunt of the beating, he refused to release his grip, instead rolling on to his chest where he was in position to catch her foot with his other hand as she kicked out again.

"Now I got you," he bellowed as he tripped her to the ground. Like a mule, she kicked with both feet, raining blow after blow about his head and shoulders. Still, he would not let go. Using the remnants of her dress as if it was a rope ladder, he steadily pulled himself forward until he was lying on top of her legs, pinning his wife forcibly to the ground. She wriggled and squirmed like an eel out of water, but she could not free herself from the weight of his upper body on her legs. Zutra held securely on to the belted material that encircled her waist, trying to raise himself on to his knees, but each time he attempted to do so, Avital was able to free a leg and land several more kicks to his head and shoulders in the process.

The heel of her left leg caught him square across the temple, and for a few seconds he felt dazed and woozy. That was all the opportunity she required to wiggle free from beneath him and make a desperate run towards safety. As she darted away, she ignored the final tearing of the fabric, which was still wound tightly in his hand. Shaking free of her garment, she ran to the far wall where she seized one of the burning torches, removing it from its bracket. The sweat on her body scintillated as she stalked back towards Zutra who was desperately attempting to clear the cobwebs that still clouded his brain. As he gazed upwards, he was temporarily blinded by the shimmer of flames radiating off her glistening skin. It was then that he noticed the wild look in her eyes; a murderous uncontrollable rage that rivaled his own.

Unable to rise to his feet in time to avoid the approaching torch, she brushed it up against his body. As soon as the fiery brand kissed his clothing, he was alight. 'Damn you! I'll kill you for this," he screamed as he struggled to free himself from his blazing tunic. "Shit, shit, shit," he repeated in pain as he tugged and pulled frantically while the flames singed his skin.

"I've heard your threats already," she taunted him as he danced about wildly, removing the last shreds of the garment. "Now burn in Hell!"

It was only a moment and he had extinguished the last of the flames but before she recognized his intent, he had the water cistern in his arms and flung it towards her. The size of a small barrel, its contents doused the torch as it crashed heavily into her body, winding her as it did so. The sopping brand dropped from her hand onto the floor where it sizzled and died. She clenched her abdomen, struggling to catch her breath as she buckled over at the waist.

Before she could react, he was on top of her, knocking her forcefully to the ground, his hands wrapped around her neck but unable to complete the strangle hold as she pounded frantically against the inside of his elbows. She heard him panting like an animal, grunting in pain and madness, yet the violent sensation of his flesh grinding upon hers strangely aroused her beyond all reason. Not even the mysterious oriental arts that the Princess Ti-Ping had performed on her could compare to this new overpowering force that took control of her body. The grip about her neck began to tighten, the lack of oxygen making her feel heady as everything else grew black. Reflexively she reached down and grabbed his dangling penis in her hand, squeezing it as tight as the fingers about her neck but with no intent to cause physical harm. Within moments it was rock hard and massive around its girth. Spreading her legs, she guided it past the yawning lips and well inside of her. Tears streamed down her face as she cursed her own weakness.

"Fuck you! Fuck you!" Zutra screamed and cried simultaneously as he felt himself overtaken by the whirlwind that drove him into a greater frenzy. He pounded her hips into the ground, driving as hard as he could with the hope of forcing her down into the bowels of Ghenna. Every violent thrust was met by a manic scream of her own, her nails raking up and down the length of his back until the welts and trickles of blood crisscrossed his flesh like a lattice. Each cut into his skin drove him further to the brink of madness, sinking his teeth into her neck and shoulders until he reveled in the taste of the metallic sting of her blood. He strove against the tantalizing pleasures that consumed his soul, groaning instead within the throes of intense agony from the wounds being inflicted. He drove deep inside her, but his killing stroke drowned within the coils of pulsating muscles that pulled him deeper into oblivion with each contraction. His glans became engorged, swollen far beyond its mass and whether from physical impossibility or lack of will, he could not find the strength to withdraw from her. Unable to retreat, his subconscious drove him forward, invading her hidden crevices, which then triggered a series of convulsive spasms that spread from her head to her toes.

Engaged in their titanic struggle, neither could gain the upper hand as they rolled and skidded across the tiled floor. Once on top she tightened the sinews of her thighs, tugging on his manhood so much that it was beginning to numb under the pressure. Avital became thrilled with the thought of fulfilling her needs while denying him his. This she convinced herself would suffice as victory. It made every muscle within her pelvis contract and clamp down even harder on his turgid organ.

Zutra panicked at the thought of his impending failure. The pressure was unbearable. His mind wiped clean of every memory regarding their initial reason for fighting, fixated solely on the battle at hand. Before she could drain him of his seed completely, he shifted his weight forcibly so that they rotated positions and once more, he had her pinioned beneath him. The superior position gave him considerably more room to maneuver, withdrawing mere fractions of an inch before prodding deeper than any man had journeyed before. Unable to control her own reactions any longer, she succumbed to his renewed thrusts, reveling in the transfer of the chi from the various centers of her body as it intensified. She screamed with unrestrained pleasure, flooded and overwhelmed by a thousand and one sensations.

"Damn you," she swore at him. "Fuck me," she roared. "Oh God," she prayed, all the time her hips surging upward as her back arched only to crash heavily against the floor over and over again. Her involuntary squeals of unparalleled delight revived his own numbed nerve endings and Zutra could feel the pressure building up again within his loins. His thighs clamped together as he quickened his pace beyond the point of no return. Roaring like a lion, the guttural sounds emanating from his lips no longer had any human semblance. With every pulsation, another roar shook the room, terrifying Avital's maidservants as they crouched behind the locked door of their chambers convinced that the king was killing their mistress and that they would be next in line to suffer from his depravity.

Avital's own shouts of embroiled passion were dwarfed in comparison to his howling. Their twinned orgasms lasted an eternity as they remained locked in each other's violent embrace. Eventually, having drained one another completely, they slumped limply against one another as if their bones had been reduced to a state of jelly.

Zutra flopped on to his back, stretched out exhausted beside the sweating figure of his wife who could barely catch her own breath. Looking up at the ceiling, it was several minutes before either had the coherence or sentience to utter a word.

"I think I love to hate you," she hissed between the deep inhaling breaths that forced her heavy breasts to rise and fall.

"And I know I hate to love you," he groaned in response.

Her eyes gazed into his and for the first time they could see more to their madness than they had ever suspected.

"You know that I still intend to kill your father," he broke the concentration of her stare.

"I know," was all she had to say as she nestled in the crook of his arm.

Chapter Twenty-Six

Ctesiphon: Late Spring 500 A.D.

Pouring over the set of maps spread across the series of long tables placed end to end, Patricius focused on the stretch of land that lay between the northern border of the Sassanid Empire and the Kidarites. He was oblivious to the twelve other men that were in the room with him. When it came to the strategy of warfare, he considered himself to be without peers. The land was an unknown entity, possibly inhabited by Magyars or Avars but no one was certain where these migrating hordes might be camped at any particular moment. Baron Attard peered over his right shoulder trying to guess what the Vizier was contemplating. During the time they had spent together in Byzantium, each had come to respect the immense capabilities of the other. Of all the men in the war room, Attard was the only one that Patricius gave any credit as being a professional soldier in every regard.

The Sassanid baron had been a well-decorated general in Kavad's army. He engineered the entire military operation against the invading Kindah, the nomadic warriors that inhabited the Arabian Peninsula. His prize was the daughter of a Kindah chieftain, the most beautiful women he had ever laid eyes upon, and he elevated her from the status of conquered tribute to that of wife. It was rumored that her beauty was the cause of the magus Mazdak proposing the now infamous rule that all women should become communal property within the empire. That was the day that the Emperor Kavad approached Attard requesting that he hand over his wife to the Magus. It was also the day that the baron withdrew his entire household to his estate located on the borders of the Gupta Empire, sending word back to the Magus that if he wanted his wife he would have to come and get her. From that day onward, he swore his eternal enmity to Kavad, an event that made him the most logical choice to lead the combined forces of the barons under the Emperor Jamasp.

"What do you know of this land, Attard?" the Commander finally inquired pointing to the area lying east of the Caspian Sea and ignoring all the other distinguished gentlemen in the room.

"Uncivilized. Ruthless. Barbaric. Which word suits you best," he jested.

"I was hoping you were going to say peaceful," Patricius informed him.

"Any particular reason?"

"Actually, there is." The Commander began drawing lines on the map in front of them much to the horror of some of the older barons that considered maps to be works of divine inspiration and therefore must be kept pristine at all cost. "Now that we're aware that Valentius won't be returning anytime soon, it leaves a gaping hole in our plans that we presented to the Byzantines. They are expecting a force to circle in from behind and come down this way from the north. Since I no longer have any Chinese forces available, I was thinking you could take ten thousand cataphracts and pass through this corridor between the Caspian and Aral Seas. You'd then come around the north shore of the Caspian and descend straight through Hun territory. If we time this right, the Byzantine forces will have made it from the northern ports on the Black Sea and would be joining up with your forces just about here." Patricius finished drawing his line at the town of Tibilisi."

"Euxine Sea," Attard corrected him.

"What?"

"The Byzantines call it the Euxine Sea. Only you Alans refer to it as the Black Sea. We can't afford to have any confusion if the plan is to succeed."

"Yes, of course," Patricius agreed. "Any confusion could be disastrous. So, what do you think? Can you do it?"

Attard rubbed his bearded chin as he gave the plan his careful consideration. "Well, we should be able to avoid the Avars and Kidarites if we stay close to the eastern shore of the Caspian. But when we get to about here," Attard pointed to the lands surrounding the northern end of the sea, "then we're going to come face to face with the Magyars and Sabirs. They can't be avoided and they could be a problem."

"Can you defeat them?"

"No. Not without taking tremendous losses and having nothing left to fight the Huns."

"Can you appease them in any way?"

The Baron nodded his affirmation. "They're traders. As long as we give them something of value in exchange for safe passage, they will let us through."

"What would they want?" Patricius was more than willing to make a trade.

"The Magyars will want horses; fast horses and a lot of horses."

"What about the Sabirs?"

"They'll want something to stop the Magyars on their fast horses!"

"That can all be all arranged," Patricius assured him. "If we can keep them busy with each other then they shouldn't be any problem for a long time."

"When would you be wishing I begin the ride north?"

"I would think that we'll be looking at the war beginning in earnest by next spring. Would the rest of you agree?"

The other military men nodded their heads, but Patricius secretly knew that had he asked any of them why they thought so, they'd only respond because he had said so himself. It reminded him why so many invading armies over the last three hundred years had successfully marched on Ctesiphon and taken it each time. The Sassanids, like the Parthians before them, thought everything had to do with numbers whereas superior strategy was of little significance. Ever since the time of Alexander the Great they thought and fought in the same manner. Put five hundred thousand men on the field of battle said they should win simply through the attrition rate on both sides. However, as soon as they came up against a strategist like Alexander with his forty thousand Greeks, they were routed. Patricius knew that he could not afford to have them fight in the same manner.

"I'm glad we are all in agreement," Patricius commended them. "Because we all know that the first move against us by the Ephthalites will be a political maneuvering. They have to persuade the people that supporting us would be supporting the wrong cause."

A chorus of agreement circled the room.

"I would think that would mean they will have to make a big showing on our own territory. Moreover, they can't afford to stretch their lines too far into the Empire for fear that we will cut them off. My instincts tell me that this public display will take place in Armenia."

"What type of show are you thinking?" Attard inquired.

"Right now, Kavad isn't much more than baggage to them. Unless he can convince some of his own people to follow him, this won't be a case of trying to restore the throne to a deposed monarch as it is a foreign invasion. And I would think the Ephthalites are smart enough to realize they don't have the military strength to launch a total invasion."

"Ahh... I see now," Attard clicked into the Commander's thinking. "Re-establish him in the north and gather strength as he moves south as the returning king."

"It's not as if you government has paid much attention to the Northern provinces. The only time any of you have been a presence there is when you're using their countryside as a battleground to fight the other empires. How many times has Armenia been contested between yourselves and the Byzantines over the past hundred years?"

"Too many to expect any allegiance from the ingrates of the provinces," Gurzam arrived late to the council and entered into discussion immediately.

"Glad to see you could make it." Patricius's comment was laced with a tinge of sarcasm.

"As Vizier, you should be well aware that there are always pressing matters of state that must be attended to first."

'Anything we should be aware of?"

"Yes!" Gurzam voiced his response angrily. "His royal and most excellent highness, Emperor Jamasp will not officially approve any orders to engage in battle with his brother. If we do so, we are to be considered rebels and enemies of the state should Kavad manage to return to the throne."

"Let the khar keer bokhor," one of the barons shouted which was quickly followed by uproarious laughter from the others in the room."

"I practically said as much to him," Gurzam agreed. "I even

suggested his mother was a cos eh lash jendeh!" Having said that, the laughter and comments flew furiously about the room.

"I don't think I've mastered that part of your language," Patricius leaned towards Attard and whispered.

"Don't worry," the baron patted him on the back. "You just have to use your imagination to understand."

"Oh, he said that, did he?"

"And more," Attard laughed.

"Well, gentlemen," Patricius signaled for a return to order. "I guess we're all rebels now. So, I'll keep our orders simple. Win at all costs otherwise there will be no tomorrow."

"What do you think we should do about our cowardly Emperor," some of the barons asked. Patricius deferred to the Pashah for the answer.

"We must consider him hostile to our cause," Gurzam chose his words carefully. "We still need him sitting on the throne so at least it appears that we are engaged in a legitimate war. And we must make certain that he cannot pass on word to his brother that he supports his return."

"House arrest?" Patricius half inquired; half suggested.

"House arrest," the Pashah confirmed. "As much as I'm loathe to say it, we must consider our Emperor to no longer be worthy of our loyalty."

"Not that he ever was, the kuni keerlees!" one of the military leaders cracked another insult that started the round of laughter once more.

"Don't be surprised if Kavad isn't well aware of his brother's cowardice. He's probably disclosed it to his new masters and they're all counting on it, which only confirms my assessment that they will perform some grand ceremony as soon as they cross into our territory; probably a coronation proclaiming Kavad's legitimate claim to the throne. That and a big show of arms by the White Huns and they'll have the people lining up to kiss the returning emperor's ass."

"As the Armenians have always done," Gurzam spat contemptuously.

"Why won't they move now?" one of the generals asked, unconsciously admitting that he had no understanding of Patricius's earlier estimation regarding the first engagement of the war being at least a year away.

"They won't move into our territory before they've completed their reconnaissance. I can assure you that they have already infiltrated the northern territories with their spies and are looking at the best location to conduct their ceremony for maximum impact."

"So that would only mean months away before they move," the same general surmised.

"Unlikely," Patricius explained. "The White Huns will want to parade a display of their own massive force in order to undermine any resistance. That means a lot of men and horses to feed. Considering they travel with their families and army whores in train, you can easily double the number of mouths to feed. Setting up a supply train of that magnitude would take a considerable amount of time."

"They could always take what they need from the Armenians," Attard suggested.

"Taking the food and shelter from the people you're trying to win over in the dead of winter? Not a particularly good way of celebrating the return of their monarch. I'm calculating that they'll want to appear as benevolent liberators. They'll wait."

"And what if you're wrong," Gurzam interceded. "What's the point in waiting until next spring to start moving our troops? A year from now could be too late!"

"Who said we would wait a year until we begin moving out? I said we'd be ready to engage in a year; that's an entirely different scenario," Patricius explained to all of those that still could not follow his strategy. "Attard, what's the best you can do with ten thousand men on heavy horse? Thirty miles a day? Perhaps if you're lucky, forty on a good day. From my calculations, from the time you leave Ctesiphon and reach Tibilisi, you'll have traversed approximately eighteen hundred miles. Sixty days of travel at best. Add on to that the time you'll require to negotiate with the Magyars and Sabirs, a minimum of another two months. The weather coming down from the Urals will easily halt your movements for at least another month or two. During that time, you'll have to dig in and set up encampments along the way. I calculate it will be easily another thirty days in total. From my estimation, you have three months, maximum four before you move out. Is that going to be a problem?" Patricius spoke directly to Baron Attard, ignoring the rest of the men assembled.

"Not a problem. Take me at least that long to set up my own supply train."

"What about recruitment?"

"Ten thousand cataphracts shouldn't be too hard to assemble."

Waving a finger in the air, Patricius wanted to make a point. "They have to be the best. You'll be on your own for quite some time; no communication with the rest of the army. Facing who knows what exists in unchartered territory. We can't afford any weakness within this force!"

"There won't be," Attard reassured him. "I'll take them from the units within my own tribes. Totally loyal, and enough encounters with the Gupta that they're battled hardened and fearless."

"Wait!" Gurzam shouted. "If you take most of the eastern units, what does that leave for the rest of us?" His concern was shared by the rest of the barons in the room who began to grumble at Attard's arrogance to select the finest from their battalions.

Turning upon the rest of the military advisors, Patricius's face wore a scowling mask. "Are you all telling me that you fear for the loyalty of the troops under your own command? If you think your men will desert in the face of combat and run to the other side, then now's the time you better tell me before I put my life on the line leading a bunch of miserable defectors!"

"I am certain that the nobles are only commenting that their men are not seasoned like Baron Attard's," the Pashah spoke on everyone's behalf.

"I hope for all our sake that is what you mean," he challenged the noblemen, "Because if there is any doubt, you have only one year in which to make them totally loyal. By next summer we'll be marching north and establishing our presence at Erzurum and Tabriz. I will personally lead the expeditionary forces to Erzurum. Hermantius with his legion of Alans will come with me. Mar Zutra with his forces will join us as well, along with another ten thousand cataphracts. Once there, I expect to be joined by another force from Byzantium of equal numbers. We will then drive against the Huns stationed in Armenia. That means I'm relying on the rest of you to form a defensive wall at Tabriz that must hold. I will tolerate no question in their loyalty. With my men coming from the west, and Attard from the North, the Huns will be squeezed on the East by the Caspian Sea. They will be forced directly into your wall and we will slaughter them to every last man on the plains of Tabriz." Patricius hammered his fist against the map directly over the province of Media. The noise was enough to make some of the barons jolt upwards. "To victory gentlemen!" he shouted confidently.

"To victory!" they all shouted in unison.

Chapter Twenty-Seven

Mahoza: Summer 500 A.D.

"How long are you just going to sit there and stare at me?"

Unable to conceal the bemused look on his face, Mar Zutra was content to watch forever if that was possible. "They look identical," he responded as he continued to watch each child wrestle with the nipple in their mouths while their hands kneaded and stroked their respective breasts.

"What nonsense are you talking about," Ti-Ping chided him. "Little Zutra looks exactly like his mother Avital and Yanqa has unmistakable features that make him look almost Tartar. And are you so blind that you cannot see that Yanqa has reddish hair? They are different as night and day."

"When they're pressed up against you like that, they look identical," he repeated.

"Are you looking at your children husband or my breasts?"

"Both," he chuckled.

"At the speed they're growing it won't be possible to nurse them at the same time much longer. Then you will see how different they are."

"I still don't understand why you named our son after a horse?"

"I told you so many times already, I did not name our son after the ponies in northern China." She took a deep breath as she tried to explain it once more. "All I said was that he shared his name with the breed of horse but I named him for the precious pearls of Buddhism. He is the Yanq, the light and warmth of the heavens." She looked up at Zutra only to see him chuckling at her consternation as she tried to explain what he already knew to him once more. "You are making fun of me, my husband," she pouted.

"No, I am falling in love with you all over again," he insisted. "I love to hear you talk about our son that way. Every time I ask it is only to hear you say that he is our little bit of heaven on earth."

"And little Zutra is your son too. You must remember that husband. We must never look upon them any differently."

"Do you think I was right in taking him from his mother? Do you ever wish I hadn't?"

"Do not be silly," she scolded him once again. "I love him as if he came from my own belly. How could I ever regret that I've suckled him as my own? The real question is do you regret that you've taken him from his mother?"

"I am confused Ti-Ping. My mind is so muddled. I don't know what's right or what's wrong any longer."

"Do you wish to talk about that day husband?"

Zutra knew exactly which day she was referring to. When he had returned to their chambers that night, she was horrified to see the scratches and bites all over his body, but she never said a word; merely prepared a disinfecting solution with which she bathed his wounds, applying a salve to the worst of them. She never asked nor had she ever commented about them since. He was silent for the longest time and then finally blurted out, "I tried to kill her." The confession brought tears to his eyes. "I think I actually would have done it, with my bare hands. What kind of man can do that?"

"But instead, you made love to her," the princess consoled him. "Whatever evil you may have intended, you replaced with love."

"I don't even know if you can even dare to call it love," he shook his head. "It was insanity. It was stupidity. It was…"

"It was love," she filled in the last words for him. "The emotions of hate and love are so intertwined that often we mistake one for the other."

"Then I must be insane because I hate her, yet I made love to her in a manner that defies explanation. Like a starved animal. It wasn't even love," he practically stuttered. "It was lust, violent, cruel and a hundred other words that don't have any bearing on the true meaning love."

"There are many forms of love," she explained. "Just as there are many words for love. What you experienced was the Shin, the darkness that overcomes men. It is the fire of the dragons. It burns as a different passion in the soul but it exists in all men. Sometimes, it is the only kind of love that two people will ever experience. But it burns so strongly that they only end up destroying each other in the flames."

"I would never do that to you," Zutra reassured her. "My love for you is pure."

"I know that husband. Now you understand why our son is named Yanqa. What we share is the opposite of the Shin. If I thought our love would be anything else, I would have never married you." Her enduring smile teased and caressed at the same time.

"But it's in me," he sounded scared. "It could come out again," he warned. "I had no control of myself," he tried to explain. "I might actually kill her the next time."

"If you wish to lie again with your other wife then it will most certainly be so. In order for you both to love each other, you must do it through hurting one another. That much you both know. That is the curse you each bear for one another."

"I don't want to share any curse with Avital. All I wish for is peace in my household. Is that too much to ask?"

"No husband, it is what everyone wishes for. My father prayed for it but found such a thing was not possible with a hundred wives and over a hundred sons. It broke his heart when he saw that they could not live together in peace. My brother said in his letter that our father no longer wished to live in a world where his own sons would slay one another. I think it was more correct that he did not wish to live in a world that he could no longer manage."

"You're trying to tell me something, aren't you?" Mar Zutra knew his first wife well enough to know that she rarely wasted words without a deeper meaning. "So was your father wrong?"

"Yes, he was wrong. You cannot control your world. No man can."

"So, you're suggesting that I should give up trying to control Avital, aren't you? At least if I wish to preserve my sanity."

The broadening smile on her face meant that she had finally made him understand. A beguiling smile that always made him feel like he was the only man left in the world.

"But then you also realize that you're telling me that I should not have taken little Zutra from Avital. That I did so only as a means to controlling her. Are you willing to let him go?"

"I love him like my own son," her voice cracked. "But he is not my son by the flesh. He is her son, and she still has milk for him. I would only be guessing through a woman's intuition, but I would think that a mother that has not dried herself off still yearns to have her child back. And now that the boys are bigger, I do not truly know if I can feed both. What you now decide may also be in your son's best interest as well."

"So, you're telling me that I should return little Zutra to his mother."

"I am telling you that you must do what is necessary to bring peace under your own roof, for your own sake husband, not hers."

"How did I ever get blessed with a perfect wife that has the Wisdom of Solomon?"

"You got lucky husband," she tittered. "I have been reading your books and now know who this Solomon is that you speak of. He was not so wise. Now do what you must do!"

"Did you come to see if I can make you bleed again?" she bared her fangs as the words slithered through her lips like the violent hiss of a serpent.

As he stood in the half-open doorway to her quarters, Mar Zutra could not help but admire the lithe body distinctly outlined beneath the thin silk robe that draped her from shoulder to floor in a luminescent elegance. So beautiful he thought to himself and yet so deadly. "As always, you look lovely dear Avital," he complimented, taking instruction from the Princess to try a different approach.

The two guards posted outside her chambers remained expressionless, as the exchange between the two adversaries continued unabated.

"I suppose there is a reason for this visitation? Could it be that your little princess no longer satisfies you?" The acid dripped from her tongue, each word designed to hurt and offend.

"The Princess Ti-Ping is well, and she wishes you well," Mar Zutra withstood her onslaught. "In fact, she apologizes not having had the opportunity to visit you since the birth of the children. She misses the time you spend together."

"I just bet she does," Avital hinted at their intimate relationship.

"Perhaps she needs a good tussle beneath the covers to stimulate her blood as well?"

Remaining totally composed, the exilarch was amazed following his talk with the Princess how little he was now reacting to Avital's continuous abuse. "No, that won't be necessary," he continued. "I believe she's quite satisfied by my efforts as they are, even though by your standards they would obviously seem dreary." He quickly bit his tongue sensing the momentary spurt of sarcasm that passed through his lips.

One of the guards flinched, but quickly resumed his stone-faced stare into nothingness before the king would notice. Both men wished they could be posted to any other duty than where they were at that precise moment. They knew their mistress well enough to know how this exchange of banter was likely to end.

"Dreary? Dear husband, I'm surprised that you are so kind to yourself. Imagining the two of you coupled would be better described as pathetic. Why don't you come in and I'll remind you what a real woman can do?" Her laugh was sterile and cold.

"As much as the pleasure of your company might entice at a more appropriate time, it is not why I am here. I'm sorry if this disappoints you."

"Then why are you here? Did you expect to see me crawl on my knees, begging you to touch me? To make love to me while you try to kill me?" She let her tongue roll around her lips suggestively.

"Actually, I am here to show you love," he replied. "But not in the fashion that you are accustomed to." Clapping his hands, Zutra summoned the Princess's maidservant from the shadows. Neatly wrapped in its swathing blanket, she carried the delicate bundle in both arms.

"What is this?" the Lady Avital suddenly looked weak, her legs giving way momentarily as she asked.

"This my wife is our child. Your child. Young Zutra who has come to be with his mother.

Avital reached out to steady herself once more but there was nothing to grab, her hands fingering nothing but air. Her knees buckled and she found herself kneeling before the king, unable to rise. Rather than enjoy her humbling moment, Zutra knelt down beside her and extended his arm to lift her face by the chin so that he could gaze into her eyes.

"Why?" she gasped as the tears streamed down her face.

"The boy should be with his mother," he consoled her.

Still unable to believe that her child had been returned, her spine stiffened for a moment and her eyes squinted. "This is some trick you're playing. You've come to crush what little spirit of mine is left!"

"No trick; no illusion," he reassured her, stroking her face softly.

Her hands raced up to his, clasping his hand between her palms as she held it against the side of her face, the tears flowing in a steady river from her eyes. "It is true then," the words barely escaped between the sequence of sobs and stifled wails.

"He has come home," Zutra confirmed. "I will visit more frequently to see that mother and child fares well." The king waved for the maidservant to bring the child forward. Kneeling on the ground beside them, the girl extended her bundle, passing the baby over to the waiting arms of his mother.

Rolling the edge of the blanket back, Avital gazed upon the face of her child whom she had not seen since the day she gave birth. She was breathless, wiping the tears from both her cheeks and then looking into her husband's own mist darkened eyes as her lips parted into a grateful smile. "Thank you," she whispered as her head nodded perceptively in an expression of appreciation.

"No, thank you for providing me with such a fine son."

Cradling the child with one arm she held out the other towards Mar Zutra. He took her hand in his and patted it delicately.

"He's really here to stay?" she still could not believe her change in fortune. Zutra helped her from the floor, leading her back into her chambers where she could rest on one of the sedans until she regained her equilibrium.

Turning to the two guards at the door, he gave them clear instructions to see that no one interrupted mother and child for the rest of the day. "And men," he cautioned them, "Not a word to be spoken of this otherwise you will find your next duty on the borders of the Gupta Empire. Do we understand each other?"

"Yes sir," they saluted simultaneously.

Once the doors swung closed behind them, Zutra and the handmaid helped the Lady Avital to be seated, the girl positioning the baby so that it was nestled properly in his mother's arms. The baby let out a howl as he opened his eyes for the first time since his return to his birth mother.

His cries caught Avital by surprise, and she looked to the handmaid for advice.

"He is hungry my lady," the girl answered. "He's always been a big eater. Whenever he wakes, he demands to be fed immediately."

"Like his father probably," Avital commented for the benefit of Mar Zutra. "What should I do?" Avital was genuinely perplexed not having nursed her firstborn Hanai when he was a baby.

"Allow me, my lady," the maidservant helped lower the gown from Avital's right shoulder, letting it slump beneath the curvature of her breast. Instinctively Avital pushed his face up against the breast, but little Zutra continued to scream rather than find his way to the nipple.

"If I may?" the girl sought permission.

"Yes, yes," Avital urged her to continue.

Placing the nipple between thumb and forefinger, the handmaid rolled the nub gently, massaging along its length until it stood erect and engorged. A few more compressions and the first drops of milk squirted from the breast, scattering a spray that showered the blanket. The cries of hunger ceased immediately as the baby turned his head, searching responsively for the milk-soaked nipple.

"At this age they rely almost completely on smells," the girl explained. "You had not fed him before, so there was no odor to guide him. Now he understands what you were offering him. You are lucky that you have not begun going dry."

"I believe it is because I always knew he'd be coming back to me. I must have known."

"You will have lots of milk from now on," the girl advised.

"A prize cow to breed," she directed her comment towards Zutra, and they both laughed contagiously.

"I guess you won't need me for this," Zutra excused himself as he rose out of the chair.

Looking up from the greedy face of her child, Avital gave Zutra her most beautiful smile, a smile he remembered from his youth and which had been absent for so many years. "Thank you," she repeated with all sincerity.

Nodding in acceptance, Zutra winked knowingly, pleased with himself, and genuinely happy for his son's mother before he exited her chambers.

Chapter Twenty-Eight

Perso-Armenia: Spring 501 A.D.

"Any idea where Attard and his men might be by now?" Zutra questioned the Commander as they sat around a warming campfire at the centre of the army camp.

"Wouldn't have a clue," Patricius shook his head as he admitted the lack of communications was exactly as he had predicted.

"How about a guess just to make me feel a little less uneasy about our chances here!" Though Zutra tried not to sound too worried, the fact that they had now been encamped a week along the shores of Lake Urmiyah outside of the town of Quvoy without any indication of the enemy's whereabouts was quite distressing.

"Don't worry so much," Patricius soothed his uneasy feelings. "I told the Princess I would take care of you and I'm not about to break my promise."

"It's too quiet for my liking," Mar Zutra complained.

"That's the problem," the Commander asserted. "Both you and I have been sitting around palaces too long to appreciate what peace and quiet actually sounds like, especially in your palace. The place is in constant turmoil! Out here a man learns to value the sounds of silence."

"Silence has its rewards; I just didn't expect to find it out on the battlefield."

"Here, take a good look at that coin." Patricius flipped the silver dirham over to Zutra sitting across from him. "What does it tell you?"

Turning the coin over in his fingers, Zutra read the inscriptions and examined the engraved portrait on the obverse and picture of the altar with both Emperor and Empress standing to each side on the reverse. "It tells me that Kavad is still a very vain person," he commented. "The portrait makes him look at least twenty years younger."

"Besides that," Patricius urged him to go on.

"It proclaims his reanointing as Emperor in his twelfth year."

"Exactly," Patricius congratulated him on his accuracy. "It means that our enemies have just recently completed the inauguration ceremony and also made claim that their Ephthalite princess is now the legitimate Empress of our Empire."

Zutra did not appear too overwhelmed by the breaking news.

"It's a good sign, Zutra," the Commander tried to reassure him. "Everything is going according to our predictions. In fact, better than I hoped. A Hun empress will not go over that well with the people."

"You mean as compared to no empress because the current Emperor's predilection is towards young boys."

"I'm betting the populace would still prefer that over a Hun."

"Assuming that there is any difference," Zutra jibed. "From what I heard they're built exactly the same."

"Ah...see...everything isn't as bleak as you think," the Commander bantered.

"It's the waiting that bothers me the most," the Exilarch complained. "I'd rather be fighting than just sitting here."

Puffing out his chest, Patricius prepared for one of his standard lectures that he was prone to give new recruits. "It's a little-known fact, but the key to a victorious army is patience. Those that run headlong into battle are doomed to failure. The war must be fought in your head long before it takes place on the field with the clash of swords. Know your enemy. Understand how he has laid out his forces. Estimate his strengths and weaknesses. Predict what will be his series of moves. Undermine his strategy. Then once you have done all that, engage him in battle."

"And what about when you can't make an assessment because you can't locate your enemy?"

"Then pray like hell that he doesn't find you before you're ready!" Patricius wisecracked. "But that's not going to happen. "This is land that we Alans have lived in for centuries. Hermantius's scouts will provide us with reports of any movement days before anyone can be upon us. For now we just sit and wait."

"Until?"

"Until we hear word that our allies have arrived in Erzurum. Then we'll combine our forces with theirs."

"That still doesn't locate the enemy for us," Zutra tried to pick a hole in the strategy.

"That's the beauty of this plan. We don't have to. They're going to find us. When Attard and his cataphracts start their movement south accompanied by the two Byzantine turmas, they'll sweep everything out of their way that's in front of them. We'll now well in advance when the Huns are on the move southward."

"Assuming this all works to plan, where's the problem?"

"There is no problem," Patricius declared proudly. "Sometimes, my friend, you worry too much!"

Summer had already started when the first scouting reports indicated that the Ephthalites were on the march towards Lesser Armenia. Accompanied by his own forces, Patricius rode at the front of five drungas of Byzantine infantry that had been sent to Erzurum. It was less than the total number he had hoped for, being no more than five thousand men, but these were the kasallarios, the best of Anastasius's heavy troopers. With their steel cap and its small red crest, they were easily recognizable from the regular infantry. A long mail shirt covered them from the neck to the thighs, with gauntlets, grieves and steel shoes covering the rest. They wore a light surcoat over the mail, most commonly adorned with a fantailed cross emblazoned on both the back and the front. Anastasius appointed Johannes as their general. Surrounding him marched the buccellarii, his own personal bodyguard consisting of two hundred of the very best fighters Byzantium offered.

"Where do you estimate we'll start the encounter," Johannes deferred to Patricius's better comprehension of the strategy at hand.

"Just outside of Kapan,' Patricius replied, having mentally marked the positions of all the forces before they began their own march. "That should happen by tomorrow noon based on their current speed. Attard and Diogenes should have reached Ganka by now, which puts them only sixty miles to the north of the site. I figure they should be arriving by tomorrow evening at the latest."

"Not if I know Diogenes," Johannes revealed a personal fact about his colleague. "He likes the glory too much. He'll push his men as hard as he can so that he can engage them first."

"I can live with that," Patricius was nonplussed by the revelation. "It doesn't matter to me who draws first blood as long as we win."

"I agree wholeheartedly," the Byzantine general concurred. "No one remembers the first to die. Only the one left alive at the end to claim all the spoils."

Looking over at his Byzantine co-general, Patricius appeared astonished. "I almost hate to admit this Johannes, but I think you're beginning to think like me."

"You always were the ultimate survivor," he lavished the Commander with a twisted insult.

Kicking his horse into a canter, Patricius shouted behind him, "And I intend to keep it that way."

Riding to where Hermantius was marching the Alanine troops on the left flank of the army, Patricius pulled his horse into a slow walk beside his cousin.

"And how's that son of a donkey's ass," Hermantius inquired.

"The same as always," Patricius responded. "But at least I know that he wants this victory as bad as any one of us do. He'll put up a good fight when he's needed and that's all that counts."

"I still don't trust him," Hermantius reflected on his years at the court in Constantinople. "He'll just as easily twist his knife in the back of a friend as he would an enemy."

"And that's why I have you cousin, to watch my back."

"Consider it done, cousin."

"And how fares our King?"

"He's a quick learner," Hermantius lauded. "The Four Hundred are seasoned fighters but he refuses to slack off even one iota. He's as much out of the saddle as he is in it, marching alongside his men. I think he knows everyone by their personal name."

"Makes for a good military leader," Patricius grunted.

"He's got more backbone than most royals, I'll give him that," Hermantius sounded impressed.

"Did I ever tell you when we were attacked by the assassin's guild, he put up a good fight. I knew then he wasn't the usual peacock we've grown accustomed to."

"Let's just hope we can keep him from doing something foolish," the Alanine general sounded cautious. "These untested ones always think they have something to prove; placing themselves in danger when they don't have to."

"You watch my back, I watch his," the Commander instructed. "His wife would kill me if anything was to happen to him."

"Which one?" Hermantius had a good laugh.

"Does it matter? Both of them can be deadly."

"So I've heard, cousin, so I've heard," Hermantius winked.

"Keep you dirty mind to yourself," Patricius warned. "I don't need you spreading any rumors when we're about to go into battle!"

"Me, Sir? Perish the thought."

"Get your men to step up their pace, General. They're beginning to lag behind and we have a date with destiny at noon tomorrow."

"Yes Sir!" Hermantius saluted as his commander rode off in the direction of the armed contingent from Mahoza.

Riding his coal black steed through the ranks, the passing of their commander was enough to raise the spirits of the men that served him. The legendary invincibility that marked all his campaigns served to pacify even the rawest of recruits. From the Mediterranean to the Great Eastern Ocean, the stories of his military prowess were unrivaled. Those that served under him previously knew they already had the odds in their favour that they'd be returning home. Each time he passed one of his tribunes, each in charge of their own numerus, the Commander would slow to pass them the word. "Tomorrow at noon, tell your men." They all met the news excitedly, knowing that there would be dreams of glory during the night.

He reigned in his horse alongside the gray gelding upon which Zutra rode. "Guess you've heard by now? Tomorrow at noon."

"Yes," Mar Zutra nodded. "The news is spreading fast."

"Nervous"

"I'd be a fool if I wasn't," the king replied honestly. "It's one thing to dream of battle, another to actually fight in one."

"You know, no one would think less of you if you stayed to the rear of our lines."

"I would."

"You probably would but placing your life in harm's way proves nothing," Patricius conceded to his monarch.

"You should understand best of all what it's like to be descended from a long line of warriors," Zutra appealed to the Commander's own sense of historical responsibility.

"But my family have remained military men generation after generation," Patricius attempted to explain the difference. "Yours may have been great warriors but that was long ago in the past. Since then, you have been more... more scholarly."

"Scholarly? Is that the best you can come up with?"

"You know what I mean. Your days of hand-to-hand combat are as old as the bible itself. You family hasn't really engaged in warfare for hundreds of years."

"Then perhaps it's time we revive the old ways," Zutra suggested. "Ever since we took on the Romans, we've become nothing but flotsam floating on the ocean of mankind."

"See, that's exactly what I'm talking about," Patricius interrupted. "You're sages; you're poets, not fighters. What you said was very poetic, but it doesn't mean you have the ability to fight!"

"The only reason we have survived for fifteen hundred years is because we have been fighters. If we let our enemies forget that, then this world will eventually destroy us."

"So, you think tomorrow you're going to change all that? You're going to prove to everyone that you Jews are a force to be feared."

"Perhaps not in one day," Zutra acknowledged, "But whatever I do tomorrow will make our enemies think twice about attacking us in the future."

"I'm not going to change your mind, am I?"

"I will not disappoint you."

"I'm not worried about you disappointing me," Patricius admitted defeat. "I'm worried that you may not survive. At least take my advice and stay at the centre of your Four Hundred. Agreed?"

"Agreed. They wouldn't permit me to fight any other way."

"Then at least your Four Hundred have some common sense."

The sun sat high in the midday sky over the plains of Tabriz. The air was moist and sat heavy upon the sweeping grass that swayed gently in the faint breeze. To the north, the dark cloud of dust moved steadily towards the quiet village of Kapan. Overhead a flock of gulls squawked noisily as they circled monotonously as if waiting; waiting for something only they could anticipate from their bird's eye view of the countryside.

A few of the villagers hastily packing their belongings on to the backs of donkey carts, then escaped via the roads leading southward towards Tabriz. They had seen the dark cloud too many times before not to recognize that it meant nothing but trouble and death. The old and the infirmed huddled in their mud-walled huts praying that the dark angel would pass over their home leaving it unscathed. It was always an unanswered prayer but nonetheless, this time they hoped that Ahura Mazda would heed their solicitations.

Emerging from the distant cloud, the first of the faceless riders appeared on the horizon. They wore leather caps over their long, matted hair, their mail and leather armor trimmed with fur while hinged metal plates covered a few of the more vital organs. Their horses were more refined than the heavier mixed-breed draught horses predominant in this part of the world. Longer legged and finer boned which provided them with greater speed than the cavalry patrols the villagers had grown accustomed to seeing. The closer the riders approached the town, the easier it was to distinguish their small box like saddles that gave them greater freedom of movement to control their steeds with only their legs while they swung their short bows in any direction, firing their arrows at either a pursued or approaching enemy. At first, only a few hundred could be seen dotting the horizon but soon, they were followed by thousands as they rode hard down upon the tiny village. Kapan prepared for the worst.

The riders from the steppes filled the plains with their massive numbers, curved swords dangling from their belts while on their backs were strapped quivers half spent from a prior battle. From the speed they were travelling, it was clear they were not looking to stop their mad gallop; Kapan was not the refuge they were seeking. The closer they approached, the more obvious it became that a significant number were wounded, barely able to keep themselves upright in the saddle as they fled from what must have been a recent encounter with the enemy. What Patricius had originally perceived as an attack was in reality a controlled flight. Taking advantage of their faster horses, the Huns decided that the best route to safety was south into the wide-open territory of Media.

As soon as the Huns came level with the outer reaches of the village, the trumpets blared sounding the attack of the combined forces under Patricius and Johannes. Emerging from the low rise of hills to the west of the village, they bore down upon the first wave of Huns that flooded the plain. The timing had to be precise as each drungas of infantry targeted a sector of the plain, anticipating where the Huns would be at any specific time. As their commanders had been trained, it was the only way that foot soldiers could successfully launch an attack on mounted horsemen.

The Kasallarios under Johannes took a different approach, as they lay low in the grass waiting for the Ephthalites to move unsuspectingly in their direction. At the last moment, they raised their lances, cradling them upon a bent knee, letting the horses' own momentum bury the shafts deep into the chest, throwing the riders to the ground, where they were quickly dispatched by the concealed Byzantines.

The combined strategies were never intended to destroy the invading forces of the Huns; an impossibility whenever infantry was in pursuit of cavalry. Its entire purpose was to cause panic amongst the Ephthalites and direct them on the path towards Tabriz where the main body of Sassanid forces under Gurzam awaited them. The 'wall' as Patricius had outlined it during his strategic war council. A barrier made up of soldiers so thick that it was impassable by cavalry. Once the horses were left with nowhere to run they became easy prey for the cataphracts that would be in pursuit from the north.

"Looks like Diogenes bloodied them first," Johannes gloated to Patricius whose men were dispatching the last of the stragglers that failed to pass through the vicinity of Kapan.

"How do you know it wasn't Attard's men?" Patricius bellowed back.

"Because the wounded were bearing sword marks not arrow wounds," he brazenly pointed out.

"Well then they must have gotten a lot closer than I had expected," Patricius conceded the first blood to the Byzantine general.

The last of the White Huns were fleeing from the battlefield when the Commander grabbed hold of his cousin who was about to launch a pursuit and questioned if he had seen the whereabouts of Mar Zutra at any time during the confrontation. Hermantius shrugged his shoulders admitting that he had not.

"What about his guard?" Patricius inquired further.

"I may have seen them moving towards the southern outskirts of the town. But I'm not certain," Hermantius recollected.

"Come with me and bring your men," Patricius ordered.

"But what about the ones escaping?" the Alan general whined.

"They're not going to get very far. It's far more important we find Zutra and see that he's safe. Quickly, on the double."

Totally disregarding any of the townspeople that pleaded for help for their wounded, Patricius raced past them, feeling anxious that he had lost sight of his king during the skirmish. Once they had rounded the stone gates at the opposite end of the village, they heard shouts and the sound of swords clashing in battle surfacing from one of the small farmlets that ringed the village.

"There! That one!" Patricius shouted and pointed to a field where the wheat had been allowed to go to seed, the stalks standing as high as a man's shoulders. Approximately a hundred of the Hun riders had tried to escape through the crop-fields, only to find that the stalks provided an impenetrable barrier to their mounts, the shafts of the plants so closely knit together that they wrapped around the fetlocks and snared the beasts. The infamous Four Hundred could be seen circling the still dangerous Huns with their curved swords and short bows, looking for an opening through which to attack.

Hermantius was about to order his archers to nock their bows and end the matter quickly, but Patricius countered the command, telling everyone to stand down. "Let's just watch cousin," he advised. "They do not appear to be in any danger. If that changes then we can intercede. You know better than to steal another man's glory."

Grumbling some unintelligible comment, Hermantius folded his arms across his chest and did as he was told. They watched the intricate dance played to an imperceptible song that only the combatants could hear. Man and horse involved in a series of complex steps that culminated in death. For Patricius, it was the first time he had ever seen the legendary Four Hundred perform their artistry. Their movements were fluid, like a river passing between the rocks of a chasm, bobbing and weaving, ducking and leaping until they had gotten close enough with their long double-edged swords to pierce the enemy's guard and land the fatal blow. The warrior art of the dervishes had been practiced for over a thousand years until each movement became a ritualistic dance of death. Born in the deserts of Yemen, no one knew exactly how it began. But to watch it practiced to perfection, it became quickly evident how it would end.

"Look there," Hermantius pointed towards to one of the men engaged in their twirling dance of the macabre. "There's our King!"

He calculated that it was too late and too far to reach the combatants in time to pull Mar Zutra away from the danger. However, in the end, his fears were unwarranted. Mimicking the style and grace of his select guard, the Exilarch evaded the short stabbing thrusts of the Hun he fought, moving from side to side, slicing both man and mount as he passed. Collapsing to its knees, the horse and rider were hapless until the man's throat became level with the arc of Zutra's blade. It sliced easily through the rider's exposed neck, the body remaining upright in the box saddle for several seconds before it toppled over to one side.

"It looks as if he has been studying the finer arts under the tutelage of his bodyguard," Hermantius commented.

"Not bad," Patricius commented to his cousin as they watched the engagement.

"Not bad? Bloody good if you ask me. There's more to that king than you would guess at first!"

"That there is Hermantius. Far more than anyone would think,"

Patricius winked.

"What about your promise to the Princess to keep him out of harm's way?"

"It would appear that he has everything under control here. No reason to worry as far as I'm concerned. We need to order our forces and begin the pursuit of the enemy. I don't want any of them avoiding the wall at Tabriz. Have the trumpeters sound assembly and let Johannes know that were moving out."

Riding furiously, the Ephthalites crossed the plains only to find themselves caught in the jaws of the vice that awaited them at Tabriz. Marshaled along the northern outskirts of the city, the united forces of the barons stood frozen like statues. Not a sound, not a movement, just a wall of men and horses packed solidly with barely a hand's breadth between any of them. As the Huns came over the top of the rise along the main road into the city, the futility of any direct assault became immediately evident. Even if the force of their charge managed to crack the front lines, they would have only mired themselves in row after row of the enemy, with no room to maneuver. Blowing two piercing blasts of their horns, told their warriors to pull their horses sharply to the left as they rode the length of the human wall in search of its end.

A warrior's natural instinct is not to challenge and charge a fortified wall of defenders and Patricius had gambled that even the Huns without any of the formal discipline of most military units would still adhere to the established rules of common sense in combat. His second assumption was that they would abandon their search for the end of the lines, turning back to the northeast towards the village of Ahar. The lie of the land made it the most obvious destination where the Huns would regroup and reassess their remaining options. It was the place he had instructed Attard to wage the final battle. The location where he prearranged all their forces should meet.

No sooner had the White Huns turned to the northeast, convinced that the barons' armies were inexhaustible the order sounded for the wall to begin its march north. Like a massive broom, it swept everything before it. Though the wall was only five rows deep, the spreading of five thousand men to a line, the intermingling of cataphracts, infantry, and bowmen created the appearance of an army far larger in size and strength than it actually was. To Gurzam's credit, through the force of his own will, he was able to maintain the unity among the various barons, avoiding the commonplace bickering and one-upmanship that had plagued the Sassanid forces throughout time immemorial. Everything proceeded to perfection.

Approaching Ahar, the Ephthalites were still unaware of the deadly trap that awaited them. Their path appeared clear all the way to the forests on the far horizon. The Huns liked to deal in simple strategies; make it to the woods and they assumed they would elude their pursuers. However, as soon as they were within a quarter mile of their destination, they understood that today there would be no simple solutions. Emerging from the brink of the forest the combined forces under the commands of Attard and Diogenes sealed off any opportunity to escape. On their left flank, the armies under Johannes appeared from behind Ahar, having used the town as a shield to conceal their presence. The Huns looked to their right but there they could only visualize Patricius moving quickly to seal off all available routes. With no place left to turn, the White Huns utilized their only option, throwing their horses upon their adversaries as if they were battering rams and fighting for survival with every remaining breath. Hopelessly outnumbered and hemmed in from all sides, it was only a matter of a few hours until the combined forces of the Byzantines and Sassanid barons eradicated the Ephthalites to the very last man.

The victorious leaders met at the centre of the battlefield, standing amid the rivers of blood that threaded their way through the dense tufts of grass that now blanketed a once great seabed that had receded long before the age of recorded history.

Slapping Attard across the back, Patricius congratulated the Sassanid general on his overwhelming victory. "I'm sorry we missed what must have been a magnificent encounter when you first met the enemy to the north," he apologized.

Attard looked over at Diogenes for any suggestions on how to appropriately respond to the commander's praise, but none were forthcoming.

"We had no major contact prior to this one," Attard admitted. "When we came across the enemy army, we launched an attack against their rear guard but that was our only skirmish. It set the main body of their warriors, which were still several days ahead of us in flight to the south. When we saw this particular division returning north, I assumed that you must have wiped out their main force. Most of these were just from the rear guard that we first encountered."

"This was the only force we saw," Johannes interceded, sounding alarmed that the main body of the enemy was still on the loose somewhere in the countryside.

"I estimated sixty thousand men in total that I saw as I passed north to join with Attard," Diogenes reported, fueling their discussion. "That's why we decided not to attack outright waiting until our forces were united. We would have been far outnumbered to go it alone."

Scanning the field, Patricius watched as the men under their command removed their own dead and wounded, leaving the enemy to be heaped into pyres. Quickly estimating the losses on the other side, he turned to his peers and made his grave announcement. "There's only twenty-five thousand of the Huns accounted for here. Where are the rest of them?"

The question was of grave concern putting an end to their short-lived victory celebrations. There were close to thirty-five thousand Huns and fifteen thousand of their retainers roaming the countryside somewhere unopposed and not a single one of their scouts had reported back where.

"It doesn't make sense," Johannes protested. "We moved continually east and our other forces had them hemmed in on both the northern and southern fronts. It's impossible we missed them unless...unless..." Johannes turned white as the worst-case scenario filled him with dread.

"Not possible!" Diogenes exclaimed. "The Huns have never shown that level of tactical coordination before. Impossible! They are simpletons, barbarians, nothing more."

"We never took into consideration that there may be more of a Persian element among them than we thought. What if they've been placed under some of Kavad's old generals? He would have still retained some old loyalties."

"Not many," Patricius tried to reassure Johannes.

"But enough," the Byzantine general countered. "Enough to take us on at our own game and make us look like fools. We were lured here while their main forces have double backed."

"We don't know that for certain," Patricius tried to calm everyone down.

Johannes knew that it most definitely was a certainty, cursing in a continuous stream of expletives until he exhausted his frustration. "If it was you in charge of their horde, what would you have done," he challenged the Commander.

"I would have split my force, drawn the enemy away from what I considered the real prize, and then capture it while they had their backs turned."

"God damn right!" Johannes shouted. "I would have done exactly the same thing. How could we have been so stupid? Dispatching all of our forces to chase a decoy."

"You forget that this decoy represented almost two fifths of their fighting force. Hardly what I'd call insignificant. Who would have thought an enemy, even the Huns, would have been willing to sacrifice that many men?"

"Someone who was not a Hun but was in charge of them would. Someone who had everything to gain and nothing to lose," Johannes reminded Patricius of the obvious. "Kavad's a wily old fox and we overlooked that. While we were protecting one hen house, he's gone and feasted at the other."

"The other?" Attard couldn't follow the conversation.

"If Persia is one hen house, then Byzantium is the other," Patricius clarified. "Johannes is right," we've been played for fools. The Ephthalite chieftain has used Kavad as much as he was using them."

"So you're saying that the main force of the Ephthalites is now across the border in Byzantium territory."

"We were so focused on Kavad, trying to anticipate his moves in order to reclaim the Sassanid Empire, we never thought about the White Huns desire to take Byzantium. Who said they had to win back Kavad's kingdom first?"

"They don't have enough men to take on the Byzantines," Attard argued with the Commander.

"Not with the number of men spotted in the north. The sixty thousand was probably only a fraction of the number the Huns had streaming down from the Urals. Whatever they lost here will be quickly replaced by their recruiting efforts. They'll be gaining them fast now," Diogenes inserted himself back into the discussion. "I should know; I used to be in charge of disciplining the eastern provinces of our empire. The populations there would turn on us without any provocation whatsoever. Their origins are so mixed they don't have loyalties to anyone in particular. Remember, it wasn't so long ago we conquered the territories off you. Some are probably even praying for the day when they can be part of the Sassanid Empire again. Whatever number of men they lost this day will be replenished easily from new recruits taken from the provinces. I can guarantee it!"

"So, what do we do now?" Attard looked at continuing the pursuit of the remainder of the Hun's army.

"We will retrace our steps and discover exactly where the enemy is. That does not include having your Persians marching through our territories. If we already have one invading army within our borders, I'm certainly not permitting a second foreign presence." Johannes was adamant in his refusal of any aid from the Sassanids.

"So, it is fine for your Byzantines to move unmolested through my country but we're not to be trusted enough to assist you in yours. Which part of our alliance did you not fully understand?" Attard moved menacingly towards the Byzantine general.

Zutra held out a hand to stay the baron, pressing it against his chest. "This is not the time to play partisan politics," Zutra spoke up for the first time. "You have a possible crisis," he spoke directly to Johannes, "And you are refusing aid from an ally. I am in agreement with Attard. How quickly you have forgotten that you are a Byzantine army currently on Persian territory. When it comes to dealing with a mutual threat to both our empires then this is not the time to enforce boundaries. If you still insist on refusing the barons from setting foot on your soil, then at least accept the presence of my men and the Alans under Patricius. We are no threat to furthering any instability within your provinces. We are not Persians and therefore you can have no objections. But you will need our aid!"

"And why should I agree?"

"Let me point out the obvious," Zutra continued. "Whether you choose to recognize me or not, I am King of the Jews. I presume we will be heading directly towards Erzurum. Since Diogenes has explained that he used to govern the area, then he will be able to confirm my next statement. Ten percent of the population in the Van is of Jewish extraction. I can ensure that none of them will be willing to support Kavad and his Hun allies. My vizier here, besides being a former Caesar of your own empire is still the most prominent leader of the Alans you have. Which means a large percentage of that population that doesn't listen to me will listen to him. Do you think that you personally have that much influence over the people in the area? I doubt it. That's why you will want us to come with you. Now think about what I have just said."

Johannes stared blankly at Patricius for anything he might have wanted to add.

"You can't refute the logic, Johannes. It makes perfect sense to me," was all that Patricius had to say.

"Okay, you both can come with your men, but the Persians must stay on their side of the border! That's my last word on the matter!"

Chapter Twenty-Nine

Erzurum: Summer 501 A.D.

Wearing long woolen robes that cloaked them entirely from their necks to their toes, they walked through the streets looking no different from many of the other denizens of the city dressed similarly. With keffiyehs over their heads, they successfully masked their appearances just in case any one of them on the rare chance should happen to be recognized.

"I'd appreciate if you would tell us where we are going," Johannes tried once more to learn of their destination.

"I will tell you all when we get there," Zutra promised.

"We've spent two weeks surveying this city from the hills and we're no closer to freeing it from the Huns."

"Patience, Johannes," Zutra urged.

"How can I be patient as I remain idle while my empire shrinks by the day?"

"The time will come to claim back your city. But for now we must learn everything we can about the enemy. They have not come to rape and pillage. More so, it is obvious that they've come to stay. Don't you think that is highly unusual for a nomadic people?"

"All the more reason we must drive them out before the people become too comfortable with their presence," the Byzantine general insisted.

"We must only show our hand when the hour is right," Mar Zutra advised. "If we act too soon then we are handing them an easy victory. Too late and they become entrenched."

"And that's your advice?" Johannes questioned. "Wait for the right time? How would you even know when the right time was present?"

Zutra continued to walk towards the city center followed by the rest of the party but still not answering the question. The others followed behind blindly still waiting for his response.

"When will be the right time?" Johannes pressed him again.

"There is a synagogue in this city," the Exilarch began to reveal the full extent of his plan.

"There are many synagogues in this city," Diogenes criticized. "A lot of Jews means a lot of synagogues. "

"Have you gone mad? What are you thinking? Are we going to pray for an answer from your God?" Johannes became quite sarcastic.

"Our God," Zutra corrected him. "Yes, in a sense that is exactly what I'm going to do," Zutra remained cryptic. "I have heard that there is one synagogue where they say a prophet resides. Do you know of that one Diogenes?"

"An old fool that even more Jewish fools have talked about in defiance of our ordinance that Jesus was the last of the prophets. I have never given it any credence. Anyway, that was years ago," he added. "He could very well be dead by now."

"But do you know where that synagogue is? I only have a vague idea."

"Follow me." Diogenes took the lead of the group and moved purposely through the labyrinth of streets.

"Has it come to this?" Johannes whispered to Patricius. "That we are looking for answers from seers. Have we actually become so desperate? And what of you? A Caesar, a soldier of Christ, and now nothing more than a lapdog to this Jewish pretender to a throne."

"I have learned not to underestimate this young king. Neither should you," Patricius commented privately so as not to be overheard by anyone other than Johannes. "If you had the opportunity to serve under him you would learn fairly quickly that he is being guided by a higher power. Our God as he stated so correctly."

"Don't tell me that you are abandoning your Christian heritage with such blasphemy," Johannes sounded shocked at Patricius's revelation. "Are you a Jew now too?"

"One can still be a Christian and still believe that the Lord moves in mysterious ways. If He chooses to guide the actions of a descendant of Aaron and David, who am I to question Him? After all, he was their God first!"

"They would call such a belief sacrilege back at the court," Johannes cautioned.

"They call anything they don't like sacrilege back at the court," Patricius laughed. "Why do you think it has been so easy for me all these years to stay away from Constantinople? I prefer to do my own thinking?"

"Sounding more and more like blasphemy to me," Johannes snorted as he stifled his resentment.

"Me?" Patricius pleaded innocence. "You're the one that's attached to the court and is now going to visit some old Jewish sage for advice. Do you remember the bible story of Saul and the witch?"

Johannes reflected upon the story from the Book of Kings, his anger dissipating and soon afterwards he smiled, appreciating the irony. "I guess today I have now become a blasphemer too. My list of sins is growing rapidly as long as I remain with you!"

"As with us all," the Commander added. "Are we okay?"

"Yes," Johannes agreed. "We are okay."

"This is it," Diogenes hailed the rest to follow him into the limestone brick building.

"Doesn't look like much," Johannes commented on the undecorated structure.

"Considering how often the synagogues are either stripped of their possessions or razed to the ground in this town, less is more, if you understand," Zutra explained the lack of any exterior decoration.

"If you're implying my people have anything to do with such events then you are sadly mistaken," the Byzantine general quickly defended himself. "We have ruled the city benevolently."

"No one ever does," Zutra taunted. "They just burn to the ground spontaneously."

"Enough!" Patricius ended any furthering of this particular conversation. "In case you may have forgotten, we are trying to be discrete and remain undiscovered in what is now enemy territory. If the Huns should find us within the city, the only thing burning will be us tied to stakes! Are we clear on that?"

"I was just reminding the general of our history. If he misunderstood my intentions and believed I was accusing him of such atrocities, then I am truly sorry."

Johannes searched for the words, but he could not find any for the moment. He extended his arm in mutual apology waiting for the words to spring from his mouth. "If my brashness and my limited exposure to your world provides the mistaken impression that I could be one of those men, then I too am sorry."

"Well received, now Excellency, if you don't mind getting on with the reason you brought us here before we should happen to be discovered," Patricius urged Zutra to move quickly.

Ascending the flight of stairs, they found themselves locked out by the heavy plated door that was clearly barred from the inside. Clanging the massive iron ring that hung head high on the door, Zutra waited for a response.

The voice was feeble and hesitant. "Who is it and why are you here?" it asked warily.

"A close friend and relative of Mordecai bar Kahana seeks the seer known as Isaac," Mar Zutra shouted through the heavy door.

"Everyone knows that Mordecai bar Kahana is dead," the answer floated back.

"Yes, he is but that does not mean his friend and relative also happens to be dead,"

"But he could not have sent you if he is dead!" The custodian refused to open the door.

"Oh, for crying out loud," Diogenes could restrain his temper no longer. "Open the bloody door for your king, you old fool!"

"Which king would that be?" the custodian challenged them with another question. "Of late we've had so many passing through this land; it's difficult to know which one is king today."

Diogenes prepared to shoulder the door, though the prospect of dislodging it from the hinges was an impossibility.

Waving his hands to stop, Zutra tried a more subtle approach. "The one king, the only king, from the lineage of kings anointed by Samuel."

"Is it truly you master?" The voice wavered, disbelieving at first.

"I am that boy the seer sent word to Mordecai to protect. Now will you let me see him?"

"Of course, come in, come in," the custodian sounded excited as he rolled back the bar and opened the door to the synagogue. No sooner had the door opened the four visitors stepped into the temple foyer. "Oh, no," the custodian moaned nervously as he eyed the three others that accompanied Zutra, whom obviously were not Semitic.

"It's all right," Zutra comforted him. "These are good men. They are not here to hurt you. Now please, take me to Isaac."

Leading them from the foyer along the corridor that circumvented the sanctuary, the custodian took them to a sleeping room behind the altar. No light escaped from the room when he opened the door. "Wait," he instructed them. "I will light the lamp."

They heard the sound of the flint striking, saw a stream of sparks and then a small flame danced on a piece of twisted hemp that extruded from the clay pot. The custodian popped his head out the room and invited them to enter. "He will see you now."

"Was he sleeping," Zutra asked politely.

"Isaac is blind," the custodian explained the lack of any light in the room.

"I am sorry," Zutra regretted the seer's infirmity.

"Don't," Isaac responded from his seat in the corner of the room. "I would gladly trade my sight in this world for the visions I have of the other." The body was old but the voice was young and vibrant.

"I am…"

"You are the Exilarch," Isaac interrupted Zutra mid-sentence. "We were expecting you."

"You were?"

"I wouldn't be a very good seer if I couldn't even predict what will happen next in my own life."

"Then you know why I am here."

"People come to me so I can predict the future. But I'm not a mind reader," the old man laughed. "Pose to me your question and I will see if the Lord has already prepared your destiny. That is how this works."

"Like an oracle," Patricius added for Zutra's benefit.

"Yes, like an oracle," Isaac agreed. "God has seeded the earth with many gifted people. And certainly, those of us that fulfill our purpose tend to live our lives in a temple. Greek temples, Indus temples, and even this humble temple, it's all the same. So ask me what it is you need to know."

"Though you cannot see us, I am here with two generals from the Emperor Anastasius. I am here with my Vizier who also represents the barons of Persia. We made mistakes and let the Huns overrun this province. They have taken control of your city and Kavad acts as their governor while he prepares to recapture his old empire. We have to know what we must do to restore the order to our two worlds. I fear that on our present course we will engage in a war that never ends. Many innocents will die as a result. If we are to succeed, I need to know what sacrifice has to be made. I need to know what the Lord has decided for me."

Tilting his head upward, the unseeing glazed eyes gazed upon the emptiness above. The seer began to cant an old prayer, the words lost to another time when prophets freely roamed the earth. No one made a sound as the indecipherable words immediately took upon a life of their own, a small gust of wind circling through the room that caused them to pull their cloaks tightly around their shoulders to stave off the sudden chill. Johannes made the sign of the cross fearing that he was now vulnerable to Jewish demons.

His shoulders jerked and the old man's head momentarily tossed from side to side until it came to rest rolled back between his shoulder blades. His mouth continued to move, as if speaking but no words ushered forth. Zutra made a move to rush forward and see if the seer was all right but Patricius immediately held out his arm to block any movement by his king. The vizier had seen all this before by those that still survived at the ancient oracles strewn across Asia. All those gifted with the art of prophecy underwent a similar transformation. He didn't have to restrain Zutra for long before the prophet began to speak in words they could understand:

> *'Seven wishes for seven dreamers for seven years,*
> *Only to have the dreams fade into mortal tears,*
> *When all shall come to pass all will again be the same,*
> *Brother against brother shall bear the blame.*

One ancient crown that will be split into three,
But only one branch will continue to be free,
The old king returns to regain only what he had,
In a time of peace, the twin eagles will be glad.

Mourn for the one that brought it about,
When all is at end a tiny kingdom they will rout,
By betrayal and lies they will sweep it away,
And few will remember what happened this day.

All will be as all once had been,
Armies at rest along the Euphrates,
Dust will settle on the staff and the rod,
For man has turned from the ways of God.'

Lowering his head, the old man sighed heavily, the trance-like state lifting from his opaque eyes. Though he could not see Mar Zutra, he turned directly towards him sensing his presence. "I am sorry, my King. I am very sorry."

"No need, Isaac. You gave us what we needed to know. My family has grown accustomed to riding the waves of fate."

"At least the Lord has not forsaken you, my King. Three lines shall stem from you. Your family's time will come again."

"Reward the prophet," Zutra instructed his vizier. "And then let us return to camp. We have much to discuss."

"But what about scouting the city?" Diogenes inquired.

"What more you may learn will not change what has already been predetermined. We know what will happen. It is up to us now to do what is necessary to see that it does happen." Though the prophecy was clear to Zutra, his companions were not as confident in its infallibility. Nevertheless, the Exilarch was not to be dissuaded from his decision to leave the city. Eventually the others agreed that it would be best to return to their men and digest Isaac's words before they proceeded further.

Pacing back and forth outside the tent, the worried expression on Patricius's face let everyone know that there had still been no word from the camp physicians. It had been days now since the fever took hold of the young king, and thus far every treatment known to the medics had failed to break its death grip.

"Anything as yet?" Hermantius asked his cousin.

"They keep telling me to go away every time I step inside the tent. They warn me against its spread, yet they don't even know what it is. What is there to catch if there is no name to it?"

"Still cousin, it is good advice," Hermantius consoled him. "He is young and strong; he will survive this."

"I know you mean well." Patricius pushed Hermantius's sympathetic hand from his shoulder. "But this is not a disease of the human condition. It is a curse. The mind is not able to handle such things. No man is permitted to know his future; not even s scion of David!"

"Now you're beginning to sound like Diogenes," Hermantius cautioned him. "He's been saying exactly the same thing. It's a curse from God; a divine punishment. Bullshit! I've been a soldier too long. It's an illness plain and simple even if we don't have a name for it."

Stopping his pacing, Patricius went over in his mind the last few sentences from his cousin. Something clicked but he couldn't quite put his finger on it as yet. "Say what you just said again," he ordered his general. "Something bothers me."

"Which part?" Hermantius sounded confused by the request. "An illness plain and simple?"

"No before that!"

"What, that Diogenes said it was a divine punishment?"

"Sometimes cousin you can be absolutely brilliant," he said jubilantly as he pulled back the tent flaps and rushed inside.

"What? What did I say?" Hermantius questioned, his words trailing off as the Vizier disappeared into the tent.

Once inside Patricius practically bowled the physicians over with his entrance. "What can cause a fever of this nature that isn't a disease?" he demanded to know. "Can poisons do it?"

"Well, yes," one of the physicians replied hesitantly. "But the signs are different."

"What do you mean by different," he pressed them harder for answers.

"Well, first of all, the King is showing all the signs of black bile. He sweats, he is hot to the touch, and he is not lucid at all. In fact, he sleeps close to death."

'And why is that different from this poison you spoke of."

"Well, a poison such as nightshade can cause the fever but then it will either kill the victim or it will be flushed eventually from the body. It would not linger as is the case with the king."

"Not to mention he has no hallucinations nor are his pupils dilated," the other physician piped in.

"And nightshade will always do this?"

"Yes," the first physician stated emphatically.

"That is not always true," the other quickly countermanded his associate.

"I hate to disagree with you Theodosus, but it has been my experience that the signs are always the same," the other physician argued but the quivering of his neatly trimmed gray beard upon his chin indicated that he was not as positive as he claimed.

"But you have never been outside the Empire," the elder physician named Theodosus reminded his colleague. "I have and I have come across at least five different varieties of nightshade and all of them have similar yet different properties."

"Different in what way," Patricius demanded to know.

"One variety I noted never caused sedation. The affected individual actually became highly agitated. A completely opposite reaction to what is ordinarily anticipated."

"Then it wasn't nightshade," the first physician stated rather emphatically.

"But it was Kronus. It definitely was. Slightly different in color but the same family of plant. That I can assure you."

"Could it be possible for there to be such a plant that behaved in the manner we now are seeing?" Patricius was even more convinced now that the young king had been poisoned.

"If Mar Zutra came across the berries and thought they were grapes, depending on the amount he had eaten, then it could be possible. They do look similar. But we have no way of knowing what variety of the plant he may have stumbled across."

"Stumbled across...yes...that must have been what happened," Patricius parroted the physician's words but the doubts raced around within his skull. "How do we rid him of this poison if that's what it is?"

"If we knew he had eaten any part of the plant, we could have emptied his stomach by making him swallow salt. However, it is too late for that now. The poison would already be throughout his body by this time."

"There has to be a way to neutralize it."

"Only one that I know of," Theodosus responded. "In my travels to Asia, they showed me a wondrous plant, with thick leaves that produced the sweetest nectar. They called it an agave and said that it neutralizes many of the known poisons. They mentioned nightshade was one of them in particular. I recall that fact succinctly."

"In Asia? It's only in Asia, you're telling me?"

"No, not at all!" Theodosus exclaimed proudly. "I brought shoots of the plant back with me. There is a large patch of it in the royal botanical gardens. In fact the Emperor has a drink made from the plant daily. Why do you think he looks so healthy for his age?"

"Thank you. Thank you so much." Patricius was overjoyed, grabbing Theodosus's hand and shaking it furiously.

"But the Emperor is very exclusive in the use of the plant," the physician warned him.

"That won't be a problem. I have my connections. Now, I need the king prepared to travel. Can you do that?"

"But we don't even know if we are dealing with nightshade poisoning," Kronus protested. "If that should be the case then by moving him you are signing the King's death warrant."

"I'll take my chances,' Patricius excused the medic of any further responsibility for his patient. "When I return shortly, I want him ready to travel." Stepping outside the tent, the Commander was prepared to shout for his general to present himself, but it wasn't necessary; Hermantius had never left, remaining outside the tent flap all along, listening intently to the discussion.

"I'll have a squad of my men accompany you," he stated before Patricius could even ask the question.

"What distance are we looking at from here?" he posed the question to his cousin.

"About six hundred miles."

"Too long!" Patricius exclaimed. "He could be dead by the time we arrive."

"Not if you go by ship," Hermantius suggested. "You can board a sailing vessel at Trabzon, just north of here, and be in Constantinople in five days if there's a good wind.

"Perfect," the Commander sounded pleased with the time frame. "Be careful Hermantius. I don't want to come back and find anyone else accidentally poisoned."

"Accidental. Pah!" Hermantius snorted, knowing full well what his cousin meant.

Chapter Thirty

Constantinople: Summer 501 A.D

"Relax Paddy," Empress Ariadne stroked his temples and tried to comfort him but to no avail.

"I'm failing him, Dinah. Time and time again I am placing him in harm's way and my stupidity may very well get him killed next time. This is my entire fault! I should have anticipated this."

"But he isn't' dead," she consoled him. "And my physicians say he will make a full recovery very soon. You may remain as my guest until he is fit to travel once more. Do not worry; I will take care of you both."

"As always, I am in your debt."

"And you know sometime in the future I will be calling that debt in," she made him aware that she always called in her debts no matter how great or small.

"I wouldn't expect any less of you Dinah," he chuckled. "But the way things are going, I may not be around too much longer for you to collect!"

"Don't be so melodramatic!" she scolded. "Having Erzurum fall to the enemy is only a temporary setback. It would have happened regardless since we were not properly prepared for a war against the Ephthalites. Now we know their intentions and we will take the war to them."

"You've always been a woman that knew how to get what she wanted."

"Not always," she admitted. "Now and then something I want does get away from me." The demure look she flashed towards him tugged at his heartstrings.

"It would be a shame to have to lose it again," Patricius stirred the memories.

"I think you are getting soft in your old age Paddy. First, you become emotional over your relationship with your king and now you're becoming a hopeless romantic. What's happening to you?" she quipped.

"Maybe I'm developing a conscience," he responded.

"Maybe you should have settled down at some point in your life," she offered a more likely answer.

"I have a family," he revealed. "Strange as this may sound, Zutra is like a son to me. I don't know how it happened or when it happened but it did. It is as if we are tied by blood."

"I know. I could tell the way you've been hovering over him since you both arrived here. Just like a mother hen."

"I guess you're thinking what an old fool I have become?"

Ariadne shook her head in denial. "No. I'm thinking how wonderful for you. You have something I can never have now that my son is dead. Cherish it Paddy. I actually envy you."

"He's a good king," he defended his behavior and reason for the attachment. "There's nobility that he manifests that defies explanation. It's almost as if I'm honored just by serving him. I know that sounds strange. It's difficult to explain."

"So why are you fighting with yourself over your relationship with him. What's really bothering you?" Her dark eyes pierced deeply into his soul.

"I never could hide anything from you. Besides all the reasons I've given you for feeling his current predicament is my own fault, I'm concerned that we can't win this war."

"Because of legitimate military reasons or because you visited some blind Jewish seer and he filled your head with so much doubt that you're afraid to make a move lest it result in the death of your king."

"I told you what the prophet had to say. Mar Zutra had no doubts that it was the truth. In his mind I know he's already preparing for his own death."

"So you've surrendered before you even made your first defense? Is that what this self-recrimination is all about?" Without warning, the Empress brusquely slapped him across the face.

Patricius rubbed the sting in his cheek. "Stop doing that! What was that one for?"

"That's for becoming an old fool and forgetting who you are. You are Julius Flavius Patricius, son of Aspar Flavianus, former Caesar of the Empire and the bravest man I have ever known. You fight for honour and you fight for those that are unable to fight for themselves. At no time have you ever turned your back on a battle and I'm not going to permit you to do so now! Are we clear?"

Nodding his head sheepishly, Patricius agreed. "Crystal! I deeply regret my momentary lapse, my Lady. I beg your pardon. Julius Flavius Patricius fights to his last breath," he pledged as he bowed over-dramatically and then stared up into her face as he winked.

"Good! Now that we have that settled, I think it's time we go before my husband and settle this other matter. You will explain this nonsense of a prophecy and tell them all how we're going to win this war. Moreover, whatever you do, pay no attention to his advisors. They are nothing but fools."

"As you demand, your Highness," he acquiesced as he mock bowed. Escorting the Empress along the corridor, they moved steadily towards the massive polished brass doors that guarded the throne room which swung open immediately as they approached.

Heavy in discussion with his political and military advisors, the Emperor failed to even acknowledge their entrance, never looking up in their direction as they strolled towards the dais where he sat pensively upon his jewel-encrusted throne. The Empress waited patiently for the opportunity to speak; her presence still not acknowledged by Anastasius. Patricius weighed the heavy political atmosphere and immediately assessed that something had changed significantly from the last time he visited Constantinople. The Empress it would appear had been shunted to the periphery, no longer able to dominate over the aging Emperor as she had done previously. This was definitely not a position that Ariadne was accustomed to or one that she would easily tolerate. Clearing her throat loudly she interrupted the conversation between her husband and his chief of staff.

"Oh, my dear wife Ariadne, I am so sorry," Anastasius apologized, "I didn't realize you were standing there."

It was so far from the truth, it was practically insulting, but the unspoken overtones were even more telling as far as Patricius was concerned. Reduced to wife, the Emperor made no illusions of her status at this meeting. Even the reference to her personal name was in itself condescending, implying she was a familiar of no higher status than anyone else was in the room. Inwardly, the Commander considered the situation quite volatile; knowing Ariadne well enough to expect that at some point the Emperor was going to pay dearly for this intentional slight. Ariadne was not a person to easily forget a transgression.

"And I see you've brought General Patricius as I requested," Anastasius continued. "I hope you don't mind General, but we have had difficulty in interpreting the exact ramifications of the prophecy that you related to us. Perhaps you can provide us with a more personal insight since you were actually there at the time."

"Thank you, Excellency," Patricius saluted and bowed courteously. "I would be pleased to explain it to you."

Gripping the arms of the throne, the elderly ruler half raised himself from his seat as he leaned forward. "More importantly, I want to know how this prophecy justifies the loss of part of my empire and why I shouldn't hold you personally responsible for this fiasco!"

"Because Excellency, it would be for the same reason you cannot hold the people of Erzurum and the rest of the Van responsible for surrendering their cities to the Huns without a fight. To do so would eliminate the opportunity of destroying our mutual enemy in its entirety as you can so wisely discern," the Commander answered confident that he would come to no harm even with his brazen response.

"And you know this because..." Anastasius scratched his head in bewilderment.

"It's in the prophecy," was all that Patricius said rather benignly.

Looking to his advisors for further comment none was forthcoming and the Emperor turned back to Patricius seeking him to expand his explanation.

"The prophecy was in three parts," Patricius detailed the words delivered by Isaac. "The first part foretells that we will suffer these setbacks initially. So why try to fight the inevitable?"

The Emperor's expression soured. "Because Diogenes warned me that unless we stop this prophecy from unraveling it will be the end of our world. What have you to say about that?"

"He is wrong," responded the Commander. "Diogenes cares about Diogenes; nothing more and nothing less. So he focused on the first part and ignored the rest."

"Diogenes is a loyal servant," one of the advisors spoke out in his defense. "He cares only about the well-being of the Empire!"

"My wife's nephew cares only about laying his hands on the Empire," Anastasius countered. "Let's be serious! Still, why would our attempts to prevent the fulfilling of this prophecy be catastrophic? Why should we willingly accept defeat?"

"Because it's not defeat," Patricius tried to explain again patiently. "It's a respite. It's to your advantage to have the Huns hemmed in behind walls. That will become their undoing."

Tapping the side of his skull, it finally dawned on the Emperor where Patricius was heading with his revealed strategy. "We make certain they can't leave the city," Anastasius exclaimed.

"Precisely. We keep them boxed in; fight a war of attrition and everything falls into place exactly as the seer predicted. Everything will return to its proper place when seven years have passed. That's roughly in five more years from now."

"That's a long time to conduct a war of attrition, General. A very costly five years I might remind you. How can I afford to keep the greater portion of my army stationed in the northeast corner of the Empire all that time?"

"The enemy will sue for peace. The Huns will retire from your territory and you'll get everything back and more. The length of the Euphrates becomes your new boundary."

"But it also means that Kavad is sitting back on his throne as well. What's to stop him from starting a new war?"

"The Kavad that will return as the Great Shah will be nothing compared to the one that was deposed; nothing more than a shadow staving off the threat of yours and the Ephthalite's expansion. The only way he'll be able to do that is to continually sue for peace himself."

"I don't understand," the Emperor shook his head. "I see no advantage to you. None of this benefits you and your king. Why are you so willing to accept this prophecy?" Clasping his arms over his chest, Anastasius waited for an appropriate answer.

"You're right! There are no benefits; no rewards for my master. In fact, the fulfillment of the prophecy means that he will most likely be killed."

"Then why not fight?" The expression on the Emperor's face indicated he was quite perplexed by the incongruity. "Who accepts their death so willingly?"

"If you knew the Exilarch Mar Zutra well, then you would understand," was all that Patricius would say.

"I'm an old man," Anastasius drew a comparison, "But I have no desire to forfeit my life as yet. How can you ask anyone to understand? Is there is some secret that you have not yet revealed to us?" The members of the Emperor's council mumbled their confirmation of their ruler's suspicion.

"No secret, no trick, no deception," the Commander stated emphatically. "Just a man that is willing to accept the fate that God has doled out to him."

"Are you implying that we're not men of God," one of the advisors hurriedly piped in, feeling offended by the comment. "If God wanted us to martyr ourselves, we would willingly do so."

"Then be glad that he's asked a Jewish King to do so, on your behalf and stop looking for evidence of deceit where there is none!" Patricius knew exactly what kind of men the Emperor had surrounded himself with and quickly assessed not a single one of them would gladly lay down their lives for any cause no matter how noble.

"Still, even a martyr strikes a bargain in exchange for his life," Anastasius suggested. "It is the nature of man."

"Lord Zutra knows that with his death his throne will be split into three. Mahoza will no longer be an independent kingdom, but he has the Lord's reassurance that his lineage will continue well into the future. One line of descendants will continue to rule somewhere else in the world. He is satisfied to embrace his fate having that knowledge. Do not try to compare him to any other man. He is a breed apart."

"And all this on the word of a Jewish seer," the advisor admonished the Commander. "Even General Diogenes wrote to us that in his estimation it was a dubious source. Had the seer been worthy then he would not have allowed himself to be trapped like a rat within the city."

The Empress Ariadne was unable to restrain herself any longer, having listened to the whining and complaints of her husband's inner circle of advisors and found them to be an annoyance. "Perhaps a reminder that all prophets according to the Bible were Jewish would convince Lord Darius that the source is reliable. Or would that also be too distasteful to acknowledge that our own Lord Jesus Christ was a Jew. Which Jewish prophets should we believe, and which ones should we refuse to accept? The Bible tells us that the true prophets all suffered for their insights. If Lord Darius on the advice of my nephew has a better insight in this regard, then let him speak up."

It was a bitter slap to his ego to permit the Empress to berate him publicly in that manner, but the counselor knew better than to challenge Ariadne openly. Though she may have been out of favor with the court at that moment, she was still a very powerful woman that had proven herself in the past to also be extremely dangerous.

"Let it go Darius," Anastasius cautioned his advisor. "My wife is right. Whether we like it or not, God has spoken to these Jews and will continue to speak to them. He cannot go back on His promises to them. So let us assume that this seer is accurate in his foretelling of events. And let us not forget that Diogenes is a soldier who will have very little to do in the coming years if we only fight a war of attrition. The prophecy is not in his best interest. Nevertheless, it could very well be in ours. So tell me, General Patricius, how would you suggest we conduct our campaign for the next five years?"

Patricius took the opportunity to demonstrate his mastery of all things military. "Gentlemen and of course your Highnesses, if I can have your undivided attention, please!" Hovering over the map displayed in the centre of throne room, Patricius picked up the pointer that lay on the trestle table. The enemy is situated here at Erzurum." He pointed to the fortressed city drawn on the map. "But that still places them well east of the Euphrates. If you were to reinforce the cities of Elasik and Gazantep, it would prevent any advancement of their troops into the Syrian province. Along the entire length of the river between those two cities, the construction of a series of outposts would prove a strong deterrent to the enemy. The same is true for Trabzon on the southern shores of the Black Sea. We strengthen and fortify the port there so the Huns can't receive any supplies except over land. That decreases their ability to reinforce as well as stretches out their supply line over a vast distance which I'm willing to gamble will cause them to stay put in the region around Erzurum rather than risk being caught too far from the supply train. Then, heading north from Elasik to Trabzon, we construct another series of outposts. That will then become the new border for your Empire; easily defensible and providing you with the capability of launching raids into the Van without taking too much risk."

Clearing his throat, one of the military attachés among the Emperor's adjutants raised a bone of contention. "General Patricius, if you draw the line along the Euphrates, you're placing our city of Amida beyond the defensible line."

"The city of Amida is already beyond your defensible line," Patricius stated firmly. "Trying to defend a city that is a hundred miles inside enemy territory is illogical. Let me rephrase that, it's not illogical, it's foolish. The population isn't even Byzantine; it's Persian. Trying to hold on to that particular city will drain your resources, and the loss of men it would entail cannot be justified!"

"Easy for you to say!" Lord Darius shouted. "What's it matter to you if we give up our valuable tracts of land that we fought hard to obtain?"

"Amida is nothing more than a trophy city. An opportunity for you to crow that you took a major town from your enemy and that you now have a presence deep within their kingdom. But as you may recall, the agreement with the Emperor Jamasp was for a total withdrawal of your forces once the tributes were paid. Your men shouldn't even be there. So, pull them back, defend what is a much easier position, and stop pretending that your army is invincible. It isn't!"

"We may pull back," Anastasius hesitatingly agreed, "But we will not give up Amida. Some cities are not negotiable."

"And why we're busy doing all this, what will your armies be doing?" Lord Darius challenged the Commander.

"Exactly what your men will be doing," Patricius offered. Drawing the pointer across the map, the Commander outlined his own defensive plans. "We will be digging in along this line from Mosul to Irbil, five hundred miles north of our capitals and four hundred miles south of the front."

"What good does that do?" Darius inquired haughtily. "You're too far from where the war is being fought and so remote from your own cities that you wouldn't be able to defend them."

"True, very true," Patricius concurred. "I can't deny any of what you've said. But if you look at the map, should the Ephthalites or any of Kavad's forces that he raises from the Van get past those two cities they would be in the valley between the two rivers. They wouldn't need their supply lines any longer and there'd be nothing to stop them from decimating the population. That's our final line of defense, in fact our only line of defense. If we lose there, then we've lost everything!"

"And you're willing to give them all your northern territories without even a fight?" Darius was astounded.

"Ideally, if your armies do their job and contain them in Erzurum then they shouldn't have the opportunity to take the north. Should they start migrating south then something has gone terribly wrong. Also remember, according to the prophecy this war ends with a treaty; they go back to where they spawned from. The borders are all reestablished and there are no battles on our home soil."

"And you seriously believe that is the way this will all end? Then explain how is it that your King is predicted to die if it all ends peacefully?" the Emperor sounded dubious.

"As you are all aware, he is only now recovering from what could have easily been a fatal assault. No weapons, no war, only the vile act of the poisoner; a coward that attempted to circumvent the prophecy by interceding in such a malicious manner."

"And what makes you so certain that the attempt on Mar Zutra's life was made by someone that was aware of the prophecy?" Darius insisted on knowing.

"Quite simple," Patricius was pleased that someone had actually raised the attempt on his king's life while in the presence of the Emperor. "The prophecy foretold his death through betrayal. The individual that attempted to poison him would be thinking that he was only fulfilling his role in the prophecy. It said that we would mourn for his passing which would

indicate that his end would come during this present crisis while we're all still around to mourn his passing. The rod and the staff are to be covered over by the dust of ages. You all know your Bible well enough to understand the concept of the rod and staff. It's indicating that his murder will be by someone who also understands the heritage that those two items represent. That would mean he was poisoned by the hand of either a Christian or Jew. Since those Jews that would be capable of such a dire deed are currently with Kavad, it is unlikely that it would be any of them. That only leaves those that were present at the time of the foretelling of the prophecy and I know for a fact it wasn't me."

"That doesn't leave too many options on the identity of the individual, does it?" Darius tried to prompt the Commander into listing the possible suspects which he knew would be condemned by the rest of the council as a serious accusation without proof.

"No, it doesn't," Patricius remained calm. "Just two come to mind. Nevertheless, we would be wasting our time in trying to identify the culprit. Instead, the word should be spread that the Exilarch is not to be harmed; otherwise, it would be contrary to the prophecy's first line. There are seven dreamers for seven years. Not two years but seven! If someone was to alter that prediction, then the results could be disastrous for all of us. To do so would be tempting fate and defying God's will!" he warned everyone gathered in the room playing upon their superstitious natures.

"And have you identified the seven dreamers it speaks of," Anastasius inquired.

"Of course, you are one of them, your Excellency. But so are the six others that dream of ruling over kingdoms."

"Six, what six others?" the Emperor counted out the other players on his fingers.

"There is Kavad and his brother Jamasp. The Ephthalite chieftain is now added to that group. Then of course there is Mar Zutra and his brother-in-law that now rules as Emperor of China."

"That's only six of us in total," Anastasius pointed out the error in the math.

"And why should we overlook the one that has guided me from the moment I first returned? That she is the daughter of Emperors and the maker of Emperors. We can never omit the Empress Ariadne from that group. To do so would be foolhardy." Patricius intended his comment as an admonishment to the Emperor; a reminder that he should not consider himself so safely entrenched in his throne that he could overlook or dismiss her continued support. Though the advisors gathered in the hall quickly took offense to the inclusion of the Empress in the circle of monarchs, Anastasius quickly silenced them with a wave of his hand.

"Yes, I can see that," the Emperor admitted. "My wife is key to everything that is germane to our current situation. I hope that she will assist with this long period of attrition we are about to engage in should we follow this plan of yours. Building all those fortresses ad outposts will prove be a very costly undertaking. It may be necessary that we require some of her family's wealth in order to complete the construction."

"And I would willingly give to the well-being of the Empire," Ariadne sealed the offer. "The future of Byzantium must be safeguarded at all costs and those that rule it must be secure in the knowledge that they have made the right decision!"

"Well General," Anastasius concluded, "It appears we will fight this war your way!"

"As always, your Excellency, your wisdom is enlightenment to us all," Patricius bowed courteously to the Emperor as did the other advisors following his lead.

Chapter Thirty-one

Mosul: Late Fall 501 AD

"Your right, I don't understand," Zutra freely admitted.

"This is the way it has to be," Patricius insisted.

"Surely there is a better way than spending months sitting and waiting for nothing to happen. At least if we joined with the Byzantine forces outside of Erzurum, we could possibly lay siege to the city."

"Have you ever laid siege to a city," the commander inquired, knowing the answer well in advance.

"No, but it has to be better than sitting here and doing nothing," Zutra protested.

"I told you that it would be best if you returned to Mahoza. Be with your wives. See to your children. Govern over the people. You don't have to be here!"

"And what am I supposed to tell everyone? That we are sitting and waiting for events that aren't happening? Those are not the answers they want to hear."

"We are merely fulfilling the prophecy that you purposely sought out," Patricius reminded his king. "This is the balance he spoke of. Wars of attrition cannot be measured in lives but in patience. We wait out the enemy, and the first one to blink, loses."

"There is no glory in this!"

"You're right, there isn't," the Commander confirmed. "It is the costliest of all wars that are waged. They are endless, yet during that time the troops must be fed, entertained and paid. Our great advantage is knowing that the distances to maintain those supply lines are far longer for the Ephthalites than they are for us. Furthermore, they have the additional costs of trying to administrate the cities they now occupy. Just trying to

339

maintain the infrastructures will be a burden that will drain their coffers at an alarming rate. Especially since nomads have no understanding of what is required in the first place."

"So, when does it end?" Mar Zutra's impatience was flaring.

"As the prophecy indicated, it would be seven years in total. We are well into the third year now since Kavad made his escape."

"But can't you see, the longer he has a presence in the north, the more time he has to regain his influence over the northern tribes."

"As our intelligence indicates he is already doing so," his Vizier stated factually. "We are well aware of it. It was an educated risk that we assumed from the beginning. But as long as they stay north of this defensive line, we are content to let him have them. Think of it this way; more mouths to feed and a lot more pockets to line if he is to remain secure."

"And what happens once he rebuilds his army?" Zutra voiced his concern.

"Hopefully it will put a strain on his relationship with his Hun overlords. Once Kavad considers himself strong enough to break their tether, then he might actually revolt against his new masters."

"And if he doesn't?"

"Then he's going to eye the south and want it back. You will have your battles of glory then!"

The Exilarch paced back and forth in his tent while he contemplated what he should do. "If nothing changes in six more months, then I'll return to my palace," he said definitely.

"Nothing will change," Patricius urged him to return to Mahoza now.

"Yet I can tell from your voice that you cannot state that with one hundred percent certainty."

"Nothing is one hundred percent in this world!"

"So what's the worst scenario?"

"That Anastasius blinks first!"

"And then what?"

"Then you won't have to worry about your kingdom because it won't exist very long after that!"

"My kingdom is doomed then," Zutra bemoaned, sensing something ominous in the vizier's warning that he was reliant on the Byzantine

Emperor's steadfastness.

"If the prophecy proves true, then yes," Patricius confirmed.

Zutra continued pacing about the room his motions appearing somewhat frantic. "There is no doubt to the prophecy. Isaac has never been wrong before! We are fighting a battle that even if we should win, I lose."

"If that was true then there would be no need for generals. Our fates would be sealed from the day we are born. Over my lifetime, I have chosen not to believe that. Instead, I choose that God shows us what will happen if we choose to do nothing. That is the nature of free will. I have never been one to do nothing!"

"Nor have I," Zutra agreed, "But I am at a loss to understand how we can stop Anastasius from choosing the option of Pax Mondi that is foretold by the prophecy. It will be too tempting an offer for any ruler under the strain of financial ruination to ignore."

"Then we must find something more valuable to offer him instead. Fortunately for us the prophecy has given us enough time to think of what that might be."

Diogenes and Johannes sat around the table with the other generals that had joined them on the campaign. One in particular, Justin, had gained tremendously in favor with the Emperor as a result of his military brilliance demonstrated against the Goths in the west. Count Rusticus and Count Romanus were also present but only because Anastasius wanted them as far from the capital as possible, their piratical raids against the coast of Italy having caused a major dissension between the Emperor and his western counterpart, Theodoric of Rome.

"Must we always argue every time we sit around this table?" Johannes begged for order.

"Must you always pretend that we enjoy each other's company?" Rusticus fired back. "And who put you in charge anyway. Both Romanus and I outrank anyone else here!"

"Only through an accident of birth! Nobility doesn't count on the battlefield," Johannes challenged them. "You bleed the same as us."

"And last time I checked, I was still the nephew of the Empress,"

Diogenes added. "I think that still places me in the royal family of which neither of you have any claim."

"Then make some decisions and get us out of this hell hole," Romanus complained. "And what are you looking so smug about?" the Count turned on Justin.

"I was wondering how long it would take both of you to get irritated once you could no longer rape and pillage defenseless people." Justin interspersed his comment with a mocking laugh.

"They were enemies of the Empire!" both of them roared.

"Only if you consider the Western Empire to be an enemy of ours. I always thought we were essentially one great empire with two Emperors. Of course Theodosius might have second thoughts about that after what you two have done!"

"Are you accusing us of treachery?" Rusticus exclaimed.

Slamming his scabbard and baldric down on the table, making us much noise as he could, Johannes put an end to their accusations. "As far as we're all concerned, I am still the one in charge here. Until the Emperor says otherwise, that is the way it's going to be. Anyone that disagrees I will personally lock in the brig for treason! Now, are we all of a mutual understanding?"

The counts continued to grumble despite the warning. "And what exactly are you in charge of? The soldiers grow fat and lazy sitting behind the lines. They have nothing to do since it's obvious the Ephthalites have no intention of attacking. It proves they are weak. We should be looking at a strategy to drive them from Armenia rather than letting them die from old age. I say we take the surrounding towns and drive into their own Empire. Let them worry about how much they're losing while they sit around fat and they'll be scurrying back across the Urals before you know it," Romanus offered his alternative plan.

"The losses in doing so cannot be justified," Johannes argued. "We sit tight, fortify the stranglehold we have on them and eventually starve them into surrender. We need to think siege mentality and continue with the initial strategy that was agreed to!"

"You actually mean you don't want to upset your Persian and Jewish allies by expanding our empire. Isn't that what you're really saying? You'd be doing them a favor since its obvious they don't want to fight either."

"They might see our occupation of their lands as a declaration of war against them as well!" Johannes warned the others.

"So what? They're in no position to defend themselves. I say take what we can and the hell with the rest."

"You would Romanus. As long as you get what you want, you don't care about the rest. But that's not going to happen here. We're not about to open another front. The Emperor is trying to pursue a plan of stabilization and that means we don't double-cross our allies."

"Phah," Romulus spat. "I'd rather make a deal with the devil than with Jews and Persians. We have become weak and that is why the Empire is beginning to crumble."

"And here I thought it was because you went and attacked our fellow Romans in the west," Diogenes interrupted the discussion. "When Romans start killing each other, burning entire villages to the ground, we're sowing our own destruction."

"Don't fool yourself," Romanus laughed. "The Ostragoths control Rome. That part of the Roman Empire died a long time ago!"

"And you certainly did your part to drive the nails into its coffin," Johannes injected his own poisonous barb.

"We are all that is left of the ancient empire," he defended his actions. "We must prevail; we must survive at all costs. If we take everything of value from the western half, then we leave nothing for our enemies to use against us. What's it matter if the corpse has already withered?"

"You would dare try to make your justification sound reasonable."

"Because it is reasonable," Rusticus defended his besieged colleague. "We are at war! Christianity is being attacked from every direction. We are all that is left to uphold its legitimacy as the spoken word of God. Instead, here we are, allied to heathens, Jews and fire worshippers. Do you truly believe you are doing God's work?"

"I am doing the Empire's work!" Johannes argued, resenting the intimation of failing his obligations to Christianity. "There is no difference!"

Stifling a yawn, Count Rusticus tempered his reply. "If you say so General. After all, I'm not the one to pass judgment. That will happen soon enough when we reach the gates of heaven."

"For those souls that head in that direction," Justin was quick to point out. "It might be worthwhile to give your destination some consideration Count."

"Are you attempting humor, Justin?" Rusticus frowned at the insinuation. "It doesn't suit one nicknamed the Grim Reaper. All of you will be as answerable to the Lord on that day just as I am."

"If we can return to the issues at hand," Johannes was not willing to brook any further discussion. "We need all the men under singular command. Otherwise, we make ourselves vulnerable to attacks as they strike at us piece by piece. A united force provides not only a siege wall made of wood and stone but one of flesh as well."

The suggestion was met with immediate displays of acrimony.

"I have no objection as long as that command is mine," Justin stated.

"The command of this war has been placed under my direction," Johannes reminded everyone in the room. "The Emperor has made that perfectly clear."

"Yes, the command is under your direction," Justin reaffirmed, "But that has nothing to do with the direct command of my men. I have no objection to you directing this war, but my men report only to me!"

"Here, here," the other generals agreed.

"It cannot work if we are not unified," Johannes warned. "I need all of our men to work as a single entity. We cannot afford to have them wage this war independently of each other. This is a different kind of war from those waged on the battlefield. It is neither one of martial predominance nor impending glory. We need to entrench ourselves around the city, control all means of ingress and egress, and govern over the surrounding populations in order to maintain them on friendly terms. We cannot do that if each one of us feels entitled to move our men where and when we please."

"You will not have my men!" Count Rusticus shouted as he slammed his fist upon the table.

"Nor mine," Romanus agreed.

"It would appear that we are at a stalemate," Justin tallied the score for Johannes.

"This is a sad day," Johannes scolded them all. "Whereas we may have been able to bring this war to an early end by starving our enemy into submission, we have now succumbed to fulfilling the prophecy by guaranteeing it will go on for years."

"So be it," Rusticus defended his decision not to release his troops. "If this Jewish seer is as accurate as they claim, then we are only doing what we are supposed to do."

"I am not willing to engage in an argument over your adherence to some prophecy. You freely admitted you share no respect for any Jewish belief. How strange that now you are willing to acknowledge this one when it suits your own purpose!", Johannes challenged Rusticus.

"As I recall, you were the one that willingly went to see this prophet." Rusticus's smug grin purposely mocked the general.

"What are you implying Rusticus?"

"Oh, I don't know Johannes. Aren't there a lot of Jews in Scythopolis? That is where you're from, isn't it?"

"I don't like what you are intimating," Johannes scowled, his face flushed with anger.

"My, my," Rusticus feigned innocence. "This does appear to be a sore spot with you. Perhaps there is more to your cooperation with this Jewish King than we're aware of?"

"You even dare to raise such an accusation and I will have you quartered. That is a promise!"

"What do you think Romanus? Do you think there's a possible truth to the rumors?"

"I don't know Rusticus," Count Romanus played along with the game. "It's always been said that Johannes has been stolid in his Christian beliefs. Though no one can exactly say for certain when they've last seen him in a church, any church. That is a bit peculiar when you think about it."

"Both of you are treading on very dangerous ground," the General warned them. "If you are even suggesting that I am anything but a devout Christian then I will have you both in front of the Ecclesiastical Courts before you can say another word!"

"He is very defensive about the issue," Romanus concurred, "Don't you think?"

"Too defensive in my mind," Rusticus replied. "What say you about the matter Justin? Your faith is without question, and they say that at some time in the future you'd be in line to sit on the throne. Do you believe there are Jews in your army masquerading as good Christians? I would think that would be considered intolerable?"

"Save your mind games for someone else," Justin warned them both. "I for one will not participate in them."

"There is no game afoot," Romanus suggested, "only a simple statement of suspicious circumstance. If the rumors are false, then prove them otherwise. That's all I ask. This is not only as a matter of principal but is in accordance to our own Church edicts. I for one will not take any instruction from a Jew or a Jew sympathizer. That is within the law after all!"

"Truthfully, that is the law," Justin admitted, "And in matter of laws I am bound to adjudicate by authority of the emperor. So, I beg you Johannes, stop their nonsense now before it goes too far and prove it otherwise."

"What will you have me do, Justin? Raise the skirt of my tunic and show you, my foreskin. I am from Scythopolis; we practice circumcision there."

"See, I told you so," Romanus said pointedly in a very accusatory tone.

"Many cultures circumcise!" Johannes turned on the Count with a ferocity that was practically at the boil. "Are you going to accuse all them of being Jews as well?"

"If the shoe fits…" he let the few words linger.

Reaching for the hilt of his sword, Johannes felt his hand firmly in the steel grip of Diogenes. "Don't do it friend. As much as you may be in the right, he is far more connected than you will ever be. And that means I would be obliged to defend the royal pain in the ass much to my own chagrin."

The pressure on his wrist caused him to release the leather wrapped handle without ever drawing it from the scabbard. "He has insulted me," Johannes fumed.

"And he is an insult to the Empire, so call the score even. What little he has said about you in truth is nothing by comparison. Let it go before he raises the issue as a matter of law. Do nothing to provoke him."

"Truth bothering you," Romanus taunted.

Johannes began to resist the downward pressure being exerted by Diogenes.

"I think there is justification for an Episcopal investigation," Rusticus raised the issue to a much higher level. "I wish to raise the issue to a matter of law!"

"What are you talking about," Diogenes questioned as he struggled to keep Johannes under control. "There is no justification for your allegation."

'Let our silent comrade speak on this," Rusticus threw the question to Justin who sat patiently scrutinizing the interplay between the other generals. "It is clear that the accusation of being a Jew has sorely troubled General Johannes. True? So much so, that you can see his hand firmly on the hilt of his sword as we speak. I see that as both threat and attempt to take the life of our colleague Count Romanus. Now I ask, would such an accusation raise such ire if it did not have an essence of truth. Most others would just laugh it off as nonsense. Now even if I did not believe it so initially, I now have reason to suspect it's true. As soon as he touched his sword, it is now a matter of law. Do you not agree?"

Adjusting his position, Justin made little attempt to engage in the banter. "I have no opinion either way."

"No opinion?" Romanus practically launched himself across the room to land in front to Justin. "How can you have no opinion? You have been posted to this council on behalf of the Emperor and as adjudicator in all matters pertaining to the court. In the first matter, a Jew practicing to be a Christian under pretense is to be considered a heretic. By law, a heretic must be condemned. In the second matter, an officer has made a threat against a noble of the Empire, which we have all witnessed. How can we place our trust of command in a man that not only threatens his superiors but may not have the protection of Our Lord? We could all be doomed because of him. As representative of the Emperor and as a military man you must have an opinion!"

"You're obviously trying to make a point Count. Why not just get to it and save us all this blathering." Justin's role as outsider was stretched to the limits.

"There is an issue regarding lack of confidence in our current commander. I for one cannot trust to have my men released to his command. Nor will I follow a man that has made a threat against a noble. As a member of this military council, I say we must put it to a vote."

"Put what exactly to a vote," Justin wanted further clarification.

"The ability of Johannes to lead! I say he must be stripped of command!"

"Nor will he have my men," Romanus added. "There is an obvious lack of confidence amongst the council and that means we must put it to a vote."

"Do you have anything to say on this, Diogenes?" Justin inquired of the remaining general.

"Forgive me Johannes but if word was to get out that you were under suspicion as it surely will, knowing the true nature of these two others to spread dissent, then it would even be more foolish of me to release my men from under my command. I am bound by the law and in this they are right, we must put your command as general to the vote."

"Forgive me as well Johannes. I for one was never fond of this strategy of starving the city into submission," Justin stated in a closing comment. "We can react much faster if we remain under separate commanders. I think we have to rethink our strategy. The issue of your Jewishness is nonsense, but control of the army is a viable question. We need to vote."

"What are you saying?" Johannes was both distressed and flabbergasted by Justin's ruling. "If we don't besiege the enemy then we cannot exhaust their supplies. If they are not sealed within the city, then they will have the superior situation since they can draw sustenance from the surrounding farms. Only maintaining the siege wall can prevent that. If you do this foolishness and put my right to command to the vote, then you have tossed away all we have gained thus far."

"Let them foray outside the city," Romanus bellowed. "My men will cut them down as soon as they show themselves. That is the way wars are fought. We will have lost nothing by dropping the siege."

"This is madness," Johannes beseeched Justin to reconsider.

"I'm afraid the matter is settled," Justin responded. "We must put it to the vote. Whatever the result of our deliberations, you must step down from command until we hear word from Constantinople confirming the matter."

"More madness!" Johannes howled in desperation. "That could take weeks, even months until we hear back. How can you even be party to this lunacy? You know this is wrong. I beseech you to reconsider!"

"If war isn't madness, then what is," Justin philosophized as he drew the discussion to a close.

Chapter Thirty-two

The Van: Winter 501 A.D.

Sitting high in his leather box saddle, Patricius surveyed the surrounding countryside. "Well, you got your wish," he suggested to Zutra.

"And what wish was that?" the Exilarch inquired as he strained to see in the distance and determine what his vizier was observing.

"Two wishes actually. One that you no longer had to stay cooped up in Mosul and the other that you'd be able to blaze a path of glory in battle."

"Your eyesight is obviously better than mine," Zutra queried his commander as he still could not see anything unusual on the horizon.

"Dust," Patricius pointed to a small cloud in the distance. "Lots of it! Probably three thousand men based on the size of the cloud and the distance."

"You can tell all that from a cloud?" Zutra was impressed.

"Actually, I can tell that form the report I received back from my scouts earlier in the day," Patricius laughed. "So, we better find the better ground to meet them on before they reach Amida."

"What was in the scouting report?"

"They said there was an army coming this way," the Commander smiled. "But don't worry; it's only one of Kavad's Arab allies. Na'man of al-Hirah. Easy prey if the reports are proven correct. Isn't that right Eugenius?" Patricius questioned the Byzantine Duke seated on a gray mare to his left.

The Dukes appeared haggard and drawn, having travelled several days to join with the Exilarch's forces at Mosul and begging them to aid his cause to have his town of Melitene liberated from the invading Huns. "Let us pray it will be that easy. All I want is my town back and my people freed."

"I promise you that will happen," the Commander reassured the old

Duke. "But let's not forget that none of this would have been necessary had you not let the noblemen Rusticus and Romanus pillage the city of Nisibis."

"I had nothing to do with that," Eugenius refuted. "They are scum and have been returned to Constantinople to answer directly to the Emperor for their sins."

"Those people were allied to our cause," Patricius wailed. "Half of the city was Byzantines. Your own countrymen! They slaughtered the children and raped the young girls!"

"It was a sin and they will be held accountable." Eugenius held up his hand signaling that he had heard enough.

"Sin or not, it was exactly what Kavad needed to break free of Erzurum. You never should have permitted those two entry into your territory. People from all over the countryside have now joined in Kavad's cause. They feared your two Counts more than Kavad's punishment for deserting him in the first place. Now he looks like the liberator, not us! If only you had left Johannes to run the war. None of this would have happened. Now look at the mess we're in."

"Johannes was a good general," Eugenius agreed. "But he is the past. I hear he refuses to take the field again, even now that his name has been cleared; a matter of foolish pride."

"As a fellow general I can understand completely. 'If my compatriots have no faith in me, why then should I serve my country?' Every general worth their salt operates by that code."

"Is that how you became to be fighting for this Jewish King? You who were once Caesar are now not even willing to call yourself a Byzantine anymore." Eugenius asked purely out of genuine interest, his question not intended to be offensive.

"Let us just say you're not wrong. There will always be other reasons but they are of little importance now." Patricius dismissed Eugenius with a subtle warning not to pursue the matter any further.

"So what is your plan?" Eugenius quickly switched the topic.

"Quite simple actually. Na'man is obviously not in communication with the Shah, so we can assume he is beyond any immediate assistance."

Mar Zutra who had been listening quite intently at this point felt compelled to ask his burning question. "How can you make that

351

assumption?"

"Easy, my Lord. Where is Kavad right now?"

Zutra decided to play along. "Outside Amida."

"And how long has he been there?"

"Several months." Zutra was bewildered by the line of questioning. "Why are you asking me what you already know?"

"You will see soon enough. And how is the siege of Amida fairing?"

"You know as well as I do that it's been a disaster thus far."

"That's right!" Patricius shouted jubilantly. "It's been three months and Kavad and his Hun allies have lost close to ten thousand men trying to take the city. He can't even get close enough with a battering ram without the Amidenes dropping hundred pound stones on his men. So, bear with me, what has Na'man been doing for the last three months?"

The light of realization donned on Zutra as he suddenly saw through the Commander's line of questioning. "He's been raiding the Harran countryside, plundering and taking captives. If Kavad knew what he has been up to while his men are busy dying, he'd have Na'man stuck on a pole and eaten by crows."

"You see, I told you that you'd understand," Patricius congratulated the King on his insight. "In order to be a good strategist, you must learn to read the signs," he tutored. "Na'man has ensured that he is far enough away from Kavad that he isn't receiving any communications so that he can avoid being summoned to Amida."

"So we attack Na'man on the plain knowing that he won't receive any help and wipe him out!" Zutra exclaimed eagerly.

"Not exactly," Patricius shook his head. "We chase him. We chase him all the way back to Erzurum, putting even more miles between him and Kavad. I'm betting the Huns left behind to garrison Erzurum will slam the gates shut on him as soon as they see us on his tail. We'll slaughter him to every last man in front of the city wall. Then I'm willing to wager as soon as the garrison witnesses the slaughter, they'll swing open the gates and surrender themselves to us."

"And what if they don't?"

"If they don't, they'll be in even more trouble because the citizens of the city will know that their liberation is waiting outside the gates and they will rise up against their oppressors. An angry mob bent on vengeance will convince the garrison that surrendering to us would have been the wiser and better option. Would you not agree Eugenius?"

"A most ingenious strategy," the count nodded in agreement.

"Then let's give the orders to engage," Patricius roared his instructions to the tribunes.

Like clockwork, everything took place exactly how the Commander had described it. Within days Erzurum was once again a Byzantine city, freed from the Ephthalite occupation that had been perpetrated for well over a year. Word of the reconquest of Erzurum by Count Eugenius and the Vizier Patricius spread like a wildfire across the subcontinent. The news was greeted euphorically throughout the halls and council rooms of Constantinople, dismissing the mood of doom and gloom that had hung over the city ever since Justin as acting General-in-Chief had dismissed the combined forces in the northeast and let each army fight independently with disastrous results.

Once more, the war had shifted into a stalemate with neither side demonstrating any momentum to strike the knockout blow. Nevertheless, as far as the Byzantines were concerned, this Christmas was the most joyous they had experienced in several years as most of the cities in the Van had been returned to their dominion. Only Amida remained threatened, unable to withstand the siege through duplicity of some of its own denizens.

On New Year's Day, the sentries stationed on the tower gates blew their horns shrilly, a resounding alarm that awoke the soldiers in the barracks below. Approaching the city, the kasallarios marched steadily in their long mail shirts extending well below the knee. Their light surcoats over their mail were hardly enough to keep the winter chill from penetrating straight to the bone. From each of their steel-capped helms protruded a small crest of purple plumage that danced briskly in the bitter northerly that blew down from the Urals.

From his perch on the western wall, Patricius quickly estimated at least forty thousand men, both infantry and cavalry approaching under the Imperial banner. "Well I'll be damned," he muttered to Zutra and Eugenius, who had assembled beside him as soon as they heard the blast from the horns. "Looks like today is going to be quite interesting gentlemen. How many people can say they receive a visit from the Emperor wishing to extend a New Year's greeting?"

The procession filed through the opened gates of the city, met by a festive atmosphere in its wake as those citizens that had gathered to watch now cheered heartily as Anastasius's gilded carriage rolled past, even if only the faint outline of their divine ruler showed through the heavy fabric drapes. Ignoring the cold and the bite of frost in the air, no one returned to their homes until the procession had moved off towards the fortress occupying the entire eastern suburb of the city. It was a momentous occasion as a visit from the Byzantine Emperor was an extremely rare occurrence. In fact no one presently residing in Erzurum could even remember the last time any had done so.

Anastasius stepped down from his coach, assisted by an aide on either side of the stairs ensuring that the aging monarch did not misstep and fall. His eyes fell upon the group of officers that had retaken the city and he smiled. "Well done," he congratulated them. "Well done, all of you."

Trailing behind the Emperor, they followed him into the officer's mess where it was his intent to talk further with them. Anastasius's own officers deferred to the conquerors of Erzurum and let them proceed immediately behind, while they trailed at the rear. The two aides helped Anastasius into the barracks commander's chair and for the moment, the Emperor appeared lost in thought, his eyes glazing over with a faint mist. "It's been a long time since I've sat behind a desk like this one," he commented. "Most of you probably think that I was nothing more than an accountant keeping the books for Leo, but there was a time I did hold a military office; a very long time ago indeed. Sometimes you do miss the simple pleasures in life," he reminisced.

Those that had gathered in the hall remained absolutely quiet, permitting the Emperor his dalliance with the past.

"I know you're thinking what a foolish old man," he continued. "How could the Emperor ever want for anything? Let me give you some advice if you're willing to listen. Enjoy what you have; it is often better than what you think you desire." Looking upon the faces lined before him on the other side of the desk, Anastasius broke into a warm smile for an old friend. "Eugenius, you old fox! Still willing to place yourself on the front lines. You're going to have to learn to leave the fighting to the younger ones eventually. Nevertheless, well done! The Empire is in your debt. And Patricius, you have continued to amaze us with your ability to size up any situation. Had you not been sworn to another liege I would have surely appointed you as commander of my forces. But alas, you are so, and as you know no one but a loyal Byzantine can hold that position. But I will forgive you the affront that you brought Persian troops on to Byzantine lands against my general's warning."

"It could not be avoided, your Excellency," Patricius replied calmly.

"Of course it couldn't," Anastasius nodded. "Just don't become too comfortable while here."

It was obvious to Patricius that the offer of a return to Byzantium was never on the table. The Emperor no more wanted the commander back in Constantinople than he wanted the hemorrhoids that forced him to fidget restlessly as he tried to sit comfortably.

Anastasius had to momentarily catch his breath, hacking a moist cough as he did so. His aides reached down to lend assistance but the Emperor waved them off. 'Nevertheless, I can appreciate your military genius and I need your continued alliance if we are to regain our lost towns and cities. Therefore, I will not insult you by placing those lesser qualified to command above you. Justin as you know has been dispatched to take care of a situation in the west that has arisen. Johannes has officially retired and refuses to break his retirement in spite of my ordering him to the contrary. Counts Romanus and Rusticus, both of whom I have received numerous epistles regarding their behavior will no longer trouble you having been dispatched to the west as well. So, what am I to do? I have exhausted my list of capable generals that you would willingly serve under."

Patricius was about to protest that he served his own king and did not take orders from any of the Byzantine generals but decided to let the matter drop while Anastasius continued to speak.

"It leaves me with only one solution. To place the armies of the east under a general that you could ably work alongside. I know what you're thinking! That would be a recipe for disaster; two cooks in one kitchen cannot brew a stew," the wily Emperor mused. "It won't work unless the cooks are family and therefore willing to extend themselves to cooperate. Lord Patricius, I give you your nephew, Areobindus. May the two of you strike as a unified blow!"

Stepping from the crowd of officers that filled the hall behind them, Areobindus moved towards the desk as his fellow officers separated cleaving an open path. Patricius was obviously shaken by the announcement, his eyes tearing and glazed, as he fought hard to resist letting his emotions run free. Through the mist, he could see that his nephew bore all the same features of his long-dead brother. In size and strength, he was an even match to the much older commander. Standing toe to toe the two of them eyed each other carefully but restrained themselves from displaying any overt emotion.

"Relax gentlemen," Anastasius laughed. "You can forget about the rest of us and behave like normal people for once in your lives," he instructed.

Almost immediately they let down their guards, embracing one another. Patricius fought hard to choke back any tears that tried to escape. "I thought you were dead?" his voice cracked. "No one told me you had survived. Not even Hermantius mentioned anything to me."

"It's my fault. I made him swear to say nothing to you," Areobindus explained. "I knew that if you were made aware that I was alive you would not leave Constantinople when you first came unless I agreed to head east with you. You would have felt obligated to your brother's memory to stay behind as my protector if I refused. It would have been a decision you'd be made to regret for a host of reasons. You had to leave and that meant you could not be permitted to know." Uncle and nephew held on tightly to the other recapturing all the lost years that had passed between them.

"Alright Generals," the Emperor intruded. "Let's not get carried away. We're all glad that you've been reunited but there are other matters besides your family reunion. There will be another with you Commander, my nephew Hypatias. I wouldn't want you to become sorely tempted now that you've found each other to become disenfranchised from the war and disappear again to the east. Not that I believe you would but Hypatias will guard my interests just in case. I know that you will find this arrangement acceptable, Lord Patricius."

The Commander merely nodded knowing that he had no choice in the matter but still grateful and overwhelmed with the happiness of seeing his nephew alive. Hypatias stepped from the crowd and approached Patricius, extending his right arm as he did so. Showing no sign of disaffection, the Commander clasped the general's hand in friendship. Slight of build, and short in stature, Patricius was left to wonder just how good a military man the Emperor's nephew could actually be.

"And now I wish to spend some time with my royal brother Mar Zutra," Anastasius informed everyone to their surprise. "Help me out of this chair," he commanded his two aides. "Where's a good spot for us to commune away from the rest of you?"

"There's a peristyle garden directly behind this meeting room your Majesty" Eugenius pointed the way.

To his own surprise, Zutra found that the Emperor had wrapped his arm around his as he dismissed his aides with an imperial wave of his hand. "Let's go for a walk my young brother." His entourage began to fill in behind as the pair started to move towards the garden doors. Frowning, Anastasius glared at his staff and officers. "I do not recall saying let us all go for a walk in the garden. I would like to spend some time alone with the King if you all don't mind. Go do what it is you're supposed to do and plan how we are going to win back our remaining territories. Now leave us alone!" In spite of his age the voice was stern and commanding.

Passing through the archway, the Emperor instructed his aides to close the doors behind them so that they were sealed off from everyone else. He nodded his approval as soon as the doors clicked closed behind them. "Come walk with me young Zutra. There is much we have to discuss."

"It would be my pleasure Excellency," Zutra agreed graciously. "I am honored to have this time with you."

"Wait until you hear what I have to say before you speak so loquaciously," he warned. "You may not be so pleased after I say my peace." They strolled deeper into the overhanging arboretum, with its dense foliage that still managed to resist the winter's chill in this sheltered location.

"I doubt there is anything you could say to me that could surprise me Excellency. Since the prophecy I have known that I am nothing more than a pawn in this war."

"Hardly a war," Anastasius corrected him. "More of a bartering. And you should be aware that Shah Kavad has sent to me a delegation with his requests. He has grown tired of his Hun overlords. Now he wants them gone."

"I presume he has stated his price for this negotiation?"

"Of course! What kind of barter would it be unless it had its price?" Anastasius patted Zutra kindly on the back as they strolled together. "He sent me back Count Rufinus as his first sign of good faith."

"If I recall correctly," Zutra interjected, "You had sent Rufinus in good faith to Kavad in the first place. Whom he took prisoner and then subsequently attacked the town of Amida."

"Yes, true, very true," Anastasius tutted. "But he could have killed Rufinus at any time. But he didn't. He sent him back to me unharmed and that was a good sign."

"He sent him back to spread the fear of what had been done in Amida," Zutra still refused to concede that Kavad had shown any intent of negotiation. "Eighty thousand killed and horrible atrocities performed on those he took as slaves."

"Such is the price of negotiations," Anastasius conceded. "But what you do not know is that he also sent Rufinus back with a message. Send a sum of money so he could hire Arab mercenaries and he would turn his attention on the Huns and not on Byzantium."

"And you are sending him the money," Zutra bemoaned.

"No, of course not! I am sending him Areobindus and Hypatias. Areobindus has twelve thousand men with him and Hypatias has a further six thousand to add to your army. I will send him a message in blood. I will not pay for a truce until I have all the lands and cities back that belong to Byzantium. Then and only then shall he have his truce."

"But there is something more you wish to say to me." Zutra detected that the Emperor had not disclosed Kavad's entire message that he sent back with Rufinus.

"You are very perceptive," Anastasius mentioned with a hint of admiration. "Shah Kavad had a message he wished delivered to you personally. He says that he will not permit your kingdom to exist on his soil. You must be expunged and swept away like dust into the air, never to be seen or heard of again. He will make peace with your people but not with you. And with your death he has promised to let your descendants live."

"Is he expecting a reply from me? He should have known my answer before he even sent his messenger." Zutra was firm in his resolve. He would not surrender to the Great Shah.

"It need not be this way," the Emperor suggested. "I have given it careful deliberation and I believe there is an alternative. I only ask that you hear me out."

Mar Zutra already knew that he was not going to be comfortable with whatever Anastasius was about to recommend. Out of respect, he withheld his pride and acquiesced.

"Though I know not how it is possible, you are the living embodiment of the King of the Jews. Such a title flaunts in the face of Our Lord Jesus Christ and is sacrilegious to even consider such a person could exist. Yet you stand here as living proof that such a king does exist, whether we like it or not. I have never doubted it because my beliefs are monophystic, I personally do not feel threatened by your existence. But the Nestorians will howl like dogs braying at the moon." His hand waved frantically mimicking the distress his adversaries in religious doctrine would experience. "Since they insist that Jesus had two separate natures, one divine and the other human, then they will not agree that a continuation of his human line survived past his crucifixion. And further protest that the human line continues to be Jewish in its religious adherence, a fact that will send them into a murderous frenzy."

"They should have known their bible better," Zutra criticized the Nestorians. "God does not pronounce statements haphazardly. When he said the rod of Aaron and scepter of David would not fall from between the legs until the end of time, He meant the end of time, as He knows it; not in human terms. Therefore, my line is here for an eternity and just because a bunch of doddering old men wish to believe otherwise does not make it so."

"I have no reason to doubt," the Emperor agreed. "In fact, I would think the presence of your royal line intermingled with the princely lines in Byzantium would do much to enhance our royal stature. I would even be prepared to return to you your kingdom in Jerusalem to make it so."

"But as with all good barterers, there is a price to pay," Zutra smiled sardonically, waiting for the Emperor's next statement.

"The world has changed. Religion has changed. You represent the old, we represent the new order."

Looking at his benefactor, his body bent and shriveled with age, Zutra could not help and admire the irony of the Emperor referring to himself as 'new'.

"If you could only find it in yourself to embrace the change to Christianity and realize it is not that different from your own beliefs. We have emerged from your own womb. We are your child and like most children, it is their obligation to supersede their parent. The transition would be easier than you think. I could make it easy for you. Your people will follow you. They will do as you say. Imagine their joy and jubilation to have Jerusalem returned to them. It is within your power to make all this happen."

"I do not disbelieve that you have it within your power to give me what you say but what you fail to see, what all of your predecessors have failed to see is that it matters not what we choose to do, it is what God chooses for us to do. Not you, not even I can make the choice. Only He has the power to do so!"

"But he sent us His only son," Anastasius declared. "He was telling your people then that you should choose a new path, a brighter destiny!"

"If that was the case, then I would have to agree with your Nestorian counterparts. I cannot exist. However, I do exist, which means God did not tell us that we had to abandon our old ways. Otherwise, He would not have continued to preserve them!"

"I am giving you a chance to live. You can be with your family. You can rule over your people. Do not turn down this offer so casually."

Placing his hands on either side of the Emperor's extended right hand, Zutra held it comfortingly between his. "I do not reject your offer of life lightly. Oh, how my heart struggles with my soul as we speak. To live my days out with my children, to watch them grow into strong men; what more could any king ask for? But God has sent me a prophecy and the image you have offered is not what He has presented to me. I must accept my death as inevitable for the Lord has spoken. Who are we to question His wisdom?"

The Emperor knew any further words on the matter would be futile. Mar Zutra had put him to shame for he had witnessed how true faith clearly marks the man and knew that he paled in comparison. "I can understand what your Vizier meant when he told me that he was in awe of you. It would take someone very special to make Patricius consider himself unfit to tie your bootlaces. What would you have me do?"

"A simple thing," Zutra replied. "At some time in the future I will send one of my sons west to take up the mantle of spiritual leadership that has become absent in Tiberias. I ask that you give your permission for him to do so."

"You ask a lot from me," Anastasius sounded distressed by the request. "It was one thing to let pretenders to Jewish leadership head the community but now you want a fully blooded king to do so. It would be a recipe for disaster. Why would I agree to such a thing?"

"If you truly respect who I am, then you will do so," was all that Mar Zutra had to say on the matter.

"I need time to think about it," Anastasius mulled over the probabilities.

"As I said, Excellency, it will not be until later on in our future. I am certain you will have your time to think and do what is right in your heart and in the eyes of God."

"And what of your other child?"

"His destiny lies elsewhere. I must make that secure for him as well. Similarly, that of my brother Hanai must also be secured. Contrary to what the Great Shah thinks, the kingdom in Mahoza will continue. That much the Lord has shown me to ease my departure from this world."

"How I wish I could face the prospect of death with the same self-assurance that you do," Anastasius shook his head wistfully. "Here I am approaching the seventh decade of my life and I fear my death far more than pain and discomfort this frail body makes me suffer. Yet, here you are, young and healthy and you show no evidence of fear at all. How I wish I had the strength of faith that you possess."

"It is the fear of living life in bondage, my people enduring hardship and denied God's blessing that makes me cringe most of all, Excellency. In death I return to the Lord's embrace. Why should I fear that? He is calling me home. I am going home!" The old Emperor was warmed by the young king's confident smile, as Zutra patted the back of his hand. It was then that Anastasius understood all, and he cried.

Chapter Thirty-Three

Amida: Spring 502 A.D.

Surveying the landscape from his concealed position in the surrounding hills, Kavad quickly counted the number of enemy troops marching across the plain. It seemed too good to be true. A little more than ten thousand he estimated and from the look of them, they appeared to be mostly raw and untested recruits. He turned to his commander to confirm his assessment. "What do you think General?"

A dark and brooding man, Constantine folded his arms across his chest as he cleared his throat while preparing to give his answer. He was very familiar with most of the units of the Byzantine army, having personally commanded several of its legions in the not-too-distant past. Unfortunately, with each battle won, he had been passed over for promotion. He considered his allegiance was being tested until one day he could not feel the slightest increment of loyalty to the Empire any longer. "That's Areobindus down there. I can recognize his armor or should I say his dead father's armor; quite distinctive with all its feathers and plumes. Looks like a bloody peacock."

"Yes, yes," Kavad agreed. "But what about the fighting strength of the men under his command?"

"He's exhibiting the same cockiness his family was always famous for," Constantine spat. "He's a fool to think he can take us on in the open field with so few. And yes, you're correct; most of them haven't even been blooded. It should be a quick rout your Majesty."

"Then let the attack begin," Kavad commanded.

Pouring down from the hills, Constantine led his twenty thousand troops, the very same units that had cruelly slain the Greek citizenry of Amida, against the exposed right flank of the Byzantine force. Having the high ground and overwhelming numbers, Constantine didn't bother with strategy. His orders were to charge and slaughter everyone in their path.

Areobindus proved that the ability to command ran deep in his family's veins. Like a specter, he appeared magically at every point that the two armies collided, rallying his soldiers, urging them on, leading them into foray after foray. By the will of one man alone, the Byzantines were able to break the backbone of Constantine's much larger army and send it fleeing towards the town of Nisibis. In their panic to find refuge behind the gates of the city, the Sassanids crushed several thousand more of their own troops in desperation. Though Constantine tried repeatedly to turn the tide, his trumpeters blowing the orders to reform their lines, the calls went unheeded as the panic settled over his far more seasoned soldiers. Still well-protected and concealed on his perch overlooking the valley, Kavad lowered his face between his palms and moaned heavily. How many more times he cursed would he have to bear witness to the ineptitude of his own forces. Once again, an easy victory had escaped his grasp. Turning his horse, he rode back with his escort to remnant of his forces, determined more than ever to find a way to win that all important first and decisive victory.

Once the news reached the combined Parthian and Byzantine forces that Kavad's forces had withdrawn to the northern territories to lick their wounds and await the end of the rainy season, it gave Patricius free reign to do as he pleased with the army under his command. Aerobindus's victory was enough to remove any threatening presence of the former Shah's army along all the major battlefronts for several months he calculated, and he seized the opportunity. Along with Hypatias, he made the decision to undertake the siege of Amida during the Great Shah's absence. It was a simple strategy; surround the city with a ring of men so thick that no one could leave or enter into Amida. Once the citizens grew desperate for food, the combined forces of the Byzantines under Tribune Theodore and the Persians under Captain Pharazman, Governor Gurzam nephew, would roll up to the walls the three great towers of wood clad in iron that they had constructed, abut them against the stone defenses and then breach the interior. But with the passing of two months, they were no closer to breaching the walls and their losses were mounting each time they came within range of the defender's arrows.

"They will need to be taller," Mar Zutra criticized the current height of the siege towers, everyone was now growing impatient with their failure to take the city. .

"No they won't," Patricius responded to his King, concealing some great secret that he had not yet divulged.

"I thought we wanted to use them to jump down onto the bridgework of the city walls," Zutra expressed his concerns. "But with the Amidenes laying more bricks atop their wall, they've raised it by another ten feet. We aren't even able to look into the city, let alone jump down into it."

"I suppose you are concerned because you were intending to be one of the leaders of the sally entering the city," Patricius suggested.

"Isn't that what we're here for?" Zutra knew that his Vizier was purposely antagonizing him.

"Haven't we lost enough men without putting you into harm's way? We must seek another way. Perhaps even another place."

"Another place?" Zutra questioned, his voice sounding desperate.

"Part of my role is to keep you safe," Patricius reflected. "I can't do that if you go ahead and charge headlong into every confrontation. Leading sallies over city walls would make that part of my job extremely difficult!"

"When it is my time, there is nothing you can do to prevent it!"

"Perhaps not, but this is not that time. Now go tell your men to break camp. They'll be leaving by tomorrow."

"Leaving? Where too?"

"Just leaving," Patricius slyly replied without naming a destination.

"What about the siege? And the towers, what about them? This is madness to just abandon everything that we have started."

"This is war," Patricius corrected him. "The path is not always a straight line between alpha and beta. Now, be ready to leave," was all that Patricius would say.

"You're not going to tell me what's going on, are you?"

"No," he said sternly. "I have purposely kept you out of the discussions. If it fails, I want no one blaming you for what happens afterwards. The blame will lay with Hypatias and myself. More with me because I know that Hypatias will very likely run to the Emperor and lay it all at my feet. In the meantime, just watch and learn."

"It is unnecessary to shield me from every adversity," Zutra rebelled. "It is important for a king to know failure too. I am man enough to deal with my own failings!"

"I'm not disagreeing with you my Lord; I'm just saying that for this particular stratagem I think you're best to distance yourself as much as possible. Even our own men might turn on us all if it fails."

"Whatever you're planning I presume this is not straight from the military texts."

"More like something one reads in the classic books of Homer. Just wait and see," Patricius refused to divulge any further details. "We'll leave just after dusk. It will create a much greater impact that way."

Still having no knowledge of what his Vizier had planned, Zutra instructed the men of the Four Hundred to disassemble their camp and begin their march southward towards the forested surrounds of Mosul. Without hesitation, the men did as he commanded though they were just as confused as everyone else was pulling camp that night. The units under Pharazman had already trundled off towards an undisclosed destination earlier in the evening and in the shadows of the command tent, Zutra watched as Hypatias gave his Tribune Theodore last minute instructions. Only Patricius did not appear to be readying the soldiers under his command to break camp immediately. His would be the last of the units to vacate the plains outside Amida.

As darkness descended over the deserted fields outside the city's gates, Patricius took one final look at the city, which was now ablaze with lights and the raucous sounds of joyous celebration. Word in the city was that the enemy's soldiers had deserted after slaying their commanders and that was rumor enough for Kavad's occupying forces to begin their celebration in earnest. Even the Amidenes found reason to celebrate, most of the population now being Persian following Kavad's slaughter of the Greeks and hence their unwillingness to be liberated by the Byzantines. No one could say which occupying force was the lesser of the two evils, each highly specialized in raping and pillaging.

With one final wave of his outstretched arm, Patricius gave the signal for his archers to fire the three dark towers that abutted the city's walls. Having filled them earlier with incendiary materials, it took very little effort to set them ablaze, even with all their iron cladding. From his present location in the hills the blazing towers looked like three giant candles burning in the distance and long into the night, the heat so intense that they scorched and blackened the massive stones where they kissed the wall. To those marching south from the city, they saw it as the Vizier's final resignation that Amida could not be taken, their first true and bitter taste of defeat. In contrast, those occupying the city viewed the pyres as a tribute to Ahura Mazda, who spared their city through his godly benevolence, which called for even greater celebration with unlimited libations of wine and ale.

Early the next morning the dazed and head sore Amidenes recoiled from the sounds emanating from the plains outside the city. The bleating of sheep in the hundreds, perhaps thousands filled the air as they grazed upon the trampled grass. It was a sound the half-starved city had not heard in a very long time. As the Captain of the guard stared blankly over the wall of the city, it took a few minutes to clear the cobwebs from his addled brain. Only then did he recognize it was not an illusion and he thanked Ahura Mazda for hearing his prayers, telling his men they should look forward to the feast they would be sharing over the next few days. So many signs of godly favor in such a short period of time could not be mere coincidence. Still wary, he sent a couple of scouts into the plains to quickly assess the situation. They returned excitedly informing him that the only threat were the handful of bedraggled shepherds herding the beasts across the fields with nothing but their staffs for weapons. Another sign from Ahura Mazda, leaving the Captain with little concern as he personally led his men, unarmored through the opened gates with only daggers in their hands. Sheep for the slaughter, he mused as he watched the frightened shepherds throw down their staffs and run as fast as they could from the rapidly approaching soldiers. With thoughts of filling their bellies after so many months of restricted rations, the Sassanids leaped upon the animals, wrestling them to the ground as they slit their throats. They jeered and laughed, spraying the fountains of blood on their comrades. Some were not fast enough or adept enough and their antics as they were butted and bucked from their intended meals only brought jeers and laughter from their mates.

More so when they were seen desperately running in pursuit of the frightened animals in every direction.

"Lambs to the slaughter," Theodore chuckled to his second in command, as he lay prone in the tall elephant grass that fringed the plain. Silently he signaled the men to creep closer to the plain's edge before ordering them to charge at fall run. At the same time, Pharazman circled undetected from behind the city leading a contingent of light cavalry. Before the Sassanids had the opportunity to recognize his equestrians in similar dress to themselves as being the enemy, they found their path back towards the gates cut off. The Captain of the guard ordered his men to scatter for safety but they found themselves confronted by the more heavily armed troops under Theodore's command. The ambush was over within the half hour, the plain littered with a thousand dead and dying Sassanids.

Having captured the Captain of the guard, Theodore ordered him to surrender the city. The request was to no avail, the citizens of the city barring the gates as soon as they witnessed the slaughter of those caught outside. Leaderless, frightened and besieged without any means of defense, the Amidenes ignored the pleas of the Captain as he begged them to open the gates and surrender the city. They watched as the Byzantine execution squad impaled the captain on a pole that they erected directly outside the city gates, yet still they would not open the gates to Patricius and his returning soldiers.

Patricius shouted to those standing on the walls. "Citizens of Amida, your time is at an end. Keep your gates closed for as long as you wish. We are in no hurry. You have no leader any longer. You have no force to protect you. You only have walls to cringe and scurry behind, but those same walls will be your death. We have food aplenty as you can see, provided by the generosity of your surrounding farms. I suspect in your celebrations from the previous night you have consumed most of what you had remaining. You have nothing left. Nothing but your lives and that will not be for too much longer. When you no longer wish to die from starvation, I suggest you open your gates. We are in no hurry to leave. It is late summer and the weather is hot. Enjoy it while you can. Amida will be your tomb."

Chapter Thirty-Four

Amida: Winter 502 A.D.

Christmas was fast approaching as the war of attrition looked certain to close out yet another year and begin a new one with little change in circumstance. It was also that time of the year for taxes to be collected from the provinces. Anastasius considered the celebration of Christmas to be a festival of giving, and what better way of sharing the bounty of the previous year than reaping the taxes to secure the wellbeing of the Empire. Every citizen of the Empire realized, the giving of the tax was not optional, a lesson often learned at the end of a whip or club to those that thought otherwise.

Conduct of the war in Mesopotamia by the Byzantines was a costly affair, and word had been sent to all the tax collectors in the districts that there would have to be an additional amount freely given by the populace in order to support the war effort. Collecting additional taxes was no easy task, so a second instruction to help ensure that the citizenry of the Empire cooperated was given. Anastasius ordered the army to assist with the collection.

Zutra and Patricius found their base camp outside the village of Melitene eerily depleted with the absence of the Byzantine generals and their armies. Leaving their tents still standing, the December wind howled through the empty canvas flaps, providing a surreal ghostly atmosphere. Huddled around the fire, the officers of the Ctesiphon and Mahozan forces contemplated what was to be done over the next few weeks until the end of the Christmas celebrations by their Christian allies.

"Seems like a bloody good excuse to avoid fighting," Pharazman commented to all those warming themselves by the flickering flames.

"Aye, I can't disagree with you there," Hermantius added his opinion.

The grunts of confirmation from the other officers expressed their consensus.

"I mean, what kind of war is this where you remove all your soldiers from the field so they can shake down the villagers for the few drachmae they can offer?" Pharazman continued to complain. "You're one of them," he referred to Hermantius, "Surely you can explain to me what kind of mystic force can possess good soldiers to make them do such a thing."

Shaking his head, Hermantius couldn't provide any satisfactory answer. "It wasn't like this in my day when I fought for the Empire," he qualified. "Soldiers were soldiers, not glorified tax collectors. No way would we even consider doing such a thing. Sure, set us against a town and we'd plunder and pillage it in order to raise the money needed by the Empire, but to have us go knocking door to door with sacs asking the people to give their fair share, unheard of. I tell you, the Empire has grown soft!"

"Yeah, soft," the words echoed back and forth among Hermantius's officers.

"Well I don't believe we should just be sitting here wasting our time because your Emperor has better things to do than conduct the war," The Persian Captain expressed his bitterness with the situation.

"How many times do I have to tell you, he's not my Emperor," Hermantius growled. "The day he sent us to your lands was the day he exiled all of us. We are now as Persian as the rest of you!"

"You don't look Persian," Pharazman stated somewhat condescendingly. "And you still worship your Christian god. So how can you call yourself Persian?"

Hermantius was not one to let an insult pass easily, no matter how benign it may have been, especially after quaffing several mugs of ale. "Exactly what are you suggesting? Are you saying I can't be Persian if I want to be?"

"I think it's quite obvious," Pharazman accepted the challenge. "I'm just stating a fact!"

"Well how would you like to fact this?" Rising to his feet, Hermantius balled his hands into massive fists and shuffled his feet towards the Persian Captain.

"Sit down cousin and be quiet," the voice carried from the distance as Patricius and Zutra walked steadily towards the campfire. "We leave you men alone for a short time and this is the best you can come up with!" he scolded all of them. "Tell me it's the drink cousin and not some stupid desire to cause trouble."

Hermantius felt ashamed; more so that he had disgraced his cousin than for embarrassing himself. "I am sorry Patricius. Perhaps the ale did get the better of me."

"I hope so, because we have a lot to do in a short time and I can't afford to have you beating each other's sorry asses. Have I made myself clear?"

"Yes Sir," they all snapped to attention.

"The King here and I have been discussing our situation and we're not too happy with our Christmas gifts or should I say lack of them. In fact, we feel very short changed. No one bothered to ask us what we'd like to be doing over the festive season. The King has expressed his desire to be back with his beautiful wives and I personally don't think that would have been too much to ask for. I could have done with a few lovely maidens myself."

The officers all laughed at the Commander's inferences of soldiering intimacy. Patricius had an unerring ability to find the right words at the right time to say to the men under his command. This time he plucked the heartstrings in each of them as they took a moment to reflect on their wives and family whom they hadn't seen in well over a year.

"Well, I say it isn't good enough. If the Emperor and his soldiers are all getting presents, then we deserve some too," his voice rose dramatically as he fueled their desires to receive a reward for their loyalty. "And I think the people of Amida should be the ones to give us our presents. What do you have to say about that?"

Every officer around the fire shouted their approval.

"Now you may not realize it but the Emperor has done us a favor. By pulling all his forces out of the region to go collect his head tax, he's made everyone in Amida believe that they have two weeks to do as they please before any of the Byzantines return; two weeks to go about their business replenishing supplies and fortifying themselves. But we are not Byzantines, are we? And we haven't strayed too far away for a fortnight. We aren't on holiday gentlemen, so let's do what we came here to do in the first place! As far as I'm concerned, everything that's moving along the road to and from the city belongs to us. Every wagonload of food, merchandise, beast and woman that is outside those gates belongs to us. Wouldn't you agree?"

"Aye, Aye," they all shouted in unison.

"So, get mounted up, and move your men out because I want my presents!"

An ecstatic cheer rose from the officers as they scattered back to their tents, excited by the opportunity to plunder and pillage. The short distance from Melitene to Amida was covered within less than two hours. Setting upon the unprotected caravans, Patricius's men stripped the merchants of everything they possessed. Grain, oil, and stores of food all were taken back to the encampment in the very same wagons that had been used for the deliveries. A variety of merchandise and wares were also seized during the raid, including one wagon filled with precious silks. Not feeling especially magnanimous this Christmas season, Patricius's forces did not leave a single merchant alive to bemoan his misfortune. That was the price exacted by Patricius for doing business with the Amidenes. By nightfall all of his men had returned to their camp to enjoy their spoils, exchanging gifts of drink, clothes, and most importantly, intoxicating young women.

When the Great Shah Kavad learned of what occurred along the road to Amida he flew into an uncontrollable rage. Not only had he sent grain and oil to the besieged city, but also two wagons filled with weapons under a select guard of sixty men who now were reported as missing and presumed dead. However, what the Shah found even more insulting was that the herd of five hundred head of cattle that he had sent to feed the city was now filling the stomachs of his enemies. Moreover, each time he demanded to know from his ministers who was responsible for this travesty, the same answer was given; Patricius. One by one, they pleaded that it was unavoidable, unstoppable, that the Commander of Mahoza was divinely inspired and protected. Their responses only fueled his rage into a malevolent madness, and he kicked out harshly at several that still claimed the losses were beyond their control. Impaling those that offended him on stakes outside his camp, he gave fair warning to any others that were prepared to provide a similar excuse for their failure to protect the caravans.

Neither a novice nor ignorant of warfare, the Great Shah recognized that the seeds of self-destruction had already been sown within his council. Once the belief of the adversary's invincibility became ingrained within his troops there would be no power on earth that could change their minds. Instructing his assembled ministers and generals he gave them one order that superseded any other; kill Patricius. In order to destroy a myth of invincibility it was necessary to remove its head and hang it on a spike for all to see; everything else about this fruitless war had become of secondary importance.

"Bring me his head!" the Great Shah screamed as his generals fled from his tent.

Returning after several weeks of canvassing Mesopotamia for tax money, Areobindus was the first of the generals to rush into the Commander's tent with an urgent message.

"Quick!" he instructed his uncle, "We must leave here immediately!"

"Greetings to you too," Patricius replied calmly.

"I'm afraid Commander there is no time for pleasantries. As we speak there are forty thousand Sassanid troops converging on your position. They will reach Melitene in hours."

"This is as good a place as any to confront them." Patricius still remained calm.

"They're sending cataphracts and Hun archers. On an open field, they have every advantage from horseback. We wouldn't stand a chance!"

Assessing the situation, Patricius was still not panicked. "Haven't you learned anything by now," the Commander sounded like an old school teacher disciplining one of his students. A horse is of no advantage if they can't penetrate you ranks. Once we've assembled the troops into a floating wedge formation, those of us on the ground will have the advantage."

"I will not dispute that with you," Areobindus conceded, "But considering Hypatias has not yet returned with his forces, the enemy has the advantage simply by sacrificing their horses in sufficient numbers that when they fall they crush any formation in front of them. We don't have enough men to stave off their attack."

"Why would they sacrifice themselves so willingly," his uncle questioned.

"They're not coming to fight a war, they coming to secure the reward placed on your head. They will mass their entire strength against one single point. That point is you, and no matter how good your strategy may be, you will not prevail against those odds."

Cocking his head to one side, the Commander considered his nephew's argument and found it certainly credible. "Normally I'd say the Huns weren't capable of thinking that extreme, but this attack would most likely be Kavad's invention. Hannibal was the last general to consider a falling animal as a weapon of warfare. Of course, he used elephants and they crushed a lot more of the Romans than a horse would but then again, Kavad has no love for his men, unlike Hannibal. He'd sacrifice all of them if need be. I'll concede to the wisdom of your argument. We will retreat to the forests and if necessary, cross the river. The cataphracts won't be able to make the crossing. Go out and sound the orders for an orderly retreat," he commanded. "I don't want any of the men to think that we are fleeing because I'm afraid of losing my life."

With great haste, the encampment at Melitene was rolled up and packed onto the mule train as the forces under Patricius readied for their rapid retreat westward. Riding towards the corner of the camp where Zutra and the Four Hundred lodged, Patricius pulled his horse alongside that of the King who was already prepared to travel. "I want you to head south your Majesty," he instructed his king.

"I don't understand. We are all heading west," Zutra protested.

"Yes, we will draw the Huns and Sassanids away from your party. It will give you the time to put distance between yourself and them. Head towards Mahoza and don't stop for any reason."

"What insanity is this that possesses you? What good would my being in Mahoza serve if you're defeated here? Better we fight at full strength and not split our armies."

"Better you think like a king and protect your throne," the Commander argued. "You have a responsibility to far more people than just yourself. What about your families? Your sons for God's sake? Who's going to protect them if you fall in battle today? And what about the people you reign over. Are you just going to leave them to the mercy of the Hun hordes as they overrun your kingdom?"

"I cannot run from my enemies. I am not a coward!"

"No, but you can most certainly be a damned fool!"

Zutra was momentarily stunned for a response. Not even Mordecai would speak to him in this manner and the old Vizier had practically raised him. "You, you cannot speak to me like this!" he stuttered.

"When did my role become one of kissing your royal ass? You will do what I say because I'm the only one that is even looking out for your welfare and the welfare of your kingdom. You're certainly not!"

Mar Zutra dug his heels in, refusing to back down from his stance but he had no valid argument to refute Patricius's concerns. Knowing the stubborn streak in the King's backbone all too well, Patricius decided to end the matter abruptly.

"Captain Solomon!" he called over the commanding officer of the Four Hundred. "What is the primary role of the Four Hundred?"

"To protect and serve our King, Sir!" he snapped to attention.

"And when the King's life is placed in mortal danger, what are your primary instructions?"

"Remove the King from harm's way and eliminate the threat, Sir!"

"And when that threat is of a magnitude that it cannot be easily eliminated what are your secondary instructions?"

"Ensure that the King has been taken to a secure and safe area where the threat is avoided, Sir!"

"Well Captain," Patricius continued. "We are about to be attacked by forty thousand men on horseback. Do you consider that a threat that you will be unable to contain?"

"Yes Sir!"

"Then I suggest you implement your secondary instruction immediately and whisk the King back to Mahoza where you will keep him safe and secure. Have I made myself clear?"

"Yes Sir," the captain saluted and immediately signaled for some of his men to encircle the King.

"This matter is settled," Patricius slapped his chest in salute to his

King. "Keep well my Lord and pray for us." Turning his horse, he rode at full gallop to catch up to his men that had already begun their march westward. He knew better than to look back. The thought of never seeing the young king ever again was too hard to bear; too difficult to even contemplate. Better to think of a glorious death in battle of which children will sing about in song for centuries.

By the time they reached the Kallath River, Patricius was convinced more than ever that this would be his final battle. Over the winter months, the river had become swollen with the rains, and it now surged as a mighty torrent carrying everything in its path downstream. The sounds of the Sassanid heavy horses and the much lighter and faster Steppe horses used by the Huns were not very far off. Areobindus ordered one of cavalry units to attempt a crossing, but no sooner had the horse entered the water the current began to sweep it off its feet and the soldier barely managed to pull his animal free from the undercurrent and make it back to shore.

"That's not going to work," Areobindus stated the obvious to his Commander.

"I'm afraid we are at the end of our road," Patricius apologized to the officers and regulars that surrounded him. "Here we must make our stand. Forty thousand men attacking from our front and nowhere to retreat; I guess I don't have to tell anyone what that means. But I still think everyone of you is worth at least two of the enemy, so before we die willingly, let's see if we can even the odds a little."

Hermantius tried to work out the math on his fingers. "If we were to take out two men for everyone we lost, then we'd win!"

"There are only eighteen thousand of us," Areobindus corrected his cousin. "We're still a little short in numbers."

"Then I will kill at least three," Hermantius smiled.

"That you probably will cousin, that you will," Areobindus agreed with a jocular grin.

"Sorry to interrupt everyone's moment of bragging, but I believe the time is at hand to prove what you can do," Patricius shouted as he pointed upwards towards the eastern horizon. In the distance the line separating earth and sky was blotted out completely by the moving dark blur that rode steadily closer. It wouldn't be long until they would be able to distinguish the outline of every horse and man that constituted that line. Shortly afterwards every ring of the cataphract's chainmail would be clearly visible.

"They still have to move through that fringe of forest that lies between us and them," Patricius assessed how much time they would actually have. "I want every archer we have ready to let fly as soon as they emerge from the edge of the trees on to our side. Get ready now and hold your fire until I give the order."

The total number of archers between Aerobindus's men and those of Pharazman numbered no more than a thousand. Patricius calculated that each archer would be able to release three arrows from the time the Shah's men emerged from the forest and were on top of them. With no better than a twenty-five percent chance of the arrows finding their target, the Commander was not impressed by the potential for enemy losses. He wasn't the only one making the calculations. Every man within their army knew the odds. Within minutes, the enemy would be swarming over them in overwhelming numbers.

"Let's get the pike men in behind the archers," Patricius ordered.

Areobindus immediately relayed the instruction down the line. Patricius commanded with such confidence that the men did exactly as he said even though they knew they couldn't hold back the initial charge.

"Hermantius, get you men into formation. I want to see them in floating wedges. Three sides to the formation, not four! Do you understand me?"

"I know what a fuckin' wedge looks like," Hermantius shouted back. "We'll be ready for the bastards!" Hermantius shouted in response.

"Areobindus, get the rest of your men to the rear. They're still pretty raw, so I'd rather have them entering as a last resort. Pharazman can move his units behind those of Hermantius."

'You think they're going to break, don't you," the general inquired. "My men already showed them what we can do, don't forget that," he defended them.

"Constantine was a fool. He never took away your mobility. Here you will have no mobility, you are trapped."

"They will not break!"

"There's always a chance of a break when it comes to facing one's own death," Patricius wasn't willing to debate the matter. "This way, if they try to run, there's only one place to go; into the river and they won't take any of my men with them."

"They won't break!" Areobindus insisted.

"They'll break," Patricius had no shadow of doubt. "Just move them to the rear."

Areobindus gave the order to his cavalry units and infantry to assume a position to the rear of Hermantius's and Pharazman's men. Exactly as Patricius had predicted, no sooner did he move his men to the rear, several of his men panicked at the first hint of the Huns racing towards them, plunging headlong into the river seeking to escape. Several horsemen tried to do the same, but withstanding the current was impossible and they were swept away, tumbling and rolling beneath the waters until neither man nor animal were seen again.

Waiting until the Huns and Sassanids massed in sufficient numbers, emerging from the woods, thus leaving little room between any of their cavalry, Patricius gave the command for the archers to let fly. The first volley of arrows rained down heavily, striking with a higher level of accuracy than anticipated. But by the time the second volley was released there were so many of the enemy bearing down on them that the archers rushed their shots and most of the arrows glanced off the chain-mail and fell harmlessly to the ground.

Finding a knoll upon which to stand, Patricius exhorted his troops to stand their ground and fight. "Men of Byzantium," he shouted to the young recruits at the rear, "Do not put your race to shame. Nor should you disgrace your reputation as professional soldiers. As you have just seen, you cannot flee from the enemy, so why even bother to try. Instead, do as your Alanine and Persian comrades are doing. Fall upon your enemies and with the strength in your limbs and the fury within your heart which all men have when they face death, let's give them a battle that they will never forget!" A rousing cheer went up as he shouted those words.

"What better way is there to die than in glorious battle. Let us die on the edge of a sword, with valor so that our names will be engraved in legend and song forever. Such a death is far sweeter than drowning in the river's cold embrace! I for one will not perish like a coward! Are you with me?"

Shouts of approval rang from the mouths of Aerobindus's men.

"I said are you with me?"

This time all eighteen thousand roared their answer and the sound was enough to cause the first wave of Hun attackers to reign in their horses fearing that the Byzantines had somehow outmaneuvered them. The two forces collided with horrible impact as the pike men impaled the first riders to breech their lines with optimum effect. Nevertheless, the Sassanids and Huns kept pouring from the trees, so that for every horse and rider that fell, there were a half dozen more to replace them. Swords flailed in wide sweeping arcs as Hermantius drove his men forward against the enemy's front line. Still standing upon the knoll, Patricius exhorted more and more men into the fray until there was barely any room between the forest and the river for a man to swing a sword freely.

"Keep them bunched to the centre," Patricius shouted to Pharazman over the din of the battle. "Don't let them turn on our flanks!" It was wishful thinking on the Commander's part. In his heart he knew no matter how valiant his men fought the sheer numbers of the enemy would eventually permit them to outflank his army. "Bring up your men Areobindus. Now's as good a time as any for them to show what they can do in a fight!" Throwing his nephew's forces into the fray was a last resort but there were no other options. The devastation on the field was unprecedented but no matter how many of Kavad's men they could kill, they were drowning under a tidal wave of the enemy.

It was then that Patricius heard the bizarre sound rising in the distance. At first, he thought it was the wind, but then it became louder as it emanated from a source on the other side of the woods. "What the hell?" he swore as his first reaction.

Others on the battlefield heard it as well. Initially, it was nothing more than an eerie drone but then it grew into distinct voices raised in song; thousands of them, perhaps even tens of thousands. More bewildering were the words; in some foreign language that most could not recognize. Between the lyrics came several blasts on horns, echoing through the trees. The sounds were emanating from everywhere, and the combatants halted for the moment, each side fearing for the worst.

The words to the song carried on the pungent breeze:

'Adon oilum asher malach, beterim col, yatseer nivrach,
Leate na-ahsah behefsoh col, ahzai melech shemoh nikrah
Ve-ahahrai kichlot hacol, levadoh yeemloch noirah,
Ve-hoo hayah, ve-hoo hoiveh, vehooh yeehyeh beseefarah'

Over and over the verse repeated, growing louder and louder as the forest amplified the now harmonious voices.

"God damn it!" Patricius cursed once he recognized the language from his days in Mahoza. "Why couldn't he just listen to me for once?"

The effect the singing had on Kavad's forces was entirely different. The strangeness of the language, the haunting of its guttural sounds, the eeriness of some unknown spell that made their skin crawl caused the Huns to separate from the Sassanid Cataphracts. The were overcome by their superstitions and fear of the woodland demons. "Get back," Constantine shouted after the Ephthalite cavalry, but it was too late, as a hail of arrows emerged from behind the forest shield striking with incredible accuracy.

Patricius was both shocked and dumfounded as thousands of missiles flew from the trees, striking both the Huns and the rear of the Sassanid enemy. "What the hell is going on?" he mumbled once again. "He doesn't have any archers, dumbass!" he berated himself for underestimating Zutra.

With the enemy falling by the thousands, the song switched suddenly to a chant. "Zutra, Zutra, Zutra," the words tumbled out of the trees, rolling across the field of slaughter. A few of those Sassanids loyal to Kavad that managed to escape when their Great Shah was captured outside Ctesiphon remembered this particular chant all too well. Once again it spread panic though their lines. Charging from the shelter of the trees, the Four Hundred drove themselves upon the backs of the now terrified cataphracts.

"What in God's name is he doing now?" Patricius could not comprehend any strategy at play. "Four hundred against forty thousand? Has he lost his mind?" Though the number of the enemy had declined sharply being far less than the initial forty thousand, Zutra's men were still vastly outnumbered. As the Four Hundred chopped and slashed their way through row after row of riders, the horns continued to play a medley of commands from behind the curtain of trees. Miraculously, the four hundred had grown to well over four thousand as Hypatias's men poured from the forest.

"Well, what are you waiting for," Patricius shouted at his own men. "Do you want the Jewish King to do all your work for you? Get your lazy butts in motion and let's end this battle."

Attacked from every direction, the Sassanid and Ephthalite armies panicked, thinking only of escaping but challenged by the same horrible predicament that the Byzantines had encountered earlier. Only one route of escape remained, now that the way back through the trees was blockaded by Mar Zutra's and Hypatias's men. The only remaining option for them was to dive headlong into the surging river, and many did so knowing that survival was virtually impossible. Imbued with renewed vigor, the combined armies under Patricius's command hacked the remaining enemy to pieces as they swept through their shattered lines.

There was no other option left for Constantine as he threw down his sword and surrendered his surviving troops into the hands of his enemies. With ten thousand prisoners in tow, Patricius paraded them towards Amida as an unmistakable sign to all that would oppose him that he would extend them no mercy. Outside the city he had his men erect a crucifix for every officer that had been taken prisoner, tallying two hundred and thirty-two in number.

"You said you would spare my soldiers," Constantine protested to the Patricius.

"I did," the General explained. "I have not tortured a single one of your men. Now your officers, that's a different matter. They are not soldiers by my definition. They will be the straw that breaks the back of the people of Amida. No army to deliver them, no food to feed them, and only death on a stake awaiting them if they do not open the gates."

Constantine's men hung until the birds picked clean their rotting corpses of any remaining flesh so that the sun bleached white the bones that rattled in the desert breeze. Those prisoners, fortunate enough not to be of officer's rank, considered themselves blessed as they shuffled in chains towards Constantinople, there to feed the lucrative slave markets. As a special gift, he had the renegade general's head dipped in tartaric acid and delivered to Anastasius to do with as he pleased.

Chapter Thirty-Five

Amida: Winter 503 A.D.

"You disobeyed me!" Patricius was still furious weeks after the battle.

"What are you talking about?" Zutra couldn't believe that he was still hearing the complaint. "I saved you!"

"You put yourself and your kingdom at risk against my wishes!"

"Forgive me, but last time I checked I was the King and you were my Vizier."

"And I'm the one that promised Mordecai I would keep you safe. If you don't like the way I'm doing things, then you can dismiss me!"

"This is ridiculous! I saved your life!" Zutra shouted in return.

"I am still the commander of this army and that means I'm to be obeyed! I can't have anyone, even my king, flouting my authority on the battlefield!"

"Authority which I have invested in you!"

"No, authority which I have earned," Patricius hammered his fist against the table.

"What do you want me to say? Hey, I'm sorry for saving your life?"

"I want you to follow my commands when it comes to your safety. I want you to trust my judgment."

"I did follow your instructions," Zutra emphasized.

"Then it's Captain Solomon that I'll court martial," Patricius could not let the situation rest.

"He followed your orders as well," Zutra insisted.

"How do you figure that? His job was to get you to a secure area where you could not be harmed."

"Only if the threat could not be neutralized, remember. His first priority was to keep me safe by removing the threat. It was only when that goal could not be achieved was he to hide me away somewhere safe."

"So, what are you saying?" Patricius scoffed at his response. "That he calculated his Four Hundred could effectively take on one hundred times that number and neutralize the threat?"

"Not at all," Zutra shook his head. "But when we met up with General Hypatias along the road we knew the circumstances had changed. The odds were only two to one then. It was a good plan. It worked and you should be grateful."

The Commander's demeanor changed completely as he found the King's last comment amusing. "That's what the Emperor Hsiang said to me when Valentius found me in the opium den and gave me a purpose in life. I don't think I ever thanked Valentius in all the years we were together. The Emperor found my overt lack of gratitude odd."

"It is a difficult word to say for some." The King comprehended what Patricius was trying to say. "I don't have to hear it said to know that it is felt."

"It was still a foolish thing to do."

"If you say so," Zutra was willing to compromise. "But did you see their faces when they heard us singing. There expression looked like men finding themselves surrounded by jinn. They shat in their pants."

"You had half my men shitting in their pants too," Patricius admitted. "Your men can't sing. It was a horrible sound."

"Well good!" Zutra exclaimed. "That was what it was intended to do. If I had the time, I would have taught Hypatias's men a few other songs that sound just as bad. At least they got the chant right."

"Nice chant," Patricius complemented. "Kind of grows on you. Zutra...Zutra... Zutra..." Patricius turned the chant into a vainglorious mocking.

"Cut it out," the king punched his general lightly on the shoulder. "We couldn't think of what else to chant," Zutra explained. "So are we alright? I don't have to dismiss you or anything of the like?"

"As long as you listen to me," Patricius extended his right arm.

"Aren't you supposed to kiss mine?" Mar Zutra joked as he seized the commander's forearm.

"Let's not push the issue," the commander warned but at the same time a broad smile spread across his face.

"So, what's next?"

"Next, you ask. Next, we look at an egg."

"An egg?," Zutra questioned disbelievingly.

"You seem somewhat surprised," the General quipped nonchalantly.

"Well, I thought we'd do something a little more pertinent and energetic, like break through the walls of Amida. A little more meaningful. I didn't think seeing an egg was high on our list."

"Yes, from what I've been told a very impressive egg; so impressive that it has all my generals mesmerized!"

"When did this happen?"

"This soothsayer apparently showed up this morning from what I've been told. Claims to have a message from God, nothing more than a troublemaker as far as I'm concerned but you know how superstitious the troops can be."

"Lead on." Zutra followed his Vizier out of the command tent to the wood framed structure of the general staff quarters a short distance away. From the sounds emanating from within, it was clear that everyone inside was very impressed indeed. Loudest of all was Hermantius who could be heard oohing and ahhing continuously.

Within the building were gathered the officers and petty officers of the combined forces surrounding a frail bearded man dressed in dingy monk's robes. Between his thumb and forefinger, he held up the goose egg so that all could see it with its distinct markings.

"Commander, I'm glad you have arrived," the monk greeted Patricius as he entered. "I have a wondrous gift for you," he said gleefully.

"You wish to give me an egg."

"Not just any egg," the monk turned it between his fingers so that the design on its surface could be viewed. "This egg was laid by a goose in the village of Agar exactly as you see it now. See how there are Greek letters raised upon its surface. And two crosses which completely encircle the egg. It is a miracle!"

"You think God sent us a message through an egg?" Patricius

questioned skeptically.

"Look what it says," Areobindus pleaded the monk's case.

"Not you too, nephew? Oh, well…" Taking the egg from between the monk's fingers, Patricius read out loud the embossed words on the egg's surface. On one side, it said THE GREEKS and on the other, SHALL CONQUER.

"What do you make of this," Patricius asked as he passed the egg to Mar Zutra.

"Forgive me Lord," the monk interrupted, "But I doubt such a holy thing should be passed to a Jew."

Turning on the monk, Patricius showed his contempt by drawing his sword and placing the tip against the monk's throat. "This so-called Jew saved all of our lives. This egg as far as I know hasn't saved anyone. So when you refer to him, you say your Majesty. Is that clear or do you wish for me to carve another hole in your throat to speak from?"

"Yes," the monk trembled. "Your Majesty, though I doubt you will understand the egg's significance, I think it's a sign from Our Lord Jesus Christ," the monk insisted. "He is telling us that he will protect our men from harm. He will hand the filthy fire worshiping Persians over to you as your prisoners. You should not make light of this miraculous message."

Handing back the egg to his commander, Zutra commented simply, "I'll confirm it's an egg."

"What will you have me do with this egg," Patricius mocked the monk's religious enthusiasm. "Should I dress it up in a general's uniform and have it lead my forces. Or perhaps I am I to throw it at my enemies when they attack, and they will all magically fall down dead? Better yet, perhaps they will disappear into the bowels of the earth as did the Korahites when Moses threw down the tablets? Tell me monk, what should I expect from this miracle of yours?"

"Do not mock the word of God," the friar shook his crooked finger at the Commander.

"Shake that finger at me again and I will stick that egg so far up your ass you'll be searching for it for weeks."

Areobindus gasped at his uncle's disrespect for a man of the cloth.

"Here Areobindus." He tossed the egg to his nephew who cupped his hands immediately in order to catch it deftly without risk of it breaking. "Keep it if you want it. Perhaps monk you can impress my officers in this tent with your tricks but don't try something so simple with a man that has spent twenty-five years in the orient. They are far more artistic with their embossing of eggs in the Sin villages. As far as your handiwork, it is nothing more than a crude amateur's attempt. The Sin actually use colored bees wax that they apply to the egg before submerging it in the vinegar. Makes for a far more attractive egg, which is also definitely much easier to read that this pathetic attempt to replicate their technique."

"How dare you ridicule one of God's miracles," the monk fumed. "With His own finger he traced these letters within the ovary of the bird."

"When you present me a goose that talks like a man, then you have a miracle. All I see is a trickster that I should crucify here and now. I hope your superiors made certain the goose that laid this egg has been given a priest's frock because she is certainly much holier than your sort." Grabbing the monk by the scruff of his cassock, he forcibly threw him out of the tent. "Now get out of my camp and if you ever try such foolishness again, I will have you martyred." Just for good measure, he gave a swift kick to the monk's backside, which sent him sprawling.

"You will be sorry. God will not forgive you," the monk shouted as he scurried away from the tent as fast as his bent legs would carry him.

"It is a pretty egg," Hermantius sighed, somewhat disappointed that his cousin had destroyed the mystical aura that surrounded it.

"Cousin, if you truly wish to learn how to make such eggs, I will gladly show you how. Better yet, the Princess Ti-Ping can provide a class for all of your men because she is an adept at such arts. Now is not the time to put your faith in anything but your sword and the man standing beside you when you confront the enemy. The holy relics that the Church tries to delude us with will not win us wars. We win wars. Just us and the will of God! Depend on nothing else!"

"Sorry to interrupt Patricius but I'm afraid that was also the Emperor's stenographer for recording the events of this war that you just threw out," Hypatias clarified the position of the monk to Patricius and Zutra who were not present to hear the earlier introduction. "I guarantee that egg will now be given even greater prominence than anything we have done thus far in this war. As for you two, you may find that you've just had yourselves written out of any of the reports to follow."

"So be it," Patricius remained defiant. "I don't intend to read his account anyway unless he makes a point of recording how my boot went up his holy ass. It's good that we're all here because I wanted to discuss with you my intentions for Amida. The people have been far more stubborn that I thought possible. Leaderless, starving, dying in droves, they still defy us and refuse to open their gates. It will be a city of ghosts before too long and there's no prize in handing a dead city back to the Emperor Anastasius."

"What are you proposing then," Hypatius was intrigued by the general's sudden change in attitude.

"I am thinking we should burrow beneath the city walls until we can either enter the city or the walls actually collapse around them."

"Mining the walls is a dangerous business," Hypatias criticized the Commander's plan. "The reason we burnt our siege towers in the first place was to eliminate the enemy forces and keep our men safe from any further attacks. What would we have gained if we are to suffer heavy losses by tunneling. I wouldn't be comfortable ordering my men into such a situation."

"Very dangerous work," Patricius agreed completely. "That's why we'll use the prisoners we have at camp. Should the Amidenes choose to throw rocks down upon their own people, then let them do so. If the tunnel collapses, then we just send in more prisoners to clear it out. It solves our problem with the prisoner numbers as well. Feeding them is becoming too costly a matter."

"We could always sell more of them to the slave markets," Hypatias voiced his opinion.

"The ones we kept were those deemed unfit for sale," Patricius countered. "The rest are those citizens we capture almost daily attempting to flee the city. In retrospect, I consider it good fortune that we didn't dispatch them at the time we captured them. Now we have an expendable workforce." The Commander looked somewhat apologetically at his king whom would not permit the unnecessary slaughter at the time and the only reason the captured citizens remained alive.

"To kill in battle is one thing," Zutra defended his position, "but to kill an innocent, that would make us accountable to a higher power when our days are done. We can now see it was the better decision."

"From a military standpoint I wouldn't exactly call it wise but at least we now have a solution to our issues of an expendable workforce," Patricius countered. "You may have just exchanged them a quick death for a much slower one. They will dig for their survival."

There was little to discuss before the council of generals adopted the strategy. With so many prisoners of war there had been another growing concern if they should attempt to revolt. This was an acceptable solution by all. By midday, the works to undermine the wall was already in full swing. A continuous line of diggers with pails moved back and forth from the section of the wall that the army engineers had identified as the weakest structural point. Every bucket of earth and gravel hauled from beneath the wall brought the Byzantines were one-step closer to entering the city.

Erecting a wooden shelter over the workers meant that they could tunnel without much interference from above. It was a concession that Patricius was forced to agree to as Zutra pressured him that they still had an obligation to protect the innocent. On occasion when exiting from the end of the slope-roofed shelter a stone thrown by one of the Amidenes would find its mark, but that was of little concern as there was always another slave to replace the few that had fallen. Not having anticipated a long siege, the Sassanids failed to bother gathering boulders within the city and therefore they had nothing of any significant weight to cast down upon the wooden structures. The stones and pebbles were the best the people could find. Day after day, they watched the steady stream of heavily laden buckets exit from the end of the shelter, while the mound where they dumped the soil grew taller and broader until it was a hill of considerable size. However, the task of tunneling beneath the thick walls was still a monumental one that extended from days into weeks and then into months.

On a sunny autumn day, while the generals sat beneath their palm leaf shades erected upon the hills overlooking the plain beyond Amida, they followed the approach of a Byzantine cavalry formation as it came winding along the northern road. To its rear followed a supply train considered worthy of an emperor. Several thousand horses and just as many sheep were herded along the road, while at least twenty wagons filled with supplies and equipment trundled afterwards. They watched the obligatory exchange of salutes between the legions tribune and the sentries posted at the outermost gates of their encampment. Patricius looked to his right and left to see if there were any signs of recognition from any of the officers, but none was forthcoming. He would just have to wait for the tribune to join them atop the hill and state his business.

Puffing as he ascended to where Patricius remained seated, the tribune took a moment to catch his breath before introducing himself. "Tribune Timostratus, Duke of Callinicus, requesting that I may append my forces to those stationed here at Amida Sir."

"Relax tribune," Patricius signaled to the duke to lower his salute. "It would appear that you have a lot more horses and supplies than warrants the number of men in your unit. Have you suffered great losses recently?"

"Not at all sir. We took them from the enemy," the Tribune stated proudly.

"Seriously?" was the first word that Patricius could think of. "Where and when did this all happen?"

"Five days ago, Sir. At Nisibis."

Once more Patricius looked to his officers seated on either side to see if any knew about what had transpired. "Why haven't I heard about this," he voiced his displeasure to them.

They shook their heads to indicate they had no knowledge either. None of the scouts had returned with any reports of a great battle.

"Tell me about this battle," the Commander urged him to continue. "It would appear that my intelligence officers have been slack in their reconnoitering."

"There wasn't any battle Sir."

"No battle? Did the Sassanids just give you their horses?"

The officers surrounding him laughed at the Commander's suggestion, presuming it to be an excellent joke.

"In a manner of speaking Commander, we took them."

"You took them?" Patricius parroted the words in disbelief.

Timostratus explained. "You see sir, I have six thousand cavalry under my command but the enemy refused to engage us. We have been encamped beside the city of Ras'ain for months now with little to do. My men, I'm afraid were growing fat and bored. The enemy had grown so bold as to send us word that they would be passing by on their way to Nisibis but had no grudge to bear with us. Apparently, their Emperor was sending ten thousand men, a mixture of infantry and cavalry to Nisibis in order to prepare for an attack against you. They considered us of little significance, dismissing us as if we didn't even exist. There orders were to engage only with you in battle!"

"I guess I should be honored," Patricius joked once more to delighted spurts of laughter from those around him.

"My men were infuriated by the insult," Timostratus continued. "We decided that we had to teach them a lesson of respect. Nisibis is nothing more than a back-water town. There was no way they could contain all their horses, livestock and supplies within its walls. At night, we fell upon the garrison they posted outside to tend the animals and destroyed them to the last man. Then we took everything they had."

"That provides an interesting dilemma," the Commander contemplated. "I can't imagine several thousand Equestrian without horses. They're obviously going to have to learn how to walk. Isn't that a pretty picture?" he laughed. "Not to mention they no longer have any food. I foresee it won't be long until they're chasing one other around with carving knives as well."

This time Hermantius howled with laughter imagining the sight of Kavad's men attempting to cannibalize each other.

"Yes you may join us, Tribune," Patricius assented to his request. "But I caution you, I don't think you'll find it any less boring here. As you can see, our only entertainment is watching those men down there tunnel beneath the wall's foundations. It's a slow process. They tunnel, the Amidenes try to fill it from the other side, men die and then it starts all over again."

"At least my men will be in good company while they watch, Sir," Timostratus saluted and then turned as he began to descend the hill.

"Once your men have settled in, come on back and have a seat," Patricius called after him. "We'll have to start making plans for when the wall falls."

"He's right," Areobindus commented as he watched the Tribune return to his troops. "This war is getting extremely boring."

"What shall you have me do, nephew, start another war?"

Patricius made his comment in such a manner that none knew whether he was still joking or quite serious.

"I would like to request leave with my men so that we may seek better sport in Armenia," Areobindus pleaded his intentions.

"To do so would be contrary to what your Emperor has instructed," Patricius warned him. "Anastasius said only to regain those lands which Byzantium had lost and nothing more."

"I promise not to attempt to take possession of any cities while we're there, uncle. Amida is enough to keep us busy. But I know that if I do not take my men into the field soon then I will have greater problems to deal with."

Rubbing his chin, Patricius thought about the request and the possible repercussions. "If you go, take this Tribune Timostratus and his cavalry with you. They are of no use to me laying siege to a city and he certainly seems eager himself to engage in real battle. I don't need his men making a nuisance of themselves if they remain here. Go with my blessing Areobindus. And may God grant you the victories you seek."

"What about me?" Hermantius whined.

"You will remain here with Pharazman and clean up the mess after we breach the walls. If you wish Hypatias, you may take your men wherever you please as well. There is not much for you to do here either."

"I think I will stay Commander if you don't mind," Hypatias answered. "My instructions as you know were to keep an eye on you. It's best to do as I was instructed."

"So be it," Patricius assented. "As for you Zutra, go home. Be with your lovely wives, sire some more sons and get on with ruling your kingdom."

"I will have to give it some thought," Mar Zutra considered the instructions.

"What's to consider? You overheard me tell Timostratus exactly how this will continue. We will dig the shafts, parts of the wall will fall, the Amidenes will fill in the shafts from their end and we will dig more tunnels to replace the ones they filled. Our men will shoot arrows over their walls to try and keep them away and they will throw down pots, kettles and whatever other garbage they still have remaining behind their walls. Some of our tunnelers may die in the exchange but more of theirs will die in the process. In the end, eventually, Amida will fall."

The other generals nodded their heads affirming what Patricius had described as being accurate. There would be nothing for Zutra to do.

"All right, I will return to Mahoza," Zutra finally acquiesced. "I do miss my Princess."

"Good, it is about time. I fear your Princess more than all of Kavad's armies," Patricius smiled broadly. "If she was to think that I was purposely keeping you from her then I would have hell to pay! Our parting will give us a reason to celebrate tonight. We can slaughter some of those sheep Timostratus has brought us and see if there's any wine in those wagons he confiscated. It's been a while since we had a real occasion to feast!"

Chapter Thirty-Six

Mahoza: Winter 505 A.D.

"Hurry husband," Ti-Ping urged as she pushed Mar Zutra from their bed. "Lord Patricius will be arriving any time soon and you're not even dressed.

"His last instructions to me were to go make babies," the King defended his laziness as he pulled the robes over his head. "How can I do that if you force me from our bed?"

"He told you that well over a year ago and I would think from the number of times you have taken me since you returned that I should be giving birth to a litter by now," she giggled seductively as she patted her belly, which only now was beginning to protrude. Her actions only enticed him to climb back on to the bed.

"No, you have had enough!" She kicked out playfully. "I have had enough. Go see your other wife or your concubines before I fade away from exhaustion."

Grabbing her ankle as it swung by, he pulled her from the bed. "You must get dressed too. The audience is before King and Queen, remember?" As he held her petite foot, he gently kissed the inside of her ankle, which sent a shiver of pleasure down the length of her leg.

"Stop that," she shouted in ticklish torment.

"Only if you allow me back into your chambers tonight." His tongue teased the flesh along her inner calf.

"Yes, yes," she screamed. "Tonight! I'll see you tonight! Your are insatiable!"

Holding her to her promise, Zutra let her extended leg fall gently back to the bed. "Now hurry and get dressed," he prodded her. "You're going to be late."

Mar Zutra waited until everyone was assembled within the throne room before making his grand entrance. The dignitaries from Ctesiphon had arrived earlier, with Gurzam prominently standing closest to the dais. Both of the royal wives were already seated on their respective thrones; Ti-Ping immediately to the left of Zutra's empty throne chair and Avital on the right but a step lower in height.

At that moment, everyone's eyes were transfixed upon the Vizier who had just returned with his victorious army from the north. He had spoken to no one since arriving, requesting that everyone wait, and everything would be divulged at the time of the audience. It was an unusual request since affairs of state were usually discussed in private first, but as everyone in the twin capitals over the years had come to realize, Patricius was far from ordinary. If he wished to make a public pronouncement, then there had to be a good reason.

With much fanfare, the court chancellor finally announced the entrance of the King. Accompanied by the heralding of trumpets, Mar Zutra entered, followed by his half-brother and his two sons into the great hall. The young lads seated themselves on the bottom tier of the dais while Zutra climbed to the top where he took his place between his wives. All heads bowed as he passed, the only permitted sign of respect permitted in Mar Zutra's court. A bow from the waist was prohibited as the King claimed men should only bow in that manner before God.

Taking his seat, Zutra nodded his head acknowledging the return of his Vizier from the warfront.

"Welcome Patricius son of Aspar. We are glad for your safe return and grateful for your good health. News of the cessation of the war has preceded you. This is a happy occasion for all. Tonight, we will celebrate your safe return and award you for your success. What further news have you brought from the front?"

"I am afraid all is not as well as you think your Majesty," the Commander replied in such morose tone that it began a shock wave that ricocheted amongst all in attendance. His pronouncement was not what anyone had expected, the word circulating through the countryside being that Kavad had capitulated; complete and total surrender.

"But I heard that Kavad sued for peace?" Zutra sounded confused by the Commander's bitter response. "The war is ended. We have won!"

"That is true your Majesty, the war is over, but the concessions he received makes one wonder who actually surrendered to whom."

The assembled guests grew nervous as they rocked back and forth on their feet, not entirely certain what message the Vizier was exactly trying to convey.

"Elaborate for me dear Patricius because I must confess that you have me at a disadvantage. How can we have won and lost at the same time? That makes no sense at all."

"As you are well aware my Lord, before you returned to Mahoza I gave my permission for General Areobindus to take his men into the Armenias to make his fame and fortune."

"Yes, yes. And from what I heard, he made quite a name for himself," Zutra agreed.

"My nephew proved himself very successful over the following months. In but a short time, he had defeated a standing army of ten thousand Armenians fighting for Kavad and took captive thirty thousand of their women and children. Along the way, he plundered and burned numerous villages taking everything they possessed. In the end, he made himself and his men very rich in the process, tallying in total one hundred and twenty thousand sheep, oxen and horses, along with the percentages from the slave market sales. But he was not finished. Returning from Armenia he took the roads past Nisibis as the Tribune Timostratus had unfinished business there. They attempted a ruse, one which you are aware, had worked successfully for us in the past. By dressing a small platoon of men as shepherds, he herded a portion of the sheep past the walls of the town. Starving, as they must have been since the time that Timostratus last took all of their stores, the Sassanid General sallied forth out from Nisibis in an effort to seize the sheep. Those dressed as sheep herders feigned fear and fled from the field. The Sassanids thought them easy prey and gave chase, separating themselves from the protection of their town. Seven thousand of the

Sassanids fell to the ambush Areobindus had set for them. Fortunately for all of us, the Sassanids have never learned anything from their past errors and keep making the same mistakes over and over again."

That last comment brought a round of laughter from the assemblages of guests and courtesans.

"The remaining forces in Nisibis were under Mushlek the Armenian," Patricius continued his story. "Upon witnessing the death of Kavad's men, Mushlek surrendered with all his men and swore allegiance to the Emperor Anastasius. There was nothing left for Areobindus to do in the area, so he returned to my camp outside Amida. That as you know was several months ago."

"Glorious news, Vizier," Zutra shouted his praise. "A great victory for us and surely what spelled the end to Kavad and his ambitions. So where is this message of doom and gloom that you have delivered to us?"

Those in attendance broke into loud applause again upon hearing the Vizier's recounting of the fall of Nisibis and Zutra's subsequent praise. Patricius waved his hand suggesting that they should cease their applause. Zutra recognized the dower expression borne on the Commander's face an knew that whatever victories had been won were about to be reduced to insignificance by what would be said next.

"Yes, we all know of Aerobindus's success in breaking the back of Kavad's army. We should be celebrating, not mourning such a feat but when he arrived back in my camp, the world as we knew it was changing. The situation in Amida deteriorated even more rapidly now that Nisibis had fallen. Without food the people within the city began to cannibalize one another."

There was the sound of horror-filled gasps as the dignitaries listened to the tale as it unfolded.

"The scent of roasted human flesh filled our nostrils but there was little we could do about it. The people still would not open the gates to the city and let us put an end to their misery. My men were disgusted and sorely pressed me to burn the city to the ground to end such demonic behavior but as you know, the city was prized above all others by the Emperor and we had orders that it must be returned intact. Oh, how I wish I put that accursed city and its people to the torch, as it deserved."

"Hold, Commander." Zutra raised the palm of his hand to signal a cessation to the report. "Enough of such evils before my children," Zutra beseeched the Commander. "I do not wish them to hear further of atrocities of this kind. Chancellor, take the children back to their apartments immediately."

Nodding his head, the chancellor immediately did as he was bid, leading the children from the hall.

Once the children had exited, Zutra waved his hand to his Vizier to continue. "Please tell me that it doesn't get worse than this, Patricius!"

"There can be nothing worse than the depravity of a mother boiling their own baby, your Highness. The mayor of Amida could not abide it from what I've been told. He threatened anyone caught killing another citizen for food with death. But what do people care about the threat of death that are dead in their soul, already? I could not bear to witness such unrestrained evil any longer, so I sent my men out into the countryside to subdue the rest of the population. Alas, we had been equally infected by the curse of Amida, and my own men became guilty of the wholesale slaughter of innocents. They were infected by the blood lust and there was nothing I could do to stop them. Every male child my soldiers found, they felt justified in slaughtering. The woman and girls were raped repeatedly until they died from the physical trauma. Entire villages were razed to the ground without provocation. Entire communities were sealed in their temples, unable to escape while my soldiers put the buildings to the torch. I had no other choice but to reassemble my forces and lead them into the wilderness east of the sea before there was neither a single man left alive in the villages nor a single building left standing in all of Mesopotamia."

"I do not blame you or your men, General," Zutra reassured his Vizier that even such horrible acts could be forgiven in time of war. "Such is the madness of war. Only God can judge such things."

"Then he must have judged us and found us guilty of sinning beyond measure! After all that we had done, the Great Shah knew that my men would not be sated until we had annihilated every one of his men and supporters until not even one remained. For this reason, he sent his envoy to us in Amida. However, this ambassador was under instruction not to speak to me directly, insisting that he would only talk to the representative of the

Emperor, his nephew Hypatias. I'm afraid that my absence from the negotiations was God's punishment for the actions my men had performed and in turn has spelled our cruel demise!"

"What are you speaking of?" Zutra questioned the Vizier's reference. "Because of your leadership there is peace between the two Empires. No other man can take credit for that. Surely, even Hypatias could not deny that no matter what atrocities were committed by our forces, they pale in comparison to all that had been committed by Kavad and his army."

"No, I have failed you all," Patricius cried out. "I came back with our men as soon as I heard what Hypatias had done. We all have been named as the price of peace and Anastasius has agreed to it. Blood for blood, was how Hypatias described it!"

Gurzam turned white upon hearing the Commander's words. There would be no peace for Ctesiphon or Mahoza. "Are we all to die?" the Pashah inquired.

'We are to be wiped from existence," Patricius answered. "We have been betrayed! After they exchanged high-ranking prisoners, Hypatias then gave the Sassanids and their allies leave to exit Amida under his protection. In return, Anastasius was given back his prized city that so many had lost their lives for. The boundaries between the two Empires have been redrawn in Byzantium's favour and the respective forces have withdrawn safely behind them as agreed. The Emperor has even sent a large sum of gold to the Great Shah so that he can drive the Ephthalites from his lands once he has subdued the pockets of resistance within his own kingdom."

"And…" Zutra attempted to draw out the rest.

"All allies of the Byzantines residing in Mesopotamia are to be afforded no further protection by the Emperor. We have been cast off! Sold out! Abandoned!"

"I still fail to see the advantage to Anastasius in all this. We would have been able to give him all the same and even more!" Zutra interrupted.

"All that we had promised, the cities, the territory, the trade routes, Kavad has agreed to. The yearly tribute from the Jew tax, the entire flotilla that was being built for the Huns, all will be handed over to Constantinople."

"What more could he possibly want?" Zutra was still not convinced.

"Our deaths. Anastasius has agreed that there will be no repercussions should we be annihilated. Even now, the Great Shah is assembling what remains of his army to bring them against our two cities. We are all accused of being traitors to the Empire and we are to be exterminated!"

"How long?" Zutra demanded to know.

"Having decimated his armies as severely as we did, I would guess that he won't be able to mount a significant force before the autumn months."

"Half a year at best then; there is no time to waste. We must tend immediately to those that must be safeguarded and transported to safe havens. Pashah, see to it that from among your people those that must flee are readied within the next quarter. I want every available ship and caravan made known to me. There will be no wholesale slaughter of our peoples for Kavad to feast upon. I promise you that! Our people will not die at the hands of Byzantine treachery." The words were spoken with such an imperial air of dignity that no one doubted Mar Zutra's commitment to save them all.

"Where should we go?" Gurzam inquired. "We cannot expect protection from anywhere in the two empires with such a treaty."

Reaching to his left, Zutra clasped the hand of the Princess Ti-Ping as it rested on the arm of her throne. She knew immediately what he was thinking. Looking deep into her eyes, he smiled but the effort was strained. He could tell that she was aware of his every thought. "Those that wish to live should prepare to go east with my wife," Zutra answered the Pashah. "The Queen and I will send word to my brother-in-law, and he will receive you there. I must send you to the ends of the earth in order to keep you safe."

The reaction to exile in Northern Wei was one of shock and dismay to many of the Persians who had never been beyond the borders of their country. Most were stunned into silence, shaking their heads but aware that there was no other solution.

"Patricius, I will need an escort for the Queen and our son."

"I will send General Hermantius with two cohorts of men, your Highness. The general has always had a desire to travel to exotic places."

"And now as to the matter of where I will send you, Patricius."

"What do you mean, my Lord?"

"There are still places you must go before your duty to me ends."

"I am going wherever my King goes," he stated adamantly.

"You know I must remain here," Zutra advised. "You cannot stay! I am bound by my prophecy. Nothing that you have revealed to me is a surprise. The curse of the prophecy was always there to be seen. The betrayal was always expected. Now I must see it through to the end if the rest of you are to survive. The prophecy must be fulfilled to guarantee all your safety."

"And as such you know that my destiny is bound to yours. I go where my King goes," Patricius was just as stubborn regarding the matter.

"No, you must protect the Lady Avital! I am commanding you to do so. You will take her and our son to Constantinople with a letter that I will send personally to the Emperor. Whether he recognizes it or not, he has an obligation to me. I will hold him to a promise he made me as God will bear witness should he ever attempt to break his oath!"

"Zutra, don't do this. Let me stay with you," the Vizier pleaded. "There are others that can escort the Lady Avital. I must remain with my King!"

Some of those assembled in the hall were awed by the Commander's expression of familiarity to address the King by name but admitted now was hardly the time for proper protocol.

"You must follow my command. You have sworn to do so. The Lady Avital and my son are dear to me and only you can see to their protection. I ask you as a friend, will you do this for me?"

Bowing his head, Patricius agreed to the request. "As a friend I will do as you've asked."

"Thank you, my friend. I think we all have urgent matters to take care of for the time being. This audience is over. I'm afraid there will be no great celebrations and feast tonight. Best that we all spend tonight with our families and thoughts of what is to come. Hold on to those you love, cherish the time you have together, and know that whatever happens is God's will. I think I would like to be alone with my wives now!" The King dismissed himself from the assembly, taking the hands of both Ti-Ping and Avital in his own as he led them from the great hall.

Chapter Thirty-Seven

Mahoza: Spring 505 A.D.

"I don't know what to say in response, General. This is most unexpected." Zutra reclined back into the nook of his throne, thinking long and hard about the request that had just been presented to him.

"But it can be done, your Majesty, is that not so?"

"Yes, it can be done but you must also recognize that it can never be undone should you and your officers go through with this. Once you have committed to such an act it is irreversible, otherwise you will be outcast from the community. Excommunication is not something you would wish upon yourself while residing in a strange land."

Standing before the throne, Hermantius remained calm with his head bowed, while his officers stood alongside assuming the same reverent posture. None dared to raise the line of sight from the tiled floor until such time that the king provided a favorable response.

"Do you even know what is involved," Zutra questioned the general once more to ensure that there would be no change of heart or any regrets. "It is a most difficult undertaking, and each step will be scrutinized heavily. Do you understand this, General? This is not a matter to be decided upon lightly."

"It has always been the way of our people, your Majesty," Hermantius explained. "In order to serve our rulers properly then it is mandatory that we become united not only in cause but in faith as well. It is not as if we Alans have been Christians for all that long that we have abandoned all of our customs and beliefs. Religious unification with the state and monarchy is still one we adhere to strongly."

"Am I safe to assume that you are all committed to this decision then?" Zutra was still hesitant in granting his permission for the conversion of his officers. "This must be a choice freely undertaken. If you have been coerced in any manner, then speak up now."

"If we are to protect the Queen and her two sons, then we can only do so if we are not only bound by duty but united in faith, your Majesty." Hermantius clicked his heals loudly as if to emphasize his statement.

"And are you so certain that my next child will be a boy as well," Zutra mused at the general's confidence in making such a bold statement.

Raising his head so that Zutra could look directly at his broad smile, Hermantius responded confidently. "It has to be my Lord. I know my bible stories and it's all your family ever produces, a continuous line of male heirs."

Zutra burst out laughing but quickly suppressed his amusement at the expense of his general. "I'm afraid General Hermantius that the bible may have misled you. It's not that my family didn't bear daughters, only that they were never deemed worthy enough to be recorded by the biblical chroniclers. Nevertheless, I hope you are right. I would dearly cherish another son. However, if it should not be the case, then I would love a daughter equally as much. Now, let us return to the matter at hand. You and your officers have raised a request to convert to the Hebraic faith. Although I am pleased that you have expressed such a desire, I will still need proof that you all have made this decision willingly and freely of your own accord. There was no pressure from anyone for you to do this. Is that correct?"

"Yes, your Majesty," they replied in unison.

"And you wish to do so because you feel it is only fitting that as the honor guard for the Princess Ti-Ping that you share the same faith as the royal family as is per your custom as you have made a point to stress."

"Yes, your majesty," they responded to the man, a second time.

"And you realize that if you adopt the Hebraic religion then from henceforth, you all will forever deny Jesus Christ as the son of God, and you will be branded as heretics should you ever return to Byzantium. You may even face punishment by death if you did so. You all know that is the price of heresy, correct?" Zutra paused to give them all time to reflect on his last statement.

The officers all looked to their leader, Hermantius to reply on their behalf. "We've had a good long talk on that one your Majesty and it would appear that all of us are in agreement that it would seem Jesus was the one who abandoned us in the first place. Hard to think that if he truly were the son of God, he'd let Anastasius cast on the dung heap, especially after all we did to save their asses back in Constantinople. Pardon my language, my Lord, no offense intended but the Church was feeding us a lot of bullshit in my opinion."

"And none taken Hermantius, please continue." No matter how crude and rough the general presented publicly, Zutra always saw him as the most affable of men.

"So, like I said, we can't really believe in someone if he doesn't believe in us. Especially after all we did in his name. Figure if he did exist, then he was what the Jews said all along, just another Jewish teacher that ended up on the wrong end of a Roman cross. That being the case, then we should still seek to follow his example, since we already are finding ourselves being nailed by the Romans, if you follow my meaning. If they're going to hang us, then as far as we see it, we might as well be Jewish too, if that makes any sense to you."

Rubbing the short, pointed beard on his chin, Zutra slowly nodded. "Strangely, general, it does make sense to me as convoluted as your logic might appear at first. I think it is not uncommon to find one's true faith at the time one senses they are in crisis with another. The Lord moves in mysterious ways, so who am I to disagree if he delivers more sheep into the fold."

From the expression on the officers' faces, Zutra realized that none of them actually understood a single word of what he had just said. "That egg business didn't have anything to do with your decisions, did it?" The king drew Hermantius's attention back to the event which transpired over a year ago.

"Can't say that it truly inspired us and filled us with much confidence, your Majesty. After all, it promised us a glorious reward for winning this war on behalf of the Church and instead it's like the Commander said in the first place, 'nothing more than a pack of religious lies.' Only thing we got was the shaft up the ol' arsehole! Guess, we all had to be pretty stupid to think that God goes writing his prophecies on eggshells. Next thing we'd be looking for the word of God at the bottom of latrines. Take us all for being damn fools! That's what I say. If there is no honor in what they do or say, then we Alans have a responsibility to seek our own way. We have seen over the last eight years my Lord that you and your family do possess something to believe in. You do so with all your heart and all your soul and that's good enough for us to believe in as well. You and the Queen are all the proof we need that yours is the true path."

Mar Zutra remained hesitant in giving his final approval to the general and his officers. He began to question how much of their decision was based on merely following his example rather than truly experiencing the hand of God upon the shoulder. "Anything else that you'd like to say on your behalves before I render my decision?" Zutra prompted his petitioners to entreat him with a stronger closing argument.

Hermantius sensed that the monarch was still not fully convinced that granting their request would be in everyone's best interest. He also recognized that he was being given one last chance to make a convincing argument for their case. Clearing his throat, Hermantius prepared to grasp the only straw he had remaining. It was not an argument that he had rehearsed well, thinking it sounded flimsy at best, even though it was one of the major reasons for all of them arriving at their decision. "Seeing that your Majesty has decided not to evacuate the city and has chosen to remain here even though such a decision none of us can agree with, I have done some thinking about how best to protect your children under our care when we head east."

"And through this contemplation you have attained certain insights, I can safely presume," Zutra urged the general to continue seeing that Hermantius was afraid that he may have overstepped the boundaries of his position.

Shuffling his feet, Hermantius searched for the proper words. "Pardon my awkwardness your Majesty, but it just ain't right that your children will be growing up without a father. Hard enough that you won't be there to teach them the ways of being a king but sending them to the ends of the earth to live amongst a strange people is only going to make them more confused about who they really are."

"And you obviously have a solution to this dilemma, am I correct?"

"You know we all love the Princess likes she's our own family and little Yanqa is almost like a mascot to us the way he hangs around our barracks every day. Well…if we were all to be Jewish, then we can provide him with some of that knowledge that he'll be sorely lacking through your absence. We may not know as much as you but at least we can give him some part of his father that he can cherish. More so, the Princess might even feel comfortable about his being around us and won't fear us teaching him all the bad things that common soldiers do."

Mar Zutra couldn't help but smile as he watched Hermantius painfully trying to negotiate through the slippery labyrinth that he was forging with his explanation. "General, somehow, I don't believe my wife has much hope that my son will escape the soldiering ways. Already, from much of what he has repeated after visits to your barracks, I fear it might be far too late to make amends. Donning a suit of piety will hardly rectify what has already been done."

"Oh, hell's bells," Hermantius threw in the towel, giving up the challenge to be diplomatic any longer. "We just want to take care of him in the best way we can seeing that his father wants to make a damn fool of himself and sacrifice his life for no good reason. In spite of that, we all want him to grow up to be like his father because the truth is, we all see you as one of the finest men…ah…rulers… that we have ever had the honor to serve. It would do us proud if we could even be a fraction like you. It would make us even prouder if we can teach your son to be half the man that you are." The assembled officers nodded and voiced their agreement to their general's comments. "And we can't raise him properly like you would have done unless we are sure about what we can and cannot teach him without contradicting his heritage. So best, we become like you so we can do this fit and proper like! And that's the God's truth, I swear it."

"I don't think I have ever had anyone speak to me like that," Zutra mused as he feigned shock and surprise, raising the fingers of both hand to his mouth. "What was that you called me, a damn fool? I think your cousin called me that once, but I forgave him."

Hermantius withdrew slightly, uncertain of what might be the King's next response.

"Your cousin was also certainly correct General when he suggested you won't receive too many promotions unless you learn to reign in that tongue of yours."

Hermantius was about to protest in his own defense, but Zutra held up a hand to cut him short. "Yet, I find your honesty surprisingly refreshing and yes, I probably am being a damn fool, but no man can escape his destiny. More so the fool if he believes he can circumvent the will of God!"

"No offense was intended, your Majesty."

"And none was taken," Zutra accepted the general's apology gracefully. "As you undergo your religious studies, all of you will come to realize that I never really had any choice in the matter. God as you will come to appreciate from the Old Testament makes many requests of us and usually always at a high personal cost. Not everyone was as lucky as Abraham to have the angel hold back his arm from sacrificing his son Isaac."

"We just want you to know your Majesty, that Yanqa will be raised by us exactly as you would have done. We may not be able to replace you as his father, but we will do our best to ease the loss he will suffer."

"Your love for my son is admirable, General. To be willing to make such a sacrifice, and there will be a sacrifice as you may already know." Zutra smiled and pointed towards the General's crotch. "However, you need to recognize that you are doing all this even though I will be sending religious teachers to accompany my family on the journey. This makes your sacrifice unnecessary and gives you one last chance to change your minds."

This time the King found his general flashing a secretive smile. "I guess your majesty doesn't know about us Alans. We circumcise all our boys at eight years of age. Can't take what we don't have," he smirked.

"Yes, that is something I was not aware of," Zutra replied. "In that case, I will have the priests check you all to see if it was done correctly. We do have our standards after all. Can't permit a half-assed job, you understand," Zutra smiled slyly in return with the threat of a possible further paring of their shafts hanging in the balance. Not knowing whether he was serious or not only made the officers grimace as their hands quickly covered their crotches reflexively.

The threat of undergoing the knife a second time did not seem to faze Hermantius at all as he wanted to discuss further the king's mention of the religious teachers. "Sending those others is not the same thing," he argued, then quickly begged pardon for doing so. "No teacher is going to raise

Yanqa and his brother like you would have done. For that, you have to have genuine love and I don't know of any teacher that ever loved his students from my own experience, your Majesty. In fact, I always got a caning from the bastards. Pardon me again, your Majesty."

The revelation of Hermantius receiving regular physical punishment from his tutors didn't surprise Zutra at all. He imagined the general must have been more than a handful to any pedagogue.

"Not to mention, I'm getting pretty long in the tooth, so are the rest of my boys here and it ain't like any of us our going to have any children of our own, or at least any that we're willing to name as our heirs, if you know what I mean."

Zutra simply shrugged his shoulders acknowledging that he understood completely, while he struggled to suppress any laughter that the general's crude descriptions generated. It took all his self-control to stop imagining a horde of little Hermantius spread far and wide across the Empires. "My good General, and noble officers, you have done me proud. You have done my son proud. It would be an honor to have you as his official Godparents, so-to-speak, even though the Queen may have some initial objection for my naming so many of you to this task. I will do my best to assuage any concerns she might have. Just do me a favor and try not to teach my sons any more tavern-songs." Zutra winked at the general. "I hereby grant your request to convert to Judaism. I will personally see that all the necessary arrangements are made, as well as see to the necessary costs of your training."

The men saluted in an act of respect to for God, king and country.

"I just want to say your Majesty, that we are all honored by your trust in us, and we want you to know that we will protect your wife and children with every ounce of strength we can muster. We don't want you to have any worries about that while you remain here in the city after we have gone or even afterwards from the here-after, if you know what I mean."

Zutra felt himself moving from laughter to tears. Never had any man awed him with such simple sincerity. "General, it is I who am honored. It has been an honor to have served with you. God bless you all! Now all of you remove yourselves from my presence before you see your king shame himself and be brought to tears."

Chapter Thirty-Eight

Constantinople: Summer 505 A.D.

Huddled in his mother's arms, little Zutra tried to be a big boy for his mother's sake which was not easy for a five-year-old thrust into a strange new world. Avital felt as if she had been waiting for hours outside the ornately carved and richly gilded doors that opened into the Empress's quarters. Perhaps it was no more than an hour, but the tension was already palpable. Patricius had brought her to the palace that morning and gave her only two instructions before he disappeared. One was to be patient and the second was to be honest. If she could agree to do so, then everything would be fine. He reassured her that everything had been taken care of as long as she could withhold her tongue. Patience was definitely not one of her stronger virtues.

Finally, an African slave girl unbolted and retracted the door from the inside, asking Avital to step inside alone, as she offered to take care of young Zutra while she met with the Empress. Avital's immediate reaction was to say something offensive to the servant, but she forced herself to bite her tongue and remain both civil and silent, reluctantly handing over her child. "Now you be a good boy for mama and play with this nice lady while mama's away, okay?" The child went willingly, and Avital passed through the sliver of an opening, closing the door behind.

At first the room appeared empty, a single beam of light streaking through the high-valanced window in the far-left corner while the rest of the room remained shrouded in heavy shadows. It took a minute for her eyes to adjust before she could discern that she was definitely not alone after all, spotting the lone figure sitting across from her on a wide sedan, purposely situated to capture the stray rays of the single beam of light that entered the room.

"Come in my dear. Don't be afraid," she summoned Avital to come closer.

"I am not afraid," Avital was quick to respond then clamped her mouth shut, second guessing whether or not it was the right thing to say.

"No, I don't think you are," the Empress agreed. "People like us rarely are afraid, even when we should be. Please sit down across from me and let me have a good look at you."

Avital did as she was bid, taking a seat on the second lounge directly across from the Empress.

"My, my, you are beautiful," Ariadne complemented her. "Beautiful and dangerous is how I believe Patricius describes you."

"I don't know why he would have said that?" Avital quickly defended herself.

"Now that isn't exactly true, is it my dear? You know who I am and I know all about you. So, you need not try to keep any secrets from me if I am to help you. Do you know why Patricius came to me?"

Carefully scrutinizing the features of the Empress, Avital saw that she remained beautiful even as a woman in her fifties. Barely a single line wrinkled her skin and her eyes still sparkled like those of a young girl. Her beauty further haloed by airs of dignity and grace. "I think so," Avital replied.

"What is it you think you know?" Ariadne was quite curious to hear her answer.

"I think he is in love with you."

"And..." the Empress prompted for her to say more.

"And I think you love him too."

"But we were never fated to be together," Ariadne completed the story.

"And do you know why?"

Avital shook her head.

"Because I am too ambitious," she answered her own question. "I believe you know all about that particular fault as well, don't you?"

The Lady Avital fumbled over a few words looking for the correct answer.

"Be honest," the Empress wagged a cautionary finger. "Being true to yourself is the only way we can move forward together."

"Yes," the word dropped sheepishly from Avital's mouth.

"That is how Patricius pleaded your case to me these past few days. That you and I are very much alike. Practically sisters though we were born to two different worlds. Even more than my affection I bore for him, that was the reason he suggested I should help you. That by doing so, in some way I would be saving some part of myself. Some part of my past."

"I don't understand."

"See, now you're being honest," Ariadne smiled warmly. "My Paddy has always been a clever man but this time I think he has actually outsmarted himself. Your husband apparently felt he had an arrangement with my husband, the Emperor. I feel so much better referring to them as husbands, don't you?"

Avital nodded her head, though she had no knowledge as to where this conversation was heading.

"Husbands make them sound far more human. King and Emperor I believe exaggerates their importance too much," Ariadne continued her explanation. "As humans they will be guilty of all mankind's foibles. They will say what needs to be said in order to exploit matters even though they may not truly mean it. I have no doubt your husband believed he had an arrangement with Anastasius. Yet, Anastasius is a pragmatist and he needs the accord he signed with this Sassanid Shah more than he needs your husband. Do you see what I'm saying?"

"That men will lie in order to obtain what they seek."

"Correct, unlike us, men find it difficult to be honest," Ariadne praised her response. "They say and do whatever they please and justify it in the end no matter how many people are hurt in the process. Seeing that Anastasius would not offer you and your son royal protection, Paddy knew that I was the only one that could save you."

"You have more power than the Emperor?" Avital asked somewhat disbelievingly.

"Yes, I do now, thanks to Paddy. Emperors are not any cleverer than any other man is. They always underestimate us until it is too late."

"Yes, yes," Avital agreed completely. "They use us in order to achieve a goal, then never properly rewards us for the contributions and sacrifices we make on their behalf."

"Exactly," Ariadne agreed with the sentiments expressed. "But you refused to let that happen to you."

"I was too smart for their games," Avital confessed. "I turned it on them to my own advantage." She no longer cared that she was expressing her own deep dark secrets.

"I was the same way," Ariadne reassured her that they shared this trait in common. "I would make them pay for the many hurts they had aggrieved me with."

"My father used me as a bartering tool, offering me to whomever he could gain power from. He treated me like a whore!" Avital couldn't believe she was saying such things to the Empress, but it felt good to finally express her feelings in the open.

"As did mine," Ariadne also admitted. "I was engaged to the man I loved and then my father forced me into a marriage to a man I despised."

"I was already betrothed. There existed a signed contract of marriage but my father saw a better opportunity for himself by forcing me to marry the father of my husband to be. I was a young woman. I didn't want to marry a man as old as my father. Why would he have done that to me? I thought he loved me?"

"I have asked that same question myself all these years! Fathers should love their children, but I know now it is only the rare one that actually does. Very rare indeed," the Empress waited to see if her meaning donned on the King's second wife. "But worst of all was the man I loved; the man whom I believe loved me never even fought for me. I prayed that he would rescue me from the cruel punishment imposed on my life and he never came. I despised him for it. I cursed him for abandoning me. I swore revenge against him, blaming him for my fate."

Avital felt the tears welling in her eyes. "Mine did too. But it was worse than that. He dwelled in the same house with me all that time. When his father took me into the bedroom, he must have heard me praying for God to take me away from there and he just shut his ears. I felt the blackness swarm across my heart and afterwards I prayed that he would suffer the same way he let me suffer at the hands of his father."

"Oh God," the Empress exclaimed. "Paddy was right when he said we were much the same. I never warned him when the guards came for his family. I let them kill his father and brother. I let him flee into exile. I wanted him to suffer too. Worst of all, for twenty-five years my heat ached for him because in truth I had only punished myself."

Avital's hands cupped over her mouth as she tried to suppress her own grief. "I signed the affidavit that led to his father's execution. I blamed Zutra for the shame I suffered and because of it I denied him the love he sought." The emotional impact caused Avital to lose her remaining composure as the tears flowed and sobs erupted from her mouth. "I have caused his death!" she cried in despair.

"At least you have the memories of his lying next to you for years. You've had the warmth of his seed in your belly and the gift of the child he has given you. You have a means to make up for the terrible things you have done. I was a fool for too long and never had the opportunity for Paddy to give me any of those gifts that your Zutra has given you."

Avital couldn't restrain the flood of tears any longer, her voice choking with grief so that she could no longer speak. The Empress stood and then sat herself down on the other couch, wrapping her arms around Avital as she sobbed heavily.

"There, there, my dear. Everything will be fine," the Empress comforted her.

"He only wanted to love me, and I made his life into a living hell," she wailed. "I did things, horrible things in order to have my way."

"As did I, as did I," Ariadne repeated. "I became like them, bending people to my will and using them for my own gain, when all I really wanted was the love of one man."

"Now he is going to die because of what I've done," the words foamed from her lips as the rivulets of tears streamed down her cheeks. "I did this to him," Avital sobbed.

"Do not fear for him," the Empress attempted to assuage her guilt. "He will not be alone. Patricius will be with him. And if anyone knows how to survive it is my Paddy."

"I don't understand," she sputtered. "Patricius is here. How can he help Zutra?"

"That was the arrangement," Ariadne explained. "Have you ever wondered why my husband was so eager to sign the treaty with the Shah? Did you not think it strange that he would be willing to pursue the peace when the noose had already been placed around the neck of the Sassanids? Never underestimate Anastasius. He knew that Patricius was only months from destroying the Hun alliance. Patricius who was once Caesar; Patricius who was once my betrothed; Patricius who is now the right hand of a King chosen by God; Patricius who is uncle to the most famous general in our city today. There would be no Byzantine victory if the war had continued. There only would have been Patricius. Anastasius feared that more than he feared Kavad and his armies. He needed the peace in order to stop your husband and Patricius gaining the supreme power. That is why the Emperor agreed to let the Shah live and regain power; to stop Paddy and your Zutra. The moment Paddy stepped ashore in this city with you and your son, he was a greater threat to the throne than any other enemy of the Empire could ever be. And now he's made his peace with Anastasius and you and I are the price for that peace."

"How? How is that possible?"

"He's a threat and Anastasius wants that threat removed. However, he dares not lay a hand on Patricius. Not when he is at the height of his popularity and Areobindus is within the city accompanied by his entire army. Paddy is a clever fellow too, but he lets his heart rule his mind which has always been his downfall. His love for me has always been his ruin. He offered to leave Byzantium, never to return, to rejoin your husband, but only if you and your son are installed safely in the Holy Land and I become your guardian. Areobindus has already agreed to provide you with a garrison to protect you and your family the rest of your days."

"Why would Patricius do such a thing?

"Because he knew that Anastasius was going to charge me with adultery and there was enough evidence that the charge would hold. With all the other sins of the world, adultery is still one of the few punishable by death." Ariadne noticed the look of alarm on Avital's face. "Oh, don't be so surprised. I'm not that old that I can't enjoy certain pleasures. After denying myself love for twenty-five years do you really think I was going to let him leave me again without rekindling the flames, even if it was only for a few nights? I would do it all over again if I had the opportunity." Ariadne flashed Avital a wicked smile.

"I don't know whether I should be happy for you or cry for you." Avital hugged the Empress in return, feeling both her sorrow and happiness.

"Paddy would never let any harm befall me. He had his nephew swear an oath that his would be the hand that would avenge me should any harm befall me. You should know that these Alans take their oaths very seriously. An oath between their own kind outweighs any to the Empire. Blood over honour, they claim. Then he told Anastasius that Areobindus and his men had sworn fidelity to me, binding them to my service and mine alone. He would be a fool if he raised a finger against me now and Anastasius, I can assure you is no fool."

"And then to seal the bargain he offered to exile himself by returning to my Zutra?" Avital guessed how the arrangement concluded.

"That's my Paddy," Ariadne smiled. "He's loved me to the bitter end. So, now that you are aware of the arrangement, if I am to be your guardian, I will need your full cooperation. You must do exactly as I instruct you from now on. And when your son takes over the reins of your Jewish community in the Holy Land, once he is old enough, he too must swear allegiance to this throne as well."

"I promise you," Avital hugged her again. "On my husband's sacred soul, I promise you."

"May God have mercy upon both their souls, my dear. They were better men than we deserved," Ariadne prayed as she held on tightly to the sobbing wife of a lesser king.

Chapter Thirty-Nine

Mahoza: Summer 505 A.D.

He sat motionless, staring deeply into the dark, intoxicating eyes of his beloved Princess. Her slender, delicate fingers of both hands rested gently in his, as they enjoyed the silent exchange that passed seamlessly between them, both wishing desperately that this moment could last forever.

"I don't want it to end this way," she winced at the thought of their parting, finally breaking their mutual silence.

"You know that if there was any other way, I would make it happen," Zutra shook his head. "But no man can defy the will of God. Not even a king, especially not one born into servitude to the Almighty."

"You could come east with me, my love; there is nothing more you need to do here. There is nothing left for you to prove. You have given your people everything. There is nothing left for you to offer. Why should God ask you to forfeit everything including your life? You can spend the rest of your life with me, with your children. Why would God deny you that? Is life such as sin that you will not even consider it?"

"You know the answer to that, my love. Truthfully, I am still not finished in God's eyes," he corrected her. "Until I fulfill the last part of the prophecy, I cannot rest in peace nor will any of you ever be safe. I must contract with the Great Shah to seal the bargain and confirm the safety of my people. I must ensure that there will be established the three kingdoms for the three sons as prophesized. In order to do so, I must remain here and at best safeguard my half-brother's inheritance."

"Why can't you let fate make its own solutions?" she begged. "Why must you always be the one making sacrifices?"

"You know why. I made a promise to my uncle and father that I intend to fulfill."

"Your own sons are safe," she pleaded. "Is that not enough? Must you give up your life and our love for the sake of your half-brother? Please, please come away with me now." The tears began to well in her eyes until they could not be held in check any longer, streaking down her pale cheeks.

Raising a finger to her prominent cheekbone, he caressed the tears from her smooth, delicate skin. "Can a king ever place his own safety ahead of his people? Were you not the one that told me I had an obligation to my half-brother that I had let wane? Would you still love a man so selfish to let other's die in his stead?"

"Yes, yes, I would," she pleaded, "Would it not be selfish to leave me all alone? I made a promise to love you forever," she reminded him. "How can I do that if you abandon me?"

"You have given me the best years of my life, my love. Furthermore, you now carry another child so that I may live on. Through them, I will always be with you. I will never abandon you. You have made my life complete; I am surely blessed and need for nothing more." His reassuring smile did little to overcome her distress and sadness.

Unable to quell the tears the full force of her melancholy was unleashed. "I cannot live without you," she collapsed into his lap, her face buried within her hands. "What shall I tell this baby when she asks for her father?"

"She? How do you know it is a she?" he questioned upon hearing the reference to a female child between sobs and seized an opportunity to suppress her sadness by changing their discussion.

"A mother knows these things. I have carried her differently from Yanqa. Can you not see? It is obvious to me; this is your daughter my beloved. A daughter you will never have the chance to hold."

"It tears me apart more than you could ever imagine." Zutra embraced his wife, clutching for every moment they could share together. "Yet I know that I must do this in order that I can keep you all safe. Protecting my family, her family, is the greatest gift I can give my unborn daughter. Please tell me you understand! I need to know you understand my decision."

"I don't want to live without you, my beloved, that's all I know," the tears poured into his lap as she succumbed to the anguish in her heart.

"And I cannot live without you," he repeated her words. "So, for me to send you away to the security of your brother means that I have only one fate to embrace. If I cannot be with you in body, then death will permit me at least to be with you forever in spirit." He stroked her silk black hair as she continued to cry. "I am always with you. Wherever you go, I will dwell safely within your heart. Did you not tell me once that the spirits of our ancestors, of those we loved, are always with us? It is only that thought which provides me with the courage to do what I must do. Please let me know that you understand and don't hate me for it!"

"I don't want to live without you," she wailed again.

"Yes you do," Zutra was firm. "We have a son that needs to know about his father as he gets older; a son that you will need to raise on your own and teach him to be a father of great kings. And now a daughter who will be blessed with many children and from her a great people will also rise. I need you to tell our children how much I love them; even this one in your belly that I have not met yet. She must know how I wish I could have been there when she arrives screaming into this world. How much I hoped to hold her in my arms. Never forget. Never let them forget me."

Raising her head from his hands, she wrapped her arms around his neck and pulled herself into his lap. "Cradle me tightly in your arms, my love. Let me feel the strength and warmth of your body and never fear that I resent you for the decisions you have made. I can do nothing but love you until the day I die and join you once again."

Wrapping his arms around the princess, Zutra lowered his chin onto her shoulder. "God, why have you abandoned me in my hour of need," he choked on the muffled words.

"I will do as you ask, my love," she promised, sensing his distress. "Yanqa will never forget his father. Our daughter will be provided stories that will sing of your greatness. And never shall you be far from me. I will feel you in my chest with every heartbeat."

"To go into the valley of death and not know her name is an enduring pain I don't wish to suffer."

"Then let us find a name now so you have no such worries my love, a name that glorifies her father long into the hereafter."

"And what would you suggest?"

"Perhaps we should name this little one after your mother?"

"You wish to call our child Sarai?"

"In my land a name is only one or two syllables at most. I think Sarai will be perfect."

"Sarai," Zutra rolled the name across his lips. He had not mentioned his mother's name since he stood at her grave when they finally lowered her into the earth a decade ago. "Yes, I like it. Let the Sin nation welcome our little Sarai."

"I am glad you are pleased," she hugged him ever so tightly. "And like Sarai of old, she will be a mother to a great clan."

"I see you have been studying our history. How could I have been so lucky to have you in my life?"

Before she could make reply, he pressed his lips firmly against hers, locking her in a kiss that was without end. A kiss that was only broken when both had to make a desperate gasp for air. The cycle of tears was broken by the magic of that moment.

"No luckier than I have been to find the one man in the world that I could call husband."

"How I wish I could have given you a better life," he confessed. "My own inadequacy to be the man you deserved has brought this suffering upon you."

"Shhhh", she placed a finger to his lips to stop him from saying anything further. "How can you even believe that? Never has any woman been so loved as you have loved me. Never could I have dreamed of finding someone that shared my thoughts and dreams as you have. This seed I carry within me, like her brother is blessed by our God. A God that we have even heard of and tremble at his name within the Sin Empire. How could any mother not share in the blessing of such a birth? There is nothing lacking in the gifts you have bestowed upon me, my love."

"And now what do I offer you but exile and the bitterness of my death?"

"As you explained, you have no other choice though I still beg you to reconsider," she soothed his anguish.

"Oh, that I wish I could," he regretted whole-heartedly. "But you know as well as I do that God has decided my fate long ago and it's only now with you by my side that I have finally found the courage to embrace it."

"Never would I stand between you and our God, husband. I have witnessed His hand in the many great things he has done for you over these past seven years. The miracles that He has performed have swayed me and it was your faith that has inspired me to cherish your God just as Ruth did in the Torah. Like her, I have come from a foreign land only to become the wife of the greatest Jewish leader of our time. I will take our faith back to my birth-land and there I will enshrine it and nurture it and see that it grows among my people. I will make you proud of me, my love. In God's name I will see to it that your legacy will never die."

"I have always been awed by you, my love. Never was there a moment that I did not thank God for bringing you into my life. I never would have believed that anyone could have brought so much happiness into my world."

"Are you sure my love?" As soon as the words parted from her lips, she regretted asking the question.

"What do you mean?" Zutra felt crushed by her unexpected doubts.

"That I am the only one that has brought you happiness," she prodded him towards understanding, sensing the hurt she had unintentionally caused.

"Ahh, yes, I can see where you may have concerns. And I do not want you to have any lingering doubts after I am gone."

"I am being foolish," she apologized, "and selfish. It is not my place to question such things. Forgive me."

"There is nothing to forgive and you have every right to know. I want you to know. I need you to know before we part. Obviously, it is something that I should have said to you long before this day, but I thought you already knew from every touch of my hand, every kiss of my lips."

"Perhaps I have always known," she smiled. "But sometimes a woman has to hear the words spoken as well. A queen is not expected to care, but a woman is a foolish creature that always needs to be reassured."

Cradling her in his arms once again, Zutra kissed her softly on the forehead, both eyelids and then centered on her lips. The passion of this kiss far surpassed the one previous, the flush on both their bodies causing a rosy glow that radiated with an intense heat.

"Did you see into my heart," he asked once the kiss had completed. "Did you find the answer in my touch? Who needs words when one action can provide a thousand words unspoken? Therein lays my response to your question."

"There are no doubts," she grinned afterwards.

"Nor have there been any doubts in my mind for a very long time. There was only room for one in my heart. Though once upon a time I may have confused love with duty, I have no such quandaries any longer. No other woman could ever have challenged the bonds I have forged with you."

With the back of her fingers, she softly stoked his face struggling to suppress the urge to burst into tears once again. "And no woman could have ever asked for more than what you have given me from the first moment we met?"

"But?"

"What do you mean my love?" her eyes opening wide, betraying that there was something else she needed to discuss but feared to do so.

"But I feel there is something more that you wish to ask from me," Zutra sensed the question lying behind her delicate touch and the light squeeze of her hand.

Nuzzling into his chest she blushed, "I could never hide anything from you, my beloved. Nor did I ever want to. And now that I know how you feel about us, I have no fear in asking this favor of you, my love."

Intrigued and curious, Zutra cocked his head to one side, inviting his Queen to present this burning question that she had resisted asking until today.

"A long time ago, you said to me that it was necessary for your people that little Zutra came first. I did not understand the urgency at the time but now that I am familiar with all the sacred texts, I do appreciate the burden that the rabbis placed upon you. But now, you will pass the throne of Mahoza on to Hanai, your brother; it goes not to your son. Therefore, you are no longer bound by the laws of these men that run contrary to all that I have learned in the Torah."

"Ah…I see that you have now become a sage and scholar in our laws as well," he jested. "So, what wisdom have you gleaned from the Torah, my love, that you so desperately wish to share with me," Zutra invited her to continue.

"It is for Yanqa, I ask nothing for myself. I want you to give our son your blessing as firstborn."

Rocking back on the sedan, Zutra appeared momentarily shocked. "I don't know what to say," he finally broke his stunned silence. "Zutra is firstborn. You know that. There can be no denial. It is by the laws of nature and that cannot be perverted. How can I say otherwise?"

"Was not Ishmael, Abraham's firstborn? Was not Esau, Isaac's firstborn? Was not Reuben, Jacob's firstborn son? Shall I continue my beloved?"

"I see you truly have studied your lessons well."

"Am I not right?" she sought confirmation.

"You know that you are," Zutra laughed. "Just as you know that I cannot argue with the ways of my ancestors. Not even David was Jesse's firstborn. I'm surprised you didn't mention him."

"I would have had you wished me to continue," Ti-Ping replied smugly. "So will you give Yanqa your blessing and the gifts of the firstborn?"

"With logic as impeccable as you have shown, not to mention that I cannot argue against the sacred writings which support your contention, then I agree and consent to your request. However, be aware that the golden diadem of Mahoza's king must pass to Hanai. I cannot permit you to take that back to Northern Wei, it must remain in the city as it is also his birthright since he is to be the next ruler."

"I only seek your blessing for our son, perhaps a few of the household treasures, but most importantly the holy books and sacred texts of our people that are lodged in our home."

"And that is all?" the king could see that there was still more to come that she had not yet mentioned.

"Just one more request, beloved. I seek only that which I know will serve our son well in a time of need to ensure his future. I request that you pass the suit of lights to our son so that when he comes of age he can shine like the stars in the heaven and men will be dazzled by the brilliance."

"That suit has a legacy that is tied to the land," Zutra bristled. "One day it must return to the land from which it was spun to be worn at the time of the in-gathering."

Ti-Ping looked crestfallen. Of all the objects it was the one she cherished and desired most for her son to possess. She knew such a garment once seen in her own land would cause many of the people to flock to Yanqa's side.

Zutra attempted to interject a tad of humor into their exchange. "Do you remember that first day we laid eyes upon one another? It had been Mordecai's advice that I marry all the daughters that had been delivered to me. I could not imagine the battles within my house that would have brought about had I taken his advice."

"Nor could I imagine keeping the peace between that many savage women that wished to tear each other's eyes out," she grimaced as she contemplated the scenario, reflecting upon her numerous encounters with Avital and his concubines. "And why did you not heed his advice?"

"Because after I laid my eyes upon you, I knew that there could never be anyone else. Avital, as I have come to realize was a necessity of tradition but you, my love, became a necessity to fill the gaping hole within my heart. To bring any others directly into our household when all I could think about was you , would have been the undoing of my kingdom. A dozen or more disgruntled fathers all wishing to have my head for the dishonor that I paid their daughters. It was one of the few times that I knew Mordecai's advice was incorrect."

"But you did take some as concubines?" she questioned.

"The father of a concubine cannot protest the treatment of his daughter."

"So, you are saying you felt safe then because my father was thousands of miles away and would not be able to defend my honour," she mused.

"That and the fact that I knew your guardian would not have accepted your rejection easily had I dismissed you," he teased back, sensing that he had successfully dispersed the tears that had been threatening just moments ago when he refused the suit of lights.

"You think you had something to fear from Patricius?" she jabbed him in the side of the ribs with the tips of her fingers. "You would have something to have feared from me," she assured him. "I would have shown you what a real fighter trained by the Shaolin could do." She moved her hands so swiftly across, up and down his chest, that he could not even follow the movements of each little jab that struck his body. "It is a good thing husband that you made the right choice," she jibed.

"Obviously," his eyes rounded with feigned terror, to which they both laughed. "A good thing my little Princess did not teach such mastery of these martial arts to Avital, or I would have been in serious trouble."

"Don't think that she did not ask," she grinned.

"Why does that not surprise me," he brayed. "Now that would have been a fight they would have written legends about."

Nuzzling into his shoulder, Ti-Ping diverted the conversation back to the present. "What need will there be to retain the suit of lights in Mahoza if it is only going to catch the attention of the Shah once he returns. He will never let your family retain it. The people still talk of the day you wore it at our wedding and how it filled the air with the brilliance of diamonds cast upon rays of golden sunlight. Do you think he would not desire to possess such an object for himself?"

"You aren't going to let go, are you?", he mused. Mar Zutra then became pensive, thinking long and hard about what Ti-Ping had just said, knowing that her prediction of future events was very likely. "You're right. I cannot allow such an heirloom to fall into the Shah's hands. Such a travesty would herald the ruination of our people. Nor would it serve me any better to send it to Jerusalem for Zutra to possess, since it would only capture the Emperor's envy and he would likely seize it as his own prize to display in Constantinople."

"What will you do then, husband?" She allowed the look in her eyes to plead her case for their son once more still hoping that he would see the reason of her argument.

Zutra raised his index finger to his temple, tapping it several times, as an idea sprang to life. "Do you know that they say the robe was made by Solomon originally? However, they are wrong. It was actually presented to Solomon by Nakuti, the Queen of Sheba as a gift of love and devotion. All the jewels and threads came from Africa, from a land far away from Israel. Perhaps it is time that I ask Solomon, how this ceremonial robe should be dealt with."

Ti-Ping could not comprehend her husband's intentions. "How will you ask for advice from someone dead for fifteen hundred years," she pursed her lips.

Mar Zutra was grinning from ear to ear. "He has already answered me, my love. He gave his answer a very long time ago." The king paused for dramatic effect before continuing his explanation, knowing that his wife was sitting at the edge of the seat anxiously awaiting his response. "One could not be Solomon without having many enemies. The more wives he took the more enemies he manufactured, but none threatened him as much as his father-in-law, the Pharaoh of Egypt did. Egypt and Sheba were rival powers, each trying to dominate the trade routes along the Red Sea. The day that Solomon took Nakuti into his bed was the day he offended the Pharaoh beyond reconciliation. Wiser than most men, Solomon knew that he had to prepare for the eventual attack that the Pharaoh would launch against Israel. Knowing that the Egyptians would attempt to seize the most sacred and valuable objects housed in the Temple, Solomon made identical replicas of each one. After Nakuti gave birth to their son, Mennelik, Solomon sent them back to Sheba for their own protection, along with all the original treasures that he had copied. Everyone thinks that Mennelik returned with the copies, but they are mistaken. That way when Pharaoh did attack Jerusalem, he did as Solomon suspected, entering the Temple and seizing the priceless objects of our faith, but they were mere replicas."

Listening intently, Ti-Ping connected the fine threads of the story that Zutra was weaving until it became clear as to what her husband was intimating. "So, you're suggesting beloved, that we make another suit of lights."

"Exactly," Zutra exclaimed. "Obviously not to the same exquisite detail or even close to numbering the equivalent sum of gemstones, but valuable nonetheless to someone that has never viewed the original robe. And like Solomon, I will send the actual robe to a distant land with my son, where it can be protected from those that would attempt to seize it for their own."

"You will let him have it," the Princess squealed excitedly.

"Like Solomon did with Mennelik, I will let him borrow it," Zutra winked, "only to be returned at the appropriate time in the future. How long that will be; only God knows!"

"You are wise like your ancestor," Ti-Ping cooed.

"Considering that the holy relics were never returned to Jerusalem, I don't know if Solomon was displaying wisdom or demonstrating how much he loved Nakuti."

Stoking his brow with her fingers she could see that Zutra was still struggling with his decision to send the suit of lights to the far off land of Northern Wei. "Do not worry my love. With your blessing, Yanqa will become the ruler over a great nation in the East. There they will safeguard all that is sacred to your people until such time that the offspring of your sons will be reunited to rule over the Holy Land again. Have faith in the Lord and He will see that it happens at a time of His choosing. The people will not forget the name of the Kahana. They will praise it upon their lips for an eternity."

"I doubt when you return to the Wei that they will even be able to pronounce it."

"They will try, my love. From heaven you will hear them shout your name. I promise!"

"So beautiful and yet so wise," Zutra complemented her as he held her face in the palms of his hands. "Now I know that I have made the right choice. Your faith in our religion is at times even stronger than my own."

"Then all is as it should be, my love. What will happen now?"

"The General is already waiting for you. He has made preparations for the long journey. Go easy on him my love. He is desperately trying to be a changed man for our sake."

"He is like the giant panda," she laughed. "Clumsy and awkward but you cannot help to feel affection for him, nevertheless. I will be tolerant with him, husband, but if I should hear Yanqa swearing like a drunken sailor ever again, I'm afraid the general will feel the sting of the lash."

"As it should be, my love. In my stead, you are the master of our house, and your word will be law. Even God blushes at some of the words that come from the general's mouth. But no man more loyal to our family will you ever find in this entire world."

"I am well aware, my husband. A more loyal man to care for the safety of your family, you could not have found. God has blessed us in that respect."

"Then we are agreed. I am comforted that those I love our secure in his care. Now, we make preparation to send you East. Hermantius will take an escort of two hundred of his best men and along with the house servants and my palace staff, you will make your way back to the safety of your brother's kingdom. I will also send my concubines with you to spare them the suffering they would endure at the hand of Kavad's men. Please take care of them my love. They are innocents in all of these doings. I will leave behind enough to provide a comfortable life for Hanai when I am gone but not enough to tempt the Shah to seize what remains. The majority of my possessions and treasury will accompany you so that our children will have the luxuries that I would have afforded them had they had the opportunity to remain here. Most of my library I will send with you as well. Encourage our son to make good use of the books, they are his heritage."

"Do not speak with such finality," she begged him, "It is like a dagger in my heart."

This time he placed a finger to her lips to silence her protests. "I speak only of what will happen, my love. I do not expect any other outcome. My end is near but because of you, I have no regrets. There is nothing I am found wanting, because you have provided me with an eternity of all that I need. God prepares the path before me, but your love has given me the strength to walk that road."

"How can you ask me to walk through the rest of my life without you?" she pushed the words past his finger as he withdrew it from her lips.

"I told you. You will never be without me. I am with you always. I am inside of you and as long as my memories are cherished. I will never be lost from your life. Wait for me in your dreams and I will come."

"I will be waiting for you my love," she forced a smile. "Mine will be an open vessel that awaits your arrival and we will never be apart."

"I know my sweet, sweet love." Embracing her tightly, he pressed his lips against hers, knowing that this time could very well be the last time.

Chapter Forty

The Sargon Bridge: Winter 506 A.D.

With the talents of gold he had obtained from the Emperor of Byzantium, Kavad easily purchased the loyalty of the Arab tribes that traversed the caravan routes between the three seas. They were ferocious fighters, undisciplined and savage in their combative skills, but highly effective, nonetheless. With them at his side, the Great Shah was able to drive a wedge between himself and his Ephthalite overlords. This gave him the breathing space necessary to resurrect his scattered and battered army, reunifying them into a single force of some fifty thousand men. He circulated his proclamations throughout the countryside, declaring that the Byzantines had been subdued, the revolution had been tamed, and the Huns sent back from whence they came. His agents declared him in the town squares as the only true power within the country and all those that honored him as such would be given amnesty, even if they had fought for the other side during the rebellion. After so many years of war and deprivation, all anyone wanted now was to be left alone to live out their remaining days in peace.

It gave the Great Shah time to reestablish control over his Empire province by province. When a sedan carrying his brother entered his camp, it was truly the beginning of the end. Jamasp threw himself on the ground at Kavad's feet, begging for forgiveness. Through a veil of manifested tears, he told Kavad of how he had been coerced and threatened into being nothing more than a figurehead for the revolution. He explained how he begged them not to kill Kavad when he was being held prisoner. It was not so much, what Jamasp had to say that convinced the Great Shah to spare his life, but the reputation he garnered as being merciful when he did so. Having his brother place the golden diadem on his head during a

427

well-choreographed public spectacle provided the final piece of the puzzle in heralding his return as King of Kings.

Those fighting in the resistance crumbled before his advancing army, one by one going down to defeat. In a battle south of Mosul, Attard's army was slaughtered until no more than a thousand were left, running towards the wilderness for their lives. Pharazman encountered the same unstoppable juggernaut just north of Baghdad, until he was left with no option but to retreat with his men to the protection of Ctesiphon. Unfortunately, once he reached the gates of his city, he discovered them forcibly barred to the remnant of his army, the citizens of the capital praying that their act of betrayal would earn them the amnesty that the Great Shah had promised.

Before the month of Shevat was completed, every remaining fighter in the resistance assembled within the confines of Mahoza. With the three thousand left behind by Hermantius and the thousand that survived from Attard's failed battle, along with the further five thousand from the Pashah's forces commanded by Pharazman, Mar Zutra knew that the end of days was rapidly approaching. There were too few men to fight a decisive battle but too many to feed for an extended period as they drained his city's remaining resources. Ensuring that the troops remained well fed and sheltered meant providing them with as much comfort and sustenance as they could handle in the short time they had remaining, usually at the expense of the general populace. He was relieved to know that most of the aristocracy in both cities that had been loyal to the revolution and the cause of freedom had made the trip east and were now safely out of harm's way. The remaining citizens of Ctesiphon and Mahoza had little to worry about. The Great Shah would not axe his vengeance against them. They were too unimportant to gain his notice.

On the day that the Great Shah's army appeared on the plain between the Tigris and Ctesiphon, the population of that city celebrated his return, throwing the gates open to him and making a fabulous display of their loyalty and devotion as they paraded his men along the narrow streets. Young girls wept, dancers threw petals along his path, and the thunderous ovation of their deceit shook the bricks and mortar of the ancient buildings in Mahoza located across the river. Such are the fickle fates of war.

The following morning, Mar Zutra, aroused by his Chamberlain, the king was informed that a delegation sent by Kavad stood patiently at the centre of the Sargon Bridge under a flag of truce. Mar Zutra hurriedly dressed and along with a small contingent drawn from the Four Hundred went out to meet the Shah's envoys under a similar white flag.

"Are you the one known as Mar Zutra, King of the Jews?" the chief envoy questioned as the king approached with his guards.

"I am Zutra, King of Mahoza," he replied. "There are more than just Jews within my domain."

The Great Shah Kavad, King of Kings demands that you surrender your forces immediately and in return he will spare the lives of your family. He promises to make your death a swift and painless one."

"A most generous offer," Zutra scorned, "But what of my men after I surrender them?" he inquired.

"They have fostered the rebellion against the rightful monarch. Therefore, they must die for their treason."

"Then why should I surrender at all if you intend to kill us regardless," Zutra poked further fun at the envoy's demands. "Other than my brother, I have no family remaining in the city to take advantage of your exemplary kindness."

Kavad's ambassador had not prepared to be ridiculed, stumbling and tripping over words as he fumbled for an appropriate answer.

"I have a better suggestion," Zutra rescued the envoy from further embarrassment. "Why don't you ask the Great Shah this? In exchange for the loyalty of my people, including the Jews, the Scythians and the foreigners, I ask that he proclaim my brother as the Exilarch of Mesopotamia. The position will be limited to civil matters only that pertain to my people and the citizens of Mahoza. In exchange, my brother Mar Hanai will swear his allegiance to the Great Shah and collect the taxes from our people for him. It will ensure that they remain loyal to the Empire and to the Shah without threat of rebellion in the future. In exchange, I only ask three simple things for myself. First, that he smooths the path for my brother to make this transition possible and second, to do so would mean that those that have openly defied my family and assumed power for themselves must be delivered to me and be punished for their betrayal. Reb Hanina most of all is to be among that group delivered to me personally."

"And why should I tell the Great Shah to do such a thing? The men you speak of have aided and served him loyally."

"Tell him that they were sworn to serve and protect my family through blood. Their ancestors swore, their parents swore, and they in turn swore to do so. Considering what they have done to me, how much easier it will be for them to do so to him at a later time! He will understand that men that have never known the meaning of loyalty will always bite their master's hand at some time."

"And then you will surrender?"

"No, then the Great Shah must grant my third boon, that he permits us to die without shame but instead with dignity! Let us die with glory, as warriors who have fought the good fight!"

"The Great Shah wishes to end this now. He does not wish to prolong it any further," the envoy explained. "You are not in any position to make any such demands."

"Take what I have asked to the Great Shah Kavad and let him decide! As one king to another, he will understand what honor and prestige he will gain in return by granting such requests. The people will praise him for his magnanimity and Ahura Mazda will bless him for am I not recognized as a servant of the Lord and therefore deserving of an honorable death?"

At that precise moment, emerging from the rear of the delegation, one of the men pulled off his veiled turban and stood directly before Zutra. Having wedged himself among the envoys in disguise, the entourage immediately knelt and bowed their heads responsively upon recognizing the infiltrator as being none other than the Great Shah. A large and powerful man with tightly curled black beard, he stood half a head taller than Mar Zutra. His dark eyes beneath the beetling brow and strongly chiseled features were unmistakable.

"I do understand," he looked straight into Zutra's eyes measuring the depth of his adversary. "Pardon my disguise but I wanted to see the young king that is proclaimed as the right hand of God for myself. The fact that I found it necessary to hide amongst my own men tells me what I have always known. You humble me. For seven long years, I have underestimated you and you have humbled me. Now that I have looked you straight in the eye, I understand the reason. I can only hope that I will be a wiser and a more merciful ruler because of it. I accept your terms. Send me out the boy and I swear to be his guardian for the rest of his days. You have my word on it as one king to another!"

Turning to several of his guards, Mar Zutra instructed them to fetch Mar Hanai and bring him to the centre of the bridge.

"If my death means that you will be a more merciful ruler because of it, then it is you that have honored me, Great Shah," Zutra smiled humbly. "And you will willingly give me those I seek from amongst your advisors?"

"You may have them. They are not worthy of the positions they have attained," Kavad answered. "Men of deceit and evil intent will always remain so. You are right; a dog that bites the hand of his master will do so no matter who possesses him afterwards. I will hand them over and you may do as you wish with them. Go back to your men and tell them they may die with honor before this day has ended. But have no misconceptions, you know that ultimately I will be victorious."

"Only because God in his prophecy has said it will be so, Excellency. To God and glory," Mar Zutra saluted the King of Kings.

"May Ahura Mazda have mercy upon your soul, Mar Zutra Kahana, King of Mahoza" Kavad bid the Exilarch farewell as the two kings under white flag separated and returned to their respective armies, while the sentries on the bridge awaited the arrival of Mar Hanai.

True to his word, Shah Kavad delivered all the defectors from the Mahozian community that had schemed and plotted against the Exilarch and his father. Even when they were transferred into Zutra's custody, none of the former members of the Beth Din actually comprehended what was transpiring, so shocked were they to find themselves in the clutches of their arch nemesis. From the moment they were summoned until the time they were herded across the bridge, not a single word had been exchanged between them and their armed escort. It was only when they saw Mar Zutra standing at the far end of the bridge, surrounded by a contingent of guardsmen that the rabbis realized that the betrayers had now been betrayed. Reb Hanina pleaded with his Sassanid guard that held his ropes, intoning that he had been personally responsible for the Great Shah's escape from

Susiana, but his words fell upon deaf ears. Once across the bridge, they were forced to kneel before their jailers, the ropes hanging from their hands now tied to their feet as well, rendering escape impossible. It was only then that the stark reality dawned on Reb Hanina and he understood the full impact of the arrangement made between kings. The men encircling them weren't their jailers at all; they were merely escorting them to their executioners.

The thirteen men that had once been so prominent in their community cried, pleading in vain to bargain for their lives but Mar Zutra could find no mercy in his heart. Too many had died because of their poisonous sedition and corruption. Too many had suffered because of their unlimited greed, jealousy and envy. Too many lives had been destroyed so these thirteen could squander their ill-gotten gains on a life they never deserved or merited.

"Why don't you try praying to God instead," Zutra suggested, "But I doubt he will hear your prayers. After all, He heeded mine and delivered you unto me!"

"What you are contemplating is murder," Reb Hanina accused the Exilarch.

"I believe justice is a far better word to use," Zutra knelt beside his father-in-law, whispering the words menacingly in his ear. "Justice for my father and justice for what you did to me."

"I did nothing to you. I took care of you. You were like a son to me," his voice wavered as he continued to plead for his life. Though they did not hear clearly what Mar Zutra had said, the response from Reb Hanina made the others aware that they were now living on borrowed time.

"More like a pet monkey from what I recall," Zutra shred any hope that the old man thought he could conjure by playing on Zutra's emotions. "You killed my father then paraded me around like a monkey on a chain. Making me dance and perform for all your friends. See how my monkey loves me. See how my monkey doesn't hate me for what I did to his father. See how my monkey is willing to give me his palace and his fortune when I dangle my daughter's ass in front of him like a ripe banana."

"No, no, I never did that! I loved you like a son!"

"You are unable to love anyone but yourself. The truth is written all over you like an unholy text. Even the Great Shah saw your perfidy and wants nothing more to do with you. Why do you think he was so willing to pass you into my custody?"

Seeing that his effort to make Mar Zutra feel guilt had not worked, the crafty old sage tried a different tactic. "You will be cursed by every religious leader among our people for what you are about to do. They will spit upon your name. They will curse your family. The great rabbis will vilify you and bring the wrath of the Almighty down upon your descendants. They will be cursed for an eternity! Your descendants will be cut off time and time again from our people!"

"Is that the best you can do?" Zutra scoffed. "It is now twice that you self-proclaimed holy men have destroyed our kingdoms. Because of you, we lost our country to the Romans and now you have destroyed our little kingdom in Persia. When will you ever tire of condemning your own people to death?"

"What you are about to do will not bring back your kingdom nor erase the suffering of our people for the past five hundred years," Reb Hanina spouted. "Even if we have sinned, do you truly wish to be seen as judge and executioner? No one will remember any of the good you have done, only the evil you have perpetrated as your last act. That will be the only legacy left behind for your son. He will always be known as the son of that bloodthirsty king, the son of a butcher!"

Zutra hesitated upon hearing the Rabbi's last words. The mention of his son struck a chord of doubt in the king's mind. The thought of his son being abused in any manner due to his infractions undermined his determination and confidence. "My sons are innocents, Hanina. They should not have to suffer because of me."

Reb Hanina jumped upon the weakening of Zutra's resolve, deciding to press what little advantage had been gained. "Yes, why would you condemn my grandson to live a life of shame?"

It was the wrong choice of words, and Mar Zutra was able to rechannel his hatred. "You mean sons, rabbi, I have two sons!"

"Bah, you have only one son. The other is nothing more than a demon spawned by your fornication with an animal. Sodomizer, a carnal sin for which the creature you begat will be made to suffer. That bastard offspring and the whore that bore him are already condemned." Unable to reign in his racist beliefs, Reb Hanina spewed black bile that constantly fueled his soul and displayed his true character much to the chagrin of his bound and silent colleagues.

"Animal! I will show you an animal," Zutra screamed his outrage, as he raised his sword above his head, thinking only of the oath he had sworn to Avital, that her father would die by his hand. The time had come to fulfill that oath. "May God fail to have mercy upon your black and foul souls." Drawing their swords, the garrison raised them high, mimicking the motions of their king. "I curse you all to eternal damnation," Zutra shouted. The gleaming blades slashed down without remorse, without regret.

Approaching the third bell of the afternoon, the Great Shah's generals had assembled their forces on the Ctesiphon side of the bridge. The winter sun had already begun its descent and the air was feeling slightly chilled. Standing alongside Pharazman, Zutra commented upon the state of the Shah's army assembled, appearing much smaller than the expected complement of fifty thousand men.

"That is because the other half has gone north to the bridge at Baghdad and will try to circle us from behind," the captain suggested.

"How do you know?"

"It is what I would do," Pharazman replied modestly.

"So how do you see our chances," Zutra asked.

"Chances?" Pharazman let out a burst of laughter. "There are no chances!"

"I know we have no chance to survive," Zutra agreed. "What I want to know is what will be our chances to write ourselves into the pages of history?" Zutra winked at the Persian Captain. "Surely we want this to be our finest moment."

"The longer we survive the more of them we will take into the netherworld with us. If we slaughter enough of the bastards, then their historians may have no other choice but to record the battle. That's when we will make history."

"I'd like my sons to know what we've done here," Zutra said wistfully.

"Then it doesn't matter whether we kill a thousand or even ten thousand today, that won't make any difference in the end. Your sons will know what you have done, not for what you do this day but for what you have done for the past seven years. You have given men, all men, a taste of freedom. Today we die as free men!"

"Thank you Pharazman. I will remember your words in the afterlife."

The captain was no longer listening to Mar Zutra, transfixed by a cloud of dust showing movement in the distance. Approaching from the south a force measuring no more than half a legion marched at a double step, rapidly closing the distance between their armies.

"Surely they do not intend to drive us from the bridge with so few units," Pharazman indicated his disdain at the paltry attempt by curling his lip. "What manner of trickery is this that they could have crossed the northern bridge and circled around us so soon?"

"No trick," Mar Zutra held him back. "Those men aren't attacking us. I recognize some of them, especially the golden armor of the one in front. Take a better look!"

Pharazman squinted his eyes to get a better look against the glare of the sun. "By Ahura Mazda, what in God's name is he doing back here? The fool had a chance to live. Why bother to return to certain death?"

"Why does any man do what he does?" Zutra waxed philosophically, his heart beginning to pound excitedly at seeing them approach. Anxiously, he waited for the leader of the force to jog towards them.

"Am I too late?" the Commander puffed.

"I don't understand. Why aren't you with my son?" The sudden appearance of Patricius with several cohorts of soldiers caught Mar Zutra completely by surprise.

"Your son is safe. Everyone is safe," he reassured him. "You have the word of the Empress Ariadne in that regard. She has promised to see him safely to Holy Land where she will have him instated as the western Exilarch. My duty was done there!"

Zutra was still shaking his head in disbelief. "So, you came back here in order to die. Are you crazy? That makes no sense at all."

"There were extenuating circumstances," was all that Patricius would say on the matter of his return.

"And where did you get these men?"

"Courtesy of the Emperor Anastasius. They were all condemned to die for crimes they committed while in the military. He gave them a choice, fight under me and have their slates wiped clean and their family's honor restored or watch their children be executed before they met the same fate."

"Not much of a choice." Zutra mused. "So, all of them were prisoners?"

"Not exactly all," Patricius revealed. "I bought the services of about a thousand mercenaries. I figured whatever money I paid would be replenished by you if we win, and if we don't, then money is really of no concern to me afterwards," the General laughed at his own joke.

"But why?" was all that Zutra could think of saying, "You could have gone anywhere, started over, and lived!"

"I don't know," the Commander commented as he gazed upward into the cloudless sky surveying its brilliant blue hue. "Didn't want to miss what looks like a fine day for dying."

It was the same old commander that had returned and Zutra could not help but laugh at his nonchalance. "Yes, that it is my friend, a mighty fine day for dying."

"Plus, who was going to look after you if I didn't return?"

"Well, you won't be doing that for long," the Exilarch remarked with a huge grin across his face.

"Long enough to keep my promise to your wife."

"Which one?" Zutra jested.

"Actually both." It was the second surprise that Mar Zutra had received within such a short period of time.

"So, you've come to fulfill your pledge to two women." The king still couldn't believe that his Vizier would be so willing to make the ultimate sacrifice.

"That and an attempt to gain your forgiveness," the Commander confessed, his smile turning quickly into a frown of regret.

"I don't follow you?"

"This was the only way of gaining back my honor for betraying you. There was an episode in the past involving the Lady Avital and myself that I have suppressed all these years that I need your forgiveness for." Patricius awaited the anticipated angry outburst but none was forthcoming.

"I know," was all that Zutra said.

"You know?" Patricius's jaw dropped to his chest.

"Yes, Avital told me all about it when she tried to make me separate your head from your shoulders years ago."

"But you said nothing! Why would you not have said anything?"

"What was there to say? I knew whatever happened would have been manipulated by her own hand. Hers alone! She betrayed no one but herself. You were never guilty of betrayal."

Patricius felt extremely humbled by the forgiving nature of his monarch. "But you said and did nothing," he stammered. "Why would you have not slain both of us?"

"What and lose the best friend I ever had? Don't be ridiculous. Moreover, Avital proved to be a much better wife afterwards as well. I can only pray that you have forgiven me for having led you into such a predicament."

"You had nothing to do with it," Patricius objected to the king's inference.

"But I did, my friend. If you were to examine the scenario carefully, you would see that it was the Lord's way of punishing me. I coveted another man's wife and my sins had to be paid for. Foolish pride but at least I fared far luckier than my ancestor David was when he took Bathsheba. I didn't have to kill the son I loved most because of my weakness."

"You are a very strange man," was all that Patricius could say.

"That may be the case but you're still the one who has led over a thousand men across a continent only to face certain death. That to me is even stranger. And in case you didn't notice, Kavad still outnumbers us five to one."

"Couldn't let you hog all the glory to yourself. Not to mention, I'm not the only one lacking any sense. You could have left at any time as well. No one would have faulted you. I'm certain the Princess is making my cousin's life a living hell for not going back and retrieving you."

"Common sense and love," Zutra commented, "Two things that rarely work in harmony."

"You definitely are the strangest man I have ever had the honour of serving."

"Actually, the Princess did beg me to leave with her. But how could I ever defy the manifest will of God? My survival was never a consideration. Now I must give my sons much more than a father, I need to leave them a legend to live up to."

"While you two reminisce about better times, let me remind you that we have thirty thousand men on the other side of this bridge waiting to tear us to pieces," Pharazman quickly filled in Patricius of the situation, bringing both men back to reality. "And within two hours, there will be another twenty thousand circling behind us."

"Are you asking for my opinion?" Patricius countered. "If so, then I think this rivals the Greek legend of King Leonidas and his Spartans at Thermopylae. If this doesn't make us legendary, I don't know what will."

"Perhaps some military advice you wish to offer," Pharazman smirked upon listening to Patricius's comparison to Herodotus.

"Yes, attack before the other twenty thousand arrive."

"Shall you lead the charge or shall I," Zutra inquired of his Vizier, the smile on his face indicating that he was definitely enjoying their last moments together.

"You, of course! After all, it is your legend we are inscribing today."

"Well then, shall we?"

"No, wait!" Patricius raised his hands to stop his king from running towards the bridge. "Not yet. There's one more thing we must do." Drawing his sword, Patricius raised it high above his head and paraded back and forth in front of their soldiers assembled on the eastern side of the bridge, and then brought the flat of the blade down repeatedly to beat against his shield. "Zutra, Zutra," he started to chant in unison to the hammering blows, the contagion of his enthusiasm spreading through the rank and file until all of them chanted and beat their shield in harmony. A resounding, earth-shaking chant that sent a shiver of fear through their enemies, especially to those that could remember the last time they heard that particular chorus. "Zutra, Zutra," the words sailed to the heavens, on the wings of a prayer. "Zutra, Zutra," it echoed through the alleyways and homes of the twin cities until the mortar began to crumble from the vibrations. "Zutra, Zutra," as a few drops of rain fell mysteriously from a cloudless sky, the tears of angels saying farewell to a favorite son.

The King laughed with delight on hearing his name rolling off every one of his soldier's lips.

Turning to his king, Patricius placed his sword in front of his face and saluted his comrade farewell. "Now we're ready!" he shouted.

"Alright men, let's do it," Zutra raised his sword in a return salute. He shouted his final order to begin the charge, leaping fatefully on to the bridge, "For God, for glory, for freedom! Attack!"

Epilogue

"How is it that no one's ever recorded the history of Zutra before?"

I smiled wryly. "Oh, it has been recorded. You might not recognize it, but there always has been a record of it in various forms."

"Well, I've never seen it," Pearce was adamant that it never existed.

"And when was the last time you ever went looking for the story?" I countered.

"Not lately."

"You remember that monk with the egg that Patricius kicked up the ass?"

"Yeah."

"Well, he wrote an account. Called himself Joshua the Stylite. Interesting the lengths he went to talk about the Greeks only yet still mentions that they had some Jewish and Persian supporters, even though he tries to downplay them as much as possible."

"Any others?"

"Bits and pieces by Jewish scholars and the rabbis but it had to be suppressed for obvious reasons. Mostly by the Jewish religious leaders who only refer to it as a time when terrible things were done and then state that they prefer not to discuss it."

"I can't believe it," Pearce muttered. "Who do they accuse of doing that?"

"It's hard to say for certain. At times you think they're condemning Reb Hanina for what he did to Mar Zutra's father but then you start thinking that they're condemning Mar Zutra just as Reb Hanina said they would. So overall their attitude has been to say nothing at all and hope that no one ever publishes the story."

"But what about the curse on all his descendants?"

"I think that was it. By not publicizing what Zutra had done, they attempted to curse us into oblivion. Some still spit when they mention his name but as his descendant, we can live with that. Now that the true story is out, the curse is now broken. Everyone will now know. The genie is out of the bottle you might say."

"So, Doc. Any suggestions for a title?"

"I thought that would be pretty obvious. There's only one word I think that anyone reading this book would consider befitting."

Pearce nodded his head knowing exactly which word I was talking about. "It's a good title. 'Zutra.' It does have a nice ring to it. What about his children? Anything you want to add and tell me about them?"

"Another time, another place, perhaps even another life," I responded. "Right now, I'm tired and my head's pounding like there's a hammer thumping against my skull from the inside. I'm going to sleep, and you're going to leave and let me get some rest. Remember to be back tomorrow and I'll take you over to Dongmen Square. You can get your wife something with a designer label on the cheap and lie about it being real."

"But what about that prediction of three kingdoms? You have to tell me something more and then I'll leave."

"Okay, here's something for you to investigate. Red hair, green eyes, and a mother that's a Chinese princess. How's that?"

"What's that supposed to indicate?" Pearce complained.

"Remember the suit of lights?"

"Well, yeah."

"Then know that there's something written in both Chinese and Persian history regarding a Glittering Man."

"A what?"

"Hey, remember that I've been working for years in China now. You don't think all those trips I've taken around the country have just been for sightseeing, do you? I've been putting all the clues together."

"So, when do I see what you got," Pearce inquired.

"I guarantee, if you do your homework, when next we meet, you will have another story." I laughed because I knew I had him, hook, line and sinker. When it came to the Kahana, there could never be enough legends to tell.

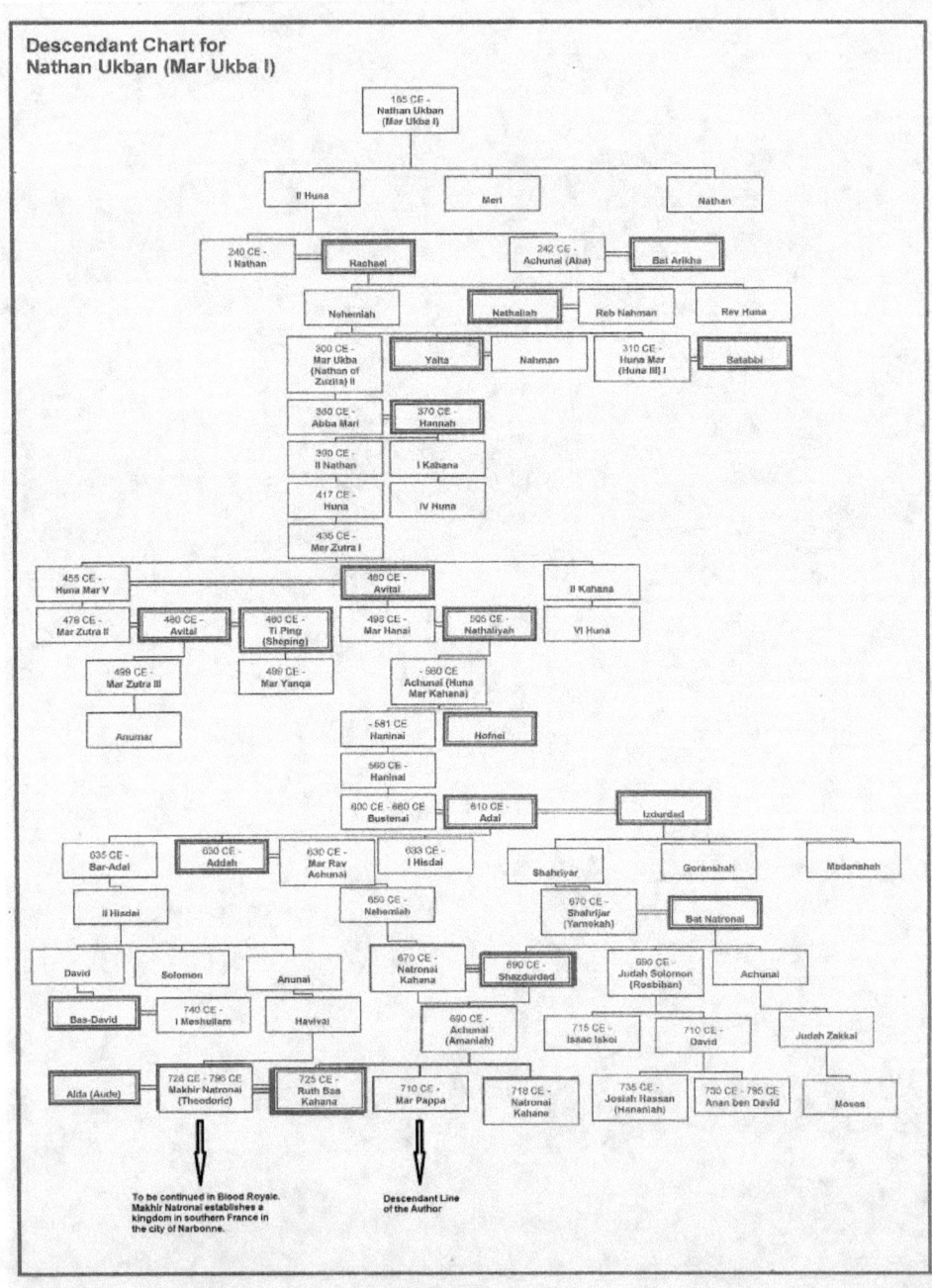

Descendant Chart for Nathan Ukban (Mar Ukba I)

www.ingramcontent.com/pod-product-compliance
Lightning Source LLC
Chambersburg PA
CBHW071635260626
47170CB00001B/114